Song of Time

Song of Time

IAN R. MACLEOD

First published in hardcover in 2008 by PS Publishing.
This paperback edition first published in October 2013 by
Drugstore Indian Press, an imprint of PS Publishing Ltd. by
arrangement with the author. All rights reserved by the author.
This book is a work of fiction. Names, characters, places and
incidents either are products of the author's imagination or are
used fictitiously. Any resemblance to actual events or locales or
persons, living or dead, is entirely coincidental.

ISBN
978-1-848636-69-9

Design & Layout by Jaharisam
Printed and bound in England by T.J. International

Drugstore Indian Press
Grosvenor House
1 New Road Hornsea
HU18 1PG
United Kingdom

editor@pspublishing.co.uk | www.pspublishing.co.uk

SOMETHING WHITE'S LYING ON THE SHORE AS I CROSS the last ridge of shingle. Seagulls rise as I trudge towards it. I'd walk on if I could be sure that it was merely a salt-bleached log, but I can't simply turn away. The ground slips and a bigger wave breaks over my knees. A hand flails, limbs unravel, bubbles glitter, and a human face stares up from the retreating sea, masked with weed.

I grab a hand, an arm. A sudden backwash almost claims us, then, in a heave, I and the body are free. I look around. Splinters of dawn light part the clouds, but there's nothing else here along this shore but me, this man and the grey Atlantic. There are bruises, scratches, gouges, beneath the stripes of weeds which cover him, but otherwise he's naked. And he's obviously young, clearly male, and still alive—if barely. I struggle to turn him over and attempt to pump the water from his lungs, but already I'm exhausted. He struggles against me and blinks.

"Who are you?"

He blinks again.

"Where are you from?"

The blued lips shape to say something, then he vomits up the sea.

Arm in arm, we stagger towards the cliffs. The many steps which ascend to my house from beside the boathouse are of age-corroded concrete. I really should lay him here out of reach of the sea and hurry alone up to Morryn—I should alert the relevant authorities. Instead, his weight drags my shoulders as we climb together and the disappointed gulls swoop. His bare feet, as they stub and blunder, begin to bleed.

At last, we reach the chimneys of Morryn. We struggle up the sloped lawn, I stab my fingers at the controls on the front door, then we slump dripping into the hall. Where to put him? I have a bedroom upstairs which I reserve for the guests who never come, but I can't face another climb, so it has to be the music room. I kick open the door, then make a final lunge towards the red divan just as the weight of his body begins to topple me.

Buffeted by weary waves of pain, I collapse on the chair beside my desk. Consciousness fades. When it returns, the figure is still sprawled across the divan. No, he's not a ghost, for there are dribbles of seawater across the rugs, and he's brought with him the smells of the shore. It *did* happen. His eyes are closed. A fallen hand twitches. It's stuck with fragments of shell, and the nails are cracked and chipped. Even allowing for the damage of our journey up those steps, his feet also look sore and abraded. Is all of this just from rocks and shingle? Standing up, I cross the littered rugs to examine him more closely. His skin has mostly shed the stripes and tangles of weed. It's blued with bruises, criss-crossed with scratches, greyed and reddened with many small abrasions, although underneath it seems softly, uniformly, goldenly, pale. His muscles are well-developed. His hair, both on his head and his groin, is drying to a darkish blonde. He could be a drowned Greek god.

"David, is that your name?"

The eyes flicker in a wet glint.

"Can you hear me . . . ?"

A trailing leg moves. He's looking up at me now, but the gaze is barely focused. Muscles rope in a spasm, then he falls back. When the eyes slip closed again, I sense that he's shutting me off. In another moment, the breathing has slowed. The eyeballs flicker. He seems to be asleep . . .

Leaving him, I close and lean against the music room door. My senses blur. Just what *am* I doing? I'm soaked, stuck with the bits of shore and weed he's sloughed off on our journey. I, too, wish I could sleep, escape . . . But I head instead for the laundry cupboard. The house implement which airs and presses my linen extends its silvery limbs as I reach to scoop up towels and blankets, but I bat it away, then struggle with arms full to get the music room door open again. Inside, the automatic piano shines its wooden sail, filled with the morning which floods through the wide bay windows. Why did I choose to put him in this of all rooms, where everything is so personal, so much a part of me? These walls lean with awards, gold disks, rare scraps of manuscript, antique concert programs, images of my husband Claude conducting the world's great orchestras. The floor is strewn with family photos, old CDs, scraps of image, my children's crayon drawings. My desk is a shrine piled high with the past. My Guarneri violin lies waiting in its case. All I am is here—everything that I could find, anyway. Yet now I've brought in this stranger . . .

My hands are trembling as I cover my drowned man with blankets. He certainly isn't starved and—despite all these many small wounds—he looks almost heartbreakingly perfect. His body hasn't been distorted or changed in the way that so many are nowadays either, and his penis is plump and jaunty despite the cold. He simply is what he is: human, young, living, male. I'd forgotten how beautiful people can be in this pure animal state. His hand no longer twitches. As I lift his head to place a towel under it, he gives a small smile.

My mind circles the obvious point. This is far from the first time bodies have been found washed up along these Cornish shores. There always have been wrecks and drownings, and the refugee ships and dirigibles of all the recent diasporas often crash or sink when they are intercepted by the guardian subs and drones. And refugees are often male and young, just as they have always been. What happens to them if they are captured alive? Sent back, I suppose, to the droughts of Africa, the sink cities of Southern Europe . . .

Outside the music room's windows, the segmented sky and

horizon remain empty. There are no ships, aircraft, or visible automata. Perhaps he's nothing more than an early-morning swimmer, caught by cramp or an unexpected current? But in that case, desperate relatives would already be searching for him. And if they were, drones and flitters would also be crawling and scanning the beach. People are easy to find now, at least the ones who are fortunate enough to live in these parts. We radiate like beacons to the waymarks which help protect our boundaries. If he were a local yachtsman heading out from Fowey or Mevagissey or Penzance, or pleasure-seeker, or cliffside walker, or merely a skinny-dipping tourist caught out by this treacherous sea, he would have been rescued long before I found him.

I study his face, trying to fix the features. Trying, as well, to remember what racial stereotype we are supposed to fear in this new century. Dispossessed Americans? Maoris? But those bogeymen lie in other decades. Now, people can make themselves look like anything. They can change their colour, re-arrange their genes. I risk raising the blankets again to check that he's breathing. He is—and everything else is still there.

Dawn has long passed. Beyond the windows lie ambered clouds, skeins of blue. Today will be cloudy-bright. It will be sunny and rainy. There will be calm and storm. Typically Cornish late summer weather, for these, my last Cornish days. My stomach rumbles. By now, I should have coaxed coffee and croissants from the implements within the glass claw of the new kitchen, and gone through my monitoring routines and taken the palliative medicines which are supposed to control my symptoms, and then started my daily practise on my violin. And then, and then—for I was determined that I would make a proper stab, a real *start*, at arranging my memories—I would begin to go over the strew of objects which covers my desk and froths from its half-jammed drawers. My head spins as I ease myself back into the chair. I've never been a great one for throwing things away, but it's not like me to exist in quite this level of clutter. But what else can I do? What other choice is there?

This house, these thick granite walls, have absorbed the sighs and screams of birth and death and every other kind of memory for the best part of four hundred years. For Morryn, it really is the start of just another day. I slide open drawers. Holiday seashells, ancient CDs, dried out pens, a single earring, my first tuning fork, datasticks and gimcrack souvenirs, all slide and roll. Here's a post-card Mum once sent me from Delhi. Tilt it at the right angle, hold it close enough to your ear, and it still activates; you can hear the murmur of traffic, smell jasmine and garbage, taste the dust of that lost city. Here's the red plastic shoe of a Barbie doll. Here's a note from Claude, scrawled in that big, elegant handwriting, which probably once came with a gift. And floating above this desk is the screen of the thing which I still think of as a computer, although it has no physical frame. Activate it, and I could wade even deeper into memory: access old school reports which Dad once hand-scanned into a computer in one of his attempts at orderliness—*Roseanna* (the teachers often misspelt my name) *is a very lively child. When she settles to a task, however . . .* —half-corrupted e-mails, videos of birthday parties, multisense recordings, and a near endless variety of my and Claude's performances. It's all there, waiting. But where to start? This is my life, yet it's far too much for me to cope with.

I'm dying. The thought still comes as a cold shock. I feel ridiculous, disappointed and—yes—angry. After all, I'm barely a hundred, and I certainly hadn't planned that my recent concerts would be my last. I put my surprising weariness down to a punishing schedule—for touring and performing is always hard work. In the space of just two months, I gave twenty-one chamber recitals and fifteen concert performances across the globe. I watched the earth vanish and the stars appear through the windows of a dozen shuttles. People, I was gratified to discover, still wanted to hear Roushana Maitland's fabulous tone, which was once famously described as being as clear as the noonday sun glinting on an iceberg. I played my violin, and the music remained immortal, and so, I thought, was I. I saved the tremors, the dizzy spells, the fuzzy vision, the inexplicable bouts of sobbing, for hotel rooms, then dressed and went out to dine in the world's best restaurants with new and rediscovered acquaintances, both virtual and real. Once, a wineglass fell. Sometimes, I forgot names. In Prague, I was unable to find my way back to my dressing room from the stage, but all these things are hardly the sole prerogative of the elderly. That was what I truly believed.

There was New Jakarta. There was Bangalore—and a forced over-night stay and listening to the hum of some environmental device as toxic rain battered my hotel window. Then came Sydney, and that last triumphant encore, and a late meal and an even later party. When the door to my hotel suite finally kissed itself shut, I was no longer sure whether I felt happy or sad that my tour was at an end. Basically, I was nostalgically drunk, and my ablutions before I climbed onto the bed and willed it and the world to stop rotating were perfunctory. No surprise, then, that it should be almost noon by the time I awakened, nor that I should have a blazing thirst. But my bed felt clammy. At first, the sensation wasn't unpleasant. In fact, I smiled through my headache as I remembered the lost times my daughter Maria had climbed stealthily into my bed and I'd been awoken by this same wetness and smell. Only then did I realise.

Back here, back in Fowey, I made a discreet appointment. I told no one, least of all my children Edward and Maria—and who else is there left to tell? The machines at the clinic sniffed and tutted at me for being the living, breathing anachronism I've wilfully become. And if some special implant or enhancement really would sort out the problems with my sight and this bladder complaint, then, well, I supposed I'd grudgingly submit . . . But I knew something was more seriously amiss when a real, human, doctor entered the bright room. His face was professionally grave as he asked me to sit down.

There are other clinics. Not those which deal with the merely living, but which cater for the nearly dead. In my hurried researches, I found that they are often housed in old buildings which this new century has emptied of their intended purpose. Banks. Churches—the un-firebombed ones, anyway. Once-modern government offices which have escaped the concrete virus.

Museums as well. But they all seem so *solid* now. They make a statement even before you enter them, and that statement echoes as you click along refurbished halls. It shines in the brass plaques which catch your face as you glance into them, amazed to find yourself finally here.

The company I chose to cheat death with, although they would never have used that term, has centres in most of the world's major capitals, as well as a conveniently local—but not too local—office in Bodmin. I was basically anonymous—music only gives you a certain kind of fame—and I submitted to old-fashioned interviews with real people, and rigorous mental and medical assessments, and to group sessions with others of the soon-to-pass. We sat awkwardly in our circles of soft-backed chairs beneath marble heads and goldlists of dignitaries long gone. Death, we were assured, is no longer a final barrier. Life can continue. *You* can continue. It doesn't require faith, and it certainly doesn't need God. Effort yes, and a little self discipline, and then some money. But what is there which doesn't need those things? Some of us penitents were far older than I was; shuffling landcrabs in their protective wires and carapaces. Some were younger. Some were plainly seriously ill. There was even one child.

I booked myself in for the necessary procedure in mid-August, almost exactly three weeks after my last performance in Sydney, and I wished it were sooner, and worried that I'd left it too late. I almost ran towards the granite pillars of Bodmin's old public hall on the allotted morning, and I was so relieved when the arms of the couch finally closed around me that I scarcely felt afraid. Then I breathed the smell of burnt bone as the crystal seed of my immortality whined its way into my skull.

I kept saying to myself—it was my mantra—that none of this was particularly strange. After all, the dead have long been with us. For centuries, their faces have stared down at us from paintings, and then those paintings became photographs, and the photographs became strips of image, and those images began to move. Soon, the dead were speaking to us from the horns of gramophones; they hovered in the dark of cinemas until they migrated into the glass screens we kept within our homes, and those screens grew cleverer and more reactive until the glass which separated us from their far side began to dissolve. The crystal fields expanded and we, the living, stepped in—or the dead, the passed, have drifted out.

Memories, I've been told, are crucial. Memories are what you are. Forget your worries about what you will become—that will take place anyway—surround yourself instead with things which are important to you, even if they are painful. Submerge yourself in time. Swim in it. Drown. Well, I'm doing that now, sitting at this desk.

My elbows slide. My fingers tremble through brittle hair. Already, the sun is surprisingly high, pushing through the clouds, catching in lazy flashes across the edges of the waves. I can't just sit here. I can't just wait. I have to do something. I can't simply die. I used to know a composer—I used to know many composers, but this was Karl Nordinger—who once told me that the answer to any problem is always there, right in front of you. But what does that mean now, sitting at this desk, in this room, with this man I've rescued—how can any of this ever make any kind of sense?

Shoving things aside, I notice something silvery lying beneath a balled-up Chanel scarf. The stuff we leave behind. A Sony Seashell, a long-defunct kind of personal music player, regards me with its shattered eye. When did I last listen to you? When did you last work? I work open a drawer, shoving the object down beneath reams of staved paper in a kind of burial, but something else blocks the way as I strain to slide the drawer back in. Reaching in and around, I find the culprit and haul it out. An old Smith Kendon barley sugar sweet tin—the sort they used to sell in petrol stations and motorway service areas for those endless journeys people once took in their hand-driven cars. Somehow, tossed aside but never quite thrown away, it's made it across all these years as far as Morryn. The round, bronzy lid resists the scrabble of my feeble fingers, then gives. Flashing with fragile light, it exhales a salty, herby smell.

EVERYBODY DOES IT, SIS. YOU KNOW THAT SMELL YOU sometimes get in the front room on Sunday mornings after Mum and Dad have had people round? It's because they've been smoking dope . . . "

Leo and I were sprawled on a rug beneath the withered cherry tree in our back garden one hot summer afternoon. I'd been mimicking my brother's lazy monosyllabism, his arms behind-the-head pose, as we gazed up at the splintered sky. Now, I had to turn. He chuckled.

"You *knew* that, didn't you? Don't you remember that time you came downstairs and Mum couldn't stop laughing when she carried you back up?"

Not that I did remember, but I didn't particularly doubt what he was saying either. It fitted some of the evidence. Windows open when it was raining. A dim memory of candlelit adult faces beaming at me through an odd dinner party haze. And yes, that smell, which I'd always thought of as pleasantly homely; like our old Hessian doormat, or bonfire smoke.

"There's no harm in it, you know. Some doctors prescribe it to help with neural diseases."

Calmly, I stroked the dry grass beside the rug. "It's a bit deceitful, isn't it? To do something without admitting . . . ?"

"That's what parents are for." Leo chuckled again. "Dad even gave me his *be careful about drugs* talk a few years back—you're probably due the same one soon. He admitted to what he called *experimenting himself* back in his student days, but that was about as far as it went. You know the top of the unit in the kitchen by the fondue set?

That's where they used to keep their stash. I even nicked some for myself a couple of times, but then it got moved, and Mum said something about people having rights to privacy although she didn't have the nerve to say what she really meant. So Leo's a good boy now. Leo always gets his own."

This was less of a surprise—my brother was, after all, seventeen—although I felt the same sense of privilege I always did when he shared something of his world with me. Despite the times we spent together, I felt that he existed at some indefinable distance from me, living a life which was bigger and more interesting. He often had a look of a deep but secret amusement in his eyes. He had it now.

"Tell you what. It's about time you tried . . . "

Already, he was standing up, and I gazed at the redbrick walls which surrounded our garden as he ambled towards the house. We were entirely alone. By nature, I was a conformist, but, like all conformists, I secretly wanted to break my own rules. And I was, after all, a child of the twenty first century. And Leo was my brother. And it was only dope.

He re-emerged with a tinkling jug of orange juice, along with a tin which had once held Smith Kendon boiled sweets. I wiped off condensation and poured out juice, pretending an absorbed disinterest as Leo unfurled a leaf of cigarette paper and snapped a steel lighter and crumbled some brown stuff. He ran his tongue along the edge of the paper and twisted it at the tip. He sneezed.

"This isn't one of my finer efforts."

Shrugging as if I'd seen better, I gulped the juice.

"Sis, do you know what this'll do to you?"

"It'll make me feel a bit happy . . . a little giddy."

"Glad they're teaching you something at school. Move over . . . " Shuffling back onto the rug, he snapped the lighter a few more times. It gave off pleasantly petroly tang. "You know you don't have to do this? I'll get into all sorts of trouble if you tell anyone—especially Mum and Dad. But some friend of yours is going to offer you this soon enough now, and you'll know what to expect, and whether to say yes or no. Have you heard of Bill Clinton, Roushana? Never mind; the trick is to inhale . . . "

The paper glowed and cracked. Warm, sweet smoke rolled from his lips. "It's not like sucking lemonade through a straw. Pretend you're simply breathing. Pretend this is air . . . "

I leaned forward, mouth agape, and I felt the papery nudge of the joint against my lips. As if it was air, as if I was diving, I sucked it in with a great inwards sweep, and something exploded within me. I rocked back, gasping, and clamped a glass of orange to my lips. Juice shot out from my nose and ran across my brother's arm.

"Hey!" Leo was laughing, and I was laughing as well, as he wiped himself on a corner of the rug, and took another drag. This time the smoke vanished within him for so long that I thought it would never emerge, and I longed to do better when he finally offered it back to me. I tried to let the smoke fall into my mouth, but most of it still erupted, and by then the joint, the roach (for these terms seemed to arrive inside my head along with the smoke) was so ruined that Leo had to unpick what was left and start again. But I was already lying back, letting the cherry tree spin about me. Thinking—this is what this feels like; whatever this is.

I don't know how much marijuana smoke I actually inhaled that summer afternoon. The day was so still, the air so pooled within the walled heat of our garden, that breathing and being there with Leo was probably enough. Someone had started up a mower a few houses off and a tiny plane was making its way from bough to bough across the solid blue. I thought of the people up there in that long silver tube. When the mower paused, I expected them to fall.

Then, and with a dope-croak to his voice, Leo began to talk about the future. How Mars would cease to hang red in the sky and turn verdant green, and Venus would shift from white to oceanic blue. Soon, long steel ships will dart from existence to

11

existence, probability to probability, world to wondrous world. It's there for us, Sis, waiting ahead in this century in which we're so lucky to have been born. Leo certainly knew that such visions were already outdated, but that didn't matter: what mattered on that afternoon was the dream, and the way he said *you and I, Sis*. What mattered was lying beside my brother on that frayed rug, and I think that Leo, for all his drawling know-it-allness, really did imagine then that the world was a place of endless possibility, a ripe fruit which he would soon reach out to possess.

The afternoon unfurled. My face felt stiff from dried-up orange juice and too much smiling. Every blade of grass grew a shadow like the tiny flecks of stubble I could see on my brother's chin, and I was studying our hands, the smallness and Indian-brownness of my own against Leo's knuckly shades of Anglo-Saxon pale, when I heard the boom of the front door, and someone calling his name. Unmistakably, it was his girlfriend Blythe Munro's voice, and was that not a small sigh of irritation which escaped from Leo's bitten underlip as he cleared the wreckage of our spent joint and squeezed down the lid of his Smith Kendon tin?

"Out here!" he shouted, but Blythe was already unshouldering her cello case at the French windows, then saying *Hi Roushana* as if she was surprised to find me here.

"Been busy, eh?" Her mouth made an effort to smile as her eyes took in the litter of paper and ash. "You *did* say I should look in . . . ?"

"Sure." I watched the way Leo stood up, how he kissed Blythe's cheek, and the motherly way she ruffled his hair. She was already a maturely beautiful young woman—in fact, it was hard to imagine that she'd ever been truly young. She smiled at me, looking as cool in a fresh white tee-shirt, billowy peasant dress and crisp new espadrilles as the day was hot. She jingled her keys as she weighed them in the cup of her hand. Blythe already had a car of her own, and not some battered banger, but little jelly-mould-shaped bit of the future in its own right, with seats which remembered who you were, and which, even then, virtually drove itself.

Unpeeling myself from my shadow, I crossed the lawn to join them as they set up music stands and opened the piano in the dining room. Even in the middle of a summer holiday, music was something I took for granted; it was simply what we did. Leo was on a music scholarship to King Edward's, whilst Blythe was studying at the private girl's school next door. They both played in the joint Music Society, and were also involved in the Birmingham Conservatoire and many of the other bands, projects, weekends, summer schools, recitals and contests into which the young and musically talented were then drawn. They were currently working on a performance of the Brahms *First Cello Sonata* for a concert at the Barber Institute and I, as was often the case, was page-turner. Of course, and as Leo quickly pointed out, Blythe should have memorised the piece by now, but it was plain as she hesitated over the first slow counterpoint when he began the languorous melody on the piano that she wasn't there yet. Despite my vague hostility towards her, I think Blythe welcomed my presence at these rehearsals. Leo's brilliance in music was brittle. He'd leap up in mid-bar to demonstrate how she should be accomplishing a tricky sequence of fingering. Not that Blythe wasn't a good cellist, but you could tell from the brisk way Leo approached her instrument that he knew he could have bettered her with no more than a few months of study. At least, that was how we felt.

And that was how Leo was: competent at most things, with brilliance never that far away in any of them. But that in itself was a frustration to him. Yes, he could play the Brahms and probably a hundred other main-repertoire piano pieces to near-performance standard. Yes, he'd won awards and had a scholarship to one of Birmingham's most expensive schools and had once performed in front of Ashkenazy, but he remained far from sure whether he even wanted to be a professional musician, and what road he might take if he did, or if the piano was his main instrument. He loved jazz. He doodled with popular tunes. He'd switch in one practice session from Bach to Chopin to Bill Evans, and never quite finish any of the pieces, and then plug the midi into the computer and work on something of his own.

This was the world which you entered when you got involved with my brother and music, and I sometimes wondered in my pre-teenage way whether Blythe only pushed herself this hard with the cello in an attempt to please him. And here I was—sitting with them: a small but slightly stoned gooseberry, and self-nominated page-turner. The French windows were open, but the air inside refused to move, and even Blythe lost something of her fresh-picked coolness as the same tricksy upwards phrase on bar thirty eight was endlessly repeated. After an hour or so of this, I was more than happy to scurry into the kitchen to make up some of Leo's special sandwiches—thick white bread mattressing layers of corn chips glued in mayonnaise.

Leo ate, but he wouldn't stop playing. He chomped and sneezed and blew his nose and cannoned at the piano as I turn-ed the pages whilst Blythe sipped a can of Diet Pepsi and the sky pooled in darker patches around the chimneys and aerials outside. Sometimes, we'd finish these rehearsals with an easier piece to which I could make my own contribution on three-quarters violin. I lost the beat as often as I found it at the tempo they played, but the specialness of making music with Blythe and Leo more than compensated. There were even times when, for just a few bars, I would get that tightrope sense of being possessed by the melody. But such moments were short-lived—the very realisation that they were happening was enough to make me fluff my notes—and they didn't come at all that day.

Without warning, Leo stopped in mid-phrase on an intended final run-through. Blythe slid to a halt a moment after, her lips jutting in wounded anticipation, but he was already pushing past us, muttering something we didn't quite catch, although the explanation became clear as we heard the raised latch of the out-side toilet which lay beyond the kitchen. The door to this Victorian relic only went three-quarters up, and the sounds of my brother voiding his bowels were unmistakable. Thoughtfully, Blythe drew a few long notes from her cello. I, meanwhile, re-con-sidered the supposed effects of corn chips and dope.

"Sorry about that," he said when he returned. "No more sandwiches . . . " He attempted a laugh. "Anyway. Where were we?"

But the session never really got started again. Leo, for whom everything had to be perfect, was too distracted and Blythe was far better at being solicitous and sympathetic than I was. Why, she'd been this way herself a week or so before. Summer flu—it was going the rounds. He'd probably even caught it from her . . .

The evening thickened. Mum and Dad returned from the teachers' union conference they'd been attending, and Blythe headed off in her clever little car towards the gates and fences which were then already starting to enclose Edgbaston's Calthorpe Estate. Forgotten, tired, sticky, I drifted out into the back garden. In those days, in that lost summer of that lost century, scarcely any stars hung above Birmingham, there was so much light and smog. The French windows still hung open, and it seemed for a moment that Leo and Blythe and I could still be playing inside. Not struggling in fits and starts through the Brahms, but making music which shaped itself like the cool flow of a midnight river. I could almost hear that lovely, inexpressible sound over the boom of next door's television and the drone of evening traffic on the Alcester Road.

Something clattered as I stooped to pick up the forgotten rug we'd left beneath the cherry tree. It rolled, shining, towards the pale solar lanterns which hung around the borders of the garden like marsh ghosts. I smiled as I picked it up.

Leo's bedroom light wasn't on when I went upstairs, but I knew that he'd still be awake.

"There." Sisterly-proud, I plonked the Smith Kendon tin down on the bed where he was lying in semi-darkness. "Saved your bacon."

"Yours as well." Rolling over, he slid out the bottom drawer of his bedside cabinet and shoved it into the hidden space beneath.

"I'd just tell Mum and Dad you made me do it."

"And I'd say it was all part of your education, which is exactly right."

Leo's room was at the front of the house, near to a sodium-yellow streetlamp which splattered plane-leaf shadows across his thin curtains, and his face had a sweaty gleam as he lay there. Seeing the stubble of his chin, I remembered the pinprick shadows of the lawn, the different colours and shapes of our hands . . .

"Thanks, anyway," I said.

"For what?"

I shrugged.

"You know, Sis, what I was saying this afternoon—it's not really true."

"You mean dope really *can* harm you?"

He gave a chuckling sigh. "I mean, what I said about the future. I was wrong. The future isn't something waiting ahead of us any longer. We're living it. It's with us. It's everything. It's here."

So this was the future, and the future was Leo seemingly recovering from his stomach upset after a few days, and then me and Dad going down with the same thing. It was trips to the chemist, a stink in the toilets, and the washing machine grinding through endless sheets, and all of us getting better, although Leo seemed to find it harder than the rest of us did to shake it off.

And the future was going to Ikea on a weekend soon after to get a new uplighter for the lounge, and the future was queuing for hours on the gridlocked M5 with Dad turning on the heater fan as the engine of his battered Renault threatened to boil whilst Leo sat beside me in the back, sweating and complaining as he stifled ugly-smelling burps. We finally returned home through the ozone evening with no uplighter, but several boxes of glass tumblers, many pot plants, a ridiculously huge wall clock, and a tinkling mountain of all the different varieties of light bulbs which were somehow then needed. There were so many *things* in that lost world. Our house overflowed with Dad's old tapes, records and CDs, and Mum's ornaments, and both of their books and magazines, and all of our musical impedimenta, and my and Leo's many toys, which we never played with, but still regarded with totemic reverence.

As Leo's unwellness continued through that hot, irritable summer, we found ourselves drawn into closer contact with both sets of grandparents. I remember the arrival of vivid trays of Indian sweets and gelid pots of restorative Irish stew, and the absent pinching of my cheek before the prow of my grandmothers' bosomy attention was steered towards Leo. Not that he was really ill, and the performance of the Brahms with Blythe and several other events still went ahead, but there was this thing, this bug, this stomach virus, a kind of summer flu or mild enteritis, which he was admittedly finding it difficult to shake.

We even spent our usual hot fortnight in one of those long, tin rectangles, named the *Clarion* or the *Belviour* which basked in lines in an arid park beside beaches in southern France. Neater versions of the post-Yellowstone refugee camps of twenty or thirty years later, they were stuffed with smaller and more temporary versions of all the things we had in our own homes. *Wine glasses, 6, frying pan, 1, corkscrew* ... I remember how I would work through the laminated inventory on the day of our arrival in the hope that I might catch a missing toilet brush or tea caddy, delaying the moment when I would have to walk the aisles between the gas bombs to face the obligatory space of playground sand where the other kids hung out. Mum might heedlessly sunbathe and ignore the glances which people gave her as they flip-flopped beside the waves, but I was just a kid, and often as not one of the few children on the site who looked remotely Asian. Mum's father Ram Ashar had come over to England from Gujarat the late 1950s in the search of a new life and a decent wage, taking a variety of menial jobs until he was able to set up a moderately thriving jewellers in Handsworth and bring over his new wife. Dad's family were of immigrant stock as well, but from a different century—Irish, and Catholic. The way things had worked out, Leo looked very much like his father, and I looked like my mother. The listless swinging on car tyres would stop as the red here-for-a-week faces of the other kids who inhabited these resolutely Anglo-Saxon enclaves of those holiday parks turned to regard me. What are *you* doing here? They didn't have say it; the question was already in my head. Often as not, I'd end up wandering the fenced pines with the sole Afro girl or the Chinese boy who'd been similarly marooned on this sunny outpost of England. Then, as at home, I'd wait for Leo to return from his book, his guitar, or the admiring crowd he was always good at attracting and rescue me. But on that last summer we spent on one of those French holiday parks, he felt unwell, and mostly sat alone.

Back in Moseley, trudging home under contrailed skies from my local comprehensive at the start of the autumn term, I'd often find my brother still sitting at the computer in his pyjamas, or banging harshly at the piano, or sometimes not even out of bed. Then, one day, I discovered Mum, who was normally out doing locum teaching, on her knees in the kitchen surrounded by sodden newspapers and wilting boxes of pizza as she defrosted the freezer.

"Roushana . . . " She looked up with a frown, wooden spatula in one hand and hair dryer in the other as she attempted to prise out another sheet of ice. "I've been trying to *ring* you. Why didn't you turn on your *phone*? Leo's . . . " She studied the pooling ice. "He's had to go into hospital. It's nothing serious—just tests, this thing that's been troubling him." She tugged at her tied-back hair. "Heaven knows why I started this. Look—will you help me put it all back. Then we can go and see him . . . "

Silently, solemnly, we re-stacked the leaking packs of ready meals, then set out through the interminable urban rush hour. Always a healthy child, I'd never visited a hospital before, and was astonished that illness should be such a huge industry. The corridors rolled on and on. Wards. Signposts. Lifts. A thousand swinging doors. People in wheelchairs and people on crutches. The nurses wore masks. Dire warnings of imminent epidemics flashed on the posters, and there were brazen glimpses under poorly arranged sheets of flesh, plastic and steel brownly encrusted with blood.

Leo was sitting up, and looking cheery, for all that he, too, had a tube running down into him arm from a crystalline sack which dangled above his bed. He and Dad, who'd travelled with him in the ambulance, both commented on the speed in which the treatments and investigations were proceeding. He had a room to himself, as well, which, along with the double doors with a code which you had to press to get through, I took at first as nothing more than the Health Service's acknowledgement of my brother's outstanding abilities.

Dad went back home through the traffic to collect all the things which Mum and I had forgotten, whilst Mum headed out along the corridors in search of a doctor, leaving Leo and I alone. As was often the case recently, we seemed to have little to say to each other. Still, the room was high in one of hospital's towers, giving a fine view across the gardens and golf courses of autumnal Edgbaston, and Leo twisted around to look out from the big metal frame of his bed as we debated whether we could see the house where Blythe's parents lived, and silently urged her expected arrival—her cool, lineney sense of calm . . .

Then we fell silent, and it was in that awkward moment, and more wanting to fill the alarming emptiness which had settled between us as the hospital resounded with distant clangs and booms than out of any real desire, that I said something to Leo which changed my life.

"I've been wondering," I said, "if I could get a bit better at playing the violin. I mean . . . " I made a clumsy, dismissive gesture. "Not that I could ever get to be as good as you are. Or Blythe. But I'd like to improve. And I thought perhaps you could help me."

Leo considered this. He made a slight raise of his chin. "We might as well," he said, "begin now."

I should have known. Asking Leo for his opinion on anything to do with music was like unstoppering a dam, and he was already deep into describing to me how practise was nothing, practise was *worthless*, unless you'd *planned* and *understood*, when Blythe finally arrived, laden with flowers, and also a brand-new Sony Seashell music player. This expensive gift was already filled with all of Leo's favourite music, and he strung its silver chain around his neck, played with it for a while, then pressed the tiny transmission stud to the lump of bone just behind my ear, and glorious music poured in. *That, Sis, is exactly what I expect from you!* We all laughed.

Was I any good at that time? Did I have an ear? Did I have a crumb of talent? Music was certainly an activity we all enjoyed and took for granted in our household, but Leo's gift was something else. It had been there from the first moment Mum sung to him and he'd gurgled back to her from his cot, and when Dad sat him on his lap before the piano when he was barely two and he prodded the notes he'd just seen played. There was never any question of them forcing him in the way that those ghastly parents with their maths and tennis prodigies then used to do. Not to allow Leo to develop his musical skills would have been like denying him the ability to walk. I, on the other hand, was as moderately competent at music as I was at most things. Mum might praise my screeching scales in much the same way she'd stick my pictures on the fridge, but I knew that I was an average child, and in that knowledge I, who stood out in other ways because of my racial mix, remained averagely happy.

Leo must have already known that I had no great musical gifts, when, back from hospital with several bruises on his arm and a whole new battery of tablets to take and a blotchily photocopied restrictive diet to adhere to, he sat me down and told me to put away my violin—which was a cheap thing in any case, coated in brittle plastic and with an equally brittle tone—and simply *listen*. Progress was slow. There were still no great new leaps, no sudden agilities of my awkward fingers, or a miraculously acquired perfect pitch. What there was instead, what mattered to me most, was a chance to spend time with my brother.

Despite his illness, Leo somehow contrived to keep up most of his attendance at King Edwards. This, after all, was the year of his A-levels when all the decisions which then so dogged bright children had to be made. Music, English or Modern History? A combined or single degree? The Royal Academy, or Durham, or possibly Oxford? Then there were the grants and bursaries to be fought over if he and my parents weren't to be burdened with a huge bill. Then there was all the revision, practice, study. Amazing, really, that Leo found time for me at all. But at least Blythe, who was faced with similar studies and decisions, had decided that she would not longer concentrate on the cello. She was, she now admitted, unlikely to be able to make a career out of music. She had also, the thought occurred to me, found other ways of pleasing Leo.

Each evening, I would gauge whether Leo was at home when I returned from school by checking to see if his bedroom window was open or closed, and it had been shut on the hot autumn afternoon when I was sent home early from school after another bomb alert, and it simply hadn't occurred to me that he might be in as I threw off my blazer and headed upstairs. My reaction to the sound which came from beyond his door was of some small disturbance—a mouse, perhaps; we'd had them before—so I headed straight in as I'd never have done if it had occurred to me that that he was in there, and least of all if I'd known that Blythe was with him as well. But there they both were, entirely naked on the bed in the unaired heat of his sun-facing room. Of course, I already knew they had sex. In that dying liberal age, my parents had made it plain to me that there were times when my brother and his girlfriend were not to be disturbed. Sex was one thing, but it was quite another to find Blythe crouching down over my brother in quite the way that she was. Blythe un-crouched and hooked a strand of hair from her mouth and her arm moved towards her breasts whilst Leo attempted to cover himself, but by then I was already slamming the door and running down the stairs.

They both came down soon afterwards as I sat hugging my knees and staring at the cartoons on the television to explain how it was entirely their fault, that they should have warned me they were in the house. But this was the future, and everything was part of it in that strange, unsettling autumn, and especially the music to which Leo introduced me. We explored the Bach *Partitas*. He played them for me on guitar or piano. He found key performances. All I had to do was listen. Leo had thinned somewhat by then. He'd turned gracefully gaunt and his skin, his breath, his whole presence, felt hot if you were close to him. He'd grown his hair longer, as well, and he looked like Chopin as he tossed back his locks and unravelled—*it's here, Sis, can't you see?*—the notes for me across the keyboard with his fine, quick hands. Meanwhile, our house had become a small battlefield in the war against whatever it was that afflicted him, with different towels for us all onto which Mum had sewn labels, constant warnings about washing hands and a permanent reek of disinfectant, but this was my escape, my way of being with my brother, and if I had not yet learned how to play music, I was at least learning how to hear it. He'd lent me that Seashell which Blythe had bought him. All the warhorse romantic concertos—the Mendelssohn and the Brahms and Elgar and the Sibelius and the Bruch—were new to me, and they were thrilling to listen to as I hunched home from school against the booming wind, alone with all the other rain-slick figures but knowing that Leo was with me amid those yearning orchestras.

Christmas loomed. Leo had another short spell in hospital, pre-planned this time, and there were more tests, and the postponement of others which, seeing as at least two girls in my class were suffering from what seemed like the same thing, he was on an ever-lengthening waiting list to undergo. He didn't come with us when we went to Christmas dinner at Mum's parents because Mum, anticipating the fuss there would be about his special diet, had decided it would be better if he spent the spend the day with Blythe's parents instead. I remember how the snow had fallen that year in incredible, world-stopping, heaps; how Birmingham, even Handsworth, looked beautiful on that slow and steamed-up journey, the houses transformed by white eyebrows and stalactite eaves.

Nan Ashar didn't bother to hide her disappointment that her grandson hadn't come, and could only manage a cursory pinch of my cheek as she filled the doorway of her terraced house. Like most Indians, the Ashars had accepted Christmas as just another festival, and plump Santas and assorted cherubs and reindeer complemented the usual pictures and figurines of Shiva and Ganesa. Then came dinner with us all jammed elbow to elbow around the oval table, and the *turrrkey*, which Nan Ashar presented with much pride and oompah, although I noticed that she and

Grandpa only pecked at the various vegetables and dips. Also here were Mum's brother and his family. Uncle Indra lived just around the corner with broad, quiet, Aunt Rupa, and had followed his father into what he liked to call "the trade".

Afterwards, I was encouraged to go off and play with their two boys who squabbled upstairs in a stuffy room over a dusty computer. The eldest, Kapil, was only a year younger than Leo, and fancied himself musical—a "deejay". As the loading bars crawled across the screen, I remembered how he'd once demonstrated to Leo what he called his *latest composition*, apparently the product of weeks of effort, and how Leo had produced something infinitely sweeter, funkier and better with a few quick prods of the mouse. But I was alone with them today, not so much a girl as a lesser boy, which was a position I encouraged in the way I tied back my hair, avoided make-up and wore big, baggy tee-shirts, often borrowed from Leo, to hide my growing breasts. Finally, a game loaded. Bright with helicopters, innards exploding, and loud clashes of flesh and metal, I discovered there was a knack to playing it which I didn't possess as, after blasting their way through several levels, Kapil and his brother finally let me have a go. In five seconds I was zapped by a many-armed Kali-thing, and they could continue playing.

New Year's Eve was at Dad's parents' house in Hall Green. At least Leo was there with us this time, but I was no great fan of this particular night with all its drink and bluster. I was allowed champagne, which I refused. I was encouraged to dance, which was an activity I then detested, and I hated the smell of cigarettes and beer, and all the jolly jostling in those tiny, semi-detached rooms. Hated, as well, the way Leo could manage to blend in with these anonymous creatures, who seemed to be mostly Gran and Pa Maitland's stupid neighbours. How *could* he cheer like everyone else when Big Ben finally chimed and link arms and then go around hugging people?

"Happy New Year, Sis." Taking my hands, my brother whooshed me up from the sofa on which I'd been hiding. He'd been drinking like everyone else, and he seemed to lean, unbalanced, across my body, and the pressure of his lips close to mine, the whole sense of being in his arms, lasted for longer than such moments are supposed to as he kissed me—and the world fell away.

Next morning, I was awoken by rattle of rain against my window, and the sound of Leo playing in the house below, as beautifully as I've ever heard it to this day, Chopin's *Raindrop Prelude*. Such sadness and delicacy: the emotion there, but held back, unshowy in all but the distant thunder of those softly rumbling middle chords. I could imagine for a while as I lay up in bed that Leo really was Chopin and I was Georges Sand, that we were sharing that grey rainswept house in Majorca which Leo had told me about, and which Chopin had so hated, and yet had managed to produce some of the world's most beautiful music within it.

Leo played the piece again, yet more quietly and brilliantly. I crept from my room and hunched on the stairs listening and watching through the dining room's open door as he sat in his faded red dressing gown, entirely rapt in a moment which I never wanted to cease. Finally, he looked around, and he seemed almost self-conscious to see me there, which was something Leo never usually was when he was at the piano. He joked as he stood up that he only dared play quietly because of his hangover, but we both knew that that he was playing as he'd never played before: that on that first morning of a new year in that still new century, he'd passed beyond mere technical facility, and was using Chopin's music to express not what Chopin had once felt, but what he felt himself.

Mum and Dad were out that morning, buying yet more *things* in one of the prefabricated cathedrals to consumerism in which people then seemed to spend most of their spare time. Leo wasn't in a good way. He muttered about his gluten intolerance as he swilled down tablets—how he'd stupidly forgotten that beer and whisky were both made from grain. Leaving the piano, he sat at the computer in the kitchen. I imagined that he was researching some essay, but there was something about his slumped posture that made me go over and stand beside him an hour or so later. The screen was stacked with websites, images.

"I know what it is I've got, Sis," he murmured without looking towards me. "It's called white plague."

Just like Mum, I'd never been able to drink milk. Leo, just like Dad, always had. It went back to our human heritage, to the tribes of Babel which once supposedly scattered themselves across this earth. Those who came to live in the cooler climes of the north became cattle rearers and husbanders and acquired by slow selection a continued ability to digest milk which those who hunted and foraged in earth's steppes, deserts and jungles continued to lose after infancy. Effectively, lactose tolerance is something which northerly white-skinned people have evolved, but which the rest of humanity mainly lacks. There are many exceptions, from the Bedouins and the Tuareg in Africa to the people of northern India. Even amongst the native Finns, almost 20% are unable to consume milk without suffering indigestion. Any virus intentionally keyed to react with the production of the digestive enzyme lactase would certainly be an instrument of exceeding bluntness with which to wage against the then-wealthy West. But it would be an instrument nevertheless.

I remember the Styrofoam cups of orange juice or coffee which I helped pour and serve from trestle tables in meetings at school halls. I remember laying out the special biscuits; flat, eggy things which tasted vaguely like pizza even when they were sweet. I remember the scrapy microphones Mum and Dad leaned into as, founder members of the South Birmingham Branch of the WRFI Society—WRFI, or Wide Range Food Intolerance being white plague's official name—they invited comments from the floor. Leo was also there at these meetings whenever he was up to it, hanging back at first but invariably pushed into the spotlight as an example of what WRFI sufferers could achieve. The local press got interested. He even gave an interview on regional news although publicity for the sake of publicity was something he'd always hated, especially if it meant giving a wide airing to his piano performances, which, despite their easy brilliance, remained an embarrassment to Leo, who could only ever compare himself to Glen Gould or Alfred Brendel. He only played in public, he once told me, because if he didn't he'd never become any good at it, but now he was accosted by neighbours about this or that lovely tune they'd heard him play, and so it went in that rainy spring of England's small monsoon, when, amid their many other activities, Mum and Dad decided to put our house up for sale. They planned on buying somewhere bigger, closer to Edgbaston or possibly Harborne, away from this place which they somehow blamed for Leo's condition, and also, although they never quite said it, from the encroaching ethnic poverty of Balsall Heath. They talked about finding a nice, big Victorian house with a proper music room for Leo and a full-sized piano, although the For Sale sign was frequently vandalised, and people were superstitious about new diseases, and the right offer never quite came.

Something between one in fifty and one in two hundred native English people were said to be suffering from white plague by then, although the numbers remained uncertain, and there were many experts who still disputed WRFI's existence as a separate condition. All I knew was that Leo had been well until that summer's afternoon when we'd smoked dope in the garden and I'd made him his special sandwiches, and that he'd never been well since. His diet—which had to cope with his small intestine's widening intolerance to a whole range of carbohydrates—was a complete minefield, and our fridge was its booby-trapped fuse. Woebetide anyone who took anything on Leo's special shelf. I never did get the talk about drugs from my parents which Leo had predicted, but I got several about my need for *caution*, for *simple common sense*, and for *responsibility*. Not that my parents weren't always acutely conscious of how difficult life could be for the sister of an ill sibling, and there were times when Mum would put an arm around my shoulder, and try to talk, or to listen, or say nothing at all. But I'd always stiffen, clam up, squirm away.

If Mum and Dad blamed themselves, or our house, for Leo's condition, I was more clear-cut. I blamed God. I took my cue from the fundamentalist websites which claimed that white plague was the vengeance of God or Allah or Jehovah, and then from my grandparents who saw Leo's illness as punishment for not having been baptised, or not having gone through the rituals of the samsaras, or simply for my parent's ill-advised cross-cultural marriage. Of course, the prayers, the offerings, were well meant, but I'd always hated those grisly images of Christ nailed to two squared planks of wood, whilst Nan and Pa's Hindu gods with their many arms and weird methods of transport seemed like a poorly thought-out set of cartoon superheroes. *Why?* I kept wanting to ask. What has this got to do with anything?

The tempests of spring finally blew themselves out with one last spectacular storm and another summer crept in on its warm heavy tread, breathing a lion-breath of carrion drains. I experimented privately before the mirror with Mum's make-up, suffered an ear infection, and had my first period. I also acquired my first full-sized violin, a second hand thing nearly fifty years old and the product of some anonymous French workshop, but with a nice, deep tone. Leo had taken the lead in its purchase, and I always thought of his voice when I played it, and his guiding hands, and the soft pressure of that New Year's kiss. Miss Freely my violin teacher, a spinsterish woman who smelled unaccountably of dog, was surprised at my sudden burst of progress. More surprising still, I suspect, was the ragged passion with which I had began to practise. *Heard you playing in your room last night*, Leo would say, bleary-eyed from another bad reaction as he shuffled down in the mornings to pick through the remnants of what he was still allowed to eat. *Lovely tone, but you need to pace yourself and slow down now you can play the phrase at that speed, especially on that last down-bow . . .*

Music spilled from our house in that strange summer as it had never done before. Leo played brilliantly now, with fire and with tenderness. Sometimes it was scary to hear the music he made, especially when he and I were alone in the house. I'd retreat to my room and lie on my bed listening awestruck as Bach unravelled below in terrifying cathedral-leaps of light. How, I wondered as I lumbered through the spiralling *Ciaccona* bar by bar on my muted violin, did anyone ever make such sounds? What sometimes made me afraid of Leo's playing now was the knowledge that, for all its soaring loveliness, what I was hearing was an expression of his illness. White plague, of course, was a misnomer. As the leaflets which Mum produced pointed out, the condition wasn't fatal, at least in countries with advanced medical services. In fact, in a world which had already experienced AIDS, Ebola, MRS, pyrexia and cat flu, WRFI seemed like a small thing to non-sufferers—after all, didn't we all have to watch what we ate? At the same time, there was also considerable ignorance and hysteria. I remember how cousin Kapil insisted it was all down to "them fucking Pakkis", whilst several Indian boys at my school were beaten up with WRFI as a pretext. Leo's diet was often characterised as being like a slimming fad, and thus no big deal. The facts that he'd suffered liver problems and a kidney infection and was still losing weight were ignored, as were the fiddly tests he had to undertake of his blood and urine each morning, and the aches and the weariness and the dreary food, and the knowledge that his illness was the main reason our house hadn't sold.

There was no longer any question of Leo going to Oxford, or to London; he would have to study at home. Blythe announced that she had also decided against the LSE in favour of Birmingham. She was a frequent visitor to our house that summer, and we would sometimes visit hers. I remember how the air in Dad's Renault suddenly seemed to cool when we reached the suburbs of Edgbaston, and the sky lost its sour tinge of grey and the trees tossed their heads as the security gates opened and we nego-

tiated the speed bumps beyond. Long lawns green beneath sprin-
klers spread towards many-windowed palaces of mock-Tudor,
mock-Medieval, mock-Modern.

It seemed like another world, although Tim and Natalie Munro
were decent people, and decently unembarrassed about their
wealth. The rich upper middle classes of those times still spent
generously on the armies of maids, minders, drivers, attendants,
dog-walkers and nannies who then kept their lives afloat. That
summer, though, there was a new device—a toy, Tim Munro
called it—which trimmed their lawns in place of their old mow-
ing service. Green and sleek, one of the outriders of the next wave
of independent labour-saving machines, it buzzed through the
sunshine as we sat around the swimming pool. Leo stayed lounging on a recliner as Blythe ploughed gracefully through the water.
He was prohibited from swimming, but he'd stripped down to his
costume, and I noticed how his ribs protruded and the bones of
his shoulders stuck out in painfully sharp angles. His flesh had
shrivelled almost everywhere apart from his belly, which projected
like a child's. He was starting to look alarmingly like those pictures
of starving people which we then saw so much of on TV. I, conscious of poor Leo, and that my own body looked nothing like
Blythe's, or even Mum's, had remained resolutely fully dressed.

Climbing out from the pool, gathering a thin wrap across her
shoulders, Blythe beckoned, and led me down through the garden.

"I wanted to show you these. See, aren't they lovely . . . ?"

A gardenia bush, draped with bridal white blossoms, was flour-
ishing in this changing climate. I, though, was more conscious of
the droplets sliding across the slopes of Blythe's bikinied body as
she stooped to inhale the creamy smell. One of the things I
undoubtedly disliked about my brother's girlfriend was that she
was rich, but that was hardly her fault, any more than her beauty.
After all, as my parents sometimes reminded me, we Maitlands
scarcely lacked for much ourselves. What I really felt, I decided as
we walked on, and the brief image arose, prompted by her near-
nakedness, of the time when I'd disturbed her and Leo in that hot

bedroom, was mostly envy, and a vague, uncomprehending disgust.

"Leo tells me you're progressing with the *Ciaccona*. He says you have an ear for Bach."

I smiled—unwillingly flattered, but flattered nevertheless. I knew that Leo never said anything about music unless he really meant it. "I've been practising a bit more."

"I still feel guilty about giving up with the cello." Her fingers shredded a fern. "Not that I have given up. But I don't think I could bear to play professionally. There's nothing worse in life, I think, than being only just good enough. I'd end up sawing away year after year at the pop classics in some provincial orchestra. Always living in hotels. Nerves and bad hands. I love music, but not that much...That's why I've decided to study law, although I suppose you think that's a cop-out."

I was flattered again by the thought that Blythe should care about my judgement. "Law's supposed to be a discipline, isn't it? One of those things that's—"

"Yes, I know, well-paid," she said, mis-finishing my sentence for me. "But I'm not doing it for the money, Roushana. I know I'll sound like some dumb beauty queen if I say it, but I'd like to make some sort of difference."

Pigeons clattered. Doves cooed. In the distance, the lawnmower droned. What difference, I wondered, and to what?

"And then my staying at home—that makes a sort of sense as well. It's what most students have to do, and Mum and Dad are totally happy to pay for a flat. They say it's a good investment. They wouldn't bat an eyelid if Leo lived there as well." She gave me a sidelong glance, sly almost, through the wet snakes of her hair. "Do you think he would?"

I shrugged, still basking in her need to confide. "It depends on how he is. I don't think Mum and Dad would mind, if that's what you mean."

"It's just so hard to know how things will work out. Now it's summer, everyone's expecting the damn virus to return. And Leo's had to put up with such prejudice. And this ridiculous business with our trip to Venice . . . "

After years of caravans and self-catering, we were going this summer to Venice, and Blythe was coming as well. But an endless series of obstacles had arisen because of Leo's WRFI. We'd had problems with the airline, the insurance companies, and then the hotel, but mostly, as the supposedly open borders of Europe slammed shut, with the British and Italian authorities.

"But that's sorted, isn't it?"

"Your mother's so *tenacious*." Blythe chuckled. "I can see where Leo gets it from."

Not that Leo was tenacious, at least in any ordinary sense—he was so innately good at things that he'd never needed to be. At least, the darker thought struck me, until now . . .

We were standing now in the blue shade of the trees which lined the furthest end of the Munros' garden. The grass here had been allowed to grow into a kind of meadow, although the flowers which sparked their colours as the trees swayed were too many and varied to have grown here by chance. Beyond, I supposed, was another garden, or the fringes of some health club or golf course, but we could have been deep in some idealised Romantic painting of the countryside, and Blythe, barely dressed as she was, was like a sprite or nymph. I realised, a little belatedly, that our walk, our conversation, our ending up alone here, hadn't been a matter of chance.

"This is my favourite place in our garden. It's where I most feel at peace—where I like to think." Taking off her wrap, laying it on a stone bench and sitting down with a small shiver, Blythe patted it for me to sit beside her. "You know, you and I, we have a lot in common."

We *were* both female, I supposed, although with she as she was, and me in baggy shorts and a surfing tee-shirt, that didn't seem like much. And we both loved Leo as well. That was it, I supposed. Whatever it was.

"Roushana, you've got no idea how much he thinks of you."

Warm though it was, even in this warm, idyllic shade, it was my turn to shiver.

"He's not always as good as he should be at saying what he means. Oh, I know he can express himself and talk passionately about anything under the sun, but that's not the same, is it? It's like talking in essays . . . "

Blythe's skin had almost dried now. She tanned well, and her colour was somewhere between mine and Leo's—it was shade which white people always wished their skin to be then, yet it seemed filled with a sort of shadowy anonymity in that seed-floating meadow.

"So I don't really know how he feels."

"About what?"

She shrugged. "I wish I knew. Me, I suppose. But—"

"You could ask."

"That's too easy. He'd see it coming a mile off."

For all my envies and reservations about Blythe, I'd always had a somewhat idealised picture of her relationship with Leo. After all, they were both so good at so many things, so surely they'd be good at being together? And perhaps they were, or perhaps they had been, but I was getting the impression from this oddly sideways—and, yet, yes, enjoyably adult—conversation that she was worried that things between them wouldn't last. Was there something I could say, I wondered, which could hasten this process, help bring at least one tiny part of Blythe's endless good fortune tumbling down? I toyed with sharing imagined doubts Leo might have expressed, or sharply casual asides about the way Blythe talked or walked or looked, but I couldn't put them into my brother's voice any more than I could phrases of frank adoration. Blythe was right; Leo was good at talking in essays but he couldn't express himself like this. That, after all, was why he played music, and that, I suddenly realised in a flash of sheer insight, was what I was trying to do as well as I scraped and bumbled my way through the towering landscapes of Bach—I wanted to say the unsayable. And Blythe, for all her proficiency and talk about provincial orchestras and hotels (which struck me then as a quite glorious way to live), had never grasped that that was what music was about. To her, it was just another accomplishment, like horse-riding or learning how to dive gracefully into her parent's pool. No wonder she and Leo were drifting apart. And, yes, I thought, he deserves better. But there was no way I could have put any of this into words, even if I'd have had the nerve to confront Blythe. Instead, I did the thing which Leo had recently explained to me most musicians are poor at doing; I let silence do the work.

I was conscious of Blythe's presence beside me—the physicality of whatever she was. I'd never really thought of her before as being made of the same human stuff as me, but, glancing down, I noticed the purple bruises of what looked like the fingertips of a grasping hand amid the raised goosebumps on her thighs, and the small crease which folded into her belly below her navel. She seemed to blur and divide. Half of her was still the Blythe of this spectacular house, the Blythe who gave speeches and accepted bouquets on podiums, the Blythe who stood in twilight at our doorstep in her beautiful clothes. And then there was the Blythe enclosed in the measly stuff of flesh and bone, which shat and excreted, which would crumble to dust and leave nothing.

"What I mean is," she said finally in her quick, clear and accent-less voice, "that if he said or did anything—if he meant anything, even if he didn't want anyone else to know or hear—you'd let me know, Roushana, wouldn't you?"

I turned to her and smiled. "Yes," I said; it was the easiest lie I've ever told.

"Good!" She patted my hand, once more the deputy-head girl. "I'm glad that's sorted. Now, shall we go and see what everyone else is up to?"

It was the day before we were to go to Venice, and almost exactly a year since Leo and I had smoked dope. There was the same texture to the heat in our garden, and the splay of the cherry tree against the sky seemed unchanged as I lay beneath it, but this time I was alone. What had also changed since the year before was the chaos which filled the house as everyone packed in preparation for tomorrow, and what had changed was Leo.

I've always hated day-befores, with their sense of blurry imminence. With Blythe coming with us to Venice as well, and because we were going by plane instead of packing everything into the car as we usually did, all the normal last-minute anxieties were magnified. Mum and Dad scurried to and from the shops for mosquito plugs, spare batteries for their handhelds, late additions to Leo's diet: more and more things. Then Nan Ashar and Gran Maitland came around, fussing and wringing their hands, leaving us with Tupperware boxes stuffed with unsuitable food-stuffs. Blythe, to her credit, kept out of the way. She and Leo would be sharing a room, whilst I would also have one of my own. I'd never thought that I'd yearn for the *Clarions* and *Belviours* with their laminated lists, but I did.

Lying in our garden, I stared up through the cherry tree's boughs, thinking through a difficult multiple-stopping in the thirty fourth phrase in the *Ciaccona* as I watched a glinting plane tear a white wake across the sky.

Leo's shadow blocked the sun. "Thought I'd find you out here," he said, then he stretched beside me on the spread rug as if nothing had changed and laid his arms beneath his head. "What are you thinking about?"

We talked for a while of musical practicalities, and he told me it was okay, sometimes, to hate the instrument you played. *Music isn't the instrument. Music is the sound it makes, and the person who makes it. Sometimes, the physical thing you use simply gets in the way . . .*

"It's the same with a person," he said, confiding to me and the splintered sky. "No matter how fond you are of them, not matter what you think you feel, it isn't *them*. It's like they're a mirror and all you can really see and feel is yourself and the thing which you can never reach."

"And you want to smash the mirror?"

He chuckled. "Yes. That as well."

I smiled up as the last contrail thinned, picturing Blythe shattering deliciously to pieces.

"Do you remember when we were out here last year?" he asked.

"Yes."

"You know, I've gone off dope. I rather hoped that it might help with the cramps I get. Or just... But it doesn't. Some other WRFI sufferers say it's the best thing since sliced bread. Not that they can *have* sliced bread. But for me, I think it might be like the taste of something you have just before you get ill. Some part of your brain you can't persuade otherwise somehow thinks it's to blame. Perhaps it's that. Anyway, I've got my stash of resin left in my tin, and you can have it if you like. If it's any use. I can't see anyone else wanting it. Unless you include Mum and Dad."

We laughed at the resurrection of that old joke, and then we lay back for a while, and I closed my eyes. I never wanted this moment to end, but, sensing the fall of his shadow, I looked up as he leaned over me.

"What?" I murmured.

Leo's hand rested on my shoulder, traced my chin, picked the sweat-stranded hair back from my forehead. "So," he asked. "What do you know about Venice?"

I was happy to prolong the moment by confessing the truth, which was that I knew barely anything. I cared even less. Venice was paintings, culture and history, and all the other stuff on which I easily grew glutted and bored. Venice was having to share Leo with Mum and Dad and Blythe. Venice was endless sightseeing. I also had a sneaking feeling, I finally said, as Leo's hands left me and the sky swirled, that it would be very busy and incredibly hot at this time of year.

The garden had fallen quiet. Even the murmur of city traffic seemed to have stilled.

"You're right, Sis. When I said to Mum and Dad I wanted to go to Venice, I didn't mean go in the way that they took it. I meant someday, somehow... But then the whole thing was already out, and they and even Blythe were conspiring to make it into this big treat, so it would have seemed ungrateful not to act surprised when it was presented to me, already wrapped up and booked and done."

"What about all the problems?"

35

"Mum *wanted* those. Battles with customs and consuls to get me there which she could fight on my behalf. How do you think she'd have reacted if I'd said, well actually, thanks, but I'm not that bothered . . . ?"

I smiled up at the sun.

"Not that I don't love the idea of Venice. Not that I didn't mean exactly what I said when I told Mum that it was probably the place I most wanted to visit on earth. But now she's turned it into a summer holiday, a trip with the family, and Blythe as well."

"I thought . . . " But I had no idea what I thought.

"It's costing a fortune, and you can imagine where a lot of the money's come from, with Blythe's parents being the way they are. Did you know, Sis, the hotel we're staying at, the Danieli, it's where Wagner used to stay, for God's sake, and probably Proust as well!"

Not that I knew who Proust was, and Wagner was low on my list of likeable composers as he would always remain, but Leo was soon talking in this same half-complaining, half-wondering, tone of Georges Sand, and I knew exactly who *she* was, and then of Stravinsky with his cats, and Henry James, and Hemingway drinking in Harry's Bar, and of Vivaldi, and how DH Lawrence had hated Venice so much he had Lady Chatterley heading there as if it was the opposite of full-blooded romance when in truth it was the beating heart of the stuff . . .

I saw a different Venice as Leo talked and I lay in the drugged heat of our back garden, and it was a far darker and brighter place than the touristic theme park I'd previously imagined. Rats swarmed in alleys beneath palaces plated with gold. Happy couples wandered between the limbless beggars in Saint Mark's Square on their way to inspect the instruments of torture in the Doges' Palace whilst paintings by Turner transformed the stones of the city into shivering water. There were the swirling saints and gods of Titian, and the romps of Veronese, and all those many films. I don't know quite how Leo managed it as he rambled and laughed and digressed, but I saw the gardenia floating away on the scummed water from Katherine Hepburn's hand, and Charles

Ryder and Sebastian Flyte arm in arm in a gondola, and Mahler's face flaking as he pursued a beautiful boy down the stinking alleys until he stumbled up the steps of a deserted palazzo as a red-caped figure, which was death itself, scurried ahead . . .

The afternoon receded and the air filled with gasoline flutters of barbecue smoke from other gardens. Then Mum returned in a foul mood from her final expedition to the shops and shouted at me to get on and finish my packing. I grumbled my way upstairs. I was half-excited now at the prospect of a quite different trip to the one I'd previously imagined, but the rest of me still felt glum and sweaty and ignored. My violin sat unplayed on a chair as I sorted through tee shirts and crop trousers, stuffing them into my zip-up bag's plastic mouth. Blythe's parents would be picking us all up at five next morning to take us to the airport in their tank-sized silver runaround, and we were all supposed to be finished and ready tonight, but I became distracted as I rummaged under my bed for lost sunglasses, last year's flip-flops and a decent swimming costume. Instead, I discovered the same Barbies whose lost shoes now litter my desk drawer, and schoolbooks written by a child who already was no longer me. Even then, I was good at keeping things, and poor at getting rid of even the most trivial of my possessions. But at least I had that Seashell, which was more mine now than it was Leo's, although it was probably too late to download any Monteverdi. Outside, the evening sky gloomed. I suppose at some time I must have gone and eaten something downstairs, but all I remember is the small chaos of my room, the sour heat, hot, falling dark and old memories . . .

Already, the shower pipes were clunking. Already, goodnights were being called. Looking in on me, her hair turbaned in a towel, Mum attempted an apology for having shouted at me earlier and I got my revenge by being monosyllabic, just as I did when Dad came in not long after. Soon, the house fell silent, but it was still early—I could hear the boom of next door's television through the wall—and sleep seemed impossible as I headed across the landing to use the toilet. I could hear the rise and rattle of Dad's snoring. Seeing as Mum hadn't jabbed her elbow to stop him, I knew that she was asleep as well. Leo's light wasn't on either, although I guessed that he'd still be awake, and there was that Smith Kendon tin he'd promised me. Still, and I hesitated outside his door, debating whether to knock, to whisper his name, whether to simply go away . . .

"Might as well come in, Sis," a soft voice growled.

Leo was sitting in the throw of streetlight beside the window. His face was striped by glints of sweat, and I got the impression he'd been there for some time, hunched by his desk in this uncharacteristic pose of underactivity. He was always so critical of people who stared into space on trains, in cars, in queues—anywhere. After all, there was always some-thing which needed doing. Notes to be made on whatever piece you were currently learning. New data on your handheld. Some book which demanded to be read. Otherwise, life could pass you by and where would you be, then?

"That tin. You said you'd give it to me."

"Did, didn't I . . . ?" He swivelled a little on his chair, but kept his face angled sideways. "Not planning to take it with you to Venice or anything stupid like that are you, Sis? Don't want to get you arrested."

There was an additional smell in this breathless air. Not that Leo's room, it has to be said, was ever particularly fragrant—after all, it was hot that summer, and he was a teenage male, and he hadn't been well—but this smell was harsh and coolly chemical, yet also reminiscent of sweetshops, and, somehow, of travel. Then I notice the litre bottle of Pernod which Mum and Dad had brought back to England from last year's holiday in a fit of Frenchness, and which neither of them had been able to bring themselves to drink, shining on his desk.

Although there was no sign of a glass, the level was a third of the way down.

"What are you up to?"

He waved the question away. "It'll be a damn sight hotter than this in Venice. Can you imagine it—getting heatstroke outside Julienne's?"

I just stood there.

"And I wasn't kidding about the beggars, either, Sis." He gave another wave, this one so emphatic his chair creaked. "And the bloody shops all full of the same old crap. Cheap glass and pornographic ties and ridiculous, unwearable carnival masks. And the jabbering French school parties. And the fucking huge Americans and the tiny bloody Japanese and the plastic coated menus and the sodding gypsies trying to nick your bag. Fuck Venice, eh?"

"No one's forcing you to go, Leo."

"No." His fingers traced the Pernod bottle. "I suppose they're not."

For once, I had no desire to get myself deeper into whatever part of his life my brother was now living. Giving what I imagined was a prim *harrumph*, I turned to go.

"You said you wanted that tin."

I shrugged an okay. There'd be trouble if Mum and Dad ever found out, and I had no plans to smoke the stuff, but I was reluctant to refuse any gift from Leo, especially one as charged with significance as this.

Carefully, unbending his back and limbs—he'd never been much of a drinker, and despised those of his age who were—Leo stood up. The chair slid away from him and his hand gripped my arm as if for balance as he moved forward, although I thought that he was playing it up a little.

"It's under here. Hardly original, I know . . ." He chuckled, sounding briefly more like himself as he began to work open the bottom drawer of his bedside cabinet. "There used to be a faint possibility that Mum might check. Not that she'd have ever said anything—and I'm sure she doesn't look now. That's the magic of white plague. Distorts everything . . ." He lifted the drawer fully out.

Leo's room was sodium-bright. The tree which had once blocked the streetlamp had died this parched summer, and I could see quite clearly over his thin shoulders into the space beneath the drawer. As well as the tin, there was a nearly folded plastic bag amid the pellets of dust, a scrunch of rubber bands and about a dozen pill bottles.

"There you go."

The tin felt slippery and hot from his hands. Slowly, clumsily, he re-inserted the drawer, then belched and slumped back on the bed, angling his elbows as if to shade his eyes from the glare of the streetlamp. "Will you bring that bottle over for me?"

"I don't want you to hurt yourself."

Don't want you to hurt yourself. He mouthed my words in silent parody. "That's the whole fucking point, Sis. Although, funnily enough, Pernod is one of the few spirits I *can* still safely drink. I had a test sip a few days ago to see if there was any reaction, then I checked it out again tonight on a WRFI webpage. So there's no worries there. It won't wreck more of my gut, and neat alcohol's absorbed mostly in the stomach, if *that's* what's bothering you. Herbs and wormwood. I'd almost recommend the stuff, if it didn't taste so bloody dreadful."

Leo was wearing the same hoop-shouldered vest and shorts he'd worn all day. With his thin limbs sprawled in this saffron light, he looked like some ancient wooden Christ.

"You could at least drink it in a glass, with water," I said.

"Then there'd just be more of it to get down, wouldn't there?"

I walked over, picked up the bottle, handed it to him.

"Thanks, Sis." He propped it on his chest.

"You told me you loved Venice."

"Oh, I *do*. But the Venice I love isn't the place we'd have been going to.

I thought I explained all of that to you this afternoon, Sis—I thought you of all people were better than that at paying attention? The whole place is sinking, and the seas are rising—don't you ever listen to the news? The sooner it's gone, the better. Can you imagine it! Seabirds nesting in the Basilica, the campaniles tilting, bridges rising from the mud . . . ?"

"They'll never let that happen."

"It *is* happening! This is the *future*." He lifted the bottle in mock salute and took a long, dribbling slug. Yellow as the light, aromatic Pernod shone on his chin and pooled in his neck. "You know, it would almost be worth the trouble of staying around to watch it happen, if everything wasn't so much of a bloody effort."

How late was it, now? I had no idea, although the usual sounds of the diminishing evening—dogs yapping, revellers swaying home drunk from the pubs, car doors slamming, a slow dulling of the endless susurration of distant traffic—seemed fallen into silence. We'd passed beyond into some nameless portion of the night.

"Sis, you've got no idea how much hard work it is. No one has. I thought—I thought, you know, that I was one of those special people. I thought that I could go through life without it touching or hurting me. I thought I could take the brick-bats and the applause and the good and bad reviews and the disappointments. But I feel so bloody *tired* every morning. It's like I've been up for six hours performing some wearying and pointless task before I can even get out of this bed. And the bloody stomach cramps, and the shits and the little emergencies, and the endless rows of fucking tablets. I've more bruises than a junkie from being prodded by syringe after syringe. And the *food!* Did I ever mention the food, Sis? You try living on diet of banana and tofu. You try going into a shop because you're peckish and finding there's not one single sodding thing on all the shelves you can safely eat. And then there's the sheer joy of relenting. You can't imagine just how sweet a Mars Bar can taste, Sis, when you're eating it in the certain knowledge that it'll bring you down for two days of fevers and vomiting, and irredeemably strip out more of my gut. My tolerance is decreasing. Who knows what it'll be next? Water, maybe. Now *that* would be fun. Or bananas, perhaps, and that would be such a fucking relief. I tell, you, Sis, whoever designed this virus knew exactly what they were doing. It couldn't be more clever. Imagine, for an infidel like me to slowly starve amid all the bounteous food we've dragged in on cheap labour across the skies from every corner of the earth just so we don't have to worry about being bored by what we eat!"

"You can't give up."

"What do you think the future holds for me? More tests, more bad reactions and useless referrals until the health service runs out of money and interest, and some fancy new disease comes along to take its place. I mean, WRFI's hardly glamorous, is it? At least AIDS had sex and drugs going for it, and CJD had all that tragic stuff of turning fresh teenager's minds into sponge, and cat flu was quick and spectacularly nasty. WRFI's a shitty condition in every sense of the word. It's slow and stupid and pointless. And I'm such a bloody *exhibit*. When I perform, when I even look at a piano, all anyone now hears and sees is this smart kid who's bravely over-coming a disease. I'm a freak. All I'll ever get is patronised."

"What about Chopin, or Jacqueline du Pré? What about all the other artists who've had consumption, AIDS . . . ?"

For once, Leo didn't come back with an instant reply. He was seriously drunk by now—his true intellect was probably already beyond reach—and it occurred to me as he took another long swig of Pernod that our best chance was that he'd fall into some kind of sleep, awake sore-headed in the morning, but at least in a fit state to get on the plane to Venice. But the thought was vague, and I think it came to him at that same moment, for he eased himself up a little and carefully placed the bottle, which was now well past half-empty, on his bedside table.

"Give me your hand, Sis. No, I mean the left . . . "

His fingers traced the calluses of my fingertips, which, much like my playing, had grown both tougher and more sensitive lately.

"It's down to you now, you know."

Changing his grip, I took his hand within mine. I felt incredible heat. Incredible lightness. Even now, I still believe that Leo was gone by then—beyond my reach, beyond my pleading.

"I was never made for this, Roushana," he told me. "If it isn't now, it'll be some other day that's so soon it'll make no difference. Some infection or glitch, or a loss of will far more protracted and painful that this. That's why I have to . . . " He thought for a word. " . . . go. You won't do or say anything tonight that'll spoil things, will you?"

Silently, I shook my head.

"Knew I could trust you, Sis."

"I love you."

"I love you too."

"Is there anything . . . ?"

"No." He smiled. "I'll be fine."

My brother would have researched what he needed to do: hoarded the right tablets in the correct amounts after having checked the precise results of their dosage. He'd get this thing right. That was how he was. I didn't doubt it. Letting go of his hand, I leaned over and kissed him. There was a moment's dizziness as our lips met—as if I, too, might tumble with him into the place towards which he was falling—and then I stood up. I turned away. Quietly, I closed the door of his bedroom.

The house spun with trapped heat and darkness. Down the stairs, the dining room door had been left open, and I could just see the smiling gleam of the exposed keys of the piano. For a moment, the air stirred, the house whispered, and I believed I could hear again, although far more beautifully than they had ever played it, Leo and Blythe performing that Brahms sonata. Then there was silence.

Back within my room, I picked up my violin. Sometimes, you hated your instrument. Sometimes, also, you loved it. There was no need, tonight, for any preliminary exercises or tunings, or even the score of Bach's *Ciaccona*. For the first time, the central melody and all phrases drew together in an endless weave, and I realised that Bach, supposedly the most chilly and mathematical of composers, was in fact the happiest and the saddest, the most warm, human and humane. I didn't doubt, as I played that night, that I was walking in the halls of genius.

SOMETIMES, HE'S SEEMED TO BE MERELY DREAMING—
my drowned man or boy. At other times, as I've sat here
today at my desk or wandered Morryn, half-dreaming, and
explored my memories I've hurried back to him in this music
room, filled with the sudden worry that he might be comatose—or
dying. Occasionally, I've become near-certain he's merely been
feigning sleep, and has been quietly watching me as I sift through
these remains of my life.

Does it represent a failure of will that I've brought him here?
Certainly, it would be nice, to leave a little mystery, and possibly
even a small scandal, behind me. *Famous violinist found dead with
anonymous male*—as if people still cared about such things. I
should report him now—alert the waymarks. Perhaps he's dangerous. He could be a compendium of every worst fear, the bearer of
some deadly new virus far worse than the antique plagues which
afflicted my childhood, or the human bomb, the patient torturer,
the rapist, the robber, the hostage-taker, the madman. But he
looks so vulnerable—so deliciously helpless . . .

I stand over him again now as the shapes cluttered within this
music room begin to blur and soften with evening. He moans
softly as I lift the blankets. On closer inspection, the scratches and
marks seem to lack the pattern which you might expect from
someone who's merely been buffeted by the sea. Illuminated in the
sun's low light, a cat's paw of cuts runs almost playfully across his
smoothly hairless chest, whilst a large lozenge of bruise shapes his

44

right thigh. He isn't circumcised. He's perfectly dry now, and he smells warm and clean. The salt would probably be good as an antiseptic. His knees are grazed. So are the palms of his hands. He could have been crawling, like some penitent from one of those mad sects. Now *there's* an explanation I hadn't thought of. Perhaps he wanted to die . . .

It's down to you now Sis. The air soars past me and my hands redouble as I look down on them. I feel as if I'm falling, but I ride these sensations. I drift apart from them. I feel as if I could pull down these old walls, tread the evening sky, burrow the earth, re-arrange everything. How much are these fugues down to my age and illness, how much is caused by the process of dying? My disease and the silvery roots of the crystal seed which was implanted in my skull now co-exist within me. They co-operate in my change and degeneration. I ride the feeling. I let it come. Suddenly, I'm exhausted—I'm tumbling towards death even as I stand here in this music room. But at least I'm not alone.

"Hey . . . " I risk nudging him. "Rip van Winkle. What's your name . . . ?"

He murmurs something, although it may just be a leave-me-alone groan. It sounds, though, like it begins with an a. *Aaddduubbnmmm.* Adam? Is he telling me his name? But it still seems a shame to wake him, and I can feel the drag of sleep as his face relaxes, his body recurls. There's something touching, almost abject, in the way he's pressing the insides of his wrists together, although around them I can see a pattern of dug-in cuts and dis-colorations. Similar marks also circle his ankles where his feet pro-ject from the blankets. It's as if he's been roughly shackled by ropes.

I go towards the windows. Winter is brewing—it comes earlier each year. I can feel it in my and Morryn's bones. Even now, on this fine evening, the wind is rising, pushing at the glass, testing the slates and eaves. I shiver, touched by outriders of the true cold which will soon turn the earth to stone, freeze rivers to grey and push the sun so far off into the sky that it will seem much as it must to those machines which mine the distant planets. But still, there is always music and the grey rectangle of my once hi-tech violin case rests on its usual chair. Keying the code, lifting my precious Guarneri from inside, I wipe an imaginary dusting of resin, then pluck each of the strings. Sensing the delayed beginning of our daily routine, the automatic piano's keys dip in response as it sounds g, d, a, e. Tweaking the adjusters, I strum back at it, then shoulder my instrument, lift the bow, and draw a longer series of open notes. The piano has fallen silent now, but a ghost I cannot see has raised his hands from the keys, and is looking towards me with a mischievous expression I recognise as entirely my husband Claude's.

We'd do this sometimes. I'd start something, and he'd have a guess, recognise, catch up. It was our private game, although we'd often do it before an audience as well. Occasionally, there was no piece, and we simply riffed, extemporised, improvised. Of course, the musically knowledgeable clapped all the louder when we'd finished. It was part of our glamour, our success, our so-called swagger and synergy—Claude Lewis and Roushana Maitland astonish the world again! Not that I feel particularly swaggerish now, standing in my music room with a half-drowned man as unwitting audience as my fingertips squeal against the cold strings. In fact, there's always this moment, this gathering barrier, when my mind feels empty and my hands lifeless. What awaits next? Silence? Agonised screeching? It will be one or other for me soon enough. But that, as much as the continued need and compulsion to practise, is why I must still go through these motions each day.

The automatic piano waits. I could announce any piece in the standard repertoire, tap in the beats, and it would start to accompany me. I can specify mood and pace. *Piano* or *forte*. But I'd rather do it this way. Stagger in, and let the damn thing catch up. So my hands pick the sliding notes of—here, and for blank moment, I actually don't know what it is myself—but, yes, it's that old warhorse, Kriesler's *Praeludium*. It pours out from my violin, and I, like the piano, must follow. Then, we are riding together. My fingers dance. The notes flutter and rise and the lid of the automatic piano gleams with the reflection of a woman who, despite everything, can still play a pretty mean fiddle.

Perhaps my drowned man doesn't like music, for he remains resolutely asleep even as, with what feels like an unnecessary amount of fuss and clatter, I put aside my violin. And I still haven't got the measure of him. He's clean-shaven, for a start—a flurry of sunlight catches on grains of barely incipient stubble—and his golden, curly hair has been recently trimmed. Why would anyone so well cared-for be abused, tied up, then abandoned to the sea? None of it makes any sense. I touch the subtle wood above the automatic piano's keys. A screen appears. The entire repertoire of Western music and much of that of other cultures is offered to me. But my bladder gives a twinge just as I settle on Debussy's *The Girl With the Flaxen Hair,* and, with an instant need which I haven't felt since childhood, I know I have to go and pee.

The first lovely fall of notes drifts from the music room as I scurry along the darkening hall, then the sound grows muffled as I close the toilet door and pluck at my clothing. The seat is ridiculously far down, absurdly cold, then, and even though I'm bursting, I have to sit and wait until the tiny dam finally breaks in a disappointing trickle. The automatic piano has chosen to play the doomy chords of *The Submerged Cathedral* by the time I'm finally empty and splashing myself in the guttering taps. My neck prickles as I bury my face in a towel. Who *is* in there playing? Claude? *Me*? Then, a wave of relief; good though the automatic piano is, you can still tell that it's just a machine.

Feeling somewhat better and something more like myself, I head back to the music room. Inside, my drowned man's sitting up with his arms wrapped fearfully around his body and his eyes are flickering wildly against the twilight as the automatic piano dips its keys. I hobble over to make it stop.

Sudden silence. The shocked air exhales.

"I thought you were asleep. I'm sorry . . . "

There's a slight change in the eyes as he stares up at me.

"You understand what I'm saying?"

He's conscious of his nakedness. A hand clutches pointlessly across his thigh.

"I found you on the shore."

At last, he blinks.

"You were nearly drowned. I rescued you. I brought you here. You slept. Do you understand?"

An almost nod.

"What's your name?"

His lips begin to shape. Could it really be Adam? But no sound emerges.

"I'm Roushana Maitland. I live here." I don't say alone. "This is Cornwall." Which could, depending on where he comes from, be either ridiculously specific, or a wild over-generalisation.

He half-raises the hand which was covering his thigh in a trembling gesture towards the space of empty air beside the piano. He makes a stuttering noise. I lean forward. He tries again. "I saw . . . "

"You saw? Saw what?"

The hand falls. His eyes trail back to settle on me. But reluctantly. Waking up alone in a strange house with a piano played as if by ghostly fingers, what is he to think?

"What did you say your name was?"

A small shrug.

"I thought you said your name earlier. I thought you said Adam."

He repeats it, but stammers the b.

"Is that you. *Adam?* Is that your name?"

"I don't know."

"You can't . . . " Slowing down, conscious of the rattle of my heart, I take a breath. "You were washed up on the beach. Do you know what you were doing there?"

He shakes his head. Again, the gesture doesn't seem quite right. A negation of sorts, but not quite no.

"Do you know who you are?"

"I thought . . . " Still afraid, he looks at me blankly.

"I'm sorry. All these questions. I'm not that used to discovering naked young men, I suppose."

It's an attempt at humour; he almost smiles.

"Were you on a ship? Some kind of boat? Were you swimming?

Walking around Bezant Bay? Flying? Did you fall from the cliffs?"

"I can't remember." The eyes don't slide away from me quite so readily now.

"Whatever it is, you've clearly had a severe shock. And I—I've had a shock too. And I've been a bit—well, I've been a bit preoccupied today. You seemed so fast asleep . . . " I trail off, conscious of the intimacy which sharing this house has already thrust on us.

He moves a hand, tracing it up across his chest as if to feel his face, then seems to think better of it. The hand falls and clutches at the towel which lies beside his bare thigh.

"What *do* you remember?"

"The shore. You were there. I was . . . " A long silence. Even with his eyes open, he's still close to sleep.

"You nearly drowned. But before that?"

He frowns again.

"Are you hungry? Thirsty? Do you need the . . . ?" My eyes, and his, can't help but travel down.

"Not hungry, no. Not . . . "

"Good. Well, I . . . " What else is there to say? He still seems scarcely here. I've had similar conversations with my son Edward when he used to sleepwalk. Then or later, nothing made any sense. "We'll have to get you fixed and dressed. Do you think you could stand up? Could you make it upstairs with me?"

I hold out a hand. With the towel still bunched in one of his hands, he takes mine with the other. He's so warm and strong and heavy. And so *tall*: he just keeps on going up as he rises. How on earth did I ever get him here from the shore?

"It's this way." Lights fan on in the hall. I hear Morryn's surprised creaks as he follows me upstairs. "Watch that low beam. Turn right here. It's through this door. If you'll just . . . "

I sit him down on a stool in the bright bathroom, then consult the faded mysteries of my medicine cabinet.

"That music . . . " he murmurs with his hands primly folded across the towel he still clutches on his lap.

"Do you know," I ask casually as I push aside yellowed bandages, "what it was?"

"Debussy. Some of the *Preludes*."

I stare back at him. "You know that?"

"I don't know why." His eyes are blue-grey, innocently clear. "It's just . . . " He blinks slowly, then swallows, as the mirrored front of the old cabinet squeaks back towards him. This, I realise, is the first chance he's had to see his own face. "Shouldn't I?"

"It's not so common, these days, to have a ready knowledge of classical music."

"But you do."

"I'm a musician. Now . . . " Slowly, lightly, deliberately, so that he can see exactly what I'm doing, I touch the digs and abrasions on his wrist, then a deeper gouge which lies amid the golden hairs on his forearm. Like two flowers, his hands unbunch. "Do you know how any of this happened?"

"The rocks? The sea?" It's a hopeful stab; neither of us believes it.

"Well—whatever it was, we'll need to fix it." I find an antiseptic spray in the back of the cabinet, then some strips of micropore, and an anti-biotic patch, a pack of artificial skin. "You'll just have to sit still and bear with me. If you want me to stop, if it starts to hurt, just say. Is that okay?"

He doesn't reply but, by the broad slouch of his body, he submits.

Beginning with the surfaces of his back, I dab and spray, dab and spray. There's so *much* of him. The notches of his spine, the breadth of his shoulders, are architectural in their span and grace. These small marks are immaterial to his beauty, although they lack the randomness which I might have associated with being buffeted by the sea. The way the ones across his back line up, a clustered series of four or five long, diagonal strips, I can't help thinking of the fall of a whip. But they're not damaging, nor deep. More consistent with playful cajoling or goading than outright torture. But why? Adam lets out a deeper breath. The muscles within his shoulders slide within the golden skin.

"It's nothing serious. If you'll just be patient . . . "

Dab and spray. My thin fingers do a spider dance. Closer to the buttocks now. There's bruising down there as well, but I decide not to go too far. His flesh is much warmer than mine. He's so much more *alive*. This process, the smell and the sensation, take me back to times when Maria, or more likely it was Edward, sat on this same stool, knees or shins or elbows brightly bleeding whilst I attended to them with what was probably this same spray.

I move up to the tops of his shoulders and wipe away a trail of dried weed. He barely moves, his breathing is easy, his eyelashes rise and fall as he blinks, although I'm conscious that my lips are intimately close to the side of his face.

"You'll have to hold still . . . " I'm a sculptor, shaping a bust— no, a whole body. I'm Michelangelo. Once again, he's David.

"Would it be better," he asks, "if I stood up?"

"No, no. Sitting is fine."

I move to his feet, his calves, his grazed and battered knees. "It's a bit worse here. Are you sure this isn't hurting?"

"Yes."

So I work on, although he's like no man I've ever encountered in putting up with all of this without the usual dramas and fake modesties. As I approach mid-thigh, and with that clenched towel already agape between his muscled thighs, he simply lifts it away. I suppose modesty must seem irrelevant when you don't even know who or what you are—but at least he's okay down there. Still, this whole male terrain seems both eerie and familiar as I dab at the lesser marks on his lower belly and ignore the dimpled stare of his navel. We never really get used to the sight of the opposite sex, although they're not so very different from us. Men also have their pectorals, their nipples. Their throats are thicker, but they share a womanly vulnerability and grace. We're all works of art, or at least we should be . . .

"Can you move your arms a little?"

I catch the soft musk of his scent as he raises them. But I'm almost done now. And what better way, Roushana, I can't help musing, to spend a little of your last corporeal time on this earth, than in doing something like this? The sheer physicality of his flesh, the things the mullahs and mystics either wallow in or claim to detest, is overwhelming. It's simply here, like a painting or a symphony . . .

As I move around to his left side, I notice that something just beneath his ribs that I'd previously imagined was mostly a bruise or a stain of seaweed is in fact a larger cut.

"Is it alright . . . ?" He breathes down at me as I stoop towards it.

"Fine. I'll just . . . " My belly drops as he moves himself slightly and the rent in his side opens a pale mouth. "If you can hold still . . . "

At least the wound appears clean, but it's so large that I can't really bring myself to look fully into it. Amazing, that some vital aspect of artery or connective tissue hasn't been severed . . . I grope for the packet of artificial flesh in the far back of the cabinet and knead and work a Satsuma-sized lump until it's soft and warm. My fingers tingle and cringe as I mould it into the cut, but he doesn't flinch.

"There." Much as a builder might cover up some hopeless brickwork, I spray a patch of waterproof covering over my bodged job. I really should get him to a clinic. There'll probably be scar tissue. What I've done is nothing like enough. A little dizzy, I straighten up. "We're finished."

"Thanks." The towel drops entirely as he stands.

"Didn't any of that *hurt*? I thought you were being brave."

"No." Another half shrug, which looks, with him standing there so beautifully naked, like the archetype of all the half-shrugs which humankind has ever made. "I just feel numb. It's odd. Look . . . " He gestures beautifully towards the scissors I used to cut open the pack of artificial skin. Stupidly, I hand them to him.

"This . . . " He grasps the handle. With slow but relentless pressure, he begins to push the tip into the palm of his left hand. The flesh tents inwards as the steel sinks down, and the scissors' point vanishes in a bead of blood.

I let out a small groan. "You can't . . . "

Then, just when I'm convinced that he's going to drive the thing through his hand, he relents, and the flesh bounds back with the elasticity of youth. It's scarcely a wound at all, although a crimson droplet dangles at the tip of the scissors as he hands them back to me.

"*That* didn't hurt?"

"I could feel it. But it's as if it was happening to someone else." Now, at last, and as if he's just realised the implications of what he's just done, he gives a coltish shudder.

"Let's get you dressed."

Morryn stirs with new presence. Our shapes turn against the windows, our shadows fall across the walls, and I can feel myself breaking through fresh layers of intimacy as I creak open wardrobes in my bedroom. Claude's black evening suits, his ruffled shirts, still have the whiff of applause about them—a spotlight gleam to the silk. I can't dress him in those, but here, in a drawer beneath, lie my husband's working clothes. Old denims. Sweats and tees. Oil-stained, snagged and holed and frayed, and then washed grubbily clean so he could dirty them again as he worked on his precious car, the DB5. I lift them out in a loose pile and hand them to my drowned man. Socks and underwear will be more difficult, and I've got rid of all of Edward's old stuff, but already he's pulling things on, bending with delicious ease, hopping toe to toe. He catches sight of me watching him just as his head disappears into a frayed crew-neck still flecked with ghosts of sump oil, the black stars of welding burns. Glancing away, I give a happy shiver—thinking how, despite everything, I'm no longer alone.

He's finished dressing. The faded denims are baggy around his waist. Much though he detested it, Claude plumped up through middle age. I hand over a belt. Adam takes it almost gingerly. His gaze is intense as he works it through the loops.

"Well," I say, "Can I call you Adam? I mean, I know it's probably not your name."

"Adam . . . " He shrugs, still searching for the belt's innermost notch.

"I'm sorry this stuff is so old. I'm not used . . . " I swallow. "You'd better put on these, too." I catch a small, sour pungency as I pass him old trainers, their doggy tongues hanging out, and remember Claude, humming *Figaro*, his hands busy with their laces.

"You must be hungry—and thirsty."

"I suppose I am."

"But first—perhaps you'd like . . . " I lead him mutely towards the upstairs toilet and he nods his understanding as goes inside. The facilities are antique, like so much of Morryn, but it seems that he knows how to lift a toilet seat, and use a flush—taps and towels, even—in the old-fashioned way which I still prefer.

There's a dog-like obedience to the way he then follows me back downstairs when he's finished. For all that mannish strength, he's timid. Yes, I think, as I steer him towards the night-segmented iron and glass claw of my new kitchen, perhaps he has been imprisoned, brutalised, hurt. It's easiest to think of him as some kind of escapee. Why, other-wise, would I be sheltering him?

"This kitchen was designed by my daughter Maria," I tell him after I've I sat him down at the counter and handed him the tumbler of water which the scurrying kitchen implements have provided, which he sips rather than gulps. "She's an architect. She lives in Barcelona. You know where I mean by Barcelona?"

"It's a city in Catalonia."

How come . . . I bite back the words. He's a child. He's wounded. He's vulnerable. And I've seen him naked. Anyway, isn't this exactly how amnesia works—or is that just in old two dimensional films?—you remember generalities easily enough, but your own life remains absent. "You really can't remember anything?"

"No."

"What about . . . Things which aren't specifically about you. You can obviously speak English, for a start. Are you English, do you think?"

"We're in England, aren't we?"

"You know that?"

"Isn't that what you told me?"

His voice, now that I'm hearing more of it, has a slight, shifting accent. A slide to some of the vowels. That stuttering b. Could be foreign. Could almost be Cornish.

"This is so *strange*." More animated now, he puts, almost bashes, down the tumbler and shoves at his dark blonde hair. His elbows slide across the counter. These are a young man's gestures, full of easy frustration and expansive, unintended, grace. Then he looks back up at me. "Where exactly did you say this was?"

"We're just outside a Cornish town called . . . " I pause: a small experiment. "I'll spell it out for you and you see if you can say it. F-O-W-E-Y."

"You mean Fowey?" Amazingly, he says it correctly: Foy

"You've heard of it?"

"I don't know. It's just . . . There."

"Perhaps you're local."

"Perhaps I am." Although he doesn't seem particularly happy about the prospect.

"I . . . " I sit down myself in this sun-segmented room. Close but not too close to him. "I decided not to report you, or take you to a clinic. Not right away. You could be—"

"What? A refugee?"

"Something like that. Some kind of migrant, anyway."

"Which means I'd be sent away again?"

"After . . . " I think about dressing it up. But what would be the point? "Yes. You'd be sent away again. Back to wherever you've come from."

"And if I don't come from anywhere?" Another small glint of humour—or mere resignation?

"That's not possible, is it?"

"No." In a more positive negative, he shakes his head. "Thanks for taking me in. I'd like . . . " His hands make a sudden gesture. "To stay. For a just a while. If I may?"

"Of course," I say. "Do you feel okay? Physically, I mean?"

"I think so. Tired, and a bit scratched, but . . . Nothing more."

"Do you know what year it is?" I gesture towards the time and date shown in one of the kitchen's displays. "Does that seem odd, or right, to you?"

"It's *there*, isn't it? Time's time. Doesn't really matter what I think." He smiles winningly, sitting here in my kitchen wearing my dead husband's clothes. Then he raises his arms and yawns. It's an impressive sight, with all those fine new muscles bunching up and the arms slowly cart-wheeling. I think of Michelangelo again—that archetypal man pinioned in all the neat concentric shapes and circles which then seemingly make up the world. He's filling Claude's clothes far more than Claude, even when he grew more softly bulky, ever did. I think, as he yawns so cavernously, of lions and other predatory beasts, then wonder at the dreams which must have possessed him as he lay all day on that red divan.

"And you must be hungry. Umm . . . "

"Please—you might as well call me Adam." He still says it in that oddly stuttering way.

"What would you like to eat? Something plain, I imagine? Do you recall likes, dislikes, preferences?"

Barriers are going up as he looks at me. He's quick—he can tell when I'm testing him. "It's like pain. Some part of me knows that I need to eat . . . But that's it. What were you going to eat, Roushana? Can I share some of that, perhaps?"

"It'll take a few minutes."

"I don't mind."

"You're a very easy guest . . . Adam."

Less and less, I see him as a danger. More and more, as a victim. After consulting what little there is in the fridge I decide on a meal, and the blades and arms of the kitchen implements soon set to work, slicing off shocked Os of bell pepper and getting garlic and olive oil sizzling with strips of chicken, pieces of crab, whilst I mostly watch, thinking as I have often thought of those magical plates and spoons which tended to Beauty in the palace of the Beast.

"That smells lovely."

"Thanks. It's a kind of Cornish paella—one of my favourite recipes, although I can't claim much credit for it nowadays." More for the sake of show than because it's needed, I add a pinch of saffron and sea salt to the bubbling rice. "There's some bread over there in that bin, if this seems too rich, or you can't wait."

"No. I'm fine."

"Do you know how to work this?" I gesture towards the space which the kitchen screen occupies when it's active. "If you look in on the news channels, it might help trigger something . . . "

Another one of my cack-handed tests, but, in what I'm coming to think of by now as his usual accepting way, Adam does what I suggest. He touches the silver ridge which causes it to activate, and images leap into life above my kitchen counter. As I taste the perfect sauce, and with a dizzying speed I associate more with my grandchildren than my children (of course, he's closer to them in age) he starts flicking through the datastream. There it is, tumbling by me—the whole world outside Morryn, although Adam's accessing it at a rate that's far too quick for me to follow. In a spill of impressions, I catch glimpses of dark shantylands and bright cities as chopped tomatoes are slid into a pan. Amid torrents of smiling advertisements for purposeless products, I see the suppurating skies and tombstone forests of goaded nature's atrocities. The scenes tumble, as well, in the stormy grey of Adam's eyes. His face, suddenly mobile in the light which plays over it, mirrors amusement, horror, concern. Steam roils whilst the armies of cults bow and raging mouths call down some fresh apocalypse. Somewhere, the heavens explode. Oceans rise, duststorms blur, and graphs of international profit and loss soar ever-upwards as I pointlessly stir the fragrant broth which the machines have made. Then there are places which might not be this earth at all. Acid plains and petrochemical swamps expand under clouds of extraordinary hue and turbulence. Is that Venus, Mars, Titan? Is that *Venice*? But it's always gone in the moment before I can grasp it.

"All of *this*—you know?" I ask him.

"Do *you*?" Adam's eyes are glittering. He's close to tears.

I shake my head as the larger implements finish laying the table, withdrawing to their discreet apertures within the walls. There's something impossibly touching about seeing two place settings facing each other after so many years of eating alone. Not quite a last supper, perhaps. But almost.

In the dark heart of Africa, the penitents of some cybernetic cult of the life-beyond-living queue up to die.

"Perhaps I should turn it off?" he asks.

"It's not helping, is it?"

He shakes his head. The screen fades. "And I shouldn't have just sat here. I should have helped you prepare this."

"No, no—I hardly had to do anything. Anyway, you're my guest . . . "

Serving by hand, I ladle a moderate-sized helping for him onto the warmed plates, and then a slightly lesser one for me. Sitting down to face him, I take a forkful and place it in my mouth. I chew and then I swallow, but my jaw aches and most of the flavour's muffled as if by some olfactory equivalent of the deafness I've long had to combat with implants. Is this what is happening to me—that I'm becoming a cold spectator of the last moments of my life? Is it an effect of my illness, or of the crystal?

Adam, meanwhile, eats gracefully. He might be hungry, but, just as his body suggests, he can't have been starved. He even pauses to make the sort of kind comments any socially adept adult would make about a decent meal, and I mumble my acceptance in return, grateful that at least someone's enjoying what my machines have prepared. I still can't work out his accent, nor the ethnic origins of the features of his face. Everything about him is so vaguely specific, so specifically vague. He has to be someone, to have come from somewhere. Those fine earlobes. That dull bronze skin. The near-perfection—despite those rope-marks, which I wonder if he's noticed—of his wrists against the ragged fabric of Claude's ancient clothes. I try looking for cultural signs. That passing of the bread basket, the way he wields a knife—it's all so elegant. An American laying aside of the fork here, a near-Indian use of pinched fingers to dab up the sauce there, and the easy way he handled that screen. How can someone know and do so much, and yet not know who they are? It's beyond eerie—it's impossible—but it's so *nice* to have a guest that half of me simply thinks of the many other days which we might, despite every-thing, still spend together here in Morryn, eating, talking, drinking, discovering each other . . . He's saying between forkfuls how he likes his name—he waves a hand much as a Frenchman might—the whole idea of being called Adam. But he still doesn't quite say Adam. There's that characteristic stumble over the d and the a which he doesn't make with any other word. Abandon . . . ? Abaddon? My icicled brain squirms. The mush in my mouth turns to maggots and the magical kitchen fades. What *are* you?

Finally, I've re-arranged the mess of the food I started with to make it look as if I've eaten some of it, and Adam's cleared both of two helpings, the second mopped clean, but not scrupulously so, by the bread.

"No . . . " He smiles and lays a hand upon mine as I attempt to move. "I'll do this . . . "

I slump back in my chair. No use pointing out that the implements will see to the clearing, for I realise from the crawl of metal across the counters he's using them already. But they don't dominate things in the way they do with me. He moves about, *possesses*, this kitchen so easily. Even since Maria designed and built it, I've always felt a stranger in this place. It's as if it's been waiting for him—for this moment.

The sea's turned dark outside. Beneath a rising moon, it's manacled with silver.

"Well . . . " Adam wavers as he looks about him at the cleared kitchen. There's a catch in his breathing. For a moment, he sways.

"Are you alright?"

He gives one of his nods, which isn't quite a yes.

"You're probably still tired."

He nods again.

"I have a bed—a guestroom . . . "

I'm not sure who's helping who now as, moving by what feels remarkably like habit, we both prepare for bed. That's the oddest thing—just how natural this seems. The finding of sheets, the hiss of taps and the closing and opening of doors and the flush of a cistern. Doors stir as I touch them. Rooms exhale.

"This was my daughter Maria's room," I tell him as we hover at the threshold. He and the light both seem to hesitate before we enter, and I'm half-expecting that heap of animated furry toys of which my daughter was so worryingly fond to still be squirming beneath the window until the air resolves into the clean and near-empty space this room has become.

He sits down on the soundless new mattress and all the towels and pillows I've given him flop from his arms. Once again, he appears dazed.

"I'm just up the corridor," I hitch a thumb, "if you happen to need me."

He gives me a smile.

"Perhaps it'll all have come back in the morning."

"What . . . ? Oh yes." I'd meant to be reassuring, but his gaze slips away.

"Anyway . . . " I turn to go. "You know where everything is."

It's down to you now Sis.

I spin back, and the room spins with me.

"What—?"

But Adam just looks up at me, innocent as always, with eyes you could fall into, a gaze you could drown in. He's lost—a blank message in a bottle, cast up on Morryn's shore. I touch his shoulder in final reassurance, then close the door. Although sleep and I are strangers these days, I head for my own bed.

MY BROTHER LEO'S FUNERAL WAS A SECULAR CEREMONY at the local crematorium. More out of habit than any remaining conviction, my parents had resisted family pressures for something more Hindu, or more Catholic, than a simple godless farewell. Afterwards, as we all stood milling outside on the blustery gravel, I was surprised to discover that you really could smell smoke. To me, this day was empty, without significance, and I resented every hug, wail and tear.

Tall, elegant, composed, Blythe Munro emerged on the gravel from a cluster of white-clad Indian relatives debating who should travel in what car back to our house. Something had hardened in her face. She had a short and efficient new haircut, was dressed in court shoes and a tight-fitting black suit, and she already looked like the lawyer she planned to become.

"I suppose these days must happen," she sighed, and I thought for a moment that she meant Leo's death. "They're just something to be endured."

I shrugged, suspicious as ever of any common ground between us.

"I'm not sure that you'll be seeing that much of me now at your home, Roushana. When I'm around your parents, I'm sure I just remind them that Leo isn't there."

"That's *not* . . ." I trailed off. I wanted to break through the bland assurance which she was able to bring even to her grief, but I couldn't. Since Leo's death, no one had asked me about what I'd known or suspected, nor whether I'd been into his room on that last night. Just as he'd wanted, it had remained our secret. Unlike my parents and the rest of the world, I regarded his suicide not as an act of madness, but as an exercise in will and logic. But as Blythe and I stood there, her expression changed and her lips parted, and I thought she was about to ask why I'd reneged on that promise I'd once given her as we sat in that glade in the far reaches of the gardens which surrounded her house, and why I hadn't tried to stop Leo, but at that moment her bracelet chimed, and then Nan Ashar spotted me and waddled over. The last I time saw Blythe Munro, she was raising her arm and whispering guiltily into her phone on the crematorium forecourt.

My grandmother had slowed and sagged recently. Life, I thought, as she leaned against me and gave off her characteristic odour of mothballs and armpits, is a series of acts which we eventually grow tired of performing. But at least here was someone who seemed to be able to accept the fact that Leo was dead.

"People, the whites, they keep saying they can't believe it," she said as the long black car which had borne Leo here pulled off, empty, along the driveway. "But I had two sisters back in the village, both gone already. Also, my mother's brother went young. Then there was a baby . . . "

The crematorium grounds through which we wandered were surprisingly large, with neat wastebins and discreet signs warning against the leaving of floral tributes, although many flowers fluttered and tumbled in their cellophane.

"Sometimes I wonder why we all came here to England at all. They told us they wanted our men to be conductors, and then they decided they didn't need them. Everything's automatic, so-called labour-saving. Even the buses."

Once I'd got past the puzzling image of Indians in tuxedos with batons, I nodded. Nan had taken to confiding in me more lately. I may have been only a girl, and a half-caste at that, but, because of my look and skin colour, she was able to relax into the supposition that I was essentially Indian.

"Glad to see you're looking so *nice* today, Roushana. Wearing decent clothes instead of all that workman's stuff you put on usually. And at least you don't dress like some girls, showing all their legs and then the belly button." She stroked my arms. "And you're got such a *lovely* skin. So pale. It will be much admired. All this . . . " She pulled a sour face and waved dismissively at the bending fir trees. "Meaninglessness. Even here in England, people are coming to see how wrong it is. It isn't about being Hindu, or Muslim or Christian. Leo was too young, too troubled, too uncertain of his path with nothing ahead of him but music, but your dear cousin Kapil . . . " She clucked and gave me a harder squeeze. "He never misses prayers, can name saint's days I've never even *heard* of. Believe, me, there is to be a resurgence . . . "

Overhead, a helicopter loomed as the cars pulled away towards home and the buffet which waited back at our house, slicing the air with storms of grit and dead flowers.

Leo was right. WRFI didn't go away in the months and years to come, but it did slowly vanish from the public's consciousness to be replaced by other, more dramatic, diseases and disasters. It had spread worldwide, and sufferers in underprivileged countries were already dying in their tens of thousands whilst even those who lived in the wealthy First World continued to escalate in their intolerances. Just as my brother had predicted, they all either succumbed to some infection, or gave up, or simply faded away.

Weakened as he was, I don't think Leo could ever have lived the musicianly life he'd wanted, although I still wish I'd said more to him on that night in his room. After all, Paganini had a genetic disorder, TB and syphilis, Pearlman was disabled from childhood polio, and Beethoven had famously fought his deafness. Even now, when I hear of someone who has battled physical odds to make their mark on the world, I think of Leo, and wonder if things might have turned out differently if I'd tried harder to dissuade him.

Dad, meanwhile, got promoted to Head of Year at his school. He threw himself into his work, as his hair, which had been denser and more ginger than Leo's, greyed and fell away in the space of that one horrendous winter. Tornadoes ripped up streets, and it rained as it had never rained. Then came sleet and snow borne on rumbling waves of thunder, and after that a glacial chill which blistered lips and cracked paving until that, too, was blown away in a fortnight of falling chimneys, shattering slates and keeling trees. The roads and the railways stopped working. The powerlines failed. The atmosphere was feverish, and with it came a new wave of flu. Everyone feared it was WRFI, or worse.

Tumbling in my bed, restless as the sky, first hot and then drenched in freezing sweat as I tried to find a position which would bring me ease, running through impossible phrases on a huge violin, it often seemed that Leo was still with me, uncurling in dizzying angles from the storm-beaten light, although his limbs were thin and contorted, and his face was masked by a vomit-filled plastic bag. Leaflets pasted the storm-swept streets for this or that extremist group whilst the television raged with pictures of yachts driven through the roofs of houses in Florida, and the endless watery wastes of poor Bangladesh.

This was the future, Sis, and Leo, who was right about so many things, was also right about Venice. Channelled by the workings of an ill-advised attempt to shield the lagoon, waves broke gleefully across St. Mark's square. The campanile keeled. The basilica collapsed. The residents fled. Amid endless talk of a restoration which no nation, in this time of numberless humanitarian crises, could possibly afford, Venice sank back into the tidal mud from which it had risen.

As with WRFI, there were many who believed that that winter of catastrophes was the work of a vengeful god. In this new world, and in this still-young century, their claims were harder to laugh off. Then came a day when the sky above Birmingham was pegged back, huge and grey and like a stained marquee, and Dad was suddenly all elbows and whistles as he banged around in the back kitchen, screw-drivering the lids off tins of paint. Still whistling, he headed upstairs with rollers and step ladders to Leo's room. The sour, homely smell of wet emulsion had just begun to emerge from Leo's room when Mum returned from the shops, dropped her bags and ran up the stairs to ask just what the hell he thought he was doing. The rest of the day was filled with accusatory silence and for years after a rollered tide of white on the wall of Leo's room ended above his bed.

The only music in our house now came from my violin. Once, experimentally, I raised the lid of the upright piano and strummed, somewhat inexpertly, the first chords of the *Raindrop Prelude*. Dad came in from next door with the numbers of a spreadsheet crumpled glowing in his hand. In a quite voice which trembled from the strain, he asked me if I minded not playing when he was trying to work. I never touched that piano again.

But I was good by then. I was no longer taught violin by Miss Fully, and in my fierce impatience with being merely good, I was already starting to have my doubts about Mister Phillips, who insisted I call him John, and was well past his prime after a life of hard labour in provincial orchestras. But I still thought of music as an abstract thing. Before I took my first journey to Cornwall with Mum and Dad in our first Leo-less summer, I'd never imagined that it might be encompassed in the swell of waves or a tumble of granite. But, as we escaped the city of our grief, heading away from concrete towns which still bore the stains of last winter's storms, then along lanes of wind-contorted trees which twisted down towards deep, unexpected valleys and framed glorious glimpses of the sea, I began to understand.

I remember the queue for the Bodinnick ferry, and the stacked rooftops of a town on the water's far side. Then came a longer, straighter road, high-hedged, with a slot of sky over-leaned by twisted oaks, and a sudden fork leading down to our rented cottage. I remember the nettle-scented twilight, the high grass which almost reached to the windows, and the absolute, whispering silence of that tiny valley. One day, I decided, this will be my home. Even now, and although the thought feels like sacrilege,

Morryn sometimes feels like second best to that cottage where I spent my first summer in Cornwall.

What would I have given then to be better than merely good? What, if I'm totally honest, would I still give now to regain the touch and finesse I once had in these dying fingers? As I wandered the clifftops and discovered squat churches and got barked at by angry dogs in decaying farms, Leo was always with me. Not now the fever-Leo of the long winter, but my companion and confidant and guide. I listened endlessly to the Heifetz recording of the Sibelius *Violin Concerto* which he'd downloaded for me into that Seashell player, which was precious to me in itself although it had already been supplanted by yet cleverer devices. I bathed in the music's icy passion as I wandered the dangerous paths along the freshly broken cliffs and turned my face to the reborn sun. This, I thought, as the wind and the music shivered through me, is how I want to play. This is what I want to *become*.

Being away from Birmingham meant something to my parents as well. Even if they were no longer capable of happiness, they sensed that I was at least experiencing my own version of that emotion in that cottage. Gone were the relentless day trips and guide book consultations of our previous holidays beside the then hot beaches of France. For them, as they collapsed in long-suppressed exhaustion, Cornwall was an escape from Leo, but for me it was a way of getting closer.

Mum and I drove into Fowey one hot afternoon. There was the traditional hunt for a parking space which the automatic machines indulge in to this day and then, as we wandered beside the new harbour workings and explored the shops, I got the impression that she wanted to talk. In my better Cornish mood, I was even prepared to turn off Heifetz to listen. I was still wearing one of Leo's old tee shirts, but today, amid the boutiques which still then predominated in such places, Mum nudged me towards trying out some more feminine clothes. I held tops and dresses before long mirrors, judging them against the chilly look which might best encapsulate the Sibelius slow movement.

I was taller than my mother now. In the wake of Leo's death, she had changed and shrunk. With their cross-cultural marriage and commitment to rational education, Mum and Dad had entered adult life imagining that they were part of what all society would eventually become. Now, as the divides widened, that belief had gone. She had a story of a nurse who'd refused to believe that she was Leo's mother during one of the times when he was in hospital. Even here in Cornwall, lads drinking outside the Duke of Prussia called down at us jeeringly as we walked past the harbour towards the shops. Mum was still an active member of the local WRFI group, but even that was starting to fade. The condition, of its nature, was almost exclusively confined to white people . . .

"Can you believe they're saying *prayers* now at the start of every meeting?" she said to me now as we bore my new designer bags back up to the car park. "Not just any old prayers, either, but exclusively Christian ones. So I just stood up and said I had no desire to participate. The ridiculous thing is, they acted so surprised. You could see them thinking—we thought you were one of us!" Mum gave the nearest thing she now gave to a smile. "Well, I told them I was a committed Hindu. *That* shut them up . . . "

Even through the worst of times, and despite the abandoned piano, Mum and Dad had encouraged my attempts to become more than merely good at the violin. But they still imagined that I was working out my grief and anger at losing Leo. Despite the enormous progress I'd made, they were still expecting me to lose interest.

"If you really want to make music a career, Roushana," Mum said as we drove back towards our cottage along the hawthorn-clawed road, "you need to think about how difficult that will be."

"Do you think I *haven't*?"

"Of course. But there's that phrase about putting all your eggs in one basket."

"Isn't that just what Leo did?"

Her hands massaged the wheel. Uppermost though my brother was in all our thoughts, it was rare for any of us to mention his name. "Leo was—"

"You think he had talent and I don't, is that it?"

"Nothing of the sort." Her mouth twitched. "But you saw how much pressure it put on him. I think, *we* think, that it was partly why he . . . Well, why he killed himself. Whatever happens, we don't want you to get hurt."

"Music is what's got me through this, Mum."

"I understand. And that's *one* thing. And no one disputes you're exceptional now—after all, you won that competition."

I ground my nails into my palms. I hated those competitions and recitals, which took place in the same dusty halls as Mum's WRFI meetings. Hated them when I won them, and hated even more when, as the upstart new girl who appeared seemingly from nowhere amid the rumours of her lost, brilliant brother, I lost.

"All I mean, Roushana, is that music's so uncertain. And you're good at English and maths—top set and all of that. We don't want you to throw any of what you can be away. You'll need a well-rounded education if you're to succeed at anything. Of course, we're proud of what you're achieved with the violin. It's almost a miracle, the way you've come on so quickly. But we'd be proud of you in any case. You don't have to prove anything. Not ever. So all I'm saying is that music's fine, but that it would be useful to have another plan as well."

I snapped, "I don't need any other plans," and turned up Heifetz on my Seashell.

I must, by any standards, have made an alarming and irritating figure as I strode about inside my arrogant, self-absorbed bubble. At school, and at music seminars and classes, I kept my head high, my gaze unfocussed, my thoughts to myself. I'd probably have been a candidate for bullying if I'd have responded in the slightest to the stuck-up Paki-girl taunts which sometimes wafted in my direction. But I didn't. I was, I was sure by now, destined for higher things.

Good was *nothing*. Good simply wasn't good enough. At night, my hands raw and aching after the four or five hours' hard private practise I now generally managed to put in at the end of the day, my head simply wouldn't switch off as I finally lay stunned and exhausted in my bed. I didn't even find the loss of sleep and rest frustrating. Yes, it was abnormal, as I'd heard Gran Maitland and Nan Ashar privately whispering, and yes I was straining myself up to and beyond the limit. But why *should* I want to be normal? Weren't the limits of so-called normality simply barriers to be broken through by people like me?

Amid those fatigue-flickering nights, in the TV-less quiet, amid the occasional sighs and stirrings from the far bedroom where my parents battled their dreams, amid the growl of the wind, and the blare of car horns and the mutter of police helicopters and the swish of the rain, many ghosts reached out to me. First came my warmest allies, my closest friends, Heifetz and Pearlman and Mar and Menuhin, and of course Barbirolli and Karajan and all the great composers, their cheeks gaunt, their eyes hollow with the pallor of grief and pain. *It's alright*, they would whisper. *We have been with you in this place. Feel, listen—we understand.* The deader they were, the better. I could barely bring myself to listen to performances given by anyone living. There was Mahler and there was Tartini, as well, and Paganini, and Chopin and Liszt . . . Wild-haired misshapen romantics all, and to me impossibly glamorous. *What would you give?* they always wanted to know. And I'd mew in my roiled sheets on those hot, freezing nights and I'd spread my arms and I'd tell them that I would give everything, and still it would never be enough. No, no, no, no, they would mutter and laugh as they filled up the shadows and crawled out from under their posters and dripped with the rain and crammed aside what else was left of my thoughts. *You don't understand, Roushana. Everything is nothing.* There has to be more . . .

I was exhilarated. I was terrified. My skin crawled. I drove myself so hard and did without sleep and ignored my mother's occasional pleadings. *This isn't the only thing in life, Roushana. You're over-stretched.* How stupidly wrong could she be! Of course it was the only thing! I wanted to be stretched so far that I snapped into disparate pieces and then to examine my flayed body and find out what those pieces were, and what lay beyond. That might get rid of this curse of being merely good. That, at last, might be something. The swaying figures surrounded me. I was touched by gaunt fingers. I felt their hollowed breath. I shared the fatigue of centuries. On summer nights, as barricades went up and the helicopters flickered closer and cars were rolled and the flaming streets of Balsall Heath played orange across thunderous skies, I breathed the acrid smoke of funeral pyres. When the rains raged and the gutters giggled like gargoyles and fish-condoms swam in the streets, my teeth were gritted with the soils of the grave. On broken-glass mornings, exhausted but elated, the taste of dried blood was still on my bitten tongue as I trudged through the blasted world. My bleeding fingers stained the strings of my violin. It had to hurt. When it didn't, I knew I hadn't done enough. I was a walking stigmata, weird Goth-girl who didn't even listen to modern music, with her eyes purple-kohled from sleeplessness and a gaze which saw right through you into the impossible beyond.

I was close, I suppose, to self-harm. But I still think that, for all the teenage drama, my self-sacrifice and self immolation were, essentially, about music. Good was bad. Good was rubbish. Good was so far off the scale as to be inaudible. The only books I read were books about music, often technical, or—as my sole relief— the lives of great composers and performers. Poor old Gustav, poor old Petyr, smashing themselves against the hopeless rocks of public apathy, but I didn't think of them in that way. The death of a child, a wife, a lover, debilitating disease, devastating shyness or critical flaying—these things weren't sad in any proper sense, because that was what life was like, that was exactly what was to be expected. Grief, hopelessness—the more raging the emotion the better—were all simply things to be captured and made sense of within the music, which would last long after the flesh had fallen from the bone. Emotions themselves were worthless spasms of chemistry and electricity.

Yes, I was getting better. It wasn't some delusion. This really was my life's work, and sacrifices had to be made. That chuckle. His rarer laugh. What remained of his scent fading from his tee shirts into the back-ground odours of this house and this century. His lips warm and hard against mine on that New Year's Eve. His room still lay across from mine, scarred as if by some wan sunrise by the white shadow of Dad's brief attempt to emulsion it, but otherwise the same. Sometimes, I waited for him to come to me, long-haired and gaunt in that old faded red dressing gown amid the other Romantic greats. After all, my brother was hardly out of place. He was beautiful and talented and dead. What did it matter if it was WRFI or TB, suicide or madness? He, too, would uncurl from the restless hiss of my breathing and the sound of my heart beating against the springs of my bed. As blind as Carolan. As deaf as Ludwig. Torn from the present, nailed to the past, he was there with me, gaunt and pale and knowingly mocking. But the closer he got, the thinner and more pitiful he became. Leo and not Leo. Not a figure of power, no—or not of power entirely. For he was the dust-picking of breezes. He was the buzzing of flies. He was the open sores of child-hoods of endless starvation and pain. He was the hopeless joy of giving in, and a distillation of suffering. He was the savage white light which lay beyond the deepest black. Sometimes, on the best and worst of nights, I let this Leo who was not Leo embrace me, and still I wanted more and more of him. For I would have given everything. *Anything*. And I knew by now he would have taken it. And perhaps he did.

Dad, in his newly exalted position of Head of Year, bought us into a family health scheme. Medical insurance, he announced when he came home with the glossy paperwork, was exactly what all responsible families obtained for themselves these days with the health service so over-stretched, and Mum and I both nodded, knowing that Leo would never have been eligible. Still, it was pleasing to think that, in those days of impossible premiums, we could now afford such a thing.

There was a plush clinic situated in a new out-of-town complex on the fringes of Solihull. Some of the buildings were shops. Some were offices. Some were warehouses, set off from their neighbours by high fences and warnings about automatic machinery. There was a lake. There were ducks. Our appointments had been spaced across the same after-noon, but Dad had had to call off because of some security crisis at school. By the time Mum and I approached the bleak blue and silver monument to wellness to which the talking card had directed us to on that breezy, gritty, sunny day, we felt nervous as penitents.

Mum's appointment was before mine, and I sat waiting and staring at the adverts which glimmered on the walls. This was more like some expensive health club than a hospital. There wasn't a single trolley, nor was there an ill person in sight. The only smells were of coffee and cut flowers.

Finally, Mum emerged. "Well, that was thorough," she sighed as she sat down.

It was my turn. The doctor who examined me hardly touched my flesh. Basically, I just had to stand, or sit, whilst things occasionally clicked or hummed around me. Tall and gaunt with Slavic cheekbones, she pursed her mouth and made small tocking sounds as she considered all the many items of information about Roushana Maitland which her many screens displayed. They were getting to the stage, she explained to me in her lulling accent, when such visits wouldn't be necessary. Steel and ceramic anteater snouts sniffed and studied me, then drifted away.

Apparently, there existed what she called *a significant measure of data* [70] about my Maitland and Ashar ancestries, for all that the documentation on Gujarati Indians and the west coast Irish was much thinner than that available for Anglo-Saxon whites. Still, she mentioned distant cousins, long-dead relatives, deaths and births and emigrations in centuries both new and old. She told me that I was tired, and that she was so terribly sorry about the tragedy of my brother, and that I needed more sleep. And then she asked me how much more about my future life I really wanted to know.

There were times when I could have turned back, requested more or less information, backed away from whatever truth she was about to reveal. But I gazed forward unflinchingly into the coming years. If I only had a short time left to make my impression on the world, I wanted to know. But my oracle was kind, her voice was soothing. The decades fell away.

"You're in good shape, Roushana. You've absorbed the strongest traits of both your inheritances. With your temperament and metabolism, you are unlikely to incur significant weight gain, nor will you suffer from any serious addiction, although of course that does not mean that high-risk drugs are safe. Allowing for normal environmental factors, your chance of contracting any of the major cancers lies in the bottom ten percent. Depression is unlikely, although without stimulus these factors grow a little higher, so I would strive to avoid large periods of inactivity."

"Who will I fall in love with, and marry?"

She smiled. "We cannot go quite that far yet . . . "

I smiled back at her—I rather liked the *yet*.

" . . . but I can tell you that you can expect to have a more than satisfactory, ah, love life. Or if not . . . " The smile between us grew mischievous; this was strictly girl to girl. "You can tell them it's their fault, not yours."

She was offering me a mirrored pool within which visions of my future came and went. What after all, did await? Whose hands would take mine, and draw me on? What would I give, and what had I already given?

"Would you like to pause, Roushana? We can cover this in a further appointment. Or it can be downloaded at your leisure . . . "

I shook my head.

"You will live, in all likelihood, to a considerable age, and in good health, both physically and mentally. You have strong bones, although you should avoid anything more than small amounts of dairy products. There are also some other substances, but nothing, I think, that will inconvenience you . . . I'll have a list prepared."

"Thanks."

"Of course, you should exercise. I suggest you will find stretching exercises such as yoga useful in later years, for the lower back and hips, especially on the right side. Before that, it does not really matter. Your heart and lung prospects are excellent, even if you are silly enough to smoke. And you are not the sort of person to sit around doing nothing?"

I nodded. She knew me so well by now.

"And you're a musician? The violin? Ah, you're so *lucky*. You have drive, talent . . . " Her gaze grew unfocussed. Perhaps she was considering the dreams which she'd once nursed in her Slavic homeland, then had to obliterate for the sake of money and a career in a foreign country.

But there was one question I had to ask. "How will I die?"

For a moment, something like surprise crossed her features. "I cannot tell you that, Roushana. All I can say is that if you treat yourself sensibly and do not succumb to something unforeseen and take care when crossing the road, you should live to witness the end of this century."

I felt deflated; a mere hundred years suddenly didn't seem long to me then, any more than it does now. "And after that?"

My doctor smiled a faraway smile. "Who knows," she murmured, "what will be possible by then?"

Like all oracles, she's turned out to be right, but not in the ways I thought. I *would* live out my designated century—but barely for longer, at least in this flesh.

Mum and I went to a shopping mall after we'd finished, clicking through the turnstiles with our IDs while the pass-less and disaffected lounged semi-threateningly outside. All things considered, I was happy with my prospects, and Mum seemed equally content. She hummed to herself as she swished around the designer shops, although I noticed that here, just as at the medical centre, we were amongst the few non-whites who weren't employees. She was wearing a sari, as well. In fact, I'd got so used to seeing her wearing Indian costume lately that it took me a while to realise just how much she stood out.

But Mum was oblivious. Mum, now that she had picked her way across the ice floes of Leo's death, was becoming determinedly happy. She'd put on a little weight too, and had started eating using her fingers, as she began her resolute drift towards Indianness. The difficulties she'd found getting people to accept that she was Leo's mother remained with her—she'd had parents at school asking what the likes of her could possibly know about teaching English, and this was her revenge. I noticed the fading henna markings on her hands as she picked at the huge muffin we shared at a Starbucks. She'd also developed a habit of talking about something called the "the village", by which I'd realised by now she meant not Moseley, but the place in Gujarat which the Ashars had originated from. She'd only visited there once, and then as a sulky and determinedly English teenager—she'd been a rebel herself in those days, and had refused to learn Gujarati—but now her conversation was peppered with *haas* and *nas* and *ajuos*, whilst her long talks with Nan Ashar had drifted entirely beyond my comprehension. "It's all about the falsity of pride", she said as she finished off the muffin and sipped her *cappuccino grande*. "Pride is *nothing*. That's the one thing you must learn Roushana. Do you understand me?"

My mother was turning into her mother. Dad and I, on the other hand, had started to grow closer in those Leo-less years. He, too, had taken his comforts in sad and angry sounding music, although for him it had been the *Sturm und Drang* of heavy metal rather than the glummer Romantics, but whatever revelation was made when he attended his re-arranged appointment at that clinic had a cheering effect on him. He set off later for work, and often walked there, and arrived home sweatily happy, his briefcase no longer straining with paperwork. When I looked inside it once, all I found were sandwiches. His taste in music changed as well. He'd always had a liking for minimalist composers like Glass and Reich and Pärt, whom I'd previously thought to be boring fraudsters, but now, as their sounds murmured through the house like the unwinding of music boxes, I came to understand them. The trick of this music lay in its simplicity. It came without emotional baggage. You could dance to it, or cry. If you met minimalism half way, it became a revelation. And all these things I learned from my Dad.

He even began to make music again himself. Not that Dad was a good musician—with the greater wisdom about my genetic heritage which my Slavic doctor had given me, I understood that my physical dexterity came primarily from Mum—but he had a good ear, and he enjoyed playing, and the slowly unfolding figures of serial minimalism suited his abilities. He treated us to a swish new computer, and spent many hours transferring and re-ordering our old family pictures and recordings. It was, in retrospect, an important task, for much of the data about my early life would have slipped between the endless waves of different formats and new equipment if it wasn't for his efforts.

I found one particularly treasured recording only a few days ago when I made my first tentative forays into this country of memory. It's audio only, but the sound brings with it everything else about that warmish spring day.

"That's fine, Roushana," the soft vowels of Dad's mild Brum accent murmur at the start. "Who needs silence? We'll make it part of the piece . . . "

Our new computer no longer came in a plastic box. In fact, it didn't really exist in one place at all, although there was a power supply some-where, and there were nodules spread like some silvery infective fungus. The part of the interface Dad was using hung before the open piano on a wing of glass, and he nodded to it as one might nod to a page tuner as the guitar arpeggio he'd recorded earlier started to unwind its way through major to minor, then climb back to its resolution. Over that he played an even simpler piano figure, which he embroidered a little each time it came around. In the recording, the birdsong, overlaid from outside through the open French windows, becomes raucous. Then it fades. For a while the loud slam of a car door somewhere down the street adds a neat counterpoint. So does the squeak of my youthful hands as I raise my violin close to the microphone. My turn to make a contribution, although it seemed a shame to add more, and I waited. I understood better now the need for simplicity; I believed in the glory of silence, and of the single well-chosen note. Then a phrase suddenly shaped itself out of nothing and I played.

When the piece finished, Dad and I gazed at each other in stunned surprise. On re-listening, the piece now sounds more pretty than profound, but nevertheless, we knew we had conjured something resembling beauty out of thin air.

"Well if . . . " Dad's voice begins.

Then the recording cuts off, and I never heard him speak again.

Next day, he must have gone off to work as usual, although I, as a later riser, have no recollection of his departure. All I remember is being summoned from lessons at school just before lunch, and finding Mum sitting waiting for me on the sofa in the head teacher's office, her face white and entirely blank. The head seemed embarrassed, and mumbled that it was probably better if she left us both alone.

The day of Dad's funeral was far colder and windier than Leo's. Huge puddles lay across the crematorium lawns, gathering and shattering the chasing sky. There were many young people there, for Dad had always been a popular teacher. His parents seemed thinned and shrivelled by the loss of their son. Granddad Maitland was especially stick-like, the tube of his neck seemingly too thin to support the weight of his head. He, too, would soon succumb to a stroke similar to the one which had felled Dad, but, for him, the process of dying was protracted. Every time that I saw him askew on his pillows with his mouth drooling and his eyes helplessly blank, I felt even more certain that Dad, by taking no treatments and whistling quietly towards oblivion, had made the right choice.

I scanned the figures standing out on the gravel, looking for Blythe Munro. But we had drifted apart in the time since Leo's death, and I had no idea whether she'd even been told about Dad. So I headed instead towards my cousin Kapil, who was looking surprisingly spruce in a black jacket and white collarless shirt, and sported a touchingly frail beard. He was considerably taller than me now—tall, in fact, for any Indian—and had become handsome in a doe-eyed sort of way.

A discreet pin badge for the RSS glittered at his lapel. Every weekend, every evening he could spare, was devoted towards the Hindutva. With brisk, decisive gestures, he enunciated how easily all the problems of the world might be solved if people could simply see things as they really *were*. The main difficulty, of course, was the Muslims. Unlike the all-inclusive Hindu faith, they clung to the arrogant insistence that all other religions were wrong.

"Don't the Christians say that as well?"

He gave a complicated shrug. "Those that do are just as bad as the Islamics. But there are long histories of tolerance. Take the Catholics..." he gestured towards one of the floral tributes. "They, too, have their major and lesser expressions of the Brahman. The Trinity. Mary..."

"So why doesn't everyone just get along?"

He sighed. If only people would see...But there was so much wrong-headedness...There were so many heretics...Hinduism was essentially the best of every religion—and it was big enough to accommodate the entire world. But there were those who fought, those who resisted—

"Hold on, Kapil. Let me get this right. You're telling me that Hinduism permits all other expressions of belief, but because other religions claim to be exclusively right, and Hinduism doesn't, you believe those religions are wrong?"

He nodded encouragingly. "I'm glad you're seeing the logic of the argument. There are so many out there who don't..." Even those, his look said, who weren't girls. And I'd read the papers. I knew what the weekends when he went off to Bradford or Luton or Derby—these so-called peaceful protests and warning marches—were really about. I'd breathed the smell of riot gas on Birmingham nights just like everyone else. I'd seen the mosques, temples and churches gutted by arson or suicide. I'd watched war spread out from Kashmir on the news and seen the atrocities in what Kapil probably imagined was our homeland. Still, it was hard not to find this newly brisk and decisive Kapil appealing.

Losing Dad was different to losing Leo, and I missed him in smaller, more ordinary ways. There was the tea he used to bring up to me in bed at weekends, and the charts of Things To Do he kept in the kitchen, which Leo and I, and often Mum as well, would often change in silly ways. There was stubble he left dotting the upstairs sink after he'd shaved, and the sight of his briefcase sitting in the hall on weekdays.

I succumbed to grief like a bout of illness. My face swelled. I couldn't eat without vomiting. I felt perpetually tired. Even music, listening, playing, the very thought of any kind of melody, became horrid to me.

Somehow, Mum managed for us both. Somehow, she carried on. She got herself up each morning, and got me up as well. Dealing with Dad's estate, she discovered he'd already secretly ordered most things in secret anticipation of this death—even going as far as putting Post-It notes on some of the more obscure accounts and insurance policies to help her through them—but she got through that, as well. She even resumed teaching. I didn't know how she managed it all; I still don't. I remember her speaking to me as I sat with knees hunched in a blurry corner of my bed. Dry-eyed, her forehead dotted red from a visit to the mandir, she said to me that life wasn't always about doing or saying the things you actually felt.

"Sometimes, Roushana, you just have to get on with it and bloody well *pretend*."

"And what's *that* worth?"

"Nothing's worth anything." She took a breath and gave a slow blink. "I've learned that now . . . The past's gone, darling. The hopes and the theories mean nothing. All we've got left is the future."

Mum never did crack. She never did give in. Sometimes, I would hear her moving around downstairs at night, or I would find her staring at some everyday object which had triggered some memory of Leo or Dad, but she always looked up at my approach, re-composed her face and drew me to her. Mum was a lesson to me in that time of aftermath. You had to move on, or give up: there were no other choices. I even found that if I picked up my violin, raised the bow and made my weakened fingers move across the strings, notes still filled the air. It was the way of the world. Cause and effect. Similarly, if you moved the muscles of your mouth in vaguely the right way, a smile still sometimes came.

With a poorish set of GCSE results, I moved school to the Sixth Form College in Edgbaston, not far from the fine houses of the Calthorpe Estate which, for all I knew, Blythe Munro's parents still inhabited. Socially and economically, though, the school belonged to the inner city. My Asian features were much less of a rarity here, although the Sheik girls hung out with the Sheiks and the Hindus with the Hindus and the Muslims with the Muslims. Then there were the Africans and the Afro-Caribbeans, and the New Radicals and the Poles and the Burmese and the Kurds, as well as the whites, who were historically divided between Catholic and Protestant. I, too, found a group I could hang out with, although the one I chose was that of the non-belongers, the Goths and the head-bangers and the self-harmers and the gays who, because of their varying glamours and stigmas, were generally left well alone.

Clustering outside in our separate groups on pavements windy with traffic as cars and lorries rumbled by in the cheap lanes and the sleek new independent machines swished along the premiums beyond, images and messages billowed from the handhelds to which our generation were welded. Synthesised glances, digitised murmurs, virtual pheromones and ai-written essays were exchanged. Drugs as well. Cigarettes, being illegal by then, were also popular. But the marijuana which Leo had favoured was now regarded as worthy and medicinal, and had been replaced by tabs and viruses, aerosols and patches—there was even a brief craze for suppositories. Not that I imbibed any of these more than was necessary to keep up some sort of face, and that the pressure was ever that great. It was okay to be square, and for every streetwise kid there were two or three neo-conservatives in tweed or burkas. Generally, though, there was still little trouble between these different species of youthful humanity, even in those difficult times.

I remember the long, drab corridors and the long, drab lessons of that era. I remember the burning ache for the hour to end. Knowing that anyone who gave off the whiff of over-achievement was certain to be sneered at, I kept my music studies as separate as I could from my school life. How readily we accepted those anthills of education in those days! The idea that you should force-feed young people random information which they were required to regurgitate, and then call it an education, still somehow prevailed.

I would often cheat the school's security systems and go out and explore the city. I didn't have the necessary permits to enter Blythe's Calthorpe Estate, but I sometimes wandered its edges and breathed the green whiff of its golf courses and sprinkler systems. I vowed that I would get in there one day, or somewhere like it, but on my own terms. In Birmingham, summers of monsoon had been replaced by those of drought, and the city shimmered and growled with traffic as reefs of concrete grew outside public buildings to forestall the risk of bombings. It was often unbearably hot, with tinny skies, clottings of dust, random plagues of insects, the scares of new diseases. Somewhat cooler was the dark interior of the Oratory Church, with its Roman Catholic scents of incense and old ladies, its door bangings and coughings, which lay next door to my college. I liked to sit in the back pews and try to out-stare the dimly gilded saints with their tawdry flames and sundry piercings. Christ presided over it all, arms raised as if to take flight, an avatar of suffering.

Amid Dad's files and Post-Its, Mum discovered that he'd insured his life for a sizeable amount. The insurance companies were folding by then under the strain of storm damage and the pensions of centenarians. Arguing that Dad had already known of his genetic weakness, they disputed the claim, but, in this as in every other battle, Mum never flinched or gave up. Eventually, they had to relent.

When the cheque came though, she announced that she would be going to visit the Ashar's family village in India. *My village*, as she was already starting to call it. She wanted me to come as well, but I'd been patronised and prodded by enough aunts here in Birmingham and I refused, and we agreed for the sake of appearances that Nan and Gran would look after me in the full knowledge that I'd be happier on my own. When she returned after three weeks, she seemed to have regained the knack of smiling, even if that smile was different. She grabbed and hugged me at the airport in a newly vigorous way. She almost pinched my cheek. Mum was pale from an enteric infection, but had lost the worst of her grief, and with it what remained of her English reserve.

Although frugal in most areas, she now took on Dad's love of gadgetry, and insisted that I don a wired VR suit and experience the virtual India she'd recorded for me.

"Roushana, I can't believe you've never tried one of these things."

Lying black and intricate and spewing wire on the carpet of our lounge, the outfit looked like an eviscerated alien. I lifted one of the arms dubiously. Like most people, I associated these things with the porn industry. "It doesn't seem very hygienic . . . "

"Of course it is—they're entirely self-cleaning."

"You're saying someone *else* has used this?"

"For goodness sake, Roushana, it was only me."

Stripping, I pulled the suit on. Stars, presumably stray scraps or static or data, flickered out from the blackness, then I was suddenly *there*.

Children with faces much like mine clamoured around Mum as she emerged from her taxi. Motorbikes phutted. Smiling aunts made namaste. The warm, virtual, air clotted my nostrils with scents too rich to be unravelled as she sat and ate balls of rice under the spine-fringed shade of bel trees, whilst the rapid conversations of the women were transformed into glowing subtitles for the benefit of my resolutely English ears. India by then was in crisis: war was spreading from Kashmir, there were endless elections, and tens of millions of refugees were pouring into Bihar from the floods in Bangladesh. Still, life went on, and Mum's village, which lay about fifty miles from the noise and high-rise Ahmedabad, was a greenly pretty place of rivers, farms and fields. Still, and Mum being Mum, she'd also recorded other scenes for me. After all, this was India, and the adivasi, the tribal people who most Indians still regarded as barely human, lived in a dreadful shanty town just a few kilometres downwind. Then there were the low-caste dalits, the so-called untouchables. Howling clouds of flies, too real to be unreal, crawled over my skin . . .

"I just wanted you to understand, Roushana," Mum said as the near-intolerable smells and sights faded from my senses and she tidied away the wires with the slow grace I was beginning to associate with Indian women.

"Understand *what*? That this is what you get if you allow a country to run itself on religious prejudice?"

She shook her head, smiled her different smile at me, and gave me a long-suffering look which I've seen many times since. It's there in the faces of Madonnas in Renaissance paintings, and Indian pativratas, and it says that that life is short, and God is gracious, that achievement is nothing, and that pain in this world is to be expected, and endured.

In return for that first of her many trips to what we were starting to call "Mum's India", we went again the next summer to "Roushana's Cornwall". Even then, we couldn't find the cottage we'd first stayed at—to go there without Dad would probably have been too painful, in any case—so we settled instead for a flat overlooking the shore and fish and chip shops of the small resort of Portreath. This was surfing territory, then. Even though it was midsummer, the waves of that season were vast as the Atlantic currents were doused by fresh water from the melting icecaps of

Greenland. Walking the cliffs and wide beaches, I became fascinated by the antics of the cloud-skimmers and body surfers.

In the mornings, incredible mists would cloak the wide arc of shore. Then came the first breakthrough of sunlight as you struggled into the glossy spills of the liquid-like, frictionless fabrics which transformed your flesh into something which could ride the waves. I learned the language of the sea, which was far stranger than Gujarati. Learned, as well, the easy companionship of the shore.

In the evenings, there were bonfires, plastic jugs of cider, wafts of chemical escape. And there would often be music: strummed guitars, voices drifting in song against the smoky thunder of the waves. I was too precious to risk exposing my violin, but sometimes someone would bring along a disposable keyboard, and I'd take it over, surprising them by what I could play. *Hey, you're not ba*d . . .I remember returning one morning and finding last night's keyboard flung over the rocks as a Daliesque offering, and still faintly playing.

As the night deepened, couples would pair off and head into the darkness of the dunes. Sometimes, a conversation between me and some boy would lengthen, and a hand would be laid across my back or brush against my breasts, but I always shifted away. Still, I knew that this sex-thing, as I thought of it, wasn't to be avoided. When I returned to my last year at sixth form college, and whilst the major part of me was preparing for my entry examinations at the Royal College of Music, the rest devoted some time to considering my choices.

Most of the lads I knew had either ceased to be virgins, or self-importantly claimed their celibacy, but I now began to regard them all with a more critical eye. By then, Mum always wore traditional dress, and I was generally assumed to be entirely Indian in my background, which left a theoretical gene pool of other Hindu, Indian lads, although I dismissed that idea right away. Next thing, Gran Ashar would be clucking about how word had reached her that I was sweet on someone, and wasn't it time we all went and had tea with their family? Was I really that calculating, passionless, cynical? The idea of having sex itself certainly held little appeal for me. I even toyed with the idea that I was perhaps a lesbian, but I felt no greater frisson at the thought, and less still at the prospect of the reality, so I decided it would have to be a male. I knew with an equally cold-eyed certainty that I was moderately attractive, or at least could make myself seem so, although my manner in recent years had earned me a reputation as being cold, a tease or, worse still, *frigid*. It didn't really occur to me that I could just go out with someone and see how we got on, and then try someone else. This was like a recital, a concert performance. It had to be right first time, or not at all.

My plans finally settled on a lad named Caspian who sat at the desk opposite mine in Geography lessons, where we occasionally exchanged mock yawns. Caspian, with his other-worldly, princely name, didn't belong to any of the obvious groups. He was good at tennis, he was bright, as well, and I also knew from his previous girlfriend—and this was important to me—that he had some sexual experience.

A bomb scare at school in the winter of the Mahashivrati atrocities meant that we went home early, and I kept beside Caspian as we swarmed out past the impotently bleeping metal detectors. It had been snowing, and the city roads were thick with brown slush as we walked together. Caspian loved books of the old variety with binding and pages, and we took a bus together down towards dusty second hand emporiums which still continued to trade around the university. He talked of first editions and put his arm around me as we walked from shop to shop through the frosty twilight. When we finally stopped to kiss under the streetlamps as the snow began to fall again, I felt both greedy and empty.

Mum had another of her trips to India planned soon after. Instead of devoting her charitable efforts towards WRFI, she now supported an orphanage near her village. Sometimes, she'd talk to me about the place as if I knew it, and I'd promise that, yes, next spring, next autumn, or when I've got in the RCM, I'd go there with her, although neither of us quite believed that I would.

"I feel so bad about leaving you again, Roushana," she muttered as she stuffed a few bras and knickers and winds of sari cloth into the small, worn bag which was all she took with her.

"It's perfectly alright."

"Of course, if you felt you could afford to slip a few days off—"

"Mum."

"Yes. Silly idea. I'm sorry." She came over and hugged me. "You'll take care, won't you?" Her bracelets jangled, her eyes were so close to mine that they merged and she smelled of mints and patchouli. I never thought that she wouldn't see me again.

"Mum, it's me who should be saying that to you."

"But nevertheless . . ."

Then we heard the toot of the airport taxi.

I'd been up-front with Caspian about what I planned for us to do on our first night alone in my house in Moseley. I'd even bought a bottle of wine from the shop at the end of the road, and he'd promised he'd bring the necessary prophylactics, although the patches felt odd against my skin, and neither of us were drinkers. We stared at the wine bottle and the two untouched glasses as they lay before us like some weird still life on the front room's low table. The evening passed slowly. Having agreed we'd make love, it seemed pointless merely to kiss. I called up some music, but for once I barely listened. I'd already allowed Caspian to massage my groin and kiss my breasts, and the sensations had been vaguely delicious. I'd become conscious, as well, of the bulge which came and went in his crotch; it was there again as we finally headed upstairs in the twilight.

You really want to do this, he murmured, his lips against my neck, as we began to undress ourselves in my bedroom. Faint moonlight trickled across his chest, his belly, then, as I wriggled from my knickers, it shone across his surprisingly-angled, tumescent prick.

I hadn't made a bad choice in Caspian; he entered me slowly and broke my hitherto undiscussed virginity with a series of polite thrusts. Soon, he was finished, and I was left with seeping wetness, and an urgent need to shower, which politeness made me postpone. We made love—fucked—whatever it was that we were doing—twice more that night, although still in what felt like a distracted sort of way. I didn't come, and as I lay in the early morning gazing at the small reddenings on Caspian's back, I decided that sex was certainly one of life's comforts, but that it would never take the place of music.

Sharing my bed with another presence, I slept oddly, drifting in some half-state until I finally awoke with a start. I'd been dreaming something about bodies darkened and twisted. Then a cold, dry chuckle rattled close to my ear, and I found myself beached alone in my bed in white morning light. I could hear Caspian moving about downstairs in the kitchen. There were banging cupboards and clatters of crockery. I could even smell coffee. I stretched and smiled. Yes, I understood now why people compared sex to food, with its all warmth and mess and physicality. Like food, as well, the sense of it lasted a while and then, once again, you were hungry. The sound of a newscaster's voice wafted up from the hall. Then Caspian's footsteps were on the stairs.

"Where did you say your mum was staying . . . ?" He asked as he stood in the doorway. Disappointingly, he hadn't brought up the coffee.

"I told you." I sat up. "She isn't—"

"It's all over the news, Roushana. A nuclear war's started. They've dropped a bomb on Ahmedabad."

ALL NIGHT, I'VE BEEN HALF-AWAKE, HALF-DREAMING. The memories which I've been circling, seeking, perhaps avoiding, have suddenly come washing over me—they're inescapable. Even now, surfacing into the frail sunlight of another late summer's morning, I can hear voices and the bang of cupboards coming from downstairs. And I can smell coffee.

How do I see death? There's no insight, no sense of profundity. Animals—all the other animals with the possible exception of elephants, whales and dolphins—have it easy. They never see it coming. But do *we*? Of course, we should. After all, it's just science, time, physics. Pluck a string, it vibrates. If someone is born, they will die—I have long known these things—but dates, times, specifics, are new to me. It was odd, how the doctor talked of seasons. This summer, yes—the summer would probably be fine. Autumn as well, although autumns now are so quick and sharp you hardly notice them passing—but winter was a shake of the head.

A blank wall looms, and I have no real idea what lies beyond. Of course, there have been acquaintances who've passed on: sponsors and business types you have to deal with if you wish to perform, and the empty spaces in booked-out concerts which are occupied by presences you barely see. Then there was my old agent Adur Foster, who told me as we sat outside a café in London that a cancer which the implants in his body had been fighting for years had suddenly won its war. Sure, he had a few months left, but to be honest he didn't want to waste it dealing with all the bullshit he'd had to put up with for so many years on behalf of what was—let's face it Roushana—an arrogant and ungrateful clientele. So Adur was doing what any sensible person did, and getting properly set up for his last, living journey. We parted on promises that he'd be back in touch just as soon, as he put it, as he got this whole bloody thing sorted. He said he might even decide to continue as my representative, although I never heard from him again.

And there was Daisy Kornbluth, whom I first knew through her husband Jorge, that fine cellist. Daisy ended up living alone in Cornwall, and we would sometimes go for walks, or cook each other meals, or simply meet up at our houses to grouse about the world. But, although we enjoyed our shared complaining, Daisy was sad in some deeper way I never felt able to reach, nor she to explain. Then, one day as we took a beer in the snug of the Duke of Prussia, she told me she'd decided that enough was enough. No, no, she was fine, fine, yes, absolutely. It was just time for a change. I went to her passing ceremony a month or so after, and wondered if I was the only one who thought Daisy's presence at what was effectively her own funeral seemed a little strange. Still, as we sat in the shade of a swing chair outside her house and watched the members of her unfashionably large family milling across the lawns, we both laughingly agreed that there was something to be said for hearing your own eulogy, and getting the chance to correct the mistakes.

"So," I asked, "what's it been like?"

She blinked at me oddly.

"The preparations, I mean."

"Oh . . . It's hard work. Surprising."

"And you really feel you're ready for this?"

I felt her hand grip mine. "The truth is, Roushana, I've come to realize that part of me has been dead for a long time already." A smile, as thin and cold as her hand, played across her face. "That's the thing I felt before, but could never explain."

"And what's it like? Do you know now . . . ?"

She looked at me. But, again, it was in a less than Daisy-like way.

"I mean, you must have a better idea by now."

"I really don't think I do, Roushana. It's like one of those journeys to a place you've heard of and always felt you knew. But the closer you get, the more you realise you don't know it at all. But I'll keep in touch, I promise." Her dry hand clenched mine more strongly, almost to the point of pain.

And she did send me flowers—a massive plume of varicoloured roses—a few days after she'd passed, accompanied by a thank-you note written in what was still recognisably her own spidery hand. We even spoke once or twice through the kitchen screen, and it almost felt like I was talking to the real, living, Daisy as she told me of the incredible things she'd witnessed, and just how happy she now was. But the real Daisy had never been happy in the way this new Daisy was. There were more flowers—that Christmas, a poinsettia—and more hand-written notes and messages urging me to keep in touch, all of which I ignored until, finally (for even the dead can take a hint) they stopped . . .

I turn over and stare at the empty, undented pillow, wondering about Caspian, and Mum, and Ahmedabad. Then I'm walking the shore, and it's yesterday, and there's something on the strand. Dead seal, bleached driftwood, pure imaginings? Like the sea itself, the image disintegrates and drags me down in a shuddering rush. Once again, I'm falling, sinking—

The bedroom door opens and a figure enters the room with a jangle of crockery. Pillows are moved. Someone I almost recognise leans over me. "Hope you don't mind me waking you." Fanned by wings of light, a face looms above me.

"I was awake anyway."

"You're not the sort of person to lie in, Roushana . . . "

I shake my head in a sort of agreement. Adam's wearing yesterday's clothes, and he's got on yesterday's smile, although his hair is damp, and there's a piney smell of soap to go with that of the fresh coffee.

"You've showered?"

"I hope you don't mind." He balances the tray on my knees.

"No. You should make yourself at home." As well as the coffee, he's found me jam and croissants, and all of it's laid on Morryn's best crockery. "This is . . . "

"Sorry. I know—an imposition."

"No, no . . . " I have to bite back tears. "It's the loveliest thing anyone's done for me in ages."

"He was a great man, wasn't he?"

Adam's been looking around Morryn, although I can't exactly accuse him of prying. There's so much *stuff* crammed everywhere. The awards and commendations. My children Edward and Maria posed in still or moving images, and all the things they made when they were young—crumpled projects in dusty paper, cracked clay or fading scraps of virtuality. Clusters of photographs of Mum and Dad in plain flat colour. And those postcards from India or Cornwall and the stranger, more recent missives which sometimes come from my grandchildren. All the posters for recitals I once gave, some still brightly alive. But above all, it seems, he's been looking at Claude.

"You recognised my husband's name?" I ask. We're standing outside on the mossy patio above the slope of garden which spreads towards the sea. The edge of the storm which brought him here has retreated, and it's another warm, bright, breezy day.

"I *think* I did. I realised I knew who you were as well, Roushana Maitland—I mean. You're both equally famous . . . "

I nod. I can't tell if he's just being polite.

"Roushana Maitland and Claude Vaudin. It's like . . . "

"Barenboim and du Pré?" I suggest.

"Yes," he agrees. "That's far better!"

"Who were you going to say?"

"Doctor Jekyll and Mister Hyde." He laughs at the thought. "I know, I know, it's stupid . . . " We walk slowly down amongst the paths and rockeries. "These things—they just come to me. It's like

91

wandering a library, taking down books at random. I have no idea what I'm going to find next. But the stuff here in this house. You and your husband. That makes any kind of sense."

"Well, at least it's *somebody's* life."

"But it's not mine, is it?"

We wander on across the lawns, stopping when we reach the low wall which defines Morryn's boundaries. Beyond lies the bite into the land which the sea has made in Bezant Bay, the waymark, a monolith of crystal, gleams up on Gribbin Head, as it looks down towards Fowey on its far side. Step too far that way, and it would register Adam's presence. He's far safer staying with me here in Morryn, at least until we get things sorted. I know time's precious, and that I need to return to what happened in Ahmedabad and beyond, but I find it easier to stand here breathing this sea air and telling Adam where I was born, and where I grew up (he's heard of Birmingham, of course, but only vaguely). Telling him, as well, about Leo. *It's down to you now Sis.* I even use that phrase, although he shows no surprise, registers no understanding; merely the same sadness I saw yesterday evening when he gazed in at the world from that kitchen screen. Then I tell him how I came to love Cornwall, and this, its characteristic sound, which—far more than the cry of these gulls and the rumble of those waves—is the near-endless hiss of the wind through hedges, over roofs and walls, around bent branches, across wavering grass. Listen: it's there now, although so subtly that you'd barely notice—like a breath, a heartbeat . . .

He smiles, and nods far more affirmatively.

Back in the house, and unaided by the kitchen implements, he makes us both more coffee—mine sweet and black, the way he now knows he prefers it—then he settles again on the stool before the screen in the kitchen and starts paging through whatever it is that he'd been looking at, whilst I, in what already feels like an act of mutual habit, head into the music room to practise. I imagine the days ahead, the times we will spend, and all the small ordinary things like this which we will do together. Morryn will turn to a changed rhythm, with dust stirring, rooms filling. Life, that most precious of all things, will go on . . .

It's an odd, lovely, feeling, to have someone other than yourself to consider. Even as I run though some Scott Joplin transcriptions, it takes me back to the hectic days of caring for the kids here in Morryn. Then further, to the days when Mum took care of me. Her arms, her smell, her laugh, touch me, and the feeling of her presence is so close that I put down my violin in mid-phrase and slump down at my desk. The music room pulses, fades, as my fingers scurry through the detritus on my desk with a sudden need. And there it is, blurring and redoubling—almost too small to be found, too light to be held, and far too brittle and cheap to have lasted through the years. But it has. It's *here*. A torn-off scrap of cheap paper, coloured a weary pink, stamped with the number 219.

LIGHTS GO OUT. CLOUDS DISSOLVE. CARS STOP IN THE roads. In the first white flash which broke over Ahmedabad at seven minutes past noon local time, and at Lahore and Jaipur, then at Hyderabad and Karachi in the beginnings of India's retaliatory strike, millions were already dead, their shadows seared into the walls. Then comes a wall of heat and wind. Roofs fly up as the sky tears apart. Buildings flatten. Flesh is seared from bone. Then, long before the beginning mushroom cloud begins to rise above the dissolving city, comes the fire.

In far-away Britain, so many things stopped working so quickly in the following hours that it was hard to believe that we, too, weren't the victims of that same spreading pulse. Even as Caspian was telling me what he'd heard, the newscaster's voice died as house computer systems went down under some predatory virus. Neighbours' dogs were barking and the sky seemed unnaturally dark as I pulled on clothes and shouted at Caspian to get back to his own home, then set out alone down Augustus Road with the vague intention of reaching Nan and Pa Ashar's house in Handsworth.

As if this moment had long been expected, the city had dissolved into delirious chaos. The main roads were jammed with the cars of people seeking relatives, or trying to flee a city which they feared would soon also be destroyed. Car and house alarms were squalling, buses lay overturned, and the pavements were already glittery from looting. But there were odd moments of calm. I remember seeing a woman out riding her horse along a side road which the stalled traffic had left clear. She smiled down at me as she went past, then dug in her heels and increased to a trot as she headed up towards Highgate Park.

News was leaking out at streetcorners and open-doored houses as people clustered around the few devices which were still functioning and receiving information. Not all the bombs had gone off, or reached their intended targets. Islamabad was seemingly intact. So, at least for now, was Delhi. But the shock waves of the weapons which had been ignited on that terrible Asian noon continued to spread. People were already calling it World War Three, or the apocalypse, and it seemed like only a matter of hours, minutes, seconds, before China and the Russian republics joined in. Then there was America and Europe and Egypt, and there was Israel, and there was Iran. And there was also Taiwan and Korea and Japan, whilst Jakarta had gone already in what remains to this day an inexplicable blast.

Things were somewhat better around the fringes of the closed estates in Edgbaston. Few of the residents here were likely to have lost anyone closer than a relative of their cleaning staff, and the high fences and fatal warning signs gleamed in an odd kind of triumph against the low black clouds. To avoid the certain chaos of the city centre, I left the roads and followed the footpaths down beside the canals. The air down beside these blank waters had settled in soft, smoke-scented waves. It was, I had realised by now, just as likely that Nan and Pa had headed towards Moseley to find me, but I kept walking.

Without the canals, I doubt if I'd have made it to Handsworth, for buildings were in flame and barricades were being erected when I returned from beneath the shelter of their bridges. It was Hindu against Muslim. It was black against white. It was tribe against tribe. As a long-festering war broke out here in Birmingham as well, bodies were dangling from streetlamps. Being female and wearing my westernly boyish clothes probably saved me, for no one knew to which of all the many sides I belonged amid this chaos until my arm was grabbed by a distant cousin as

I approached my grandparents' house through the smoke-roiling streets. Slinging the pickaxe he'd been wielding to prise up slabs of tarmac from the road across his shoulder, he led me around the flaming, upturned cars. Nan and Pa had tried several times to get out, both on foot and in their elderly car, but each time, they had been blocked, or had turned back in fear of their lives. They treated my arrival as if I was a ghost—they couldn't believe anyone could get this far across Birmingham. Uncle Rupa and a hysterical Auntie Indra were also in the house. Like Mum, my cousin Kapil was in India, although his recent e-mails had been cryptic and no one knew exactly where. Other neighbours and relatives came and went. Bricks had been hefted through nearby windows. Kitchen towels were held to bleeding foreheads. Then, with the power still off, the freezers began to leak and we had to leave the toilet unflushed for fear that the water supply would also fail, and buckets and saucepans lined the hall. Candles burned, and gunfire echoed as the long evening darkened towards what seemed like our first night in an entirely changed world.

The next morning dawned oddly quiet and clear. An army vehicle lumbered past the end of our road, guns scanning the terraces, its loud hailer clangorously warning all residents to stay inside, but by mid-after-noon, warnings or no warnings, people had began to re-emerge like the dead reborn onto the changed Handsworth streets.

News that Delhi had gone as well began to filter through. The Indian troops were said either to be still advancing, or in chaotic retreat. Jaipur was a mass grave. So, it was rumoured, was Bradford. Here in Birmingham, the troops moved into the inner city with a decisiveness which suggested some-thing long-readied. Tracked machines began to clear the barricades, then to build up new ones of their own. Our world contracted. Men in body armour and sight goggles stopped you with the snouts of their guns if you walked further than the end of your street. We lived on stale nan and tubs of liquid ice cream. People wore funerary white.

Many young men were arrested, and we tried to persuade a catatonic Auntie Indra that perhaps Kapil was better off over in India.

The air smelled of burnt rubber and raw sewerage. It was a time of paper. Burnt paper billowed in the streets, cardboard signs were hung around the necks of mutilated arsonists or supposed Muslim collaborators, old holiday photos pinned to walls and lampposts adorned with desperate pleas, whilst hastily printed images of supposed atrocities or calls to arms were passed hand to hand. Our precious digital identities, with all their clever technology, were suddenly useless. We sifted through the old medical cards and birth certificates which Nan Ashar, who knew a thing or two about bureaucracy from her younger days in India, had never thrown away. They, along with the new smudgily inkjet-printed identity cards which were being issued to all of us so-called ethnic Britons, were suddenly vital to who we were, and everything we might be permitted to do.

Candles flickered in windows. Birmingham had never felt so silent. No one knew anything for certain. India remained a blank territory. It was said that the Pakistani bombs and missiles were damp squibs, or that the Indian government had built secret shelters in which nearly everyone had been saved, then that we were being kept here in Handsworth because of some deadly new disease which was spreading across the world, or that people with European passports were being airlifted out of India, and that the British government had set up a clearing house for returnees at Birmingham's main airport.

Was Mum alive? The question felt worn-out and meaningless. Her village lay nearly fifty miles away from the centre of Ahmedabad, but no one knew how powerful the bomb had been, nor exactly where it had been targeted. And I knew Mum often went to the city to attend meetings to promote her new charity, and that the blast had occurred at noon. Then, even if she had survived, there was the aftermath, the firestorms, the dysentery, the radiation-poisoning, the Indian and the Pakistani army, the threat of more bombs, the lawlessness . . . I flickered between endless uncertainties. If I could picture anything, I saw Mum standing on the road outside her village, watching the thunderous rise of that mushroom cloud as the trees bowed and burst into flame, then walking towards it.

Some of the stories turned out to be true. Calcutta had survived, and relatives with the correct passes and permissions really were being shuttled to the airport here in Birmingham. No one knew what was waiting there, but Nan was in her element as she strove to get us passes. She cajoled. She argued. She wheedled. She marshalled her precious collections of paper. After a long night of queuing and bickering, she and I and Uncle Rupa scrambled onto the bus with whited-out windows which would supposedly take us to some kind of clearing house. The rest of Birmingham remained a shadowy mystery as we jerked and trundled over ruined roads. The people travelling with us were silent, or crying quietly.

There were glimpses through the windscreen of tanks and huge concrete blocks drawn across sliproads as the bus finally stopped and we were yelled at by guards to get the fuck out, you black cunts. I saw from the wide expanse of fencing and tarmac in the few moments we really were outside that we were in some far-flung corner of Birmingham's airport. Then guns were shoved in our backs, and Nan and I lost contact Uncle Indra as we were herded to join several thousand other Indians waiting inside a chilly warehouse, although Nan swore as we squatted on the bleak concrete floor that she'd once come shopping here for a new bathroom carpet in better days.

Day or night, the lights never went off in that warehouse, and the few toilets had long ceased to function. Demarcations were made, and small, pointless attempts at privacy were endlessly erected and squabbled over. Damp dripped down from the distant roof. Still, Nan was soon reforming lost acquaintances. *Ah, now my sister-in-law, she spent some time in that part of Bradford* . . . Big jets often passed thunderously close over-head. Word went around that similar groups of Muslims were being held in a warehouse nearby—the one, as Nan calmly informed me, which had once held an out-of-town branch of Marks and Spencers. One woman killed herself else by clambering the building's inner walls and throwing herself off, whilst a young man was found with a piece of scaffolding driven through his heart in some unknown act of revenge. It was said that London and most of the South East had been destroyed in a strike by the Russians, but news, real news, was even more scarce here than it had been in Handsworth, and the guards were saying nothing. Then, on the third day, a large loudspeaker was set up on a tall stand in one far corner of the warehouse and names, many incomprehensibly mis-pronounced, began to be called out.

We crowded towards that big black box. It was ridiculous how our spirits rose as we debated each distorted phrase, and how disputes multi-plied as a selected few were permitted to pass from this long purgatory through a small and well guarded door marked NO EXIT. I fell back into a drowse of waiting.

"That'll be us," Nan said, prodding me awake.

Beyond that hallowed door, Nan and I were instantly separated and herded along different corridors, and I didn't see her again for several days. It was getting harder to remember Mum, or why I was here, as a large, stiff-faced woman led me into a bare room and told me to take off my clothes. Finally, shivering more from the outrage of what had been done to me, dressed again, but still shoeless, I was ordered to take a seat beside a chipped desk amid many office partitions and await my turn. This was surely it—a person nearby was sobbing, someone else was shouting—but I just felt drained.

"Name . . . ?"

I shovelled my hard-earned papers across the desk. They were ignored.

"Name . . . ?"

My interviewer went away. Another came. It was like some weird form of musical chairs. There were long gaps as I just sat there with my bare feet pressed to the studded rubber floor. The woman beyond the partition nearest to me was endlessly repeating the same flight number and I longed to find the energy to tell her to shut up.

"You say your mother was working for a charity. What number is it registered as? Do you have a tax reference? What's the exact name?"

I realised that my saying Mum was involved in a charity in India was tantamount to describing her as a terrorist. Then there was cousin Kapil.

"Marriage plans, were there?"

Wasn't Mum—wasn't *I*—a British Citizen? Didn't we have *rights*? But the young man with the loosely knotted tie fought back a tired smile as I feebly attempted to rage at him. After all, he probably had as little choice as I did about being here.

I became convinced that the truth of whether Mum was dead or alive was being determined solely by this endless questioning. A mistaken word, the wrong box ticked, and she would vanish forever, destroyed not by nuclear war but mis-administration. After the most part of another day, I was given a pink raffle ticket numbered 219, with a smaller and longer unique number printed yet more crudely beneath it—more paper. Then I and a few others were prodded out into the surprising daylight to board another whited-out bus which bore us through several roadblocks to the glass frontage of the airport's international departures terminal. I'd been here before to see off Mum and visiting relatives, and this was where we'd have gone if Leo and Dad really had ever made it to Venice. It was strange to see the place like this as, still clutching our precious raffle tickets, we swarmed in.

The terminal seemed to be living out a last mad bank holiday before the world of cheap travel and falling frontiers died forever. People were sleeping on seats or curled up amid the contents of their suitcases. Others wept, sat comatose or argued and gestured towards whoever would listen. Even allowing for my own recent experiences, and my own personal funk, the smell was incredible. Stretchers were lined beside the departures tunnel, along with what could only be body bags. Soldiers milled. Bizarrely, airport muzak was playing.

None of the flight displays were working, but an old man in a Nehru hat had told me that a relief shuttle from India had just come in via Cyprus. Suddenly, people were screaming and fighting over new arrivals of body bags. Fleeing them, I ran up dead escalators to a balcony amid the shuttered or ransacked airport shops which looked down on the scene. All I saw were swarms of dark heads. Where was Nan? Where was Uncle Indra? I slumped, reduced to tears and helplessness.

It was a few minutes before I looked down again, and then with no hope of finding anything. Then, I didn't believe what I saw—it was too easy—somehow, this was and wasn't Mum—and there was something odd about the way she was turning her head. I recognised the clothes, but she was moving differently. Dazed, I hobbled back down the dead escalators. A sea of people pushed around me. Anguished voices keened. Old photos of lost family members were waved in my face. I batted them away and Mum came and went as the crowds surged between us. She still hadn't noticed me, and I'd nearly reached her before she finally turned her head and her hands began to fumble towards me, pushing though a surge of bodies to touch my arms, my shoulders, my face.

"That *is* you, Roushana."

She smiled. She was almost looking directly at me now, and I saw she was blind.

ADAM'S THE PERFECT GUEST. AFTER TAKING OVER FROM the kitchen machines to make and clear away our breakfast, he then found enough food left in my sparse fridge to make us both this passable lunch. Morning went by in a rush of memories, and it's past noon already as we sit here eating bread, which he's freshened up in the oven, and a couple of varieties of decent-ish cheese. There are even grapes, although I don't know where he got them, or these succulent slices of saucisson, from, nor this jar of pickled walnuts. To me, it's a feast, although it feels strange to be sitting here in my own flesh, in my own house, when part of me still feels as if I should be squatting with thousands of others on the concrete floor of an airport warehouse . . .

"You've been rather quiet," Adam says as he pours me water from the carafe.

"I have these . . . " I wave a hand as I dryly masticate. "Preoccupations."

"Of course. None of my business."

Is he fishing? I let it pass.

"Might as well finish this off." The tattered edge of Claude's old sweatshirt raises as he slices the remains of the cheese, and I notice that the waterproof covering which I sprayed over that rent in his side is now becoming discoloured. "I was wondering," he then says as if the subject hasn't changed, "what would happen if I left this house and kept on walking."

"I don't know..." I think again of Birmingham, of being a refugee in my own country. "If you went inland towards the road, or anywhere near a town such as Fowey, you'd probably be detected by the waymarks as a moving, human shape. Your presence would be—I believe the term is *interrogated*. If it turns out you have a right to be here, you'd be welcomed, taken back into whatever your life really is. If not, you'd be captured, imprisoned, sent away."

"Hardly seems fair, does it? I mean, I'm the same person either way."

"Things aren't fair, Adam. Don't you know that?"

He blinks. His perfect teeth bite his perfect lip. "You're too negative, Roushana." He makes a feminine gesture, which seems both sexy and charming in someone so resolutely male. "There *has* to be hope. Otherwise, we wouldn't both be here, would we? Otherwise, I'd be dead already on that shore."

"You're right. I'm sorry. Do you remember anything more now? You seem so familiar with everything here in this kitchen."

"I do, don't I?" He gives a furtive smile, then lowers his head.

"And these rope cuts..." Reaching across the remains of the food, I take his hands, turn them palm upward and ease back the cuffs, although the marks have already faded. "Have you noticed them? There are similar ones on your ankles. Don't they look to you as if—well, as if you've been tied up?"

Breathing together, sharing the soft warmth which his body emanates, we stare down at his wrists, although it seems there's nothing else to be said.

Finally, as the silence stretches, I let him go.

"Anyway," I say. "Thanks for getting this meal. You've done really well to find what you did. But I think we'll both starve if I don't get some more food in. Of course..." I gesture towards the kitchen screen. "I could order it through there, and it would come in the matter of an hour. But I enjoy shopping, and—well, to be honest—I don't think that it's a particularly good idea that we let even some dumb delivery vehicle know that you're here."

Pausing in my coat outside on the front porch, I decide to enter the command which will cause all Morryn's doors and windows to seal. Better, I tell myself, that Adam stays inside and away from harm . . .

An almost-warm wind buffets me as I follow the old road down towards Fowey. Amid its changing, booming, whispering, hissing sound, I can still hear echoes of the Sibelius which I once filled my head with as I walked the Cornish cliffs. If I squint in this lemony sunlight, the abandoned fields become sheep-cropped once again and the distant wind generators begin to turn their sails. But, thin as the breeze, pale as the light, the vast mote of some leviathan is floating across the sky as it mouths and digests whatever poisons have been cast here from other, less fortunate lands. *This is the future, Sis.* Just half-close your eyes, look up at the sun. It's that easy—that close . . .

Bezant Bay lies twinkling where the antique tarmac gives out in a freshly-hewn drop. The beach has grown slimmer in recent years and fresh rockfalls foam their jagged mouths. I'd pause here to rest, but I know I'll be kidnapped by memories if I dawdle, and I have to get on. A broader landscape unfolds as I follow the coastal footpath beyond, revealing the Fowey estuary and then the gothic turrets of Place House. Fowey hasn't changed so very much since I first came here with Mum and Dad. Clay barges still slide towards the deepwater harbour between the dragonfly boats, cars crawl along the esplanade, and the ferry still noses across from Bodinnick, even if none of these activities now require human intervention. The tightly down-tilting streets which I enter even smell the same: coaly and fishy, faintly damp, and with that sudden feeling of cold when you pass into their near-perpetual shade. As always there are people about, and many of them are real— shopping, talking and gawping in the old-fashioned way as I shoulder thinly past them—but there are other presences, trails of voice and colour like wind-blown scarves gone too quickly by for me to register them. *Ah, look...!* A voice exclaims, and hands which have no body flutter in delight. Tourists, I suppose, just like so many other of the visitors which Fowey has long accommodated, but borne here from some other place along the network of silvery veins which shine across these pavements like the winter's first frost.

I head into the market and set about filling my striped shopping bag with all the varied produce of the stalls and shops. Herring outstare me from their beds of ice. So do fat pimento-eyed olives. Some sort of consideration before I set out from Morryn as to what I needed to buy here might have been an advantage, but I still have no real idea what Adam likes, or how long he'll be staying. I aim for a scattershot approach. Effectively, I buy larger than usual quantities of all the things I enjoy—or used to. So it's kippers and taramasalata, it's brown eggs and bacon, it's freshly circumcised button mushrooms and coriander of dewy fragrance, and saffron buns and, yes, strawberries as well. The stall-holders are friendly, obliging, and ridiculously proud of their displays. This grow this stuff themselves, or smoke it, or make it, or catch it—my bacon's even labelled with the pig's smiling snout and name. I'm sure it led a happy life, just like all these happy, willing people who hand me their produce with a greaseproof-wrapped flourish and a mouthing of something approximating to my name.

I have a sort of vague celebrity here in Fowey which exceeds even Bessie the flayed but fondly-remembered pig. I'm that woman, you know, the musician, plays some sort of acoustic instrument, the fiddle or something, lives in that nice house up on Sithy Hill. They promise to attend my occasional local recitals, but mostly they don't. Even as my arms start to feel the weight of the bags which jostle against my legs, the whole exchange seems saccharine. There's no payment, for a start—I'm simply given whatever I ask for. I know that sensors are registering each transaction, but it still doesn't seem right. I'm like an extra in a film set, and the feeling is compounded by how good-looking everyone is these days. Amid the tall, the dashing, the handsome, the finely-boned and authentically ethnically-detailed, the only living ones who stand out are the few elderly souls like myself, and those yet more ancient who are supported by discreet but nevertheless distracting frameworks as they shuffle along like withered robots, clinging to this earth when they should have long done the obvious thing and passed on. *The future's here Sis.* It's been and gone. And I'm still here. And so, now, are the dead.

They're not everywhere yet. But they're getting there. The cities nowadays—London where Edward lives, and Maria's Barcelona—are filled with these spillages of strange movement which catch at the edges of your eyes. Even in solid, stolid old Fowey, it's often hard to tell exactly what people are seeing now that its main streets are enmeshed in the ever-spreading network of crystal. For most of my life, the idea of someone talking animatedly to something you can't see has been commonplace. My grandchildren chase ghosts across Morryn's lawns on the rare occasions they visit me, and that woman over there is laughingly embracing a near-invisible friend as she stands outside an antique shop and debates some purchase. The crystal fields have expanded. They lie in that extra sheen which glazes the steps beside the harbour, and in the plays of shape and shadow above them. I've seen it for years in concert halls, in the empty seats which aren't truly empty, and at parties after-wards in the great palaces and hotels. *Look, Roushana Maitland . . . Excellent performance—I don't believe we've met . . .* A swirl, a smile, a touch of impossible hands and a sense of genuine presence as I'm introduced to someone who isn't here, and may not even be alive. Mum, with her intricate VR suits and Hindu attitudes, would probably have been enthusiastic, but, just as with my old friend Daisy and my old agent Adur, I've always found it easier to step back, make my excuses, look away . . .

Now I really do have sit down and rest. I can't possibly make my way back to Morryn without doing so. I head for St. Fimbarrus' church, which I've always liked in my atheistic way, because it's old and empty, and all the more so now because it hasn't yet been invaded by ghosts. Blessed, musty calm descends on me as I bang shut the doors and sit down amid the shining rows of empty pews.

I used to come here even when the kids were young, although for Maria it was always full of signs and mysteries. Everything about this place is unchanged, and my daughter's breathy questions as she touched stones and brass inscriptions in what I used to think was a worrying reverential way still echo in my head. *Why's that man bleeding? What's resurrection? What's that thing with holes like a face?* It's a skull, darling, and why on earth should I have to come up with excuses for this misogynistic, death-obsessed mumbo-jumbo? But one of the challenges of parenthood is having to explain the world as if it's something you've personally invented, and Maria always looked so hopeful and helpless as she stood there with that protuberant lower lip of hers pushing out. There was something in her soft and somehow unfocussed eyes which I sometimes still see. The buildings she makes now all have a taint of St Fimbarrus' about them. It's most obvious in that piece she did in the square beside that church—the Sagrada Familia, which Gaudi, another religious obsessive, wasted his life on—but you can see it just as plainly in the glass and iron planes of Morryn's new kitchen.

I'm wandering, drifting—it really is time I got going again. Fumbling the plastic hoops of the once-gaudily striped bag which I've filled with my shopping, I begin to shuffle along the pews. Then, as a deeper rush of the past comes over me, I have to sit down.

M UM TIPPED OUT THE MULTI-COLOURED SHOPPING bag which contained all her passes.

"This one," she said, feeling for a white cube scrawled in with faded marker pen Arabic, "is proper *military*. I shouldn't have it at all really. But it'll get you through most of the barriers to the underground offices in NCT. Should have been supplanted, but it hasn't. Go on—feel..."

I was sitting with her in the steamy heat of a café on Maiden Lane in London. It was mid-afternoon, and I'd finished my day's studies at the Royal College of Music. The cyclists streamed by outside: mere blurs as Mum talked about her continued travels to India, each of which became epics of Mahabharatan proportions.

Here was a stopover at Aden. This was the fruit of an interview—interrogation, really—in Krakow. Some of the passes were fat and some were thin. Some rolled like marbles and some were buttons and some bore spikes for insertion into something else. Some you had to be careful with because they bonded instantly with your flesh, whilst others excreted poisons although she could tell all of them apart merely by their feel. My thoughts drifted as she continued. Then I realised from the blind glare of her ruined eyes that she was studying me.

"Are you *alright*, Roushana? You seem . . . "

"I'm fine," I said, a little too insistently.

I was fresh from the end of another short-term relationship. It had been a lad this time, although by now I'd also got around to trying girls. Somehow, the similarities always seemed great, and the differences small. The endings, as well, were similar, as I found myself in receipt of accusations and angers I scarcely understood until I'd learned to find people who could be as casual as I was about the giving and taking of physical affection. But now, even in this warm café, all I felt was cold.

In her other shopping bag, a differently-striped counterweight, Mum kept recordings of her trips. To peer inside them was to experience the sounds and smells, even the rainy light, the hot metallic skies, of war-ravaged India. Voices clamoured from the depths in Gujarati, Hindi, incomprehensible local dialects or pidgin English. As she tromped around with her two pannier bags in grey salwars and open-toed sandals, Mum kept a bright scarf tied piratically around her head to disguise her thinning hair. She and her headscarves had achieved a sort of fame in Ahmedabad Two. Some called her *ñhe gooda ladya*, others said she was a saint, a *sadu,* and their many voices called out as she pushed aside my coffee and slid the clamorous images towards me.

"No more excuses," she said. "Next time, in the summer break, you're coming to India with me. You could be useful to me now. You can make a difference. They were even playing your tune in the airport lift . . . "

In Memory of an Angel, the title pinched from Berg's Violin Concerto, which has caused confusion ever since, hadn't exactly stormed up the charts in the seconds after its release, and its two successors had done considerably less well, but they had brought in some money, and my first small taste of fame. My idealism had taken a few jolts at the RCM, although I was surrounded by some of the best musicians and teachers in the land. The flats of my cheap rent were a swamp from the risen Thames on their lower floors. Dangerous insects droned in through my windows, or wormed and burrowed in search of the comforts of my skin, sheets and clothes. Dad's insurance money had faded by now, our house in Moseley hardly paid for itself in rental, and Mum poured everything she could find into her projects. For all that I'd already achieved, for all the beds I'd briefly shared and the bodies which I'd allowed to share my own, London felt worrying empty. When a music promoter had offered me what he called star-billing to make a few recordings, I'd been interested even after I'd found out exactly what was involved.

After I'd been posed and digitised into the image of the lost, pretty, orphan gypsy they wanted, I was whisked across town to choose a new instrument at Guiviers. Stupidly, I fell for something part plastic, part metal, part made from the new synthetic woods, which functioned in any of ten thousand modes.

"And the money you've made," Mum said as the faces and hands amid her sheaf of pictures faded back into her bag, "I hope you haven't done anything stupid with it, Roushana Maitland, like put it in a bank, or invest it in property?"

Wearily, warily, I shook my head.

Our journey to India took four days. Mum, or the strange, irritating and appealing woman she seemed to have become, said that that was good; she said a great many things were good when it seemed obvious to me that they weren't. My new violin was twice mistaken at airport security checks for a weapon. I felt constantly queasy, and reeked of sweat and the failed chemicals of my self-refreshing clothes. The foolhardy or desperate souls who now indulged in global travel all had a story to tell, but I'd soon heard enough of lost families, bureaucratic malice, military ineptitude, religious hatred. As the only planes we could find began to head back-wards across the time zones, I came to long for our arrival in India simply so it would bring this nightmare journey to an end. Then, at midnight, with no lights showing and the engines stilled to an eerie glide to make us a less obvious missile target, we were finally there.

There was a smell of shit and burning as we climbed out from the plane. Even as dawn rose over the perimeter shockwire of the Blue Zone, the heat was greasily oppressive. Greenish smog hung beyond the sleepily moving construction vehicles. There were huge, swirling flocks of some kind of big bird. Then mountains—enormous, and enormously distant. So this was India, whatever India meant . . .

After several hours of hassle and form-filling in stifling rooms, we took at ride out on one of the food convoys. Fearsome autonomous tanks trundled front and rear between the decrepit lorries, and the main worry was landmines, no, it was snipers, no, it was the radiation winds, no, it was the delays for quagmires and breakdowns—or it was the UUN soldiers who were supposedly protecting us. Mum had warned me especially about the UUN. They eyed my blouse and denimed legs and stroked the snouts of their subsound guns as we shared the swaying eyrie of a half-track cabin. Many of them were software junkies: there were inflamed sensory input jacks in their arms and you'd have put them down as gangsters if it hadn't been for their various UUN sponsorship badges—Hezbollah, Nike, McDonalds—which they bore on their armour.

Sprawled outside lay the endless plastic tents and cardboard semi-shacks of Ahmedabad Two. Children and keening widows swarmed dangerously close to the caterpillar tracks. Mum explained as I told her what I saw that the big birds which seemed to flock everywhere were called kites, and how you could identify the rubbish dumps by their denser swirls, and also the places where the Parsees, who were in resurgence, laid out the bodies of the dead. But there, Roushana, those dark columns which you say hang in the distance towards the east? That's probably the real smoke of funeral pyres . . . For this was India, and the peace talks in Moscow were stalled and the nation, whilst still officially still at war, had collapsed into hostile segments, but people were still getting on with the business of living and dying just as they had always done.

The convoy divided and our half-track and a remaining half dozen lorries headed south along what had once been the Memdabad Road. I recognised the name of Mum's village on the bullet-holed sign, but it was no longer the place I had visited in virtuality. The rice fields and banyan trees which had once made this a rural haven had been swarmed over by the displaced. We disembarked into a corral formed by the remaining lorries. Dogs were barking, women and children scurried, men shouted, gesticulated and scowled, and everyone pushed forward as the handing out of sacks of supplies began.

It was chaos, and the UUN soldiers were getting nervous. Fearful that we'd be trampled, I tried to draw Mum away, but she resisted, saying she had to supervise. Then, as the sacks vanished, the flock of saris which was my aunts began to elbow their way through the crowds. Their faces were thinner, paler and older than those I'd seen in Mum's recordings and in the photographs which lined Nan's shelves. Reputedly once-wild Auntie Jilli now hobbled on a crutch, Auntie Sinra was as blind as Mum, and could no longer use her scarred and bloated hands, Auntie Oonah had died recently from the bad water, and so had baby *Timin*, whose name I'd loved.

But Gujaratis are unremittingly proud, and seemed embarrassed by any suggestion that things here weren't as good as they had always been. After the half-tracks and the lorries had rumbled away, the village headman shook my hand and attempted a welcoming speech. Like most of my relatives, he seemed to know enough English to speak to me, but not to understand what I said in return. The children pinched and butted me. My head was stroked. There were astonished mutters at how *ripe* us English-born girls were.

In some ways, Mum's village really hadn't changed. Motor scooters still puttered about on stinking clouds whilst the women mopped their porches with water and dung each morning, then scattered decorative swirls of ash and washed themselves out of doors but modestly fully-clothed. Perhaps the village deity really had been kind, even if there was drought, starvation, cancer and looting. Ahmedabad, I was repeatedly assured, had always been more than a city—something mere bombs could destroy. It was an outlook, a way of life. Consider England, I was told, where our cousins and nephews all arrived with nothing, but now own all the shops . . .

Mum and I were provided with a hut of our own for the night, with flowers in a brass vase set on the dirt floor, and we were given many bowls filled with precious food which I, still nauseous, struggled guiltily to eat. That evening, my head spinning, weary and jet-lagged, I lay on my mat whilst Mum, who needed nothing and could sleep anywhere, snored blissfully beside me. The sound of thunder, or the guns of one of the militias, rolled down from the hills. With each thud and rumble, I vibrated like a touched drum.

Being here in India was a kind of death—a dissolving of the precious identity which I had imagined was a birthright. But it wasn't—I under-stood that now. I was just sweating, transitory flesh. I wondered as I lay trying to sleep about cousin Kapil, and whether he really was still alive somewhere in this huge sub-continent just as Auntie Rupa, who sat still endlessly waiting for him beside her front window in Handsworth, claimed. I pictured him in what was left of Bombay, gamely fighting the monsters which had once populated the screens and suits of his computer games.

There was more food in the morning, and yet more relatives who'd come from further afield as news spread of our arrival. In a communal yard which was sheltered from the sun by the huge, alarming lipstick smile of an old advertising hoarding, they gathered to watch me perform. I'd never felt more nervous, standing there with an instrument which had probably cost more than everything they had ever possessed. But they even cheered my over-protracted tuning-up, and then clapped and nodded their heads as I careered through a selection of popular Western classics. I sensed from the uniformly positive reaction that this music was entirely new to them, and probably quite meaningless. Afterwards, my new violin attracted much attention, especially when I demonstrated its ability to play by itself. An impossibly thin-looking lad was pushed towards me. I was told he also played the violin. After the cheap, dried-up instrument on which he'd previously had to work, my clever instrument must have been an exquisite revelation. His small fingers, as he played ragas with staccato precision, simply flowed. He was good—he was more than good—but what was the use, what was the point?

"Well," Mum said as she felt her way around our fetid hotel room after a twelve hour journey back in the Blue Zone, "this is *good*. This is *excellent. . .* "

An ambitious charity concert had been organised for the following day, or perhaps the day or the evening after, at the old cricket stadium. I was sharing the bill with several other so-called international stars and local celebrities, and the chaotic organisation was in the hands of a doe-eyed young man named Hakim whose failed assurances and patronising manner I soon found infuriating. Still nauseous and jet-lagged, I gave a series of interviews to journalists who plainly had as little idea as I did myself of who I was and what I was doing here.

The concert in the cricket ground finally took place on the evening after the one which had been advertised. Sick, hungry, water-retentive and permanently jet-lagged, I sat alone waiting for my call beside a ruinous bank of showers in the away changing room. It was both saddening and cheering to think of men sitting along these benches as they prepared to go and do battle in the mythically happy days when India versus Pakistan could end in a harmless draw, and stopped each day for tea. Hakim had warned me about snakes here, but I'd taken his advice as another of his obscure jokes. I even remained unconcerned when I saw a ribboned gleam emerge from a heap of fallen tiles. The cobra seemed too beautiful, too smooth and stately, to be dangerous. It and I regarded each other, and I felt a resignation come over me which I learned afterwards wasn't uncommon. Its tongue sipped the air. Outside in the stadium, music blared, the crowd stamped and seethed, but the space between this creature and I remained entirely silent. Somehow, I found that I was willing the creature to come closer, but its tongue flickered again and then it slid away. All I was left with was my own rising nervousness and a sense of empty disappointment.

The concert was as big a mess as the botched rehearsals which had preceded it. Standing in a pool of light amid squalls of rain as the stadium glittered and dissolved into a placeless blur, I couldn't hear what I was playing, nor if there was any applause.

"And this as well. You must wear this."

It was my last full day in India and Mum, who would be staying on, was sorting through passes in the depths of one of her striped shopping bags.

"What use—"

She was holding out a strip of off-white card with a safety pin yellowingly Sellotaped to its back. "No, no. Not for the journey. You must wear this now—today. And a suit as well. Hakim promised to get me one—where on earth is he? Otherwise, you will not be safe."

The radiation suit which eventually arrived was a thing of treated transparent polythene which smelled of its previous inhabitants. I felt ill as soon as I pulled it over my head.

The sun and the moon both hung in the dust-wreathed sky beyond the bullet-proof glass of our half-track. This was a different kind of aid convoy; more overtly military although at first there were the same endless shanty towns, running children and pleading, rag-and-bone women. Then we passed the dangling bodies of looters, left to hang as food for the kites and it became harder to tell just how many of the rubbled buildings were still inhabited, and how much of their destruction was caused by the bomb, or by the subsequent chaos. Then the damage became unequivocal. Walls leaned. Scraps of roof and concrete gouged the earth as if strewn by giant hands. Soon, everything was flame-blackened although there still remained flashes of fresh plastic, swirls of new smoke, dangles of washing, sour odours of lingering humanity. But perhaps the last was down to me, sitting sweating and gut-aching inside this ghastly suit. Once or twice I thought I glimpsed faces in the glittering holes of blasted-out windows and the soot-shadowed backs of twisted buildings, but it was hard to be sure.

"Can you see anyone?" Mum asked, rustling within her own malodorous sheath of plastic. "Of course, they don't trust us. They never have. Why should they?" Her fingers squealed over my hood. "You *are* still properly sealed in, aren't you? What colour is that badge of yours?"

It was still safely grey, but I felt iller than ever. I'd already had a bad bout of the runs this morning, and wondered how you were you supposed to deal with such a situation inside this suit if it returned. Things were different here in Ahmedabad One, but kites were still circling, a troop of thin-looking monkeys ambled along the ridges of an old car showroom, the skeletons of trees glinted with fresh bottle tops and failing diodes of roadside shrines, and a large lizard clung to a stone. Inevitably, it was the dalits and the untouchables who now lived in this ruined city. Nothing, here in India, ever really changed.

We stopped. Considering their masks and armour plating and the size of their guns, the guards seemed nervous as we climbed out into silence and settling dust. Mum, clinging to me as I helped her through the side hatch, muttered that they were afraid of the ghosts.

A soft wind was blowing, tinkling the shards of glass which dangled from the freshly growing creepers. A beaten pewter moon still hung above the twisted bars of broken concrete but the sun had vanished, and the heat was intense. The sky seemed even darker ahead towards the burnt-out plain of ground zero which lay between the river and the post office.

The citizens of Ahmedabad One were slow to emerge. They came like the dust, in drifts and whispers, and were equally pale. Their hair was sparse. Their eyes had hollowed. They wore scarcely any clothes. Yet they seemed almost sexless, nearly ageless, chalk and charcoal sketches of humanity—half-finished beings discarded by some god—who spoke only in muted squeaks and groans.

I was conscious of the steamy muffling of my ridiculous plastic suit, and of the warily masked and lumbering UUN soldiers. Perhaps the citizens of Ahmedabad One imagined that this was how everyone now looked and feared to leave. Not that the pickings here were bad. The city, wrecked though it was, was entirely theirs and there were houses stuffed with useless affluence, and shops, entire streets, which they would once have been considered too stained even to sweep clean which they could now roam at will. Anything which the firestorm had spared was now theirs. But life would be short shuffling these ruins, toying with melted handhelds and bracelets, picking over the wreckage of better lives amid the ash and bones. Apparently, the bomb which had ignited =in the space of sky between the river and the post office had been loaded with contaminants, and, as the dalits of Ahmedabad One clustered around us, I saw how their smooth, near-naked bodies were often distorted by goitrey lumps, swellings, and wet, red sores. I glanced down at the strip of my badge, but the winds were kind today, for its colour had barely changed. Or perhaps it didn't work. Or perhaps it didn't matter.

I was more worried for Mum than I was for myself. She came here regularly, and was alarmingly casual about the seals of her suit. Indeed, I wondered if, with her thinning hair and the hidden griefs for her lost life which had somehow borne her this far, she normally wore any protection at all. But at the same time, and as the dalits of Ahmedabad One circled us and gathered up our offerings of thermal blankets, painkillers, water tablets, I understood. Not India, but Mum. That the only way that she had been able to come to terms with the loss of Dad and Leo was to confront death. And death was here.

The dalits of Ahmedabad One sensed that I was different, and I tried not to shrink back as, fingers wavering like the tubers of frail plants, they strained to touch me. Eyes glittered. There were gasps, lickings of tongues and soft chuckles like the sifting of dust. A thin bare hand pressed my gloved one, then I was looking into the hollowed face of a young girl as a package, passed from hand to hand, was presented to me.

"What is it?" Mum asked, pressing close as well, her hands as eager as the dalits'. "What can you *see*?"

The package was a baby, squirming inside a stained cloth. I didn't know much about babies then, but this one seemed to be extraordinarily light, and extraordinarily young. It was like those children you once used to see in incubators. Its ribcage fluttered like a bird's. You could see the pulsation of its heart. The child mewed. Its gaze was ancient. Did they want me to keep it? Was this some kind of exchange? I didn't know what to say or do, so I simply held the softly squirming child until, after a long moment, it was lifted from me, and passed back to the girl, who fled into the ruins, her quick feet raising puffs of dust.

The rest of the dalits of Ahmedabad One were also disappearing, clutching their supplies, whilst the UUN soldiers were eyeing the haven of their half-tracks and thinking of the comforts of the Blue Zone. But Mum hadn't finished here yet, and she snapped at their commander that they would have to wait. These men were, I suddenly realised, almost as superstitiously wary of my mother as they were of the dalits.

"Here..." Her grip tightened on my arm. "There's a leaning telephone tower that way isn't there?"

I shrugged a yes, then realised she wanted me to lead her towards it.

We passed blasted shop-fronts, Maruti cars twisted and piled bumper to bumper, scarred and peeling half-adverts for Maha candy and Kingfisher beer, old Starbucks signs, and a melted heap of custard-yellow plastic buckets. I stumbled and wavered far more than Mum did as I tried to describe all I saw.

"Is this a corner? Are there traffic lights where it goes downhill? Is there a pink-painted wall opposite, and a sign for the buses?"

All of these things were, or once had been, here.

Mum smiled. "This is where I was when it happened, Roushana. I was crossing this very road. See, how you can see from here right down into the heart of the city? Of course, my mind was occupied with other things that morning. We were planning legal action—now, can you believe it?—over some tiny bit of land. And I was crossing this road, which was a feat in itself, but something made me hesitate. It's the first thing that happens, you know—the flash. There's no way of telling. But I looked towards the sky over the post office just before it came . . . "

We stood amid the torn tramlines at the centre of this once-busy road. Down the hill, tumbling out of the business districts and towards the river, scrawls and tangles of burnt-out wreckage became one indecipherable mass. It was dark down there and a kind of blackness towered up into the sky. I cringed when something flickered, although it was nothing more than the beginnings of this afternoon's thunderstorm.

Still, I had to ask. "What did you see?"

"I saw the Brahman," my mother's hands dug into me. "I saw God."

The hot skies churned and rumbled as I stood on the runway of the Blue Zone beside the churning engines of the plane which would bear me away from India. It was said that there might still be a proper monsoon this year, which would be good for the crops, help reduce the famine, but would also displace the hundreds of thousands of refugees from the war who were living along the flood plains.

"I'm really not sure that you're the same, Roushana," Mum murmured into my shoulder as she hugged me goodbye. "You've changed."

"Of course, Mum—didn't you say that India . . . ?"

Her hands ran questingly down my sides, across my belly. Her lips lingered against my neck. Then she leaned back. Behind us, the engines of the plane were getting louder still, but the grip of her hands was strong, and the glints in her eyes were piercing. "Whatever you do next, Roushana, I want you to take care—for me. I don't normally say that, do I? I'm not that selfish. But I'm saying it now. Take care. Not for yourself, but for your mother. Will you do that for me . . . ?"

Back in England, I finally took notice of all the signals—the belly-aches and water retention, the missed period which I'd put down to stress—which my body had been sending me all the time I'd been in India. The patch for the pregnancy test was the same shade of grey as the badge Mum had given me. Then it turned blue.

The father of the boy child I knew I couldn't possibly have was a fellow musician named Snow. He'd been easy, smooth and sinuous—a little cold, as well—and the end of our short relationship had been there from the start. There'd been few hard feelings, although we hadn't really spoken to each other since, and I had no intention of speaking to him now. But something amid the cocktail of prophylactics we took in the brief time we were together, an overdue implant, a software glitch, or mere bad luck, must have let us down. All I thought, all I saw, was that thin, lost baby in Ahmedabad One. That, and my musicianly career in ruins.

I did what I had to do. There were surprising, atavistic pains, and a large amount of blood. Afterwards, I felt immensely relieved, and hugely reprieved. I showered myself raw until I was squeaky-clean as new plastic, as brushed steel. I told myself that that was it and that nothing had changed, but the new violin which I had nursed so carefully through all the waits and the arguments with security to and from India no longer seemed to belong to me. I came to hate the smoothly clever weight of it, the suspension-bridge sheen of its strings.

I parcelled it up carefully inside its case, took it to the local UPNS and addressed it to the lad in Mum's village who'd briefly played it. I didn't really expect it to get to him, but the thing didn't feel like mine and I wanted it to go somewhere—out into the world. I had dreams long after of some shadowy figure playing it amid swarms of smoke and birds, but I never saw a face.

I T WAS GROWING DARK BY THE TIME I'D FINALLY ROUSED myself from inside the church and climbed the long hill back here to Morryn. Adam was touchingly worried, but soon set about preparing an excellent meal from the somewhat squashed and wilted produce in Mum's old nylon shopping bag. As he worked, chopping and cooking things by hand in the way he prefers and with all the machines put away or ignored, I showed him some of Mum's pictures of India on the screen above the counter, and told him about Gujarat One and Two, and that ridiculous violin. I even mentioned my lost child. Yes, the pain's still there, but I realised as he served out the meal that it's hurt me more in all these years I've kept it hidden. There's no doubting, as well, that Adam's becoming part of the process of my remembering. He listened as we ate, and the food, even if I can't now quite remember what it was, was dreamily delicious. If there's a question of any sort—the plain, simple ones of when and where and how—he simply asks. He accepts the litter of my life so readily. Perhaps he hopes he will even find something there of his own.

Despite my long day and the hard climb back up from Fowey, I felt surprisingly sprightly after we'd finished eating. Even though it was dark, I decided to give him a belated version of the tour of the house I once always gave all Morryn's guests. Morryn's first foundations and cellars go back to the rebuilding which took place around Fowey after the town was sacked by the French in the 1500s. It's expanded higgledy-piggledy since, growing and shedding various outbuildings and extensions. The house was requisitioned during the first two world wars because of its commanding view sea, and was even briefly a school. Mostly, though, it's simply been a place where people live.

I told Adam about the changes Claude and I made. How we replaced the ugly flat roof which had covered part of the ground floor with a proper one of Cornish slate, and restored those lovely chimneys. And I told him how Edward had spent his childhood years in the room where he now sleeps, and how Maria had slept next door in a place which is still filled with stuff she won't let me throw away. My daughter takes after me in that respect: I told him that as well. I found a torch and took him into the yard, and showed him the old two-seater loo, and the garage where Claude once kept his beloved Aston Martin DB5, his James Bond car, which is now a home for nothing but dust and spiders. Standing out in the starry darkness with Morryn hunched under a bright moon, I was better able to explain how the old kitchen was replaced by Maria's bold fan of seaward-looking glass, and I could also talk about the other kind of activity of which this house, like all old coastal Cornish houses, once partook. Those midnight arrivals, muffled oars—however it is that do you that—and the roll of barrels. The old boathouse below the cliffs is as much cave as it is building, and Claude used to claim that there was once a way down to it from the cellar. But Claude would. Back inside the house, I got Adam to pull at the rusty hoop of the hatch beneath the stairs, and he helped me down into the dank space for—what?—the first time in how many years? The torch played over the remains of my husband's wine collection. I rarely ever drink now, especially after what happened to me in that hotel in Sydney, but Adam was curious to try one of these expensive vintages before it went forever to waste, and I, to be honest, didn't put up much of a resistance.

Back the kitchen, and now that he's banished the implements, Adam had to search though a whole lifetime of old-fashioned utensils before he found a corkscrew, which I could picture Claude's darker fingers enclosing as he peeled away the foil and addressed it to the bottle. We retired with our glasses to the music room, and Adam suggested that I play something for him. It doesn't seem strange by now that he under-stands what it means to own a Guarneri, and that one should hold it correctly without touching the precious varnish. I was almost expecting him to start playing, but he simply handed it back reverentially. So I played him some Kreisler—so briskly that the automatic piano was struggling to keep track, and then *Les escaliers de Montmartre,* which I ended up doing solo as a sort of jig, I was playing so devilishly fast and well. After that, I performed some reels, and Adam clapped along. In fact, he kept excellent beat, urging me on to ever greater extravagances as he stood up, and, quite unprompted, did a quick, whirling, dance. I thought of finishing with a heavyweight show-piece, perhaps some Paganini, but that would have spoiled the mood. Music doesn't have to be difficult or complex. Music can simply be *fun*. How stupid of me to have ever forgotten that!

I think Adam drank more of the wine than I did, although I can't be sure, and I was never a connoisseur, but nevertheless, tonight's vintage tasted extraordinarily fine. I can still feel it flooding into me, rich and dark as the night sky beyond these windows, as I haven't done in years. Giggling like a schoolgirl, I virtually floated up the stairs when we'd finally finished playing, and it took more than the usual effort of will to perform the tests and treatments I'm supposed to perform on this aging, stupid body of mine before I got into bed. Tomorrow, I have my weekly appointment at the clinic in Bodmin. But tomorrow can wait. It just feels so good just to lie here with Morryn's walls still ringing from the music we made, and the taste of wine, which for me will always be the taste of Paris, on my tongue.

WHAT WAS IT LIKE? OVER ALL THE YEARS SINCE, I'VE been asked that question so many times by so many people. The names tumble off their lips. Harad Le Pape, of course, and Karl Nordinger with his churning melodies. But to be there—in Paris, and then, of all times. You and Claude Vaudin. Claude Vaudin and you. The stolen Giaconda. The riots in the Orsee. The concerts. The deconstructions. The deaths. The famous heap of dog shit outside the Pompidou. Bicos. Max Rochereau. Could you smell it? Taste it? What was it like? To be there.

After London, Paris was gripped by a wilder kind of turmoil. Closer, as ever, to the heart of Europe, though that heart was frail. The great new virtually-clad buildings, vast expressions of civil pride, guttered in the smog and rain. Crippled and diseased soldiers from the latest North African adventure begged and stole in the streets, whilst my tenement in the 10th arrondissement clamoured night and day with arguments in two dozen languages. Adverts taunted across the clouds. Buy this, buy that. Invest, invest. They were selling mining rights to the Ocean of Storms by then. On rare, clear nights, lasers fingered the moon: another crash waiting to happen—you could imagine it rolling down from all that weight of spoiled expectation and splashing right into the Seine. There were bombs outside the mosques. There were crucifixions in the churches. Walking to the Metro each morning on my way to the Conservatoire, I was accosted by Bible-sellers, prophets, mothers with babies, and the sellers of stolen umbrellas and salvaged pros-thetic limbs. But I was young and sharp-elbowed enough to dodge and swear my way around them in French, and I soon learned to carry my violin out of its case. That way, people assumed that I was merely a busker.

Was I more than good by then? I'd got this far, hadn't I? I was a budding soloist, a name to be looked out for, even if I could scarcely afford to buy food. Shouldering through the smoke of chestnut vendors amid the jostling Parisian crowds, dodging the ghost vans and the moaning flagellatees and the water sellers, sitting in muggy cafes and queuing for the free benches at concerts, I carried my caseless violin as if it was the brimming receptacle of my carefully nurtured talent, and a statement of naked intent. *It's down to you now Sis,* and at last I was proving that I could make my mark.

At last, I felt happy, although it was worry rather than happiness which filled my head as I carried my violin beneath my coat through the freezing January rains, dodging rickshaws, cyclists, fountaining puddles and ghost vans on my way towards the apartment of the famous Harad Le Pape. Harad was an inescapable presence for anyone who cared about art in Paris then. There were inner circles, outer fringes, nodding acquaintances, latest discoveries, sell-outs and cast-asides—there were even those who would never, ever, hear mention of Harad Le Pape's name—but to be entirely outside of the scope of Harad's influence would have been cultural suicide, even if such a thing were possible. Harad's finger wasn't on the pulse. Harad *was* the pulse.

And, finally, I'd been noticed. My bracelet had chimed with a message telling me that I was invited to see Harad Le Pape. It seemed impossible—inevitable—or a total hoax. I felt lucky, but I also felt that this was no more than my due, as, drenched and nearly late, I gazed up at the spectacular apartments along the Marais. Here, even the ubiquitous advents no longer stained the clouds' undersides, and the rain had sluiced the pavements nearly clean. This was a different Paris to the squalling squats I'd grown used to, but it was somewhere I was desperate to enter, whatever the rules of its games.

A young man, sodden and weeping, was sitting at the entrance to the building which contained Harad's apartment. He looked up at me with what could have been either pity or envy as I passed him. On through the revolving doors, I entered a marble hallway which looked more like the atrium to a large bank, but nevertheless bore odours—of cooking, of a variety of pets, and, more faintly, of toilets—which weren't entirely unlike those which greeted me in my tenement each evening. I dripped and squelched my way towards the lift and pressed its ceramic button.

The door on floor 5 was mysteriously open, and I wandered in through a series of echoey rooms where gilt furniture and cherub-encrusted ceilings battled for attention with torn canvasses and virtual projection equipment. There, quite alone in a last greyly empty space, sat Harad Le Pape. I'd expected some sort of never-ending party—the comings and goings of writers, dancers and body artists—but the only sound which touched the bare walls was that of the rain.

Harad's big body bulked awkwardly erect on a large divan chair before a huge, dead fireplace. The rampart jaw, the needling eyes, the slicked-back reddish hair—it was all there. The hands were delicate. The big feet were encased in brogues. Harad was wearing a dark blue suit, part mannish, but set with florid eruptions of butterfly silk at collar and neck. I could have minutes, hours, seconds, to make my impression. Apart from the divan, which Harad Le Pape already more than fully occupied, there was nowhere else to sit.

"So . . . " The pinhole eyes stared nearly, but not quite, at me, and I was reminded of Mum. Even though that gaze reputedly never missed anything, Harad had the intense, unnerving stare of the blind. "You brought your instrument?"

I was starting to shiver as I produced it from beneath my sodden coat. "I haven't brought any music. But I could play—"

"No. *Please*. No music. Least of all today. I've heard you, haven't I? It's not as if you're some performing monkey. I know you have the facility."

Uppermost in my mind as I hugged my violin—I couldn't help it—was the much-debated question of Harad Le Pape's sex. He or she seemed to be an indefinable mixture of the broadly mannish and the delicately feminine. Not that sex changes and even neuterism were uncommon in those days in Paris, but the messages here were far more complex. A couple of years earlier, I'd been assured, Harad had borne the overdecorated mannerisms of a camp male. Before that had come a stage of matronly print dresses. The cleverness of Harad's trick—and not that anyone would have ever dared call it a trick—was that the signals never stayed the same.

"I'd been told you were English?"

"I am." I shrugged. "It's just—"

"But you're *not*, are you. Don't know where you belong. How about *here*? Does this feel like home?" Again, almost a smile. Harad spoke clear, accentless French with cold puffs of condensation in a graceful alto. "I don't mean this apartment. I mean Paris."

"I don't think so. Not yet, anyway."

"Good. Artists shouldn't have homes. Think of what happened to Monet at Giverny. Mould growths in oils. Better to be like Conrad. Becket. Igor. Write, live, in a foreign tongue. Tear down the walls. Be blind as Joyce. Drink like Hemingway. *Taste* the alienation. Then you can say something worthwhile about your home. Or, better still, realise that nothing remains to be said and give up entirely. Pity we can't travel to the stars yet, eh?"

This was, as I soon discovered, a typical conversation: cryptic, rambling, one-sided. You always got the general impression that things were making a kind of sense, even if you were unable to work out what it was. There had been a famous review, back in the days when Harad still did reviews, of a new exhibition of scent and shape at the Pompidou Centre which had described, in Proustian detail, the texture and appearance of a pile of dog mess which lay outside on the pavement. The piece, and the dog mess, which had been stolen and then lovingly re-created many times since, had easily outshone and outlasted the exhibition inside.

It would have been easy to dismiss Harad Le Pape as a comic turn, or an expression of the bankruptcy of culture, and we did sometimes doubt and snigger, but never in Harad's presence. For

Harad had discovered Karl Nordinger, Harad had popularised Jane Affray, and if Harad was right, and culture really was bankrupt and there was nothing left worth believing in except the external manifestations of art itself, which in themselves were hollow, he or she was also our only salvation.

Harad's response to the apparent pointlessness of art was to decide to cease to be a critic and then, after a suitably dramatic pause, to astound Paris by announcing that he'd—or she'd—decided to become an artist him or herself. Above us on the 6th floor, Harad was preparing an epoch-defining cultural statement. In a sense, there was little mystery about what this statement was, for Harad talked at length about this crucial work in progress, and had enlisted the contributions of many artists. It was certainly multi-sensory. And it had to be large. Huge action paintings, Renaissance ceilings and rare perfumes had all been absorbed into it, along with bones from Père Lachaise, streetsigns and the scrambled texts of great works of fiction. Would this piece, this construction, this world, floating just above us on the 6th floor redefine our perceptions and bring about a new sense of purpose? Would it be the last expression of the pointlessness of everything? Harad seemed to imply both of these things, and many others as well. Sometimes, the piece was pronounced to be near completion. Unveiling dates were even mooted. But many of these had come and gone long before I first became a visitor to the rue de Turenne.

Silence fell. So did the rain.

"Roushana. Tell me. Why are you studying music?"

"I . . . " It was a question I'd been asked many times. I had a dozen different answers, and not one of them mentioned Leo. "It seemed to be the only thing I was particularly good at."

Harad harrumphed. "And you're happy being *good* at something are you? If you'd have been good at bricklaying, would you have done that instead?"

"Of course. Well, perhaps."

"Good—you don't like the word, so why use it? And that performance you gave. That piece by Ibrahim. That was more than good."

"Thank you."

"It was terribly good."

"And what," I snarled, finally goaded, "does *that* mean?"

Even the rain seemed to pause in surprise at my small outburst.

"Well . . . " Imperturbable as ever, Harad pursed his or her small lips.

"About time, I think, that you left behind mere stupid facility. You musicians—the pompous fuss you make. Have you met Karl Nordinger?"

"No."

"Well, don't. I've had it with you musicians. Music alone is the sound of dead things rattling. No one gets it right. Apart perhaps from Claude Vaudin. It's a dead area, and Claude's the night-watchman. You should seek him out. You might learn something."

The club, Le Chien Heureux, was the kind of place you'd go to if you wanted the latest drugs which were hard to get above ground even here in Paris—that, or wanted to watch people or animals having sex—but music was wafting enticingly from up the dank steps on that first night I went there. Someone, quite brilliantly, was playing the piano as I headed down into the fog and smell.

The ceiling dripped. People were swaying, sweating, clapping. On a small stage, a naked woman with tiger-striped flesh was dancing. Colours flared across the walls in response to her frenzied movements. But, despite everything she did, most of the attention was rooted on the man who was up there with her playing the piano. Tall, lithe and ebony-skinned, he was standing at the keyboard and dancing as well, shaking his head to the slanting rhythm he'd somehow shaped from his instrument.

The music went on—it poured out of him—as the crowd leapt and surged. Drinks were spilled. My ribs were bruised. My buttocks were felt. Then, finally, as the dancer's sweat-flung hair glittered as she threw herself into a dervish state, the music slid to an end in a last, tantalising twinkle of notes. At first, the applause which followed was shocked and sporadic, then it grew raucous. Claude Vaudin nodded and smiled. He lifted the collapsed dancer in his arms, then stepped back and bowed as someone threw them towels. With animal grace, he leapt down from the stage and strode for the bar. Shrugging off clusters of admirers—who were mostly gay, female or transgenic—he headed towards me with a bottle of wine and two glasses expertly raised in one of his big hands.

"You're that violinist, aren't you?" he shouted in English as the PA began to announce the next attraction.

I tried not to look flattered. "And you're that conductor."

"Why weren't you dancing?"

I had to lean close to hear what he was saying. "Why should I? I was listening!"

He put a hand just beneath my left breast. His face was shining. He smelled male and warm. "I'm sorry."

"What?"

"You can't be Roushana Maitland. Not if you weren't dancing—not the way I've heard you play." He gestured towards a table. "Let's drink . . . "

I was pleasantly conscious of the shift of emphasis that Claude Vaudin's singling me out had caused in this club. The tiger-striped woman—whose name, prosaically, was Jill, and who remained conspicuously under-dressed in that towel—trailed over and purred feline pleasantries at us from over her breasts. Claude was warm and polite and charming and flirtatious with her and all the other habitués who drifted towards us, although something about his manner signalled to them that he'd rather the two of us were left alone.

"This," he told our latest visitant, slipping easily from lightly-East Coast accented English to entirely demotic French, those same fingers which wrought such magic from the piano now nestling on my neck and twisting casually amid my hair, "is the violinist Roushana Maitland. You haven't heard of her? Well you have now, and you will, believe me . . . "

"I thought," I countered when we were sitting alone again, "you

said I couldn't play or wasn't listening or dancing or something."
Already, he'd signalled for more wine, and my head and my tongue
were struggling to keep up.

"No no *no . . .*" He waved a waggish finger. "Roushana, you're
the best I've heard. And I don't say that to all of them either." A
beautifully-timed glance and pause. "Or if I do, I certainly don't
mean it. But I think you should learn to dance."

I smiled. I wasn't exactly going to say no to Claude Vaudin, who
looked and sounded just as elegant here in the flesh as he did in
the many interviews and performances I'd already witnessed. His
face was chiselled, his eyes were brown and dark. His chin was
dimpled. His nose was both Negroid and aquiline.

He smiled back at me. His hand shifted from my neck. "You're
just humouring me, aren't you?"

"No, no. Of course not. But—"

Then he drew me up. And we danced. Or rather, Claude
danced, and I tried to follow him, which turned out to be impossible, although being here and being with him—and all the drink,
which I wasn't then used to, and the hallucinogenic smoke which
wafted from many people's lips, and the pheromones which per-
vaded the air—all certainly helped. The music, as I remember, was
North African. It had a complex beat, shifting from 4/5 to 4/4,
but flowing in a way which felt entirely right to the heart and the
hips. But I suppose the fact that I was counting beats and thinking just how fine Claude looked as he moved showed just how far
from throwing myself into the moment I still was.

But to be dancing with Claude Vaudin! Not that I hadn't
encountered the famous and the vain many times already, and not
that I didn't know what conductors, of all people, were generally
like. But Claude wasn't any of the things he should have been. For
someone so mannish, his delicate grace, his lightless of tone, were
extraordinarily feminine. He's probably gay, I told myself; that
would explain those meticulous good looks and the crowd him
around him at the bar.

The evening passed. And yes, there were now animals on stage.
There were men and women as well.

"You don't mind this, do you?"

I shrugged and hiccupped. Everywhere, limbs were merging. I seemed to have a wineglass held in each of my four hands.

"Here. Have some more wine."

"No—I've had enough."

"You're not much of a drinker, are you Roushana?"

"I'm a better dancer . . . "

"Well . . . It's a close call."

It was very late—even the adverts had deserted the skies—and very dark as we crossed the Canal St-Martin and headed through Saint Denis.

"Where do you live, Roushana?"

"I don't have a home—that was what Harad Le Pape told me." I gave a hiccup and a burp. "He or she was right. You're gay, by the way, aren't you?" Then my feet skidded from under me and I sprawled on the freezing pavement.

"You should get drunk more often," he said, laughing as he helped me up. "You're terrific at it. You might even get the hang of dancing. All you need to do is open up, let go."

"You're not so very bad yourself. I'm not drunk. Or not very."

"At least we can agree on something . . . "

Then we were rattling upwards in a gated lift inside some kind of warehouse, no, it was an apartment, although the space it occupied was huge.

"You *live* here?"

"Sure. Why not? What else would anyone do with it?"

He helped me towards a sprawl of sheets, and I fell towards them, then curled up and groaned as the girdered roof started to revolve. I was dimly conscious of Claude moving about in the far reaches of this space. Things tinkled. Distant drawers slid. I covered my head.

"I'm sure I've got some soberups somewhere."

"No. It's okay," I muttered. "I'll be fine."

"I shouldn't have given you so much wine."

"No . . . It's . . . "
"Here. Take this."

Then, almost instantly, it was morning and I could hear that Claude was up and about. The sheets which I was lying in smelled gingery and sweetish—more of me than of him—and I realised that I was still entirely dressed, right down to my shoes, although I wasn't sure whether this was a good or a bad sign. I risked cracking open my eyes. Light blazed, and whole aeons slid by before I tried opening them again. For once, the Parisian rain seemed to have stopped, and the many tall windows which surrounded this huge and approximately rectangular atelier were filled with a mist which wasn't pulsing simply because of the state of my head. All the adverts for porn and online virtualities were throwing their messages even through a cloudbase so low it filled this room. Reds and pinks and yellows shifted and faded. Plumes of darker pixels tunnelled and leapt . . .

And music was playing. Of course music was playing. With Claude back then, music always was playing. What I'd come to recognise as *So What?* from Miles Davis' *Kind of Blue* was pouring out from his expensive sound system with such baffling clarity that it took me a while to work out that the players weren't actually there. Not that I knew or cared about mid-Twentieth Century jazz then, but even my ignorant ears picked up on the fact that this was playing of a quite exceptional order, although I was far more conscious of Claude himself. He was naked, and dancing as if he'd never stopped since last night. Clapping, he threw his head back and laughed in happy amazement as one of the soloists executed a particularly beautiful hairpin turn. There was a piano, a big old Bechstein, and every now and then he'd slip sideways through the glowing mist to jab a note in response to something he'd heard. Even though he was competing with Bill Evans, it was all perfectly judged. Claude's fine long body shone and rippled with the changing colours, and he had an erection which bobbed and circled against his belly as it, too, executed its own mutual but independent dance. He looked so entirely lovely that even my ghastly hangover seemed to subside. Then he noticed that I was awake and wafted over just at the moment Coltrane's immortal solo kicked in.

"Hi there." He was completely unselfconscious. "Sorry if I woke you."

"No . . . It's . . . " I managed to roll over and look up at him, although I couldn't bring myself to say *fine.*

"You slept okay?"

"I'm not sure." I shaded my eyes. Mist roiled. His cock shone.

"Oh—this—" He glanced down at himself. "It's what happens when you awake if you're a man—it's just dreams."

I swallowed. Despite how I felt, he really did look delicious. And the music was fading, and I wanted him down here in this bed with me.

"You're not dreaming now," I said, opening my arms as if to welcome him to me in all my fully clothed glory before a sudden wave of nausea enveloped me and I vomited copiously across his sheets. Would I have loved Claude Vaudin without the glamour of him being who he then was, and without the music? But that's impossible to say—he simply wouldn't have *been* Claude Vaudin then. Raised in Georgetown, Washington DC, by wealthy, liberal academics, moving from the first amid virtuality stars, musicians and ambassadors, there was never any doubt about his talent, nor that he would make the most of it. So it was Phi Beta Kappa and summer camps and Princeton and Juilliard and winning Leeds and the prix d'Excellence and getting the Licentiate and turning down offers from Berlin and San Francisco to become youngest ever principal conductor at the Orchestra du Paris. None of the early worries which had beset Leo about whether to be a performer or a composer, or whether to go for pop or classical or jazz, and then whether it was possible for a mere artist to influence the world. He could do all of these things.

Only the insecure are arrogant. Only the less than exceptional care about what others think. Back then, back in Paris, Claude possessed the generosity and humility of the truly great. Sure, there were tantrums and yelling fits and the odd cancellation. Sure, there were occasional fluffed notes and people he didn't get on with and nights playing the piano at *Le Chien Heureux* or conducting when the music didn't flow in the way we all knew it should, but genius, as I began to understand, is the enemy of perfection. To get it beautifully right, you have to be prepared to get it terribly wrong. And you have to learn how to dance, as well.

Claude chuckled. His hands shaped my breasts as the glowing sky uncoiled and shadows of the rain trickled with the sweat along his flanks.

"Stand up..." His arms enfolded me. Sinatra's singing was even fresher than it had been on the coolest of all possible midnights when it was made. "Just move... Just sway..." His hands were on my belly, my hips. His reawakening cock nudged my thigh. Was this sex, or was this dancing? "Listen to the music. Don't hang up on me now—just listen to what the man says." I felt the glide of his fingers. "Under your skin. Hum to it. Sing to it. Feel it in your blood." Now he'd shifted, and was standing behind me. He led me with the sway of his hips. "Does that hurt?"

"No—yes, it does now. A little."

"But not too much?"

"...no."

"Don't worry. Relax—just let it in..."

Outside, Paris streamed with rain and colour, endlessly falling away.

Playing was letting go. Playing was bum notes and missed intros. Playing was letting exhilaration or weariness or the sweat-slide of your aching fingers lead you to some new and unexpected place. Playing was for the moment or it was nothing at all, and it didn't matter if a million people listened or you performed alone in the depths of a forest. If you played selfishly and without caring, if you played completely for the sake of yourself and didn't care about everything else—then, there was just a chance that you might get it gloriously right . . .

Music was holier than sex to Claude, and it was holier than dancing, although it must be said that all these activities often grew so blurred as we drank and played and listened and danced and fucked and talked and listened and played and danced and fucked again through that delirious spring in our atelier above the Boulevard de Clichy on the fringes of Montmartre that they became one. Then we would go out into the hailstone spring of this newly awakened Paris. We ate Indian or we ate Chinese or we ate Kurdish or we ate nothing at all and merely drank and talked, and artists of all persuasions and senses would join us from gardens of the Gare de l'Est. For wasn't that Claude Vaudin, and isn't that Roushana Maitland? Even before I realised what was happening, we'd become the couple of the hour.

It was all so quick, so giddy. One day, I'm a promising but obscure soloist. The next, I'm doing interviews, virtuality shoots for *Le Monde*, and, through a series of suspiciously convenient cancellations, Claude has arranged for me to perform the Sibelius Concerto for a stellar benefit at the Opéra for one of his many charitable causes.

I remember a day when we were sitting in a café after a long and somewhat grumpy rehearsal session at the old radio buildings. Claude, as ever, had much to say.

"Forget all the crap people talk about Sibelius, Roushana. Forget all the rubbish about fjords and Nordic gods and forests and snow and polar bears dancing. That isn't what he's about. Imagine he's Spanish, if that helps. Think how *hot* his music is, not how cold—"

Then the door from the street bashed open and a white-faced figure with a Hitlerish cowlick of hair shook off the rain from his grubby coat.

"Ah—" he hissed in off-accented English, ignoring Claude and pointing directly at me "—you're that *musician*, aren't you? The one who plays . . . " His bloodshot eyes bulged. " . . . what is it, the fucking fiddle, the bloody violin?"

I shot Claude a look in the hope that we might manage the sort of escape we were starting to specialise in. But Claude just sat there, and—after a series of volcanic sneezes which, after this winter of pandemics, soon had the other habitués of the café shifting away—this odd little man dragged across a chair to sit with us.

"No, I don't want anything." He snapped at the waiter. "Just bring another glass, okay?" He wiped his nose with the back of his hand, then smeared his hand down his trousers. He smelled like an ill, wet dog. "You know who I am, don't you?"

I shook my head.

"Well—" Claude leaned in, but our guest banged the table.

"I'm not *that* idiot. And you're two love birds, isn't that the latest trick, the new gimmick?" His breath and his smile as he leant towards me were equally sickly. Beneath the table, I had to jerk away my leg as his hand grabbed my thigh. "The best way to prostitute yourselves to the stupid public is by pretending to be everything you're not."

"So you always say, Karl," muttered Claude, who seemed to be taking this with surprising tolerance.

Again, the man thumped the table. His wineglass leapt. "I told you. No bloody, bloody names." He turned to me as spilled wine dripped into his lap. "So—are you going to change the world of music, is that your game? Or are you just hanging around with Claude so that you can fuck and get drunk and have your own measly slice of fame?"

"I don't see that I have to justify myself to you. Whoever you are—"

"*Whoever*! Ha! That's rich." He laughed, and the laugh turned to phlegmish hawk. He spat, narrowly missing me and the table. "And I suppose you know all about doing *good*. Have you seen— what's it called, Claude—" He tilted his head. "The something something for music something?"

"The Project? Is that what you mean?"

He didn't bother to nod. "Taking in those North African kids.

Saving them from the sex traders and the cults. And for what . . . "
Leeringly, he mimicked the playing of a violin. "Do you expect
them to make a living doing *that*? Do you expect them to live at
all? They'd all be so much better off being whipped, sodomised or
sacrificed in the name of whatever deity happens to be the craze of
the moment. And they'd be better at it as well . . . That's what
young flesh is for, or didn't you realise? It's there to be maltreated
before it loses its elasticity and goes old and wrinkled and sour."

It was quite a performance. Soon we were the only people left
in the café, and I was almost beginning to understand Claude's
complaisance in the face of this seemingly unstoppable tirade,
although not quite why we were still putting up with it.

"Anyway, who are you?" I asked. "You still haven't said."

"My Christ . . . " Spreading his arms, he looked at the bottle-
hung ceiling as if pleading for help. " . . . the stuck up little cunt
still wants to know." Then, just as suddenly as he arrived, he stood
up, glared around at the empty café, and staggered back out into
the rain.

Claude began to smile as the door ceased swinging. Then he
started to laugh. "You *really* don't know who that is, Roushana?"

"No—and you're starting to sound like him!"

"I'm sorry . . . " He blinked and regathered himself. "That was
Karl Nordinger, the world's greatest composer. You should count
yourself extraordinarily lucky that you've met him."

It was teeming rain and freezing cold, but Paris was warming—
Paris was hot. I jammed with Claude at the *Le Chien Heureux*. I
learned how to trade fours, and how to mess things up. I listened to
Grappelli, and discovered—instead of merely knowing about—
rock and jazz. At night, we lay awake half-drunk or half-dreaming,
floating in some strange equilibrium on a cocktail of soberups,
wakeups, upups and downers, our limbs so closely entwined that I
often didn't know whether it was my flesh or his that I was licking.
It was lovely and sinful and onanistic—we even tasted the same. I
played the *Ciaccona* for him. I told him about Leo, and my lost

138

baby, and he told me about the women and men he'd had—and, yes, Tiger-Stripe Jill as well—and how he wanted none of them now. *Just you, Roushana ... Just this ...* Claude danced.Shamelessly, he did things for me alone, and I did things for him.

There were endless parties. There was a cold snap. Briefly, the Seine froze. Then, suddenly, the mornings were wreathed in sunlight and steam. And we were busking in Montmartre, and coming up quite spontaneously with that tune which everyone in Paris was soon humming, or walking along the Champs Elysées where the fashion dummies writhed like the figures at *Le Chien Heureux*. Then along the Boulevard de Clichy, and watching the whores in all their enhanced finery, and inspecting, amazed and curious, all the many devices and appliances on sale in the shops. Up the hill in Montmartre there were other temptations. We ate *hombard persillé* and drank *pastis* for lunch. These sloping streets had become fashionable once again, and were filled with exotic emporia and antique shops. We debated whether this cabinet by Gallé wouldn't just fill the far corner of our atelier, or if that crystal scent bottle really was a Lalique. I watched our reflections move in the glass cases and mirrors: Claude, in his red scarf and black coat, the pulse in his throat and the crease which gathered in his left cheek when he smiled, and the way he and I somehow just *matched*. I'd always thought all those operas and musicals about falling in love were essentially ridiculous, a mere artistic device, but now I understood why, even in these moments of seemingly everyday life, people might want to burst into song.

"Why are you smiling?"

"Why are *you* smiling?"

Hand in hand, arm in arm, swinging our bags, pushing past the dervishes and demonstrators on the Sacré-Coré steps, noticed but uncaring—famously, obliviously happy—we wandered on. We found a shop filled with first editions, engravings, architectural blueprints and daguerreotypes of maids from *La Belle Époque* servicing moustachioed men. On the fall wall, almost buried behind a gilt washstand, hung a painting.

"Not for sale," muttered the Moorish proprietor as he noticed me squeezing towards it.

Nothing more than a few brushstrokes, and delicate blue and rosé wash, but it was plainly of Venice, perhaps viewed from the island of Saint Marco, or possibly further off. The detail was scarcely there, yet the sense of a summer's dawn over that lost, drowned city was intense.

"How much?"

"Not for sale. I told you."

But we knew about Paris by now, and we knew about shop-keepers, and I really was Roushana Maitland, and this was Claude Vaudin, and money is only money, but art is always art.

"You want it don't you?" Claude's mouth nuzzled my ear.

Was it really a Turner? At the price which Claude was soon haggling, it seemed possible, although I still don't know to this day.

"Well . . . " Once more, Claude's arms surrounded me. "We've really done it now. We'll be poor and happy forever."

The Opéra de Paris Bastille loomed under flashing clouds. With its acid-corroded glass and greened concrete, it looked like something washed up from the distant sea—a giant sea anemone, which had sucked the juicy currents of all of socialite Paris into its gleaming bowels of grey granite and black leather.

The first half performance of *Eine Alpensinfonie* was already crack-ling through the monitor speakers when I flashed my pass and was admitted through the shockwire. There was barely enough time for me to change and tune up, but that was exactly how I'd planned things. In my dressing room, there were flowers, messages of encouragement, boxes of candy and chocolate. I was already shoving everything aside before I realised that a violin case already lay on the dressing table. I sighed.

Some cock up. The wrong room. But a note hung by a ribbon from the handle.

this is for you
you deserve it
no good luck
no excuses
just play
C
x

With screens and panels to control humidity and temperature along its top, the case was an impressive object in its own right, and nothing like my own battered example. The air it exhaled after a series of clonks and hisses was rich with rosin and varnish. The instrument at rest inside made me exhale as well, but already my hands were reaching for it, and the bow which lay beside, and their feel was like nothing else I'd ever touched. It was already tuned— it was already *everything*—and the sound it gave off and the sensation of playing it were equally lovely. *Wo*w... Was I doing that? I ran through, as I still always do with any fresh instrument, some Bach phrases. But they'd never sounded like this.

I held it up to the light. The wood was surprisingly pale and the f holes weren't even. Rather like the sound it made, the finish was beautiful, yet eccentric. Then, like any other ignoramus handling a great violin, I tried peering inside.

Giuseppe del Gesù Guarnerius.

A Guarneri. My skin grew cold. Of course, anyone could fake a label, but I was far more certain than I'd been about the Turner that this was the real thing. Compared to the decent but anonymous mid-nineteenth century French instrument which I still used for my concert performances, this was like touching the hand of God.

From above, applause boomed. When my dressing room door opened, Claude didn't even wait for me to put aside this impossible object before giving me a hug.

"How on earth did you get this?" I gasped as I eased it out from between us.

He sat down on the edge of the dressing table and stretched out his long legs. "Apparently, it's the 1734 Duc de Camposelice, whatever that means. It's been owned and played by Ricci, Kessler and Lin, and there's nothing worse than keeping these things in a bank vault, is there? So when I heard that it was available, I thought it might just suit you. Have you tried playing it yet?"

"Of course I have. It's . . . "

"Good? Bad? I've heard these posh fiddles can be a lot less than they're cracked up to be. We can sort something out if there's a problem. And there's always some rich idiot collector somewhere. If you don't like it, just say."

"It's the most beautiful thing I've ever heard, held or seen, Claude. How the hell—"

"No, no." He waved a finger. "Never ask about gifts—or don't they tell you that back in England?"

I subsided. Of course, I wanted this violin. But, reluctantly, glancing at the clock, I moved to place it back inside its intricate black shell. I'd one last performance to give with my old violin before this Guarneri took over my life . . .

"Hey—what are you doing?"

Already guessing what Claude had in mind, I shook my head. "You've got no idea how much work it takes to get familiar with a new instrument. It'll be great, it'll be fabulous, but—"

"Play it, Roushana. Play it this evening. It's working, isn't it? It's not cracked or buzzing or distorted?"

"It's even in tune, for fuck's sake. But no . . . " I gazed at him: that limpid smile which could make me do anything. "I really *mean* it Claude. You don't understand about violins. They're not machines. Every one feels entirely different. It's gorgeous and I love it and I love you and I don't how you can possibly have managed to get hold of such a thing. But absolutely, definitely, no."

Ten minutes later, I was standing in the wings, Guarneri in hand, watching as Claude led a quartet of kids from his Project through a rumbustious performance of *Les escaliers de Montmartre* which the audience clapped along to gleefully. I was in a cold sweat. Claude had reassured me a hundred times that this whole concert was really about showbiz and money, and that the music didn't count in the way it always should. But this, I knew, as the members of the Orchestra du Paris moved back to their places, was my big moment. I could either take it or throw it away. The worst thing I could do was to play with average competence—be merely good. Everyone would then assume that I, instead of any of a dozen star violinists, had simply got this gig because I was screwing Claude. Better that I made a complete mess of it. Better that I didn't turn up at all . . .

Finally, the orchestra had tuned up and re-settled. Claude re-emerged, climbed to the podium, acknowledged his players and the audience, then gestured towards the space in the wings where I was standing. My feet felt light. There was an odd ringing in my head. People were clapping, then silence fell. I was conscious of a pulse to the light which washed through the enormous glass ceiling, and of the thud of my own heart. Why on earth had I agreed—although I was certain I never *had* agreed—to the totally ridiculous suggestion that I use the Guarneri tonight? The tone, the volume, the sound, the simple feel and weight and balance of it, were all entirely different to the instrument I'd rehearsed with. Claude looked down at me. Although it was the last thing I felt like doing, I lifted the centuries-old violin to my chin, and raised the bow, and gave a nod.

Of course, Claude was aware of my nervousness. But he waited and waited. The hall remained hissingly silent, but I could sense the beginnings of puzzlement spreading across the audience. Was something wrong? Then, just at the last possible moment before stirrings and coughings began to arise, he counted in the beat, and a mist of sound arose from the strings, and, more by instinct than thought, I made my entry in the third bar. The melody unwound, and the woodwind joined me and the tympani rumbled, and the oddest thing of all was that I'd never been less conscious in my life of the instrument I was playing. All I could hear was music. I was far too caught up in the moment to think through such thoughts as played, but the effect was probably like that which a runner or a boxer experiences when, after months of training weighed down

143

with weights or heavy gloves, they finally shed their encumbrances for the big event. I was flying. The Guarneri was mine and, just as Claude had long been telling me, I knew that this concerto was all about heat and passion, not ice and snow. By the time I'd poured out the first stuttering cadenza and the orchestra's big theme was starting to emerge, I sensed that something miraculous was happening. Of course, the players were surprised by all the shifts in tone and timing I was making with the Guarneri, but they responded brilliantly. Their playing was dark, dynamic, energetic—it poured from the heart, and Claude urged them on as he swayed at the podium.

It just got better and better. Slower and sadder. Lighter and darker. More volcanic and, yes, scary as well. There was nothing on earth that wasn't there in this music. As the swirling dance of the third movement commenced, I sensed the whole audience give a startled jump. I wanted to show them. I wanted them to laugh and weep. I wanted them to *know*. We all did—the whole orchestra. The strings were percussively sharp. I took the melody, I twisted it around, threw it back at them. Then we were together, and I didn't want this to stop. Not ever. The basses growled as I floated by them. Then the threads were gathered as I made staccato interventions and the great musical beast against which I'd been pitting myself, which was by now something more than merely an orchestra or even Claude Vaudin, roared, then collapsed and died, impaled on my last high C.

For a while, I was so stunned by what had just happened that I barely heard the applause. What I sensed instead was a falling realisation that what I'd just experienced had gone, followed by a determination to recreate something like it as soon as possible—among its many attributes, performing music at this level is an incredibly addictive drug—then the sense of the audience intruded. They were all standing, and the orchestra were standing as well. I looked towards Claude, but he was gesturing towards me as the roar in my ears increased and I remembered to bow. Even as he came down to me and took my hand as I disappeared behind bouquets of flowers, the roaring went on and on. The only way we could ever have shut them up was by playing something else. We ripped through Ravel's *Carmen Fantasy*, which wasn't just the usual stock encore to get the lights up and the seats emptied, but a matter of playing for sheer joy. And still everyone was clapping. I shot Claude a look, and he turned to the audience, made a gesture, a signal. The falling away of sound in this huge auditorium was eerie. He controlled them as easily as he controlled the orchestra by now.

His footsteps rang as he stepped over to the piano at centre stage. He gestured me to join him.

"What are we supposed to be playing?" I hissed, but Claude just smiled and kissed my hand.

A deeper quiet fell. For the first time tonight, I was fully conscious of all the thousands of watching faces, and the millions out there in virtuality, and that this moment was entirely unplanned. But, through a series of signals which may or may not have been rehearsed, a pair of percussion mallets were handed to Claude. Leaning into the piano, he ran a glissando across the bare strings with the end of the stick, followed by a ringing sequence of notes, then glanced towards me. Already, I was raising my violin. I recognised this tune, although we'd only played it once in our atelier, and that was mostly naked, and entirely alone. *She Moves Through the Fair* is an English folksong—a kind of music which I'd previously imagined was about Morris dancing and the odd decent bit of Vaughan Williams. But this particular tune is about death and loss, and the melody is far more icy and strange than Sibelius. Even as I drew out the first note, and Claude responded at the piano with eerie plucks and resonances, I felt coldly afraid. Not now because I doubted my ability to play, but because of the desolation of this song, which I suddenly felt mirrored so much of the world which lay outside this warmly lit concert hall and all the fuss and bustle of life in Paris, and the unknowable future into which we were heading. Drifting towards a quite dissonance which felt like the end of everything, then drawing the melody out again in the most achingly simple way, we shaped the empty air. I was shivering and exhausted by the time the piece had finished. There wasn't another note I could possibly play.

Claude and I stood there together. Silence filled the Opéra de Paris Bastille. The audience just sat, barely breathing, for far longer than any group of so many people should ever remain. Then they erupted.

Everyone who was anyone—those who were at the concert and those who weren't, but by now were claiming they had been—was there at Harad Le Pape's apartment later on that evening. The tall, empty rooms were suddenly stuffed to their ceilings with the gestures, voices, faces, fames, cleavages, rivalries, star turns, reputations and egos. Harad was holding court—but I was as well. Everyone wanted to double-kiss and congratulate me, then to remind me of the word they'd put in for me, how they'd always known I was the one to watch. Interviews were arranged. My words and gestures were even more lavishly recorded than my performance has been. Claude, normally the kingpin on such occasions, was characteristically gracious in his role of supporting act. I took the toasts. I gave a stumbling speech. The fact that the Guarneri had made all the difference—that, through nerves and inexperience, I'd probably have played with nothing but cool efficiency without it, and that Claude had guided the orchestra so brilliantly, and then come up with that cataclysmic second encore single-handedly—all of these things my lover let pass without mention, and for that I loved him all the more.

Harad was dressed tonight in silk slippers and an embroidered Chinese robe. The effect was less camp than feminine, and the general opinion was that he or she was drifting back towards a more womanly phase. I was granted a warm smile, then a surprising hug, for Harad Le Pape never hugged anybody. This, with the entire Parisian world watching, was far better than any review.

"I'm so, so, sorry for you, my darling," Harad then murmured loudly enough for the onlookers to hear. "I thought you were going to be a marvellous failure. I thought you were going to eke

out your life in some dreadful high-rise and die an early death surrounded by bottles of absinthe and vials of float. Instead, you poor
thing, you've got this—success. Just remember, though, that this
is just the beginning." I was drawn even deeper into an unlikely
Chanel-scented hug. "And take proper care of Claude . . ." This
time, Harad's voice really was a whisper. "He's far more easily broken than he seems."

Not only this, but a dissonant phrase from our performance of
She Moves Through the Fair would, like shells from Proust's imaginary Balbec, and the alternate pages of *Finnegan's Wake* read back-
wards, be contributing towards the great work which Harad was
creating on the floor above. And wasn't that Max Rochereau? And
that's definitely Agnieszka Perrot. Soon, even Jane Affray was talking to me in her animatedly verbose way about how she longed to
write a song cycle without words. And I'd perform it, wouldn't I?
And I'd be sure to be here, and read this, and listen to that, and
taste these, and sample those, and look in there? Dropped calling
cards, the leaf-falls of fame, purred their dying voices across the
wine-spilled floors. Soon, people were gathering at the lift and trying promising doors in the hope that they might find a way up to
Harad's famous 6th floor.

I found Claude talking animatedly to a tall, good-looking
woman who seemed to be in her early thirties—although, in Paris
of all places, it was getting ever-harder to tell. This was Mathilde
Irissou, recently nominated by the PS, the French socialist party,
as their candidate for the summer's presidential elections.

"You must be so weary of people congratulating you," she
cooed in perfect English. "But you deserve it. Half the audience
were in tears, you know."

"I certainly haven't got tired of praise. I hope I never do."

Mathilde's Irissou's straight hair, not so much blonde as amber,
was cut at shoulder-length in a neat bob. In a style she'd pioneered
after recent seasons of epaulettes and coxcombs, she was dressed
severely but elegantly in a dark suit which nevertheless gave discreet prominence to her superb figure. Of mixed Algerian and
Polish blood, a self-made product of the dire estates beyond the

Periphique, she looked every inch the up-and-coming politician, although her main claim to fame until this year had been as the latest incarnation of bare-breasted Liberty emerging from the barricades. In England, there would have been sniggers. In France, it meant they took her all the more seriously.

"I'm sure you already know how much I admire Claude." In this age beyond make up, Mathilde's lips were naturally, unnaturally red, her teeth were whitely perfect, and her eyes were diamond-bright. "You share our commitment to a just, socialist Sixth Republic?"

"I'm all in favour of equality, if that's what you mean." I'd already realised that I didn't like this woman, or the way she looked at Claude, but I pushed such thoughts aside. For Mathilde Irissou was a billion times better than the fatly smug Blaise Boullard, present occupant of the Elysée Palace. And I understood enough from Claude by now to know that politics wasn't about looking for perfection and rejecting everything else. *It's the art of the possible. It's what can be done, Roushana. Here and now. In this imperfect world . . .*

"We need the support of people like you, Roushana. I hope you don't mind me saying this, but you and Claude are an important couple, and I don't just mean artistically, although that's obviously true. He's a black American, you're an Asian Englishwoman, and yet you've both chosen France."

"Actually, my father was Anglo-Saxon."

"Is that so? Well, all the better. And your mother—the work she does for the poor and radiation-poisoned in India. You're a stunning example, Roushana . . . " Taking my hand in both of hers, she squeezed it and slipped into passionate French. "Between us, we can change the world. These elections aren't just about who's going to make the necessary alliances and choose a compromise president for the next five years. You might think you know what Boullard is like, but you don't. Naturally, there are the deals, the corruption, the brazen inefficiency. Naturally, there are the contracts for buildings which never get built. But that's just circling around the pot. And it's getting far worse. This will be the most brutal of all elections. Look, look, over there . . . "

Despite it all, I was flattered by her warm urgency. Had she really said *change the world?* In this strange and sudden process of my rising, in the fever of Paris in that gathering spring, anything seemed possible.

"Ah," Claude, a fresh glass of wine slopping in his hand, rejoined us and noticed the direction in which we were looking. "That fraudulent slug. I know that Harad's a great one for irony, but inviting creatures like that here tonight is just taking it too far..."

If anything, the most distinguishing feature of the man standing awkwardly at the edge of a group was his absolute ordinariness. Everyone else here tonight possessed some combination of talent, fame, power, good looks or money, but, scruffily dressed in jeans, rain-sodden sneakers and a loose, grubby smock, he was their antithesis. His skin was so oddly blotched and mottled that he looked as if he might once have been badly burned, and he was plump and unattractive. You could even see the gleam of his scalp through the greasy hair which, in an almost touching attempt at vanity, he'd attempted to comb across it. He was so unprepossessing it seemed ridiculous that he should be here, but at the same time he radiated a sort of composure—an arrogance, even. And he was oddly familiar...

"Hey, Christos!" Claude shouted over the heads which surrounded us, "how about some water?"

The man didn't seem to hear and shuffled in his slightly lopsided way towards another oblivious group. But now that Claude had said the name and mentioned water, it all fell into place. He'd shouted worse things, and thrown objects, at this so-called Christos as we lay in bed and flicked from channel to channel on what was still then called the TV. There were many prophets and messiahs back then in Paris, but Harad Le Pape had shown his or her usual judgement by choosing Christos out of all of them to invite here tonight. He was the phenomenon of the season. You saw his disciples handing out apocalyptic flyers and selling cheap bottles of water on almost every street.

"You know," Mathilde murmured, "there's every chance the funda-mentalists will have the swing vote in the next Assembly. In effect, and if Boullard gets the presidency again, they'll probably dictate the choice of Prime Minister. From there, we'll have a ban on birth control and all forms of abortion. There'll be total censorship. Women will lose the right to employment. It'll be the Middle Ages . . . "

"You really think Boullard would let things go that far?" I asked.

Claude laughed whilst Mathilde favoured me with the different smile she obviously reserved for the blissfully innocent. "Boullard will do anything to keep power, Roushana," she continued in English. "That's why we have to stop him. I know it's easy to be cynical about politics, but there are times when thought and action are crucial, when the very soul of a country lies on a pivot. And this is one of them. France is close to collapsing into factions. We have to give people hope. We have to make a stand. And if that means . . . " She gave a Gallic shrug. "If that means we have to resort to clichés and soundbites. If I have to purr to the cameras and stick out my chest and do my best to look appealing, so be it. There are worse things. There are worse prices. Which . . . " Another pause; one of those random insertions which politicians use to make it sound as if what they're saying isn't rehearsed. "Which brings me to a favour I have to ask you both. That tune, the one those children played tonight at the Opéra."

"*Les Escaliers de Montmartre*?" I offered as if she needed my help.

"Exactly. I've been trying to get it out of my head for weeks. Then, every time I do, I come across someone else whistling or humming it. We're looking for a campaign tune, and my advisors' spin engines tell us that we need something catchy and without words. That tune, to be honest, would be perfect. We'd only use it for the length of the campaign. Then, and if we win as your backing would almost certainly help us do, who knows what a nation might offer in gratitude . . . ?"

This was like watching a good jazz musician improvising. The switches in gear were surprising, yet they seemed inevitable once they'd occurred. But Claude was up there with her. "There are rights issues, Mathilde, and we'd need to speak to our agents, but I'm sure we could sort something out by the weekend? Would that be good enough?"

"That would be perfect . . . " Mathilde strained forward and up. Her lips and then her fingers lingered on his cheek. Then, with seemingly equal passion, although the sensation was somewhat chilling, she kissed me. "I need you . . . " she whispered. "Both of you . . . Remember . . . Please don't forget . . . "

The hours floated on with the resolute illogic of a party. Outside by now, all of Paris might be awake or asleep—living or dead—but everyone who was anyone was still here, and would instantly start talking about whoever was the first to leave. So we all stayed. There was even a rumour that Harad might actually have decided to allow an exclusive preview of his or her great project on the 6th floor, although that was stretching things too far. Then Karl Nordinger, whom I'd been avoiding all night on the basis of our sour encounter in that café, cornered me with a characteristically disconcerting smile stitched across his face and a sickly whiff of Pernod.

"Really enjoyed your performance tonight, Roushana."

"I thought you . . . " But how could he, of all people, detest musicians?

"Can I show you something?" Unwanted possibilities ran through my mind, but I nodded anyway.

The party groups had grown denser and more agitated in their rivalries, and the far rooms of Harad's apartment, with their toppled wineglasses and discarded clothes and trampled drug inhalers, seemed storm-wrecked and empty. Nordinger took me to a keyboard which sat beside windows awash with grey rain. He toyed with its controls and music began to play.

"This is what I'm currently working on," he said. "Doesn't seem like very much, I know . . . "

For many minutes, I just stood there listening. Even from the little I then heard, I already suspected that Karl Nordinger's *Fourth Symphony* would be his greatest work. Despite, or perhaps because, of our first introduction, I'd now come to know a little more about the man. His parents had been aid workers, and he'd spent his childhood in a variety of third world countries staring out at poverty and violence through the wires of compounds. I supposed it explained a lot, not least his cynicism, and his impossible-to-place accent. He'd started out as a computer geek making dance music, then announced to a mostly disinterested world that he would reinvent the symphony. Of course, it was an absurd presumption and the few who bothered to listen laughed. But then came the First Symphony, and his suite *Swann In Love*, which Claude had espoused in his touring-conductor days. Everyone was listening to him by now. Nordinger's music was rich, and in some ways it was backward-looking, although many of the tones and references were eastern and scraps of it broke the edges of tonality, whilst others were so abrasive they sounded like orchestral heavy metal. It was as if, as Harad Le Pape him or herself had once commented in the days when he or she still wrote reviews, Beethoven had written trance music. To me, though, Nordinger was reminiscent of Mahler. Not so much in his structures and tonalities, but in grasping at the seemingly ridiculous ambition that a piece of music can encompass the entire world. And Nordinger was able to do something which hadn't been possible for composers in any previous century, although many toyed with the idea. Using artificial intelligence software, he'd created scores which evolved of their own volition. The middle section of *Swann in Love*, for example, which was once pitted with ironic interjections from the woodwind, was now filled with Proustian twilight.

"See this . . . " He silenced the keyboard and called up a section of score onto its screen. "I know . . . " He chuckled. "Sibelius—what you were playing this evening. A total rip-off."

Not that it was, although I could see what he meant in those gathering D minor strings.

"Then there's this. It's not finished."

My skin prickled. For the first time, I saw the scattered notes of the third movement's famous *Song of Time*.

"Obviously, that bit's played on the harmonics. The last phrase ends with both the first and second strings."

"It looks . . . Quite beautiful."

Nordinger made a grimace.

"No, I don't mean beautiful, I mean—"

"Doesn't matter what you mean. Could you play it?"

"I haven't got my violin here with me."

"Not *now*. I mean at the first performance, although fuck knows when that will be."

"Yes," I said. "I mean, it's so simple. But . . . "

"But what?"

"Nothing. I'd be honoured."

This was an enormous privilege, and I recanted everything I'd ever thought or heard about Karl Nordinger. No-one but a genius of extraordinary sensitivity could write music of such compassion and sadness. Even after I'd returned to the factions of the party, the purity of his melody stayed with me. Haunting—yes, perhaps that would be the closest possible word. But now things inside Harad's apartment really were starting to wind down. Farewells were being called. Couples and other alliances were reconnecting, or deciding to remain apart. There was no sign of Mathilde Irissou, or Max Rochereau, or Karl Nordinger, or either of the two Susi Broadsmeres, or the character who called himself Christos, or even Harad Le Pape him or herself. Were these, I wondered as Claude and I found our way back out onto the streets of Paris, really the people who we shared this triumphant party with? They looked so lost and pointless now, the men bedraggled, the barefoot women carrying their impossible shoes as they dwindled with their reflections along the shining pavements.

IT'S BEEN SUCH A LONG DAY. EVEN THE BREAKFAST, WHICH —still reeling from wine and the midnight rush of Paris—I took with Adam in my dressing gown, was hard work, and Adam looked a little frail himself. Perhaps he'd drunk more of that wine last night than I'd realised. Or perhaps it's something else. "I've an appointment," I told him as he topped me up with extra coffee which I knew I couldn't afford to drink. "In Bodmin. It's just a routine thing. A car will be coming, so it's probably best if you keep out of the way."

"At a clinic?"

"Clinic? Why do you say that?"

He shrugged—it was more of a shiver—as he put down the coffee jug. "Just something I thought you mentioned last night."

"I suppose it *is* a clinic," I conceded. "I'm having . . . various kinds of treatment. After all, and as you've probably noticed, I'm not exactly young. I get tired easily. I have these . . . Dizzy spells. I need to watch what I drink and eat. I have to pace myself, take rests in the afternoon."

I'd said too much—Adam had on what I think of as his guilty boy expression—but I felt angry with him, or with someone. It's the closest he and I have come to any kind of conflict, and it seemed to linger even as I went upstairs to dress, and then sat waiting for the car. It arrived at the gate, which I'd left shut to save it getting any glimpse of Adam, with predictable machine punctuality at bang on ten o-clock, and sat there on its fat tyres, looking pleased with itself with its little motor panting steam. Had I locked Adam inside Morryn this time? Was that the right or the wrong thing to have done? These were questions I pondered as I moved off inside its plastic bubble, but for the life of me couldn't work out.

Another fine late August day, and the rowans inland along the winding valley were in extravagant fruit. Half of Lostwithiel is covered in some kind of ivy: a lost village in a lost valley, finally living up to its name. Hawks floated. The empty windows of the castle stared down at my passing. The Cornish countryside is so *wild* these days but Bodmin, or at least in its centre, is still fully inhabited, and remains resolutely granite-grey. I gazed around the market square as my car left me, telling myself, despite the sudden hammering of my heart, that I've long known this place. Here was the café in the Tudor guildhall where I'd often lunched with old friend Daisy, back in the times when being alive was something we both took for granted. It was just opening for the day's business, and offering what looked like the same menu chalked on the board outside. Funny how some things last, how others go away...

There are, I suppose, many names for the building which resides on St Nicholas Street, although the reassuringly municipal words PUBLIC HALL are still carved into the granite lintel above its entrance. Climbing in three floors by tall windows and heavy ironwork to a many-browed roof, the clinic yawned dour and grey as I stood outside its railings, but no dourer and greyer than many other of Bodmin's main buildings. Inside, there's always a pleasant bustle. People were at work, coming and going. The air smells of well-polished old wood and big floral displays, and dust streamed with sunlight from the big windows which overlook the reception area.

There isn't a desk in Liang Ho's office—not a real one, anyway. In fact, it isn't recognisably any kind of office, for people work differently nowadays, but, like him, it retains a businesslike air. There are two chairs, and there's never any question as to which one Ho sits in, and which is for you. As I settled myself, I imagined the suited accountant or solicitor who probably once used to work here.

He smiled and leaned forward, tapping together the tips of his perfectly manicured fingers as if in impatient prayer. "So nice to see you again. You're looking like your real self."

"Actually," I said, taking stock. "I *do* feel a bit better."

"No problems with the treatments?" He was just being polite; news of anything amiss would have been transmitted to him already from this thing in my skull.

"None at all. It's been a goodish week. But . . . hard work."

"So—what have you been doing?"

"I suppose pretty much what you suggested. I've been thinking about the past." He broadened his smile. "That's excellent."

"Well . . . " The phrase I'd just used—*hard work*—came back to me like a sour burp. For isn't that exactly what Daisy Kornbluth once said? " . . . it's been rather odd, to be honest. I'm a bit of a hoarder. I'm not good at throwing things away. But going through everything with ah—with Morryn, has been a far more vivid experience than I expected."

"Morryn?"

"It's my house."

"Have you heard of Matteo Ricci?"

I shook my head.

"He was a Jesuit traveller to China who developed a way of remembering the characters of Chinese script. He imagined a huge building filled with many rooms, and in each room he placed a memory, and furnished the rooms with objects which would trigger the correct associations. He soon became able to wander at will along corridors, taking turns or ascending stairways, and was thus able to locate whatever information he needed. He termed this creation a palace of memory. It's a technique which has been widely used since."

"That's what I'm doing? Making a palace of memory in Morryn?"

"Of course, the crystal is co-operating. But you've probably already found how certain objects trigger certain memories." Ho shrugged. "But don't take the term *objects* too literally, Roushana. The rooms in a palace of memory needn't just be filled with things. The trigger can be anything. A smell, a taste, maybe a mixture of senses . . . With you, of course, a melody. They can all lead you into new ways of remembering."

"So I've found." *Of course, the crystal is co-operating;* another sour burp. "But you can't bring back *everything*, can you? And how can I ever be sure that the way I think things happened was how they really did?"

"Ah—the fallacy of truth! Of course, there can be no such thing as certain knowledge. We all have our own illusions, *delusions* about the past. Some things are bound to be painful, perhaps so painful that we really have no wish to revisit them. But you shouldn't worry. This isn't supposed to be some impersonal history—it's the reflection of your true nature which counts."

With the same professional ease that the solicitor who probably once sat in this room once asked his clients about their wills—not that people need to make wills now, as many lawsuits have established the rights of the dead to continue to own property—Ho then moved on to ask me if I'd had any thoughts about the details of my passing.

"No more than I had before."

"Have you told anyone? Friends? Colleagues? You have children, yes?"

"I haven't told anyone."

He nodded and smiled some more. "And the arrangements?"

"No ceremonies. No fuss."

"Of course. There's no need for anything to take place but the process of passing itself. And that can occur almost anywhere. Here in Bodmin, of course, but in virtually any location. If you wished to pass on from a hilltop, for example, a little notice would be necessary to construct the necessary field. But if you'd come in today and told me that you'd decided that you were ready, it could be done here right now."

I let that thought sink in. "But what if I *wasn't* ready, Ho? I mean, there's so much of my life I haven't yet explored."

Ho tapped his fingers. "It's simpler than that, Roushana. If you feel you're ready, you *are*. The things you take and the things you leave behind, they're simply expressions of what you are. All that's then required is letting go—a mere effort of will."

"You make it sound frighteningly simple."

"Yes." Briefly, Ho permitted his smile to fade. "Frightening, and simple. It's both of those things."

Then, just as I was preparing to leave, he announced, "Oh, and there's someone else who'd like to see you today. I mean, if you have the time?"

Ho led me to a door at the far end of a whitewashed corridor. Bowing slightly, and smiling once more, he opened it for me, and stepped back to let me in.

As I entered, as he left me and the door snapped shut, I felt an inner CLICK—a sense of some deeper intrusion—although the room inside seemed perfectly pleasant. There were oak-panelled walls, antique tapes-tries, a few elegant scraps of minimalist mod-ern furniture which didn't seem remotely out of place, but, even before I'd fully absorbed the identity of the person who occupied it, I knew it couldn't be real. Everything was just a little too intense—the colours, the sunlight, the sense that you could count every thread of those seemingly ancient tapestries, the sheer glow of the air—too obviously *authentic*. The real world, especially when you get to my age, simply isn't this clear.

Dressed in a close-fitting white blouse and a well-tailored mid-length skirt, and giving every impression of having been waiting for some little time, the image of Blythe Munro was standing beside the polished slate fireplace. She looked just as I remem-bered her—pert and pretty and young.

"I don't want to die yet," I told her.

"Of course not. No—of course."

"You *are* dead, though, aren't you?"

"If that's how you choose to put it. Do you want me to stay?"

"You need my permission?"

Blythe glanced around as if to take in this room. Outside the window, I noticed, the view wasn't of Bodmin's roofs and monument hill, but of some pretty glade. The trees, the grass, were like this room: they all had that same impossible glow. "I do, actually."

"I suppose I might once have admitted to Ho that it could be a help to speak to someone—but why *you*, Blythe? I mean, it wasn't as if we ever liked each other."

"As I say, if you want me to, I'll go."

"You may as well stay, I suppose. But I have to tell you that I'm not convinced you're really the Blythe Monroe I once knew."

"That's okay. After all, what you think doesn't decide the truth."

"You're right—I'm dying, and no one ever asked me what I thought about that, either."

"I'm sorry, Roushana. I truly wish there were other reasons for me to be here."

"And yet here you are."

Making a small game of it, she pretended to study the long fingers which had once struggled to master the cello. "Undeniably. Would it help if I told you something about my life?"

Dead or alive, I suppose, this is how it still goes. You meet someone again after a long time, and you swap useless stories as you wonder at how little or how much they've changed. Do the dead have cocktail parties? Do they have school reunions? Do they brag and lie just like us living? But I simply listened as Blythe told me about her life, how she'd become a lawyer just as she'd said she would, although expert systems were taking everyone's place by then, and concepts such as civil liberties—the whole idea that every human being has some individual merit—were on the wane. To compensate, she got involved in several high-profile human rights cases.

Our lives had passed so close. There was a professor we'd both met in Paris, she'd even attended a civil rights conference at which I'm sure Claude had spoken, and had been to a Yellowstone benefit he and I once gave in London's Festival Hall.

"I almost sent you a note backstage to reintroduce myself, but in the end I decided not to, although I followed your careers. I always felt that we were on the same side."

I had to laugh. "And you really think you're the same person, now?"

"Of course not. But I'm still Blythe—that's the whole point."

"How do you pass the time?"

"At the moment, I'm passing it by talking to you."

"After that?"

"I do other things."

"You're enjoying this, aren't you?"

"Otherwise, I wouldn't be doing it."

"But doesn't it offend you—the ghoulish way we living insist on calling you the dead?"

"There are prejudices. We've had to fight for our rights just as any other group must."

"And now you rule the world."

"We simply protect our interests."

"How long have you been this way, Blythe? How did you die?"

"That's something only the living ask."

"You're not going to tell me, are you? Am I being impolite?"

"I know it seems like a vital question. But, it isn't, believe me. What's important is what lies beyond—what lies ahead."

I stared across at Blythe—and Blythe gazed back at me, or the dying, wizened creature I've become. She still bore, I was almost sure of it, the same clean, mild scent of flesh and flowers which had always possessed the air around her. She still had that bouncy head-girl—no it was *deputy* head—let's-get-on-with-things attitude. I could see her now, so vividly that it hurt, emerging into our back garden as I lay out on the rug with Leo. *Oh Roushana* . . . This, the slow thought crept through me, both reassuring and eerie, really is Blythe Munro.

"Remember that time," I asked her, "when I came in on you and Leo in his bedroom?"

She gave a mock-cringe. "We felt so much worse about that for you than we did for ourselves."

"That was the way you both always were! It was far too much for any ordinary kid to live up to."

"But you *did* . . ." Blythe tilted her head and looked at me with

160

a sort of compassion. "We never did know each other, though, did we? We were like cats circling around Leo as if he was our territory. But it was no contest—Leo was always yours."

"Do you still blame me for his death? You did, didn't you? You're the only one who thought I could have done something to stop him."

"But what could you have done, Roushana? You forget just how strong-willed and stubborn Leo was. And how young you were."

Something flared. Even now, I thought, she's prepared to patronise me. "And what did you really do," I snapped, "with all those years you had alive? Did you have lovers, hates, passions, children? Or was law just a suitable alibi—something you could pretend to be doing instead of having a proper life when you had blood in your veins instead of digits and light?"

"No, I didn't have children, Roushana . . . " she said, and I was pleased to see how her face had become flushed, how her eyes were shining. "Like a lot of people who lived through that last century, I decided not to. And as for lovers—"

"What do you really want from me, Blythe?"

She took a step towards me. I could hear the silky whisper of her limbs. "You're almost ready. You don't know it—people never do—but you *are*. The jewel in your head is far more than just some clever device now. It's become part of what you are. It mirrors, anticipates. It *exists*. When you look at me like that, it does the same. When you laugh, it laughs. Oh, I know how difficult this is, but you're got to give way. This—what I'm now experiencing—it's everything . . . "

"Can you show me?" Even though I still wished this was someone other than Blythe, it was a question I knew I had to ask.

"You can show *yourself*." She moved closer still. I could feel, I was sure of it, her breath against my face. "Take my hand."

I did, and her grip was warm, smooth, supple, secure. She felt alive—it was no use my telling myself that it was all a matter of energies and suggestions, for the effect was uncanny, although it's harder for me to recall exactly what happened next. It was all so quick, so bright, so real. Suddenly, we were in a huge square lined with long, elegant buildings. Some kind of domed cathedral lay at its far side, with a glimpse beyond of glittering water. Bells were ringing. Pigeons swirled. I *knew* this place, these buildings . . .

"I thought," her voice murmured, "that Venice would be as good a place to show you as any."

I had to laugh, and felt as I did so the thrills of lightness and youth re-entering my body. There were wafts of a choir from the open doors of the basilica, which seemed to be made of nothing but gold. This was too, too beautiful. The sky was Bellini blue, there were Canaletto buildings, Veronese clouds, and people were eating, people were laughing. Sconces burned along the Arsenal walls, and people, up in the high windows of the exquisite buildings, were making extravagant love. I noticed a small child, neither boy nor girl, and he or she came over to me, smiling, and then we were together on a gondola, and songs echoed from the palaces along the dank walls.

"I know," said this child in a voice high and sharp and sexless. "I look nothing like Harad, not even when he or she was young . . . But you of all people understand how difficult things were after Paris. Being both a critic and an artist only teaches you how essentially worthless both pursuits are. Oh, I won't bore you with the circumstances, Roushana, but I realised as soon as I passed that there's another way." Beside us, people were swimming naked in the golden waters of the canal. They were all beautiful and they were all laughing. "The most ridiculous thing is that it's called simply living! Can you believe, Roushana—that I had to die to find that out?"

Hands clamoured around our boat, and were rocking us back and forth. It swung over, and I fell through necklaces of golden arms into sewer-darkness, and winter-cold. I was looking down on the drowned and fallen edifices of a different Venice. The basilica's dome was a sludge-filled crater. Eels darted amid the fallen pillars of Florien's bar.

"Ha, and you think *this* is what it's really like—it's far worse . . . "

My old agent, Adur Foster, more bull-walrus than mermaid with the scaled tail he now affected, swam up to me out of the gloom. Although he couldn't possibly be talking to me underwater, silver bubbles skittered up from his lips.

"Don't tell me, Adur—you now represent promising dead artists?"

"The fact is, Roushana, that I still represent quite a few living ones as well. It was just . . . " He gave his hairy shoulders a shrug. ". . . I think we'd gone as far as we could with our relationship. And, let's face it, the music of the forever dead was getting a harder and harder act to sell."

Adur swam off with a brisk kick of his tail, drowned Venice swarmed, settled, and I become conscious once again of Blythe's presence. We seemed to fall back until the darkness became blue-lit, and I realised that we were hovering far above the earth. From up here, it looked beautiful and unspoiled—a snowstorm bauble swirled by our own invisible hands.

"The future isn't the earth, Roushana. Coastlines change, continents drift and the sea soon rises to engulf every mountain. There's no escaping chaos and change. The living will die endlessly, but even the passed can't be safe down there. Ah, but that is just the beginning! You and I, we can become the breath of the sun—we can ride the signal to the furthest probe. And not just the planets. The solar system is merely our doorstep. We can escape all matter, we can reach the stars . . . "

Morryn.

This bed.

This body.

This night.

My mind sinks back to the present. I can't possibly sleep—not when my head is filled with these impossible dreams. But they were far more than dreams, and I haven't been able to sleep for days, anyway. And Blythe . . . Blythe Munro was everything I might have expected. Brisk as ever, and just as prim. Not really that youthful, for all the way she looked, but then she was never someone who was ever really *young*. More than anyone I've ever

163

known, she was born to become what she is now, although it's disappointing that Daisy Kornbluth didn't choose to come to me instead, after all the promises we made. But perhaps she was busy, and I never did thank her properly for all those flowers. Adur, though, seems to have taken to it all well enough, and to have kept his sense of humour, even if he has decided to quietly dump me from his client list. But that's agents for you, either living or dead. And Harad Le Pape . . . !

I noticed again the view through the window when Blythe and I returned to the charming virtual room she had first greeted me in. Not just that it wasn't Bodmin which lay beyond, nor that it was some predictably pleasant glade, but that it looked oddly familiar. Then I realised that what I was seeing was that far corner of the Munros' garden where Blythe had once sat me down and shared her concerns about Leo.

"Well . . . " Blythe said, and I almost cringed as she took my hand again, but this time it was only in farewell, " . . . I wish you good luck in your passing."

A moment later, and she was gone, leaving me with what felt like a thousand questions unanswered, and an odd sense of warmth in my groin. I felt another peculiar tug in my head as I left the room myself, and turned just as the door was closing, and saw how the place had emptied to a windowless square stripped of all warmth and furniture, with its bare plaster walls embroidered only with glittering snails' trails of crystal.

The sky had changed as I stepped outside the old Public Hall. The wind was trying to turn to the north, and the warmth I'd felt initially in my groin had already begun to chill. Legs chafing, thighs wet, longing to get back to Adam and Morryn, to change and shower, I stood shivering and waiting for my car in the market square as the chalked menu on the board outside the Tudor tearoom began to streak with rain.

You're almost ready.

Of course, the crystal is co-operating.

I'm still shivering now under these blankets. Crystal jellyfish, listening inside my head, you can't wait to take hold.

This is the future, Sis.

Summer is fading, and these modern autumns never last. Great hissing curtains of auroras fill the skies in winter, even this far south. The world is changing, the dead are rising, and it really is time that I left. But I'm leaving anyway—that's not for me to decide. The virus which has long nurtured itself in my system will soon destroy these very thoughts. *Everything* will go. It's going already. My incontinence will no longer be an embarrassment kept mostly under control by a careful regulation of what and when I eat and drink. My vision will fade. My hand, my limbs, my tongue, will become unruly until they lose function entirely and start to atrophy. I will become a bag of driftwood bones, withered skin, soulless pain.

There's no point in waiting, no point in beating about the bush. *Just get on with it Roushana.* Mum, who feared death far less than she feared anything, would have had a field day. Leo as well—he made this step seem almost easy. If they were waiting for me, and if Claude were there, and if Dad had passed over, too, instead of the people who seemingly have, all those useless friends and acquaintances, this process would be much easier...

I lever myself up from the pillow, then inch my legs over the edge of the bed. Silence resounds around Morryn as I move towards the door, then out along the landing, and down the stairs. Adam will be sleeping, just as all the truly living do, but Morryn watches, waits, and everything remains unlit as I shuffle towards the music room and slump down at the automatic piano which the wash of the stirring sea gives an inky gleam. Slowly, quietly, I begin to pick out the notes of *Les Escaliers de Montmartre.*

A ONE-LEGGED BUSKER, CARDBOARD-PROCLAIMED VICTIM of the Algerian wars, was playing our song when Claude and I went to take the weekly flight to Washington. The melody, that mid-beat uplift caught almost perfectly, gasped from his accordion to echo through Charles de Gaulle airport's mostly empty space. There were smiles and good-natured applause as Claude tried his hand at playing the man's instrument, made a mess of the same tune, then humbly handed it back to him. Even in this half-abandoned monument, a crowd of fellow travellers, vendors and pickpockets had gathered to watch. Lenses flickered. The tableau, totally unplanned, and thus all the more valuable, would be certain to make the major virtuals this evening. We were cheered and waved on our way.

After all the probes and scans, and a predictable two hours' wait on the runway, the elderly Eurobus finally juddered from the ground and headed towards the Atlantic. I gripped Claude's hand as I looked out of the window. Even the thought that we might not make it to the USA was exciting, and it felt like years since I had seen sunlight and blue skies.

We talked about our families as we got softly drunk on tiny plastic bottles of wine and fiddled with the broken controls for this or that form of entertainment: Claude's, but also my own. I'd rarely looked back at anything, but Claude could trace his own name to the Carolina slave plantations, and to a woman from Senegal, with whom he shared mitochondrial DNA. He believed that to recognise one's innate sources of joy and pain was a key part of being a performer.

"How much did you love Leo?" he asked as we lumbered through the skies towards the city he called his hometown. He'd already listened gravely to the few recordings of my brother's playing which I'd been able to access, making comments about the interpretation as if Leo might still hear them, and had watched a solitary video of us both performing in some school hall (me sawing terribly on that first cheap violin) which Dad had once posted online. He quizzed me about aspects of my supposedly Irish heritage—Roman Catholicism, the Potato Famine, the ongoing conflict between North and South—about which I hadn't the faintest idea. And he'd already spoken by videolink to Mum, who was only too happy to tell him about this and that cousin and second uncle. All this stuff about family seemed so unconventionally conventional for the person I'd imagined Claude to be.

We dipped into sleep as the plane chased the sun across the endless afternoon.

Claude's mother Lujah was waiting in the evening smog outside Dulles airport. A broad, busy, imperturbably happy woman who shared Claude's golden-brown eyes, she hugged us both and took our bags and squeezed our hands and breezily insisted on how tired we must be as we crossed the tarmac and climbed into the leather expanse of a massive vehicle which she hand-drove herself through the sunset back towards the city.

This was my first experience of America as well as Washington, yet many of those blurred and lush first impressions stayed with me, and come to mind now even when so much has been lost. There was some-thing sepia-toned about the clouds, something showy and unhurried about the way the big sun was hovering for so long on that space on the horizon, gleaming across the Potomac and flashing through the rising buildings of the city as if we were still racing the dateline, or as if time

167

and the rest of the world could wait whilst the sunset lingered here purely for the sake of the marvellous show it made.

After a confusion of busy roads and bridges and security cordons, we arrived at the Vaudins' house in Georgetown. I stepped out into purple twilight amid smells of blossom and wet earth beneath the benevolent glow of redbrick sash windows. Claude's father Tony was an academic of the sort for whom grand-sounding posts are specially made. His grey hair and lined smile suited him, and Lujah was hardly a lesser talent, an amateur singer good enough to have been professional who worked as a lobbyist for various blue chip charities on what she called *The Scene*. Their house was a marvel of big rooms, dramatic stairways and fireplaces, and the Vaudins filled it with the comings and goings of acolytes and message-bearers, the subtle scurryings of servants.

"I know what you're going to say," Tony Vaudin beamed from the far end of a candlelit dinner-table whilst I, pleasantly drugged by more wine and jet lag, dazedly tried to take it all in. "It's what you British always say about us Democrats in our big houses. You think we think we're socialists, and in a way we are, but it's never a word that you'll ever hear anyone say over here."

"And you can't say we're liberal either," Lujah chimed from the far end. "That's the death knell of all political influence as we know it."

"I hadn't thought . . . "

"*Of course* you hadn't, dear." Tony Vaudin leaned across the expanse of linen and silverware which separated us to squeeze my hand. The squeeze lingered. So did the grin, which was a tribute to the capital city's dentistry. "And you can say what you like in that charming British accent. No-one will mind if *you* use the S or the L word."

"So—what do you say?"

"We call ourselves Moderate Christians, Roushana." Now, in what was obviously a well-honed double-act, it was Lujah's turn again. "Not that we are Christian, but moderate's as close along these shores as you can get to calling yourself agnostic."

Tony let out a laugh. "And that's a whole other story!"

168

Claude laughed as well. Everything here—the food, the service, the china, the exquisite room stuffed with towels and flowers and chocolates which Claude and I had been given—seemed to mesh together perfectly. When he finally took me upstairs at the far end of several glasses of fine malt whisky, he bundled me through a door into a smaller, unlit room, then dispossessed and half-undressed me on a boingy bed. Voices drifted outside: Tony's, then Lujah's, as they called to the servants about the next day's arrangements, but by now it was too late for us to stop.

"This used to be my room," he murmured as he rolled off me. Now that details were coming into focus, I saw the gleam of trophies, of silk banners and crinkled posters. "That was why I wanted you in here."

I kissed him, but his parents' voices were still milling across the landing, and I didn't feel remotely comfortable. I made a desultory grab for the remains of my clothes, but Claude stopped me.

"No, no. Just leave it all here. Someone'll clear things up in the morning." He touched my breasts. "Let's just take a chance and go like this. It'll be fun . . ."

So, on the first night in Claude's parents' house, we sprinted near-naked along the corridors, and then collapsed laughing in our own huge room and, still possessed by the same insatiable spirit, made love yet again.

I awoke tired and early and happy, as I did each day we spent in Washington, and lay there listening to the quiet of that big house. This was like living in some ideal hotel—there were always gifts, new soaps, floral surprises, innovative snacks—and I left Claude sleeping, showered and dressed in my freshly cleaned clothes, before setting out to wander the pretty streets of Georgetown in the awakening morning. Of course, this wasn't really Washington DC, let alone America, but I felt a look-at-me pride as I eyed the expensive shops as they unfanned their awnings, and walked along the canal amid storms of blossom, to think that I had got here in my own way, and on what felt like my own terms.

There wasn't a brick out of place along the elegantly rising streets, the doors all shone with brasswork, and birds sang from the immaculate trees. Menials dressed in cheery smiles and striped blazers ticked about on bikes. Even the barrier fences which surrounded Georgetown made a fair stab at elegance.

Claude, who slept in far later here than ever he did in Paris, would be lazily awake by the time I returned, and we'd make love in amber sunlight and I'd shower and dress again, and Lujah would be up by then and Tony would be attired in whatever elegant suit he'd be wearing for today's round of seminars, board meetings and committees. Time assumed new aspects here: like the great buildings of State, it grew pillars, pediments and cornices.

Outside Georgetown's golden bubble, the real city, or at least as close as Washington DC ever came to reality, still waited. But meanwhile, there were leisurely receptions in big halls, and brisk rehearsals for the concerts Claude and I were to give at the JFK, and of course there were interviews and fund-raising lunches and passionate speeches by Claude, and the rejoinders which by now I was getting used to giving. I met famous faces—men and women some of whose names had adorned the Deutsche Grammophon CDs in Dad's old collection, congressmen, the last living stars of a dying Hollywood—and it seemed they all knew who I was, and wanted to hear what I thought about not merely music but the state of the world. Above all, they were fascinated by the thought of living—and then thriving, succeeding—in Paris, which most of them saw as some dream of cobbled streets, onion sellers and artists in garrets. If I was being patronised, I didn't notice it.

There were bubbles within bubbles. This froth of liberals was just a small sub-set of the greater political foam of Washington, and an endangered one at that. There had been hope three years before on Hardy Yasso being elected president that the fundamentalist doctrines which gripped most of the country could still

170

be reconciled with the liberal principles to which many in the east coast cities were still clinging. Even her sole previous claim to fame as acting the role of mother in a long-running series of coffee adverts had been overlooked. But now, with galloping recession, and the recent bloody farce of the loss of Taiwan and the sinking of the US third fleet by the Chinese, the chasms were growing larger. There was talk that one of the new virtuality stars—not a human at all, but a digital collection of lantern-jawed smiles and creaky eyebrow-raises from a popular series of semi-medieval romances—might stand for nomination. Few thought it was a joke, and even fewer doubted that he or it would do a better job than Yasso.

I was reminded of what Mum had told me of the remains of New Delhi. From the broken-tip of the Washington Monument to the tidal marks on the Jefferson Memorial, from the wingflash of the protective drones which constantly circled the White House to the constant flurries of mosquitoes beyond Georgetown's saccharine encampments, the place had a similarly languid and decrepit feel. They were both the old capitals of old empires, but Washington, still then being Washington, remained suffused with a glamour you could still imagine would never cease.

"We're so *proud* of what Claude's achieved," Lujah confided to me as she steered me between the tables towards the next important person she wanted me to meet at the end of a sit-down buffet at the Wardman Park. "It never was just about music or achievement for us. These things are hollow without some sort of moral substance."

There was nothing about Lujah which wasn't substantial. That afternoon, she'd be working at a sanatorium for breakbone fever victims. Fundraising, she insisted, was empty unless you put your own bare hands and your whole beating heart into it. She was a walking, endlessly talk-ing, advert for compassion. In many ways, she should have reminded me of Mum—if Mum had had a penchant for wearing thick gold necklaces and swishing around in hand-painted silk dressing gowns at breakfast.

"And I'm so glad that Claude's found someone," she told me in an interlude between the applause. "Everything about you Roushana—"

But now it was her turn to take the podium, with Claude at the piano as she sang Cole Porter in that sweet, near-professional contralto whilst cheques were written at the tables. And then I performed the Heifetz arrangements from Porgy and Bess, and the whole carousel of privileged Washington life continued its spinning.

"Mum and Dad do absolutely everything they can," Claude told me as we drove out later that same afternoon. "You can see that. And Gran—you've met Gran—she's the same. But I had to go somewhere else. Find somewhere more . . . " He gestured out of the window as our hire car trundled itself along wide streets of cliff-face offices. Somewhere *less*, I thought, would have said it better. Paris, for all its bustle and rain, seemed small and simple by comparison.

But I felt that I was coming closer to Claude by being here. His philosophy—a sort of happy Existentialism which said that nothing mattered apart from ideas—seemed like a cooler, more modern version of his parents' Democratic principles, which in turn were derived from the inclusive old-fashioned Christianity for which his grandmother's generation had once stood. For Lujah really was short for hallelujah, which seemed right to me now, rather than inherently comical. But the current generation of students at GWC, Georgetown and Virginia were demonstrating in favour of a war in Indo-China with as much passion as their great grandparents had once demonstrated against one, and people were speaking in tongues at the Sunday morning service at the National Cathedral . . .

As the guide-signals gave out and Claude took the car's wheel as the buildings slunk lower and turned shabbier, I pondered how Lujah and Tony had both accepted me so readily. There were no doubts, no reservations. Hadn't Claude brought other girls home? For all the liaisons he'd admitted and those which had been documented in the press, his past sexual life still remained elusive. Here he was again, talking as we passed burnt-out and boarded shops of walking with girls on the lost promenades of Virginia Beach. But with Claude the names were always too quick, and too many. Here, or in Paris, his life was like his parents' house in Georgetown. There were always new guests, dinners, recitals, rehearsals, dances, meetings . . .

We bumped over fallen telephone lines.

"I thought," he said, "I'd show you some of another side of DC."

Old women, grandmothers of no more than forty, eyed us from the streetside shade in plastic chairs. White flurries of the plastic peel-offs of drug patches, the other blossom of these other Washington suburbs, billowed across the hot streets. Our hire car, which had seemed small and dented and cheap in Foggy Bottom, suddenly looked new and expensive.

"Are you sure this is safe?"

Claude laughed. "This is *my* hometown as well as my parents', Roushana. You think I don't know this place?"

The sun hung low, just as it always seemed to do in Washington. Beneath its glare, the tarnished Anacostia River gleamed with oil and effluent. Rotting piers slumped beside half-sunken boats and wavering tendrils of reinforced concrete. When Claude turned up a side-street and stopped the car beside a burnt-out humvee. I could scarcely believe we were supposed to get out.

"Come on. We'll be fine."

Two children in motorised Zimmer frames stood watching us. They managed to look both pathetic and dangerous. Claude walked over to them, smiled, slapped hands, said something. He came back again.

"Did you give them money?"

"No, no." He laughed at my innocence. "Or not just money. I told them I'm going to see my old friend the Burger King. If that doesn't do it, nothing will . . ."

Sure enough, the shattered façade of an old Burger King franchise lay nearby, and I told myself as I stepped towards it over the rubble that we'd walked many of the more dangerous parts of Paris without hindrance. But nothing here was the same. Inside, some individuals far more threatening than the UUN soldiers I'd encountered in India lounged amid the plastic seats which remained bolted to the floor. They were kitted out with the sort of fire-and-forget weaponry which had failed the US in its recent military incursions, and it was immediately clear that neither of them recognised Claude.

"Hey—"

The argot was too thick for me to follow—I couldn't even make out what Claude was saying—but, after a few staccato questions, and some worrying glares at me, the atmosphere began to ease. Soon, there was laughter and sad headshakes as names of people were mentioned which it seemed they all knew, although I got the impression that most of them were dead.

Beyond the counter, past old frying machines and last adverts for combo meal bargains, then up a steel set of stairs, daylight faded, and music boomed with several disparate beats. There were dark curtains, sympathetically pulsing sheets of cheaply coloured scenes. I was eyed from alcoves by more men with high-tech guns, and a few sinisterly casual women. Then, in a flurry of wind-chimes and fans and yet more brightly pulsing plastic ribbons, and a final fumbling interlude of dark-ness, we were in the presence of the personage who could only be the Burger King.

Harad Le Pape had nothing on this. We were disorientated, instinctively stooping. This really did feel like a royal audience. The King was hugely fat, which in itself, seeing as he would have had easy access to the treatments which would have kept him slim, was a declaration of status. He, and the endless layers of glittering silks and prints and velvets and rare animal hides in which he was clothed, spilled and blended in confusing rococo with the gilt—or perhaps it was real gold—throne on which he was supported. Women, some real, some virtual, and all of them even more scantily dressed than those we'd passed on the way, coiled and coiled and mewed around him. Behind and around us, in the further, darker shrines and caverns of which we slowly became aware, lounged many lesser potentates.

"Slow times, Claude Vaudin—and this your—"

"Her name's Roushana Maitland. She's a famous musician."

"Musician . . . !" The skin across the Burger King's face was stretched too shinily tight for it to register real emotion, but his eyes, deep-set, another of the room's caverns, glittered with what I took to be amusement, and the creatures around him twittered in response. "I hear of you sometimes . . . Where's it called . . . ?" He raised a tiny hand from a bulk of silk and snapped a finger.

"Paris."

"Paris . . ." He nodded, creasing his many chins and looking almost orgasmically satisfied at the mention of that name. The Burger King spoke clearly enough, although he had a small voice, for someone so large, so obviously powerful. You had to listen very carefully over the submerged booming of the music to make sure you heard exactly what was said. "Don't know why you trouble with travel. You can get it all here . . ."

Stealing glances around this place as the Burger King talked to Claude in this oblique way, I became aware that we were surrounded by a dragon's horde of drug paraphernalia. There were pipes, pipettes, nano-irons, hydroponics, old PCs, vials of super-blood and esoteric electronics. Swarms of nerve parasites flittered in jars. Chalices fumed with pleasing, yet unplaceable scents. The Persian rugs and pulsing virtual screens which carpeted the floor were lumpy with wiring. Then, swirling in the darker corner was what I took at first to be the luminous void of some advanced kind of TV screen. But it was more than that. It was brighter and darker—the next great leap into a world of entire virtuality. Even in the Burger King's presence, it was hard not to keep glancing back.

My skin tingled and pulsed. Like the smoke, the women danced around the Burger King, and I found that I was following what he saying without actually having to worry about the words. It was a kind of telepathy, and soon I felt that he could understand me as well. To the Burger King, the here-place, by which he meant everything beyond that precious screen which he guarded so carefully, was pale and grely disappointing—useful only as a way of getting quickly on to the proper world, which awaited through the drugs and technologies which were so expansively arrayed. Even in terms of physical safety, he feared a viral attack from a rival monarch far more than he feared guns, car bombs or raids by the DC police. He chuckled, smiled, touched my hand, then stroked my hair and shoulders with gentle fingers as I bowed before him. This was the path which lay ahead, he explained, and like any other apostle or seeker of the truth he was merely following it . . .

My throat contracted. I wanted to sing, or dance, or do something. The Burger King, he remembered the old days when the doors into the infinities of virtuality had scarcely been open. He remembered crack and chew and all the rest. He'd tattooed his skin with implants. He'd tried the best and the worst available. Yes, he sighed, it had been a long journey. Then his hands guided my sight back towards the place where I had been longing to look . . .

"You know about this?"

His fingers massaged my scalp and the billowing carpets of this palace of virtuality all seemed to slide downwards towards that warm, welcoming pit. Towards re-birth or death—in the presence of the Burger King, it already seemed that the distinction didn't matter.

Soon, the long mornings, the golden evenings and endless afternoons, of our stay in Washington were drawing to an end. It was time for our last big concert, and then for us to head back to Paris, to our real careers and lives, the coming elections, and Claude's Project.

After seeing what I was planning to wear onstage at the JFK, Lujah Vaudin took me over to an exclusive shop in Chevy Chase in her tank of a car and found me an evening gown in blue and crimson.

"You'll find," she said as she appraised me beside a cascade of mirrors, "that you can say and do far more radical things in life if you dress according to conservative expectations."

"Radical—isn't that another word you can't say?"

She chuckled and smoothed my hips. "*You* can say and do anything you want, my girl, if you look like this . . ."

In those days, I never saw concerts as obligations, nor noticed people yawning or gazing absently at the exit signs, and I was excitedly happy as, on the last, long afternoon before the big event, I returned to George-town after a final full run-through, and sang phrases of Mendelssohn to myself as I wandered the house turbaned in towels in preparation for the hairdressers, manicurists and masseurs who would all be arriving later.

"Ah, Roushana!"

It was unusual to see Tony Vaudin at home at this time of day and he scarcely looked himself as, dressed in a tee shirt and jeans, he bore down on me from the direction of his and Lujah's suite of bedrooms. But this was a big occasion for them, too. Claude had conducted and performed before at the JFK, but never with this much media attention.

"You look a lot readier than Lujah!"

I laughed: we both knew his wife was never, ever, late.

"The house'll seem so quiet without you both." He stood in a self-consciously boyish pose I almost recognised from Claude, his big hands stuffed into his pockets.

"I'll come again."

"You will?" He seemed pleased and surprised. "And we *must* come to Paris. I know, I know . . ." He extracted a hand to give a deprecatory wave. "It's nothing like the way people say it is."

"Washington isn't either."

"Well, there you go. Two old cities facing each other across the dead Atlantic. But at least Paris is old enough to start to think about being young again. Claude was right to go there." He gave a sideways smile. "My son doesn't get much wrong, does he?"

"I suppose . . ."

He pointed towards the door we were standing beside. "Has he shown you in here?"

I realised as he opened it that this was Claude's old bedroom.

Rather than explain the circumstance in which I had seen it, I shrugged my ignorance.

"Come, come . . . " He beckoned me. "You might learn something." He clicked shut the door. "I don't know why, he's never had anything to hide, but Claude can sometimes be a little secretive."

Claude's old bedroom seemed less small in daylight. In many ways, with its football and baseball rosettes, cups and trophies (Claude having been as near-professionally good at sport as his mother was at singing), and with its long alcoves of shelves filled with toys, games and gadgets, it looked like an idealised version of the room where an American boy might once have slept. Claude hadn't needed Ludwig and Stockhausen glowering down from the walls to remind himself of his seriousness as a musician, so instead there were merely discreetly sexy posters of the last decade's pin-up females. And it was all so *tidy*, as if he'd left knowing people would visit it as some kind of shrine. The stones and shells he'd collected from some beach holiday which lined the ledges of the tall casement windows looked like something from a museum. I picked one up. It was some kind of polished fossil, and there was still a faded price tag underneath.

"Well . . . " Tony patted the space beside where he sat on his son's bed. "What do you think?"

"Of what?" I moved by him. "This? Washington? America?"

"You can start anywhere you want."

"I'm not sure I can. It's been marvellous. But . . . Maybe back in Paris . . . "

Tony nodded as if I'd said something profound and coherent, and we were pushed a little closer together by the sag of the springs. "Just keep an eye on him for us, will you, eh? The thing about Claude is . . . " He shook his head. "Well, we always knew he was so special, so unique, that there was never any thought of our having another kid. But I suppose that's a huge weight of expectation. He's so good at everything. But it's a tightrope act and we worry sometimes that he'll fall, but he never has. But now he's got you as well as us. You won't let him down, will you?"

The question raised uneasy memories, but I nodded gravely. Tony Vaudin had the sort of tone and approach which could make you accept most things. In other decades, he'd have easily made senator. In other centuries, and if he hadn't been black, he might even have got to be president.

"I hear that that guy—what's his name, Northanger?—has got a new symphony that you'll be playing?"

"That's the plan. Although I'll only be performing a few phrases."

"And he's using AI to write it!" he chuckled. "That's just what half my students do with their dissertations. But to be honest, I much prefer the ones which are written using someone's poor old brain. Computers are still useless at making mistakes. You know, we had to put a ban on A plus markings, because all of them were written by machine. So now we've got a ban on excellence—and there's *another* word you can't use in Washington these days."

I chuckled, too. Tony and Lujah never seemed to lose their good humour at the way the world was going.

"These things, these intelligences . . . I guess we really are getting closer now to a time when they really will be able to mimic human emotions and feelings. Then where will we all be, eh?"

I looked around again at the many shelves of Claude's childhood possessions. "I suppose," I said, "we'll have to leave perfection to them, and try to be as human and fallible as we can be."

Once again, Tony nodded gravely and encouragingly. I supposed that this was his tutorial mode, but our legs were pressed against each other's now, and the dressing gown I was wearing had ridden up and parted midway above my knees. As I gazed down at my thighs, wondering vaguely how I might cover myself without it seeming prim, I realised that Tony was staring as well.

"You're right," he said with soft, surprising passion. "We have to be human. We have to be prepared to be fallible." As if by accident, his fingers brushed against my flesh as he reached beside me to pick at a stain which lay on the cover of Claude's bed. "We can't all be like Claude, Roushana," he murmured. "We must all find things out in our own way—make our own mistakes . . . "

I don't know what I then said, but I managed to stand up and leave Tony Vaudin in his son's bedroom to get on with my preparations. Next day, and after a well-reviewed performance, Claude and I flew out from Washington and returned to Paris, and to our real lives.

KIPPERS FOR BREAKFAST; THE SMELL OF THEM FILLS THE house. Yesterday's rain was an illusion, and summer is holding, and I wander the rockeries afterwards in brisk morning sunlight, picking at the weeds—or perhaps they're proper plants, and as if it matters. And perhaps I don't need to sleep, dream, any longer, either, for even after these long, turbulent nights of memory, I still don't feel particularly tired. Adam sits in the new kitchen which he now possesses far more than I have ever done, or even those redundant machines, looking out at the world from the screen. Then he brings out orange juice for us both on a tray—he's long picked up on the fact that I don't like to have too much coffee—and the tinkle of the glasses takes me to the back garden in Moseley, and to Leo. Not *back* any longer. The past is here even as we sit, we talk, and Adam says that perhaps he'll do a bit of gardening himself, and I watch him as he moves with easy youth and purpose amongst the fading hydrangeas, still dressed in bits of Claude's old clothing. Then I go inside, and the sun moves across Morryn's furniture and warms the rugs. Thus, in our close but separate orbits, do Adam and I now exist.

I find him later in the music room with the Sony Seashell dangling from his hand.

"This doesn't work."

"It's old—of course it doesn't," I snap.

"But isn't this the thing that you said Blythe gave to Leo? The one with all the recordings . . . ?"

181

I take it from him and put it down.

"It's just . . . "

"Just what?"

"Well, from everything you've told me, I understand how important Leo was to you. And all those photographs, recordings, awards you said there were. But there's so little of him here in Morryn."

"Memories aren't about objects," I tell him. That's how it is with Adam. For half the time, the questions he asks, the way he looks at the things, the ways he picks them up, feel like an intrusion, but for the rest it's an unburdening, a blessed relief. Here, I show him, pushing aside some of my old childhood drawings—that flat sun and squashed people with their square-roofed house which surely must exist somewhere other than inside every child's head—is the programme for that benefit performance I gave when I went with Claude to Washington. Copper-plate paper, now yellowed, cornered with pink flecks of wine . . .

We talk, we share—or I do anyway—for that's what living's about, isn't it? We're not islands. We'd die, drown, if we were.

"So," I try asking him, "what do you remember now?"

"Many things. But none of it's personal. None of it's me. It's as if—" An expression of something close to pain seems to cross his face.

"Not even in your dreams?"

He gives another of those almost Indian sideways shakes of the head.

"But you've heard of the symphonies of Nordinger? You know what happened to Venice? You can picture the dome of Saint Paul's?"

"All of those things, yes—I can recognise them even before I call up on the screens. But they don't seem *real*, exactly. It's just *information*. It's as if I've just read about them."

"Nobody reads these days."

"Well . . . Looked them up."

"I suppose we'll just have to stick with calling you Adam, then."

"Yes. Abaddon."

He still says it in that odd way. Then he leans from the chair he's sitting in and he gives a gasp. His hands flutter towards his right side.

"It's that cut, isn't it? The bigger one? You'd better come upstairs and let me look at it again."

He nods, then submits. Upstairs, he sits on the same stool in the bath-room he sat down on—how many days ago was it? The other cuts, abrasions—those I can see anyway on his wrists and neck now he's not naked—have faded. Crouching down, I lift up Claude's old tee shirt to take a peek. Adam's skin is golden, and his belly really does look like some medieval painting, but wasn't the spear cut on Christ's other side? For the life of me, I can't remember. But, unlike the other Adam, at least he has a navel.

The waterproof coating I sprayed on peels back easily. So does most of the dressing beneath. This is all going to be fine, I tell myself. Easy-peasy. Nothing but flesh and adhesive. Then he gasps again, this time more loudly, as the last of the strip clinging to the wound resists my fingers.

"Another moment. Just hold still."

He submits, although his belly is now sucking in and out. But I need to look—what alternative is there?—and my hands, these hands which have shaped the innermost feelings of Bach, Mozart and Beethoven, are suddenly cool and firm and steady and authoritative. Adam groans as I give the dangling white tape a firm tug. I try again. His belly has stopped moving now, his whole body is arched, the muscles have turned rigid. One last pull against a momentarily stronger resistance. There's a slight sound of something parting, then something large and sodden drops with the dressing from my fingers. The wound is wide open, glistening. The plug of artificial skin I inserted has failed to meld. But there's no odour, which is something, isn't it?

"How does it look?" Adam finally hisses.

My sight blurs, although the sunlight which washes up from the sea is clinically bright. Defined within this prism, the mouth of the wound looks far wider than I remember it. The flesh seems re-shaped, peeled back as if by curious fingers, and inside . . .

"Is it infected?"

"Hard to tell . . . it's as if . . . " Not a wound, but some new orifice, thinning and gaping as Adam begins breathing again.

"Is it serious? What can you see?"

It's a tunnel, glinting but oddly bloodless. Doubting Thomas, I might almost put my fingers into it, but I refrain. My breath, with my face still close, pulses against Adam's belly. Yes, yes, of course it *could* almost be a vagina. It isn't, but it isn't a wound, either. And inside, glittering in strange encrustation, are the pillars and grottos of a crystal cave.

"I don't know," I tell him, standing up. "Give it time. No, I don't think it's infected." I lay a hand on his shoulder. "But we'd better put some-thing over it."

His breathing is easy now, and his smile, his endless sense of gratitude, has almost returned. He's withdrawn again into the pretence of being whatever he imagines he is, and I'm just a schoolgirl playing nurse. Leo, I can't help remembering as I unravel new padding, never was a good patient long before he got struck down by WRFI. *Come on, Roushana, I'd be dead already*, even when it was only ketchup sauce and old bandages. The world had to revolve around him, especially when he wasn't feeling one hundred percent. No wonder Mum became a *sadhu*, a saint . . .

Once I've done my best to tidy him up, Adam and I return to our separate but interlocking orbits. It's afternoon already, and perhaps it's time I called the kids. I try to picture Edward sitting at what he terms his desk in the garden-like space of his office. There'll be birdsong, the rustle of trees. London's so much greener now—the areas which aren't submerged. Even his house, which was once part of a substantial Chelsea terrace, looks as if it's been invaded by jungle. Grass grows in the lounge and there are useful insects in the kitchen. My heart aches to think of what this kind of bio-frippery will do here when some stranger takes over Morryn.

The last time I saw my son in the flesh, his family arrived here in a seaplane which alighted out there on the sea like origami folded by a Picasso. My grandchildren Ayana and Cornell are not-

184

quite twins; they were born within six months of each other. They're just so *big*. So *young*. So *perfect*. They talk to each other in noises I can't decipher, and lumbered around Morryn like baby giants, playing games and chasing after things which I can never see across these same gardens where Adam is now cutting and tying back the plants in preparation for the winter to come. Then there's Edward's partner Ivy, who looks like an elf, albeit a surprisingly large one, and dresses to match in bright, morris-dancy colours.

One afternoon—the only afternoon they were here with me—Ivy and the kids went off alone to explore along the cliffs and Morryn suddenly seemed extraordinarily quiet. Looking for my son, I noticed that the doors to the garage were ajar, and found him standing amid the shadows, apparently deep in thought.

"Oh! You surprised me," I said loudly in case he thought I'd been looking for him.

"This place..." He chuckled. "I haven't been here since... Since Dad died, I suppose."

I'd hardly been out here myself much in recent years. This garage, with its tools and shadows, is still entirely Claude's. Only the space where he used to endlessly fuss and fiddle over the DB 5 remains empty. I remember how he once removed and stripped down the entire engine, and then talked about it for months after—said it was as big a task as mastering the Bach 48. Sometimes, he'd summon me in and I'd have to hold the choke or rev the engine whilst he leaned into the bonnet or lay underneath. *Now, a bit more... No, no, no, no... Slower, for fuck's sake...* The garage would fill with choking blue smoke, and I'd leave with my clothes stinking and a looming headache. Still, we all loved Claude's DB, his James Bond car. It had been worth a small fortune, would be worth a bigger one now. It was just all the oil and fuss and the *stop stop stop what the shit do you think you're doing* that I couldn't take. And then Edward came along, and he was happy to help his Dad, and I was happy to let him.

"He never did quite fix that oil leak," Edward said.

We stared at a darker blotch on the old flagstones.

"Imagine, though, if Dad ever got it working perfectly!"

"What would he have done then!"

We smiled at the thought.

"They were the best times with Dad," Edward said. "You know how much easier it is sometimes to talk to people when you're not actually paying attention? It was like that in here with him. Dad said there was poetry and music in the best kinds of engineering. And I believed him—I still do. The music itself, the proper music, all that power and passion, was so much harder for me. But this..." He gestured through the dusty bars of sunlight and shade with such quiet passion that I half expected the DB's shining silver flanks to reappear. "This..."

My son's at least as handsome as Claude was. Unlike Maria, where our varying racial strands intermingled in the frustratingly incomplete beauty of her frizzing hair, that broadly hooked nose, Edward possesses good looks and an easy composure.

"You seem," I said in the silence he'd left me to fill, "a bit preoccupied. Is it work?"

Still staring at the space left by the DB, he said, "I sometimes feel that part of me's missing. It was great working on things like that car with Dad, but most of the time he wasn't here. And even when he was... Even when he was..." He shook his head and a gull tip-tapped across the corrugated roof. "I wish I knew. You're just Mum to me. When you walk out on that platform, when you pick up your violin, I've seen how you become someone else—I've watched you change. But Dad never did. He was always up on the podium. There was always an audience. Except maybe when he was with his car. Then there was that stupid accident and it was all too late..."

I can see it now: the DB, looming out of the shadows and dust. I can smell the leather, the precious fluids and oils. I can hear the engine's bumbling roar. It was perfect by the end. Claude even fixed that oil leak. He fixed everything.

Edward and I didn't say anything. We just stared at the empty space in our lives which that lost car had made. Both smiling and solemn, easy-going but private, the last environment on this earth

I'd have expected my son to be suited to was the wild disorder of world finance. I could have seen him as some kind of designer, a maker of things, but Maria—who never seemed to care about the look of *anything* and always thought in the abstract—went that way instead . . .

Maria, she divides her time between small prestige designs and more worthy projects, closer to civil engineering than proper architecture, which she risks her life and health to supervise down in the third and fourth worlds. Neither of them pays well. I'm deeply proud of her, but at the same time I also sense a sort of timidity. The undertow of her CV is that she's a safe pair of hands for the odd bit of sensitive new building and restoration, but shies away from the big statement which would define her as an architect. Perhaps if she finally got herself a proper partner of some kind . . . Now, that *would* be a change. But the dowdy ponytail she affects to tie back her crinkly Afro hair has remained unchanged for years, and so, almost literally, have her stone-dusted clothes. Everything about her—even the thought of my calling her up this afternoon—says *leave me alone. . .*

And what would I say? How can I ever tell either of my children that I'm dying? I'd do anything—*anything*—to avoid upsetting him. What-ever love is, I think I still feel it towards them, and I'm almost sure that they feel something similar towards me. But Edward's Edward. And Maria's Maria. And I'm me. It's a love between different species. I can't call them. Not *now*.

Morryn unfolds in scents, sounds and objects as I leave the garage and my son and the DB's ghost. I enter rooms. I touch memories. The sky darkens. Once again, Morryn fills with shadow and the tide comes in, and then Adam and I eat dinner. The food he's prepared, from what I can taste of it, is heavenly, although eating now has become another act of remembering—a journey into this ever-present past. I perform for him. The Prokofiev *Sonata*. A couple of Chopin arrangements. Of course, some Bach. The automatic piano sits quiet. It's a genuine solo recital, and the choice of pieces comes instantly, whilst Adam sits and listens. It's become part of our routine; part of whatever we both are. Appreciative, intent, he makes an excellent audience. When the music is playful, he taps his foot and grins. When it becomes sad, tears grow in his lovely eyes. And the other feelings, the ones which only music can express, they come and go as well on his expressive face. Sometimes, I think he knows far more about music than he cares to admit. But then he knows about everything—so why not this?

Sleepless, dreamless, helpless, I lie back in the vivid dark of my bed.

THE WALLS OF OUR ATELIER WERE STAINED WITH continents of damp when we returned to Paris. Moulds of a brown and green Atlantis had shaped themselves across the walls of our kitchen hallway and strange grey planets hung in orbit above our bed. Our sheets, left unwashed and unmade, were forested with fungal furs. We laughed and we complained, but Claude's landlady Mme. Loic merely shrugged her bosom and stroked one of her cats. After all, this was Paris, and it was summer, and what exactly did we expect? The air reeked of rotting plaster and bad drains. I experimented with smoking Gitanes, more for the smell, which we both liked, than the physical effect. Coughing, I sat outside on the narrow balcony in the sudden intervals of sunlight, surrounded by sheets and clothes and rugs and towels as we tried helplessly to get every-thing aired. Down below, through four floors of steaming washing similarly hopefully strung, the flooded, shining streets were teeming. Bells, gunshots, sirens, the calls of mullahs and the muffle of loud-hailers and stamping, trumpeting parades made strident bar marks through the roar of traffic.

Scores ran, books collapsed and milk soured. The fridge motor howled. My Guarneri swelled. As I practised, I thought of Rousseau's tigers, of swaying palms. In the afternoon, thunder always growled, and rain blatted the swinging windows. Even though we knew it was coming, we always brought our washing in just a little too late, and lived another day in sodden clothing, and made love on mushroomy sheets.

There had been a strike at the Sorbonne, and a lock-out at the Conservatoire. Concerts were held, cancelled or re-arranged according to bomb-threats or government edicts or sudden, new assessments of some dead or living composer. Wagner came and went, Boulez had his hour, and I was no longer studying, but striving to keep up with being a full-time soloist. By now, the figures which Claude and I were seeing in our bank statements were so large that the presence of a plus or a minus sign seemed irrelevant. Meanwhile, there was always the election. Mathilde Irissou had risen ahead in the polls whilst we were away in Washington, then had been dragged back by forces no one seemed able to explain, except perhaps the spin machines, and they weren't telling. The newspapers in that summer were made of an interactive plastic, and the floppy sheets we bore home pulsed like the fungus on our walls as predications and scandals ebbed and flowed. Once you'd got to the bottom of a page, you could start again at the top, and the news, the reviews, even the adverts, would be entirely changed. Even more than it had in Washington, it really did seem that France—and in particular Paris—was the cockpit in which the fate of democracy would be decided.

And in a way, it was. What we didn't then realise was how little democracy actually mattered.

Mathilde Irissou came and paced our atelier whilst outside a fleet of her armoured cars blocked the street. She, too, had taken up smoking Gitanes, and she waved her cigarette with a grace I envied, then ground it out in one of pots of orchids which tumbled around our windows. The socialists were ahead in the polls, but the spin machines were saying they had peaked much too early, and now one of the filth-sheets had found some early images of her which, while harmless enough, were nevertheless much less elevated than her famous portrayal of bare-breasted Liberty. Was it still impossible for a woman to function in politics without this stupid leering? Worst of all were the expressions of support she was now suddenly receiving from her fellow socialists. For them, with their own selfish dreams of advancement, the best thing that could happen was that she lose the election. She flicked the starter of another cigarette. Her agile lips plumed. She made neons of emphasis as it trailed in the air. Look at the people Boullard was allying himself to—goose-stepping Le Fale, that fraud Christos. He's using fear, and he can't possibly control them. It's like Hindenburg with Hitler...

"We have to attack, and the worst thing is these people aren't even politicians. Anything I say about tax initiatives or raising the rights of the individual will be treated as an irrelevance. That's why I need you. You're both important. You stand for something true which people believe in."

She'd included us both in her prowls and smiles, but now she strode towards Claude, who was lounging on his favourite stool beside the piano, and stood close between his unscissored legs. Her chin jutted. Her earrings glowed. Briefly, as new thunder cannoned and the windows swung, she really was Liberty incarnate, surrounded by barricades of cloud. It was impossible not to feel roused.

"I want you to go for those bastards," she murmured. "You can get at them in ways that I can't. Show them it isn't their stupid belief that matters. Show them there's something other than fear and superstition. Show them that the truth is what counts..."

Le Fale didn't last. Next morning, or the morning after, pictures of him far more damning than those of Mathilde Irissou were circulating. By the weekend, and just like his hero Mussolini, he was found hanging from a lamppost. But Christos was different. Christos was inescapable.

No one knew quite where he had come from, nor whether he really had grown up with that ridiculous name, but he began his rise to fame as the sort of wandering beggar-vendor who often accosted Parisians and the city's few remaining tourists. Christos sold bottled water, but he also sold visions, and a philosophy which combined Judaic, Christian and Islamic eschatology. Basically, he claimed the world was ending, and that he was its final prophet. Although there were many others like him, he drew the largest crowds. And the water which bore this name and image sold exceptionally well.

Within a year, Christos had become an industry rather than merely a prophet. He acquired the old brewery at Marne la Vallée and used its spring and bottling plant, and the abundant free labour of his followers, to out-produce and undercut the competition. His vendors, stooped with their heavy sacks, were a regular sight on the streets of Paris. People, even many of those who didn't believe, bought Christos' bottles because clean water was something everyone needed in these torrential days with the tap supply polluted by cholera B. But many did believe, and the churches and the priests and the mullahs prevaricated, and the Pope famously called him a Holy Fool—for what was so very wrong with giving money to the poor for something so essential as water? People drank Christos' product. They kept it by their bedside to ward off bad dreams. Many even bathed in it, and claimed to be cleansed, saved, healed . . .

Christos' teachings, if they could be said to make any sense at all, were based on the assertion that these were the last of days. The Kingdom of God was due to be established here on earth at any moment, although he cleverly avoided specifying an exact date. Meanwhile, though, we must all fear and obey Jehovah, God and Allah—whom he claimed were all the same deity—as never before. Which meant that women should meekly obey their husbands, bear children, and not work outside the house, whilst homosexuality, and any kind of promiscuity, not to mention birth control, abortion and genetically-based medical treatment, were evil, and all people who doubted the word of God, which was effectively the word of Christos, were blasphemers. Not that Christos actively supported violence, but his words were inflammatory enough to encourage others to firebomb gay bars and assault women who had the temerity to go out dressed in a way which might be construed as sexually appealing.

Then there were the ghost vans, old trucks and delivery vehicles spray-painted with extracts from the Talmud, the Bible or the

Koran, in which Christos' followers toured the city in search of lost souls. Pavement drunks, park-bench sleepers—anyone who happened to be momentarily unable to fend for themselves—were routinely press-ganged into his so-called Community of God. The gendarmerie did nothing, whilst the political right, who enjoyed having the dirty work of cleaning up the streets of so-called undesirables done for them, smilingly looked on. President Boullard, who knew a trend in need of riding when he saw one, even invited Christos to the Elysée Palace, and posed with him for a virtuality shoot. Compared with the self-flagellating bombers and warmongers, Christos probably seemed like a moderate, and Boullard said that he, too, was a man who feared God, and that his policies of stronger censorship, of fostering full male employment by encouraging women to go back to their kitchens, his abhorrence of same-sex marriage, even his doubts about what he called the so-called theory of evolution, all chimed with what this holy man taught. As to whether the world was soon ending, well, he was merely the President of France, and would govern as best he could until that time, but meanwhile he would urge people to pray and consider their conscience when the time came to vote. Christos then shook the president's hand, and that handshake gave Boullard another million votes.

Claude presided at a meal in a private room at Gagnaire's the evening of the live debate with Christos on the popular current affairs show *Rapport* which Mathilde's advisors had organised for him. He seemed happy and confident. Despite all the troubles which afflicted France, these were good times for us both. Claude was basking in the award he'd just received for his recordings of the Brahms symphonies, and it seemed as if the tune of *Les escaliers de Montmartre* came from every café loudspeaker, whilst I'd just learned that I'd been awarded an honorary degree, which would be presented to me as soon as the embattled Sorbonne reopened its doors. I bridled now when critics compared me to mature Heifetz, or the young Menuhin, or middle period

Oistrakh. I didn't want to be like anyone, no matter how great. I simply wanted to be Roushana Maitland.

Harad Le Pape was there with us at Gagnaire's. He or she had resumed criticism, although the subject was now life in general rather than any particular work of art. That night, Harad rustled in an entirely black outfit, all frills and puffs, and bore a small, silkily feminine, mous-tache. He or she had reviewed the recent killings amongst the far right as a Dadaesque tragedy on a par with Godot. Other recent missives had focussed on the conjunctions of adverts and clouds over Chaillot, and the smears of tomato sauce left on a plate. Harad's great work on the 6th had been finally pronounced complete. The struggle was over, but now like a fine wine, like a good cheese, like a newborn infant, the creation had to learn to breathe. Meanwhile, we all must wait.

If Harad seemed relaxed and expansive, Karl Nordinger was barely recognisable that night as the sour man I'd first encountered. The program which would create the ever-changing final version of his *Fourth Symphony* was working fully, and had just been sold as a conceptual framework to a multinational software company. After years of nothing but good reviews and artistic acceptance, he was suddenly inordinately rich, and seemed to be enjoying it. He'd been down to Monaco with two succulent heiresses of the old nobility, and had returned to Paris with three.

It seems to me now that almost everyone who had ever been anyone in Parisian intellectual society was with us at the long table at Gagnaire's that night as we drank and laughed. I'm sure that Nadia Kakkousis was there, fresh from her triumphant *Rosenkavalier*. So was Max Rochereau, typically ebullient and talking happily of a return virtuality to paint. So was Alain Riboud, then at the sparkling height of his momentary fame before the match-fixing scandals which destroyed him. And so was Dorina Three, who had surpassed even the pervious Dorinas in her pallid beauty. As I look along the table, and Claude raises a toast to humanism, the candles seem to multiply amid the forests of bottles. For surely Picasso's down there as well, dining out as he has been for years as the one artist of integrity to remain in Paris when the Nazis came. And so are Scott and Zelda Fitzgerald, soused of course, but still in the brief, prime time when the words flowed out and they were truly happy. And there's Hemingway: where else, tonight, would Papa be? And Marcel Proust has made a rare excursion from his cork-lined room, and we're all wondering if the funny or profound things we say will re-emerge in that endless book he claims he's writing. There, further back, are Diaghilev and Monet and, yes, there's Georges Sand and Frederick Chopin, both at the pinnacle of their love and fame. Near beside them sits an even more familiar figure. Knowing everything, understanding it all, Leo smiles at me and raises his glass, and I raise mine back to him.

There was *truffel feuillete* and there was *croustillant de lamb,* and all of it was washed down by *Chateau Beychevelle*, which had been young when I was young, and still tasted of the sunlit earth of the once-fine vineyards of Bordeaux which are all now dead. Everyone had suggestions as to how Claude might finally nail Christos in the coming debate for the hypo-critical slug that he was. For a start, there were the so-called miracles. And how many wives was he now said to maintain in the huge encamp-ment in the ruins of Disneyland? And how did he square all that love-thy-neighbour crap with his attitude towards gays and women? He was a sitting duck, fishes in a barrel—an easy, obvious target . . .

The evening was passing: it was time for tides to be turned, for history to be made. With the bill settled by our PR company, Claude and I tumbled out into the streaming streets. Despite their promises of support, the other guests soon faded in flurries of excuses of new master-pieces in need of writing, fresh lovers wait-ing abed, bare white canvasses, the latest unexplored club. By the time we reached *Le Monde's* studios, we were alone.

Claude took a couple of soberups and then, uncharacteristically, a small handful of calmdowns as we sat waiting in a green room and tonight's news tunnelled across the screens. The govern-ment in Tokyo was close to collapse and the ripped up paving stones of tonight's demonstrations lay sprawled beneath the walls scrawled in luminous paint. *Under the stones, the beach* . . . Then one of Mathilde's advisors bustled in. Minor panics back at party HQ—the spin machines had ploughed through all possible scenarios, and there were worries that this interview might be becoming *too* influential. After all, Claude wasn't here to *vanquish* Christos, was he? This was merely a philosophical, non-political, debate. But the producer was already calling two minutes, and Mum was watching in India, as were Claude's parents in Washington. So, it seemed, was half the world.

The studio was nothing like the intimate space you entered when you viewed *Rapport* through the screen at home. The famous fireplace, the fine paintings—the whole warm aura of culture that this programme projected—didn't exist in reality. Assistants and re-arrangers scurried through a shiny expanse of sensors and plastics whilst, cool and distant as stars, a few spotlights glimmered far above. Christos was already hunched in one of the big leather chairs. The middle of the triptych was the presenter, a smug septuagenarian named Micel whose face had been stretched by many surgeries into the look which the French termed *Le Chinois*. Claude was on the left. Sensor-operators gesticulated. The theme music began.

Christos seemed uncomfortable from the start. But he had, I decided as I watched him, the same compulsive, hypnotic quality which all of history's famous madmen had probably possessed. Rasputin had had it, certainly. So had Hitler and Napoleon— Christ and Mohammed, would have had it, too, if they'd existed. Yet he was so ugly and sweaty! For all his blotched skin, he looked as if he hadn't washed, or changed, or even slept, for many days. He stuttered and rambled in that strange voice which never seemed to settle on one pitch or accent, and made a weird variety of gestures which mimicked the sensor operators and suggested his body was barely under his own control. Cast onto the dangerous streets, raving to the tourist queues beneath the Eiffel Tower, gathering a giant following amongst the bitter and dispossessed—all of these things were easy enough to believe. Claude, with his elegant good looks and his American-tinged French accent, truly looked as if he belonged in a different world.

When invited to condemn violence, Christos prevaricated in a low growl. When asked if he really thought that women were lesser creatures than men, he merely smiled and said that God had made Adam first. Just as we'd suggested at Gagnaire's, Claude then tried to question him about his miracles. Could he really heal the sick, bring death to the dying? Which of the stories were true and which were false? But Christos just kept saying all the things we'd heard him say too many times before. That the world would soon end, that it was time to heed the scriptures, and make peace with God and help build the foundations of his city here on earth. Otherwise, he said in a dry whisper, those who denied his word would burn for all eternity in the fiery pit of hell.

Christos simply rambled in response to Claude and Micel's attempts to use argument and logic against him. Then he began to seem bored. As he slumped in his chair and his gaze wandered the studio, it even lingered on me. Undeniably, I felt a strange sense of power. What *was* it, I wondered, as I struggled against a strong impulse to look away. Then I realised something about Christos which all the ridiculously idealised images of his face which you saw in all the adverts and on the labels of his bottles failed to depict. His left iris was brown, but his right was blue.

It was obvious to me by now that the entire debate was going to be as inconclusive as such things always are. How stupid of us to have imagined that something as simple as the truth would ever come out in a current affairs programme! As Micel steered *Rapport* towards its end, he looked towards Christos, although he no longer seemed to expect more than a final shrug. But, in a startling movement, Christos suddenly unbent himself from his chair. Leaning his body towards Claude, he muttered a phrase which I and the microphones didn't catch. But I got an impression that it was something personal about Claude. You some-thing some-thing . . . Or you're—something like that. Claude's face contorted, then his fists bunched, and his body followed. If Micel hadn't stood up between them, there seemed little doubt that Claude would have struck Christos some kind of blow. Then the credits rolled.

I sensed Claude's anger and frustration as we lay that night in bed. "So," I murmured, my hand on his chest, feeling his heartbeat, "what did he say?"

Claude drew in a long breath. "That guy—he sells bottled water, for fuck's sake! He says nothing matters and we should all give up and just buy his product because the world's ending. And he makes a *fortune* doing it—and then he kidnaps people in those bloody vans! How the hell is anyone supposed to swallow all of that?"

"But they do." I stroked his belly. "You saw what he was like. He appeals to ignorance and fear and hopelessness. And he's slippery as a snake."

I felt Claude nod in the darkness.

"Then tell me. What did he say?"

"I'm not sure, Roushana. I'm really not sure . . . "

Inevitably, that final image—Claude lunging towards a cowering Christos as the elderly Micel struggled to intervene—defined the *Rapport* debate. It was on all the newscasts. It was plastered across the morning skies. People, even the many who had no belief in the coming apocalypse, went to work with that moment from the end of *Rapport* endlessly repeating across the fronts of their shirts. Most, though, thought it merely funny and interest soon moved on. By lunchtime, they were downloading something else.

That same afternoon, as I remember, Claude and I went to look at an abandoned tobacco warehouse near our atelier he was considering buying for his Project, which currently resided in a jumble of buildings beyond the buried wastelands of the *Periphique*. People were afraid to go that far out from Paris, and the kids' performances were thus always poorly attended. It made every kind of sense to move the concern closer to the centre of the city.

Claude worked open a metal gate in an alley a few blocks away from our flat. The roof of the tall building with its acid-corroded façade was whole, but its windows were gone, and the concrete floors inside were littered and puddled. Claude always liked big, open expanses. And he liked, as we clanked up the many rusty iron stairways, the dominating views they gave through the swirling rain towards Notre Dame. It was amazing, really, we decided as we stood looking out from the lip of a wide opening in the top floor, that the place had been ignored for so long.

The rain finally stopped for more than a few hours. The sun came out. The streets exhaled steam. I performed recitals. I went to parties. I gave interviews and delivered chaotic workshops to leftist students who had no time for anything so bourgeois as formal study. I endorsed a variety of products and services. I sere-naded billionaires. I avoided seductions. I went to yet more parties. Being recognised soon lost any sense of novelty, especially when, like all modern-seeming women, I was harangued by Christos' bottle vendors as a godless whore. So I wore dark sunglasses and a Chanel scarf, and was often mistaken for a Muslim, and had different curses shouted after me instead.

The first round of the elections came and went. The Christian and the Sunni candidates, and the token Fascist who'd been put up in place of Le Fale, were all pushed aside. Just as everyone had always expected, it was to end up as a fight between Pierre Boullard and Mathilde Irissou. It was June by now, and the Paris skies had cleared to a bluish haze through which the campaign adverts flickered their auroras. And it was so *hot*. The tar began to melt as the power supply stuttered under the pull of millions of air conditioners and fridges. People suffocated on the Metro, but the water-sellers still shouted and shuffled relentlessly through the shimmering streets. People routinely bought two bottles: one to drink; one to tip over themselves. Even I succumbed. Whatever else Christos' people were, they were certainly well organised, and their whited-out vans, with their implied threat of kidnapping, crawled through the pestilential heat.

There was always a smell of smoke in the air. It was no longer a question of individual riots and demonstrations, but of a continuous bloody carnival of sit ins, road-blocks, barricades, so-called *events* and burnings. Claude and I, as we showed our solidarity with the encampment around the lock-out at the Renault Factory, or our opposition to the equally entrenched fundamentalist demonstration around the Musée de Evolution, grew used to the thump of riot shields, fusillades of stones and rubber bullets. In those searing times, the police water cannon was almost welcome, at least until you were hit in the belly, and the irremovable orange dye with which the jets were infused soon became a campaign medal, and the most chic of fashion statements.

Managing the crowds as easily as he managed an orchestra, Claude gave impromptu speeches balanced on burn-out cars. Twice, he got himself arrested—although, much to his disgust, the CRS let him go both times as soon as they realised who he was. But I was getting tired of endless demonstrations, and I often began to find myself alone in our atelier late into the evening. I knew that Claude was be out debating, or leading a fresh picket line, or drinking in one or another bar with his new-found political cronies. But he and I were musicians, weren't we? That was what we lived for—not this. Although I would never have admitted it to Claude, I longed for these elections to end. When he did finally return, he'd be sweaty and tired, and drugged or drunk to one degree or another, and jerkily over-active. I'd urge him to stop talking and pacing and come to bed—not to make love, but simply so he could sleep, for I knew he'd have to be up as early as the water vendors next morning for another day of recordings and rehearsals. But Claude found time for everything—that was how he was, then. He remained keen to experiment with the latest drug or virtuality *de monde*, at least those which weren't ridiculously dangerous, but, much though I then enjoyed drinking wine, the few I tried left me dizzy and confused. Ever-protective of my musicianly core, I soon began to refuse. Once, and having heard my story of Leo, Claude managed to get hold of some genuine marijuana, but even that wasn't the same: it left me numb, speechless and cold.

I began to think of our atelier—that big space with its twin centres of gravity of the piano and the bed—as a haven from the turbulent world. I wasn't exactly lonely, but, on those hot evenings with shouts and sirens ricocheting up from the streets, I felt that my relationship with Claude had taken a different turn. But I felt pure and focussed when I played my Guarneri and the sounds of Paris made a turbulent counterpoint to the Bach *Partitas*. I was still mostly happy, and deeply in love.

Karl Nordinger would sometimes call in. More often than not, as Claude was usually out, he and I would sit alone. By now, he was affecting colonial silk suits and fedoras which were to become his trade-mark, and an ebony cane which he claimed had once been owned by Debussy. He owned a luxury modern house near Fontainebleau which was said to be the site of a near-perpetual orgy.

"You can, you know, get sick of the taste of caviar and pussy. Believe me, when you've seen one rich cunt spread out on a Louis XIV divan in a chateau, you've seen them all . . . "

But I was no longer bothered by his attempts to shock me. The fact was, we'd come to enjoy each other's company. He'd sit at the piano, pick out the things he was working on as he finished his *Fourth Symphony,* and I'd watch how the changes of the music were expressed across his surprisingly agile face, or he'd get me to play something, and he'd listen in absolute stillness.

I once asked him what he was thinking of writing next. He laughed and shook his head. "I think, maybe an opera. Something about what's happening now, or perhaps the Merovingian kings. Then I decide, that's too big, so maybe a series of miniatures. Of course, I can't just do another symphony—so part of me says, why the fuck not? Something big and grand and stupid and comic. Or redefine disharmony. Shittiest thing is, I could do all of those things easier than pissing." He gave another laugh and played a lovely, astringent discord. "So I do fuck all except fuck and spend my fucking money."

Sometimes, we'd access his symphony, and listen to it whole, and smile and shiver at the subtle changes which were beginning to affect it. It really was assuming a life of its own.

"Are you available," he asked me one night with uncharacteristic hesitancy, "on the third Sunday in July?"

"But that's the day of the election."

He rapped his stupid cane. "Exactly."

"You're not thinking of having the premiere then, are you? And isn't that when Harad's saying he'll unveil the 6th floor? Won't your work get drowned out in all the other things?"

"What if it does? And who cares about that mess of Harad's? Harad's just a fucking *theorist*. Harad wants do something creative which defines this shitty era but can't and won't. Still these elections probably are a turning point, just like you political groupies claim—although perhaps not in the way anyone imagines. The symphony will be different after-wards, so I might as well nail it to a recognisable moment in history. Who knows, perhaps that guy who claims to be God is right. It could be the first and the last performance. Now, that wouldn't be such a bad way to end!"

The air-conditioner sighed weakly. Karl was leaning against the frame of one of our atelier's big windows and his face was half-dark, half a red gleam.

"Have you spoken to Claude? Have you booked the hall? What about the orchestra?"

Have you. . . ? What about. . . ? His face twisted as he mouthed my questions back to me. "Hey, and aren't you little Miss Prissy, ticking off dates in your fucking diary? If I say it'll happen on that day, we both know it will. This isn't about arrogance. And neither is it about stupid modesty. The symphony's a work of fucking genius. You know it and I know it, so grow up and stop all the Barbie-doll pretending. It'll play on the day I decide it'll play, and that's that. And Claude'll conduct it, too, even if he never, ever conducts anything else again in his pompous life. The only thing I wasn't sure of, Roushana, was you . . . "

Claude came back soon after Karl had left, smelling of the Gitanes I'd given up smoking. He sighed his frustration at the chaos the *Fourth Symphony* would cause in his already over-crammed schedule. But Karl was right: he didn't resist. With Claude, music always came first. By now, the political grouping with which he was most associated had coalesced around an agit-prop group of artists. Many were merely street performers—fire eaters, contortionists, stilt walkers, pavement pornographers: not proper artists at all to my way of thinking—who'd published a manifesto stating that their aim was to orchestrate the elections through a series of "happenings". Some of them, such as the release of the penguins from the Paris Zoo, had actually come off, although I found it hard to attach any meaning to them. I unclothed Claude and helped him shower as he talked of tonight's event in which a banner condemning the repeal of the divorce laws had been released down one entire side of the Pompidou Centre—a great success, apparently, even if the words had been upside down—and I stroked his resolutely flaccid penis, and removed a medium-length strand of amber hair.

I'd received several calls from Mum announcing that she was heading for Paris. But finding the right sequence of flights which would get her here was complex, and then there was always the next emergency, let-down or crises in India which prevented her from coming. After many broken promises and near things, I'd decided that she'd probably never make it here when a fresh message chimed on my bracelet one morning.

"Is that you Roushana?"

"Of course it's me, Mum."

"I really don't how I'm going to find my way to you."

"Never mind. It'll sort itself out in time."

"The thing is, I'm a bit lost."

"Lost?"

"Well, it's so hard here to understand what people are saying. This man keeps trying to sell me what is it—oh? But doesn't that just mean *water*? I've tried asking about landmarks. What's that thing called that looks like the Blackpool Tower?"

Finding a small, lost, blind Indian woman in a city the size of Paris took some time, but Mum had nurtured her own small portion of fame in post-holocaust India, and she bore it with her as a neat, jagged and resolutely self-contained package. She refused to share our atelier with us, or a decent hotel, and chose instead to stay in a rundown hostel in the Opéra area, which was over-occupied by families of Algerian immigrants. But Mum was immovable, and Mum was irresistible, and Mum was Mum, and her safety and the worry that she wander off and get lost again was a perpetual headache. Not that she was bothered. So what, if she got mugged or kidnapped or run over? After all, Roushana, my dear, do you think I can't cope with a city like Paris, when I manage quite well on my own in Gujarat?

Her presence generated a flurry of interest from the media, which she, as ever in pursuit of funds, did her best to maximise. There were inter-views. There was a reception where she met Harad Le Pape, and asked loudly if he or she was a ladyboy. Even President Boullard made a passing comment about her work during a speech in Arles and Mathilde Irissou met Mum at a well-publicised reception. She was obviously expecting a sweet, blind old Indian lady, but what Mum wanted was unequivocal support, and money. How much, in their first budget, would a socialist French government commit to foreign aid, and then, specifically, to India? Mathilde, who had been all smiles for the initial image shoot, was soon in retreat.

Meanwhile, Claude and I were showing Mum around Paris. She insisted we visit all the famous sites, all the well-known places, many of which I had never yet been to myself. So we stood with a few other sight-seers on the top of the Eiffel Tower, and wandered the deserted Louvre, and she asked us both to describe the smile on the famously forged Giaconda. *What does it look like? What do you see?* For someone blind, her approach to the world remained extraordinarily visual. She had an especial fondness for Manet's *Le Dejeuner sur l'Herbe*, and insisted we go for our own picnic on the same stretch of river despite the risk from the knife gangs. I wouldn't have been that surprised if she's started removing her clothes.

Claude took to Mum from the start. His touchy-feely Americanness seemed a far better match for her busy Indian grabbiness than what I was starting to realise was my essentially English reserve. He was always taking her into embraces, and steering and helping her at times when I knew she would have batted me away. He roared at her stories of Maitland and Ashar family life, many of which I barely recognised from the events on which they were based. *You were there, Roushana, don't you remember, and the look on your face!* Mum chortled and flapped her hands with equal delight at Claude's Washington stories and all the ridiculous things which had happened to him here in Paris and when he was on the road. Amid this mutual admiration, and all the meals out and the endless sightseeing and the boat trips along the Seine—*now, tell me exactly where we are now, Roushana, and what is that noise coming from our left*—I sometimes felt left out, and my face ached (*what kind of expression do you call* that, *Roushana?*) from the sharp prod of Mum's fingers, and from rigidly smiling.

"I'm so glad I got to meet Claude and see Paris," Mum sighed as she lay back in a deckchair on a strip of sand beside the Seine on the last afternoon before her long flight back to India. "You really do seem well made for each other. He's a charmer. And you don't need to be blind to tell he's fabulously handsome."

"Thanks, Mum. Claude's—"

"Just as long," she cut across, "as you remember he's not Leo."

A rehearsal of the Nordinger symphony took place in the Opéra de Paris Bastille a few days after Mum returned to India. Despite the expense, Claude always maintained that the feel and acoustics of a rehearsal hall never told you enough about a piece, especially if it was new. From high in the balconies I watched him at work down on the podium. By turns laughing and serious. Those big gestures. The little signs.

The printouts for the *Fourth Symphony* were still changing and the final version probably wouldn't be ready until the day itself. Any orchestra would normally have hated this, if Nordinger's piece hadn't been the masterpiece it so plainly was, and if they hadn't so adored Claude. As it was, they performed the reshaped fragments with verve. Many of the chords and colours had darkened. Like all great works of art, even those which had been fixed for centuries, there were always new discoveries . . .

Karl Nordinger himself strolled down between the empty seats, acknowledged my presence with a rise of his silly cane, then sat some way off to listen. The orchestra were getting restless by the time I went down to join them for my contribution to the third movement. They'd never seen the need to have a soloist for such a few phrases, and they wanted their lunch. But I knew Claude well enough to understand that the timing was deliberate. *They play best when they're annoyed and hungry*, he often used to joke. He smiled down at me now as I raised my bow over the strings of my Guarneri. That violin, more than any other I have ever played, has its moods, and it felt incompliant as the orchestra swelled and then fell into that hushed tremolo, and the phrases of the *Song of Time* came out angular and harsh. I played each note of that aching melody with an angry, near-screeching tone. It should have sounded ridiculous, yet it fitted perfectly, and we carried on playing, drawing on through the entire movement to its fading.

Claude looked down at me. I looked up at him.

"That doesn't happen very often," he said eventually. "Just play it like that on the night and we'll bring the house down . . . "

With my part in the rehearsal finished, Karl Nordinger summoned one of his limousines to take us back to the atelier. The bustle of Paris seemed as remote as the movements of the denizens of some exotic fish tank as I sat with him in the car's cool interior. It was already Thursday, just three days from Sunday's election, and the last opinion polls had just been published, and were typically inconclusive. Claude was off to make another speech to another demonstration, but I felt as if there was nothing left I could do.

Opening windows, setting out bread and cheese and best English grapes whilst the fans of the air conditioners twittered in useless complaint, I told Karl about my trip of the week before to perform in a festival at Avignon. It wasn't just Paris which smelled of burning. This summer's forest fires in the south had been the worst in decades. Thousands had died already, whole towns had been consumed, and the fringes of Marseilles were being evacuated.

"It's easier to understand once you leave Paris," I said, "why people—rational people—pay attention to the likes of Christos."

"Ah . . . " Karl smiled uncharacteristically broadly. "It'll make no difference who gets elected on Sunday. You know that, don't you? Boullard can't make it rain. Irissou can't make the wheat grow. Neither of them can combat cholera b. No wonder people look towards God, now they've realised just how useless the politicians are. They have to have someone to blame . . . "

"You can't . . ." I put down a plate of olives.

"Can't what?" Still smiling, he popped one of them in his mouth. "Give up hope? Let the baddies win? Give way to superstition? Loose faith in the betterment of humanity? Curl up and die? Something like that?" He extracted the stone from between his lips. "Isn't that what Claude would say?"

Remembering once again why it was never a good idea to talk politics or philosophy with Karl Nordinger, I sat down and cut myself some bread and smoothed it with butter. He was so, so *negative*. And there had to be hope, didn't there? If you didn't believe in hope, and in love as well, what was the point of anything?

"At least Claude cares," I said as I cut and stabbed a large slice of Brie. "At least he believes in something. So tell me what exactly do you believe in?"

"And you're expecting me to say—nothing."

"Karl, I've heard you say it often enough before." I chewed angrily at my food.

"Not that it matters, I suppose . . . " He stood up and went over to the hi-fi screen and I watched, half-curious, as he accessed the database of his own symphony and paged down the floating menus, then set it to play. Cleverly rendered by a virtual orchestra, it sounded very different—like a photograph of a place rather than the real thing—but still moving and impressive. He remained staring at the unfolding score for a while, considering the recent changes it had made to itself. I studied his thin shoulders, the crescent of sweat which had formed across the back of his rumpled silk shirt. Dressed in the mock-formal manner he now affected, Karl Nordinger looked like some colonial civil servant from the days when Africa had been governed by Europe. You could imagine him scowling beneath a circling fan in some tropical office, surrounded by papers which meant nothing to him. A life of gin and easy boredom would have made a perfect match for his cynicism. Instead he'd been given the gift of making brilliant music, and it hadn't made the slightest difference to him. " . . . I suppose you've heard enough of this," he said as he sat down at the table again, although he'd left the symphony playing.

"I don't think that will ever happen. By the way, is this it?"

"What?"

"The thing you believe in."

He coughed on some crumbs. "That would be too easy, wouldn't it?"

He pushed away his plate. "I'm just the conduit."

"You've said that before."

"You don't understand. The music writes itself long before it gets to this stage. It doesn't care about me and what I am—it just comes out of me—so why should I care about it?" In the background, both sombre and mocking, the big surge of the first movement's finale was unfolding. "Listen. See the way the emphasis has changed on the horns even since the rehearsal this morning?"

I nodded. The effect was subtle but significant.

"And the whole movement would be different if we were to start it again. It's changing at a huge rate. The bloody thing's *alive*, Roushana. People say that, but they don't understand what it means. It doesn't need us now, and it doesn't even need Claude's performance. It's simply there. It seeks immortality in its own way."

The music crashed. Themes collided. When it faded into the second movement on the thin vein of a single note, I felt goosebumps rising across my arms.

"That's not such a bad thing is it?" I said. "Doesn't every artist want their work to be immortal?"

Karl Nordinger just gazed at me. There were butter stains on his expensive shirt. There was pain in his bloodshot eyes. All the success and the money only showed up the essential emptiness of his life more strongly. The world, like the music which was unrolling in the back-ground, seemed intent on playing some endless and inexplicable practical joke on him.

"I'm sorry," I muttered. "Life's been . . . distracting lately."

"The way you played that theme this morning, Roushana. It was stunning."

I almost blushed. I was used to praise by now—but not from Karl Nordinger. "But you didn't think it was a little too harsh? I was taking—"

"It was *perfect*. Maybe you won't play it that well in the performance or ever again. But when you do play it, I want you to remember whatever it was which made you play like this today. Will you do that?"

This was still so full on, so straight, that, from him of all people, I wasn't quite sure how to deal with it. "Yes—but who am I doing this for? For you, Karl, or for the symphony?"

He barely blinked. "You're doing it for *yourself*, Roushana. You doing it for whatever it is that makes you do it. It's not Claude, is it? It's not even really the bloody, fucking music. It's certainly not me."

We looked at each other.

We'd both stopped eating now, yet we were still sitting at the table. Then I found that I was leaning towards him, and that he was leaning towards me, and then that we were kissing. Karl Nordinger tasted surprisingly sweet for someone so sour and sickly: of grapes and of olives. It was one of those moments when, even though our minds are slow to catch on, our bodies are reacting. Plates crashed and rolled across the floor as we shoved them aside. Olive pits dug into my thighs as I straddled the table. Nordinger's silk shirt was a struggle—his arms were buried in sleeves we couldn't seem to unbutton—then all the expensive hand-stitching gave way in a single cataclysmic tear, and his hands were on my breasts, then frenziedly helping to release me from the rest of my clothing. In the background, a counterpoint to the hot rumble of Paris and the squeak of the air conditioners and the creaking of the overburdened table, the second movement of the symphony had ended and the third had begun to seek its shivering resolution.

By any standards, it was a Karl Nordinger moment. That melody as counterpoint to our unspoken need, and the low comedy of two people attempting to have sex on a food-strewn table. But we remained in each other's arms and swayed over to the bed, and laughed as we swiped the breadcrumbs and squashed grapes from each other's bodies. The *Fourth Symphony* had just begun the long crescendo of its own climax when Karl Nordinger and I reached our own. As I fell back, and the music rose into its final hammerblows, then died in that resonant discord, it seemed to me that it had shaped itself around us and this large room. An odd sort of silence, almost a continuance of the symphony, took its place. The Paris traffic seemed to have stopped. Even the water vendors had ceased their cries.

"Listen . . . " Karl murmured.

"Yes . . . " Absolute quiet. "Strange, isn't it?"

"*This* is what I want the symphony to become."

The heat pressed down. We lay sweating, listening to our hearts and the changing of our breath. But, Karl being Karl, I knew the moment couldn't last. For all his near-autistic outbursts, he wasn't stupid and he knew that Claude and I were still a couple. So it was almost a relief when he broke the silence with a series of suppressed chuckles. He raised his hand to his mouth as if to stop the staccato bursts escaping. But they still did, and I rolled over to join in, smiling, and wondering when Claude would be back, and how quickly I might get these sheets cleaned. It was only then that I realised that Karl Nordinger was sobbing.

I found myself walking with Harad Le Pape in Père Lachaise on the last afternoon before the election. Since Mum had visited Paris and Claude had become so busy, I'd continued taking in all the sights I'd previously ignored, and he or she made an entertaining guide. Not that I was planning on leaving Paris, but I already felt that this city wouldn't be the same after the weekend. Even in the quiet of that huge cemetery in those days when the dead still didn't trouble the living, you could feel the onrush of change.

"You have no idea, my darling Roushana, just how hard a life a critic has," the famous, pompous figure said as he or she shuffled beneath a black parasol. "Compared with that, compared with the struggle and rejection and sheer incomprehension which the righteous critic must battle against every second of every day, the artist has it ridiculously easy. They merely have to *perform*. The poor critic has to *understand* and then *explain*."

Here lay the graves of Marcel Proust and Jim Morrison, Frederick Chopin and Oscar Wilde, and the ashes of Isadora Duncan. Here, commemorated in far grander explosions of statuary, lay the remains of Paris's rich bourgeoisie. Here—so, so typically French—was the tomb of the lion-tamer Jean Pezon, shown riding the lion which ate him. Harad, a walking encyclopaedia, led me along the highways and byways. Here was the grave of the man who had sold the land to build this fashionable cemetery, and then had had to pay more than that fee simply to buy his own burial plot. It was a charming, comforting place.

Harad had had the builders in at his or her apartment to provide proper access for the thousands of Parisians who would be certain to want to witness the masterpiece on the 6th floor. He or she complained at length about bad manners and plaster dust, but remained serenely coy about what would be revealed at the unveiling ceremony after Nordinger's premiere. Paris was filled with

211

speculation. It was said that it would be empty, or that someone had it on good authority—a friend of theirs had actually *seen* the building's plans in the mayor's office—that there was in fact no 6th floor. That, or that Harad would simply silence years of speculation by revealing whether he of she possessed a cunt or a cock. In those fevered last days before the election, the rest of France, let alone Europe or the world, barely seemed to exist.

"Perhaps Gog and Magog really will put in an appearance and draw Satan up from the fiery pit," Harad sighed as I held the parasol against the white sunlight and we climbed the last rise of monuments. "The astronomers are still apparently searching the heavens for a comet . . . And Karl Nordinger seemed so miserably *jolly* when I saw him recently. I believe it was the first civil word he and I have exchanged since I said merely what needed to be said about the evil, rancid catastrophe—the sheer *lazy thinking*—of that disastrous abortion some people still insist on calling his Third Symphony. These are, indeed, strange, strange days . . . "

To Bezant Bay for a picnic. Adam carries the wicker basket which he's bravely evicted of spiders, and which last saw use when the kids were so-high. Halfway down the steps to the shore, I'm already sore and dizzy. Adam helps, seemingly half-carries, me the rest of the way, whilst still managing to keep hold of the basket. I can't believe his strength, nor how I got him up from here just a few days—exactly how many was it, now?—ago. Or perhaps it's down to how much weaker I've become.

We catch our breath—well, *I* do—then we head off away from the boathouse across the pebbled shore. We've both reassured ourselves that Adam will be safe down here from the gaze of the waymarks, and even though its only a few hundred metres, the whole trip has the feel of an escape, an expedition. The sky's trying to outbid the sea for the sheerness of its blue and there's barely any wind. It's almost unCornish, the weather's so warm. Adam finds me a piece of driftwood to serve as a walking stick. I tell him about the famous writer who lived in Menabilly just up the hill. He listens and swings the picnic basket. It's so nice to find things he still doesn't know.

We sit down on the hot rocks beneath the ragged cliffs. I take off my shoes and re-balance the girlish straw hat I'm wearing, although this heat, this sun, seems weak and distant after the overwhelming fug of Paris.

"You don't miss the cities—places like Paris?" Adam asks as he begins to unpack our lunch.

"I miss Paris as it was, I suppose. And I miss Claude. But so many things changed—and so rapidly. Nothing was ever the same."

"Some of the people you met, though. They're extraordinary! It's like a history lesson. I mean . . . " he shakes his head as he slices a green pear. " . . . Harad Le Pape. Not because of the sex thing, but just such a *character*."

"You should see what's . . . " I trail off.

Adam glances up, smiles, then resumes baring the pear's gritty flesh.

We eat. There are cheese tartlets. There are mushrooms stuffed with pate. Did I buy this stuff when I went down to Fowey? Did Adam make it? My hands blur as I raise the glistening objects from my blazing white plate. I'm in a hall of mirrors. There's the food itself, then all the things I remember food to be. My own children's cries are muffled by the soft shush of the waves. Did my eyesight misbehave like this before I had the crystal implanted? A bottle of lemonade, cloudy and bitter and sweet, makes my lips stiff. A distant object, flashing and turning, passes across the strengthening sun. Adam stands and begins to unslip himself from Claude's clothing. Soon, he's naked. In fine silhouette, he stretches unselfconsciously, and I sit and watch the bob of his buttocks as he wades out into the sea.

Can he swim? Well obviously. His limbs scarcely break the bay's slick water and soon, he's far out, and turning, waving. I wave back to him. He makes it look so easy. I remember my own attempts to come to terms with this element. Apparently, I always hated swimming pools, their clamour and stink, even when I was a baby. My parents both tried to teach me how to swim in the sea on our French summer holidays, although Dad was reluctant to haul me out of the shallows, and Mum was so quick to do so I always screamingly resisted. So it fell to Leo. He wasn't concerned about arm-strokes and leg-movements. He simply wanted me to understand that the sea would let me float if I gave up resisting. *It's just a matter of letting go*, he explained to me as we sat on the hot shore. *The sea wants to support you, Sis. All you have to do is to let it. The sea's where we came from. You know, our blood is exactly as salty as the sea was when our ancestors left it* . . . I looked out at the pedalos and the circling seagulls and tried to tell myself that I belonged out there. Mum, as she emerged from her brisk morning swim and the sun shone on her wet limbs, really did look as if she was made from saltwater, and Dad, in the splashing, trundling way he swam, was like the pedalos although Leo, of course, swam better than either of them. He'd competed for his school until he'd found that the commitment was getting in the way of his music. He'd even won cups.

We crossed the hot sand and waded the toddler-strewn shallows. Then, just as the shock of the water lapped my ribs, I let my feet go upwards, and Leo supported me. He floated me out as I lay back on this tickling, bobbing surface. My ears bubbled with a clamour of sea-sounds, but the moment between us was intense and quiet. As the waves lisped close to my face, I thought of the salt-blood in my veins and told myself that all I needed to do was nothing, but I was acutely conscious of the strength of Leo's arms as they cradled my back and thighs. He seemed far stronger than the sea itself. *This* I loved, the sun, the sky, the gentle water, the sense of being safely uplifted. But the moment beyond, and the effort of making no particular effort, of letting go of some immaterial *something* without even trying, was beyond me. I felt the loosening of his support, and the cold, sudden drag of my own useless body. Instantly, I was sinking, bubbling, gasping. A moment—long though it seemed—and the sky crashed back and Leo's face, laughing, concerned, re-emerged in splintered sunlight. Then my feet were back on the hot, guilty sand as I staggered sneezing and coughing back up the beach to my fortress of towels and sunshades.

And so it went. Day after day throughout that holiday. Leo wouldn't give up. The pattern repeated so often it became a sort of ritual: my brother's visionary words, his calm but persistent persuasion. Dad out there already, churning to and fro with the pedalos. Mum standing on the edge of the shore like some dark

Aphrodite. Calmly, unswervingly, the unavoidable moment came when Leo took my hand. The chuckling water deepened as he led me through the shallows until its coldness hit my lungs, and I gave way to the push of his arms, and lay back as he held me and I urged my nuisance of a body to let go until the moment of release came, and once again my mouth filled and my nostrils burned as salt darkness closed over me.

I couldn't give up, either—Leo would never have given me that opportunity—but the time of our holidays was finite, and I dreaded letting him down even more than I dreaded the idea of swimming. I rehearsed in my dreams. I pictured myself flying, floating. Every day, I really did believe that the sea would support me. But it didn't happen, and our last day on the beach finally came. As we took the boarded steps across the dunes, I already knew that yesterday and all the days before would simply be repeated unless I did something radically different. It was then, as I flapped out my towel and lay down in the hot light, that a simple under-standing came to me. Today, I really would let go. I would submit as I had never submitted before, and let the sea take me. I would simply lie back and drown.

Leo seemed to sense something changed in my attitude, and there was none of the usual persuasion as he led me out from the frothy shallows. I knew that these people I saw around me, the swimmers and the paddlers and the sunbathers, would soon be gathered around to look down on the beached and discarded body of the girl who had drowned to prove that she was incapable of swimming. The water seemed especially eager and playful today as it flashed around Leo's waist and took the air from my lungs. I lay back and submitted. Leo's head and body were haloed by the sun as he drew me out into deeper water. Certain that I would die, I smiled up at my brother as the water chanted in my ears, urging him to let go of me forever. And then he did, and for once the sensation truly was liberating. I lay amid the shifting billows, waiting for death to overcome me. I never really was conscious that I was floating until I felt Leo's grip on my arm, and the shock of his presence was enough to send me into one of my usual flailing spasms. I'd done it—I'd floated!—but I felt a weight of disappointment as we both finally clambered out from the shallows. After all, I'd tried to die, and had merely learned how to swim instead . . .

I taught my own kids how to swim in the summers we spent down here at Bezant Bay. I took them out into the waist-deep water, marvel-ling as I looked down at them at the pale slimness of their limbs, and thinking that Leo had been right—we humans really were made for this other element. I marvelled, too, at how they both trusted me, lying back with their hair fanning, and the ease with which the sea bore them. I even tried it with Claude, who'd never managed to learn how to swim despite all the pools which had once glittered in the back gardens of Georgetown, but something was missing. I loved the idea of holding him, of the lifting softness of his long body, but he always sank like a stone the moment I let go. He was happier just sitting on these rocks reading some new score, or impressing us with whatever food he'd bought for lunch. When Claude was with us in Bezant Bay, you could scarcely call it a picnic. There was white wine, exquisitely chilled and of a particular vintage which he would explain to the kids as he let them sip it, and rugs, and silk cushions. Raising his glass, serving us all crab sandwiches on fine crusty bread with golden Cornish butter, or telling us his latest story about the eccentricities of some distant orchestra—*that* was when Claude was in his true element. I decided one day as we watched the kids swim out towards that far rock that the reason he couldn't cope with the sea was because he was incapable of submitting. Emboldened by the wine, I even told him about my own struggles to learn how to swim, and how I'd finally managed it only by accepting in a childish but entirely sincere way that I was going to drown. But Claude was frowning.

"But that's the whole point," he told me. "Why *should* I give in . . . ?"

Claude never did learn to swim—but he still loved this bay, and especially the view from the top of those cliffs. He'd stop the DB when the road still went this far just to take it in. On stormy nights, he'd stand on the last of the drop, laughingly conducting the wild air like Mickey Mouse in that scene in *Fantasia*. For Claude, Bezant Bay was Isolde's *Liebestod* as she gazed out for her lover's return from these very shores. For Claude, it was the legend of the Spanish privateer with its cargo of gold coins—bezants, indeed—which supposedly lie somewhere in these blue waters, and have given Cornwall the stars on its shield. For Claude, everything was in the abstract. Everything had to be a performance. He couldn't let a single thing in the world escape his control.

Adam stands in the shallows, shining and dripping.

"Come on," he beckons. "You could at least paddle."

I lever myself up. I tuck up my dress a little. And then—for what have I got left to hide?—a little more. Adam's arm is cold and wet and strong. Mine feels thin and dry as driftwood. All the abrasions have vanished from his body. Everything about him is clean and pure apart from the waterproof patch I sprayed on yesterday beneath his ribs, which has that same air of faux-modesty which a triangle of costume possesses when it barely covers a bulge of crotch or breast. I stick to the shelf of rock which projects just beneath the tide, coyly protesting that the water's far colder than I expected—although it always is—and then that I might fall, slip. But I really *am* nervous. Adam, wading the deeper water which lies beside me, raising his arm to keep his grip on my hand, is beautiful, strange, anonymous and sea-born. He could drown me so easily. He could drag me in. His penis is surprisingly large, despite the sea's cold. It bobs and rises with the wavelets which strike his thighs. I can't remember if I ever noticed before that penises could float.

The sea's where we came from. You know, our blood is exactly as salty as the sea was when our ancestors left it...It's just a matter of letting go . . .

Suddenly, shipwreck claws are surrounding me and I'm genuinely afraid. Adam leads me carefully back to the land. Already, the tide's coming in. The sun's getting lower. Another afternoon gone, and I can't help wondering as we trudge back along the shore if I'll ever see Bezant Bay again. The steps up to Morryn blur in Escher angles of light and shadow. It's such an enormous effort to get to the top of them that I then have to sit down, regather myself and rest. Adam helps me to the bench at the sea edge of the lawn. Once I'm down on it, I grumpily decide I don't want to move. Understanding as ever, he hurries off to get me some blankets from the laundry cupboard. Didn't we lock Morryn's doors when we went out? How does he know how to get back in? The questions are gone by the time he returns, and the warm, late sunlight falls like a blessing on my face. With assurances that, yes, yes, I'll be fine, okay, alright, I persuade him to leave me so that I can just sit here and take in the last of this glorious evening . . .

A blank moment follows. Not dreams, no. Or if they are dreams, they're dreams of nothing. The sun's almost gone. The sky is lilac. The sea is blood. This is the future, Sis, where the dead fly towards the stars on wings of light, and I'm cold and stiff. Vague irritation that Adam's left me like this comes and goes with the hiss of the in-reaching tide and it's blustery dark by the time, trailing cold, damp blankets, I finally haul myself around the bench and begin to shuffle up the lawn.

Morryn blazes like a paper lantern. All its windows are alight. Is Adam really in there? Did I lock the doors? The freshening wind tugs at the trees. There are so many years I've been here alone, but it's those when Morryn was inhabited by other lives which return to me now. The children, of course. The smell of spoiled cakes and summer sweat. Even more, it's Claude. For him, emptiness wasn't tolerable. Silence had to be pushed out of the way. I can hear all it again now. He'll be playing that weird, modern, sensory stuff—it can't even be called music—which he clambered across age, good taste and common sense to keep up with, filling Morryn with machine drums, bizarre smells, tortoiseshell lights, murmurs in lost languages, shrieks like tortured whales. No melody, no exposition and resolution. Just things tipped together into chaos which Claude, who'd once listened to Miles Davis, Ella and Sinatra to unwind, claimed he enjoyed.

Morryn's front door shudders. Even now, that lost clamour is barely in retreat. My skin crinkles. There *are* voices, disturbances, shimmers of touch and taste. It's eerie. What's left of my hair starts to rise. But it's not some alien roar. It's Claude's voice—no, it's his *voices*—not one of him but many, tumbled together as if in some ghastly parody of those shrieks and flutters with which he once used to fill the house. I limp up the hall towards the heart of this disturbance , which seems to lie in the music room.

Adam's sitting at my desk surrounded by torrents of data. Images of my dead husband—interviews, performances, news-clips, nominations, speeches, fawning profiles, bitchy reviews, news and publicity shots—dance and swarm around him. Claude old and Claude young. Claude in moments of doubt and Claude in his pomp. It's dizzying. A plughole swirl.

"What the hell do you think you're doing?" I manage to croak.

Adam stills all the images. A thousand Claudes fade as he turns on my chair to face me. "I'm so *sorry*, Roushana. I didn't realise how late it had got—I should have gone outside to see how you were. But you did say I could look things up on the screen." He makes a gesture. "I got absorbed, and you said it might help—"

"—plainly, it hasn't, has it?"

He looks pained. "It was just . . . Knowing who you are. I mean, there's so much on record. About you. And about Claude. But I had no right. Of course I had no right."

I'm breathless, I'm shivering, and I'm still dragging my blankets behind me like drowned wings.

"It was only data from the public domain."

I nod, thinking how old-fashioned the expression seems.

"I really am sorry. I just got so *absorbed*. I didn't mean—"

"It doesn't matter. Forget it."

"Roushana, I didn't look at any of this personal stuff on your—"

"Forget it."

"I wasn't—"

"*I said forget it!*"

Adam cringes. My voice is a seabird shriek.

"I'm sorry," I hear myself muttering. "I know you can't just sit around.

I know you have to do something."

His expression remains pained.

"And things haven't been that . . . *simple* for me lately," I concede.

"I could go, you know." I hear the click of his throat as he swallows.

"That might be easier. Do you want me to leave Morryn? You just have to say, and I'll walk out—I'll leave."

"No. *No.* Don't do that. The fact is, I like having you here. I liked it even when you were barely conscious."

We both glance over at the red divan as if his ghost might still be lying there.

"And what I'm doing," I continue, "all the things I've told you about my life—all these keepsakes and memories. It's not just some old woman's folly, or a stupid act of vanity. All these memories . . . They're part of *me*. And the fact is—well, the fact is, Adam, that I'm dying. And the fact is—the *other* fact—is that I'm not prepared to let dying be the end. I mean, why should it? You're young, Adam or whatever your name is, even if you can't remember. You're young, and youth is . . . Well, youth is all about forgetting, although I know it probably doesn't seem that way to you now. Of course, being who you are or aren't, you don't understand. What I mean, what I *mean* to mean . . . What I mean to say is that I'm setting down my life so that it doesn't leave me . . . "

"Roushana, I understand."

"You *do?*"

After things have settled, after I've showered and changed and got myself properly warm again, I find Adam busy down in Morryn's kitchen, and the table calmly laid with napkins and glasses.

I slump down gratefully.

"I am aware of these things," he says as his hands do things to two bundles of asparagus I'm sure I have no recollection of buying. *Chop, chop.* His trim fingernails, so neatly manicured, are captured in the falling knife's reflection. "I've told you—haven't I?—that mere facts, the way the world is, all make a kind of sense of me."

"You're luckier than me, then."

He grins and twists the asparagus up with string. "You know what I mean." Then he wipes his fingers and looks towards me. "I was serious, though. What I said. My being here—it's a tremendous intrusion. What the hell business is this of *mine*? I'm not even Adam. I don't even have a proper name."

Abaddon. He stills says it in that odd way. More than ever, I'm conscious of the huge physical invasion his presence in Morryn has made. He could be anything or nothing, and I've invited him here into the little that remains of my life. But I'm so glad that I'm not alone that I find that I'm suddenly blinking away tears. "Don't go away."

"Then I won't." He shakes his head. "Who am I to pry? Me of all people, eh?"

"That's the question, isn't it?"

We both smile.

"How long do you have, Roushana? Do you mind me asking?"

"No . . . " In fact, it's a blessed relief. So I tell him what I know about the symptoms of my illness, and about my passing, which really doesn't amount to much, as he crumbles breadcrumbs and then asks me if I happen to have any apricots, or perhaps some raisins, any kind of fruit?

"But you don't feel as if you're ready?" Wearing Claude's old apron, he salts a pan.

"I don't think I'll ever feel that way—who could? But no, not yet. And I don't feel so terrible. Or not at this moment, anyway. I'll struggle on for a while yet, I guess. And need to sort out my memories."

He busies himself with the plates. He's opened another bottle of wine—white this time, to go with the asparagus—of a chateau and vintage that's probably the last of its kind in the world.

"It's strange," he says, "it's all so *vivid*—what you've been saying. Things about your life—Claude Vaudin, of course, but also growing up in Birmingham. And your mother. That time you went to India. And Leo. And Paris. Paris especially. I really can picture you, Roushana, in that red leather raincoat."

"*What* red leather raincoat?"

"Oh . . . Didn't you say you used to wear one?"

I shake my head.

He smiles ruefully, his lit reflection fanning wings against the many-windowed darkness. "And you're complaining that *you* forget."

I drink the wine, thinking of dead lands, dead vineyards and the food, the bottle, is soon finished. I watch as Adam gathers things up and washes them by hand, wondering what ritual this is that we're now performing, and if he's going to take flight, dissolve . . .

"So perhaps I could still help," he says as he turns towards me. "After all you've done for me, I feel as if I owe you so much. At least doing this would be something."

"What *have* I done?"

"You saved my life. Lying on that shore, being whatever I am, few people would have done what you've done for me. I'm Abaddon—I'm nothing—I'm nobody. I wouldn't have had a chance if you hadn't found me. It's not just the food, all the care, the hospitality. It's everything you've shared with me. But I can listen, Roushana. I know it's not much—"

"Do you think I really need your help? Don't you imagine I haven't been on my own long enough to manage something as simple and private as arranging my own memories?"

"But why *not* use me? What other point is there to your finding me? Perhaps people's lives don't always cross by pure chance. Some part of you has to believe that, doesn't it?"

"And you want me to tell you everything?"

"Just let me help you finish what we're already doing. What else am I for?"

But it's late, and I let the question wait as I shuffle up the stairs to my bedroom, where Claude's wardrobe still hangs forgetfully open. Feeling a flurry of old irritation at his careless ways, I push it shut. I cast off my clothes. I brush what's left of my hair. I cleanse my face. I pull on the nightclothes I never used to wear. Did I shower earlier? Have I been to the loo? I can't remember, but there are vital new tasks for me to perform instead. An amber bead on my dressing table sips my blood when I touch it, then communicates with another bead—this one seems to be made of tiger-eye—which I lay on my palm whilst I submit to the momentary jab as it inserts the palliatives I need to get comfortably, albeit sleeplessly, through this night.

Morryn fades the lights as I lie in bed. For a while, a precious line of illumination from the landing fans from beneath the door and I hear Adam move up the stairs and go about his ablutions. Then silence falls, picked at by the sigh of the wind. The idea of retelling my life alone suddenly seems as bleak as the coming winter. I should be grateful to Adam—and I am—but I'm Scheherazade: the more of my story I tell, the closer I come to the end.

Something hangs, resolute and dark. It's the moment itself—the endless onrush of now—which still won't let go of me. Then, in a strange shift of densities, I become conscious that another presence is beside me, breathing as I breathe, feeling as I feel, listening as I listen, thinking as I think. As it moves and the gravity of the bedsprings shifts, I almost cry out. But it's only Adam. Taking my hand, he waits for Paris to return.

THE MAINS WATER WAS OFF ON SUNDAY'S ELECTION morning. I had to rush out and buy bottles simply to make coffee, and then for Claude and I to wash ourselves. The water sellers were doing a roaring trade. Already, queues were forming and church bells, minarets, loud hailers, domestic arguments, traffic horns, dim gun-shots and sirens resonated across the rooftops as, already late, we run-walked up the hill past the cemetery to give a promotional performance of *Les escaliers de Montmartre* beside the steps themselves. We'd been expecting news media, interviews, applause, but the Metro was down and the farmers had travelled from across France to show off whatever strength they still possessed. Central Paris was gridlocked, and we ended up playing to some jeering children, a few granddames, and a flustered socialist apparatchik who kept checking his bracelet for new messages from the spin machines.

There was another media opportunity for us as we went to vote, or at least to join the long queue of other citizens who wished to do so. Yes, there was new technology, but there was also the *grande dame* at the trestle table beneath an ancient portrait of de Gaulle who would do things in her own way, and at her own speed. She took an especial dislike to Claude. Plainly, she knew who he was, and thus was particularly determined to question his identity. People had died for this right, empires had fallen or risen, and even I'd struggled to vote because of my continuing British citizenship. Looking back along the many faces peering grumpily behind us as we stood in a fog of armpits and inky paperwork, I wondered who was for Boullard, who was for Irissou. Claude and I had once made a game of this as we sat at cafés, but there was no way to tell.

We walked down through the Tuileries past steaming heaps of manure, overheating lines of traffic and building-sized objects of agricultural machinery to attend a meeting about tonight's premiere. Creative consultants, accountants, first violins, floor and lighting managers, caterers and printers came and went as Claude and I sat in the general manager's office. Claude was in busy repose, and seemed totally happy. I watched, still loved, the leonine way he moved, his looks, his easy, reassuring laugh which rang out most cheerfully at times when others were at their most flustered. Even in this airless office, he remained cool. No, it wasn't an act. This really was him, just as it had been him up on that stage playing incredible piano with tiger-stripe Jill that first time we met. The bigger, the busier, the more crisis-ridden and chaotic the situation got, the more Claude seemed to grow in power and affable control. He checked his bracelet for calls as if willing on the next crisis.

We took lunch on the Rue de Lappe, sitting outside whilst the pavement blazed under one of those steel hoods which pumped out refrigerated air. I remember that the house red was particularly good and that we shared it and a basket of bread and a bottle of non-Christos water whilst Claude checked his bracelet, summoning shapes and colours above the breadcrumb-strewn table which resolved into the image of his parents. Tony and Lujah said hi to us both, smiling from a bench with dawn-lit mountains rising spectacularly behind them. Paris sounded bad, and they were so, so grateful to have escaped Washington this summer. And here they were, resolutely doing the old American thing and living the tourist dream in, yes, can you believe it, a genuine Winnebago! They were heading west across Wyoming, and it really was beautiful here, up in God's good acre with the pines thriving and beavers in the creeks and not the faintest whiff of dirty old politics. Still bearing their smooth Washington smiles even in the great outdoors, Tony and Lujah Vaudin faded.

Then Claude's bracelet gave another chime. Slowly, it became apparent that this latest crisis was nothing to do with music, and then that it involved the tobacco warehouse which he was acquiring for his Project. The thing was this. The thing was—well, there'd been a plan, a sort of scheme: one of the events, one of the happenings, which were so much a characteristic of this particular election . . .

It was useless trying to summon a car, so once again we walked. Buildings twisted in the heat. Rooftops flared like embers. Bowsers had drawn up at street corners to dispense water, but everyone was taking the bottles which were now being given out for free by Christos' followers. How did I picture the scene to which Claude was taking me? Despite all the pranks and happenings which Claude's agitprop friends carried out, it was certainly hard to imagine that they'd have had the organisation and the nerve to kidnap the man whose face was portrayed on all those bottles. Not that Claude himself had been involved. Not greatly, anyway, but it had probably seemed like something worth trying, or at least an idea too amusing to simply dismiss. And they'd need somewhere to take him—so why not use the tobacco warehouse, seeing as he was buying it anyway for his Project?

The building seemed empty at first as we climbed through it, but, up in the ferocious heat of the top floor, a small but impressive virtual recording studio had been set up. Tiger-stripe Jill was there, although the hair which I'd once watched flail as she danced in *le Chien Heureux* whilst Claude played miraculous piano was cut short now. Here, as well, was Thibaut Effram, a novelist from the time when there had still been novels, who affected a grey beard, long robes and the distracted air of all failed artists. As he came over to grant me the sour kiss which the English part of me never wanted, I thought he made a far more convincing messiah than the figure who sat hunched amid the circled tripods of sensory recorders. But, even chained to a chair and with most of his head covered by a virtual reality helmet, you could tell this was Christos.

"It doesn't look good, does it?" Claude muttered. "What sort of image do you think this will make?"

Tiger-stripe Jill rubbed her cropped hair. "Says he's the son of God," she snorted. "He's got bones like chicken wings."

"We didn't lay a finger on him," Thibaut added. "It was just— well, he started to struggle and slipped just as we were getting him into the van . . . Then his arm puffed up. It can't be anything serious."

The doctor who'd been quietly attending to Christos was a grey-haired woman who'd been there in the anarchist riots of the old G8, but had probably imagined her anarchist/situationist days were long behind her. Wearily, and speaking in whispers even though Christos would be unable to see or hear anything within that VR helmet, she confirmed that he had a fractured humerus. Nothing too bad, she'd splinted it, given him pain-killing and anti-inflammatory patches, and was confident it would heal. But still, it was bad enough . . .

I suppose we all knew that this situation was a mess, but you could already see Claude re-arranging his reactions. Watching him as he asked new questions and made fresh calls on his bracelet, I was reminded of how he always was at the podium when things were falling apart. A phrase that wouldn't play, a tantrum in the reeds—they were the stuff of life to him. The initial plan of giving Christos a dose of his own medicine and bundling him into a van and recording his brief incarceration now seemed as stupid as it had probably always been. But to have him re-emerge now, and with clear evidence that he'd been physically assaulted . . . You didn't need to consult the spin machines to know that Boullard's people would have a field-day. All the stories about the filthy, untamed left would be resurrected. It could mean a five percentile drop for the socialists, especially with today's delays in voting, and the difference between winning and losing.

"The best possible outcome," Claude cracked his knuckles as he paced around the tripods and wires, "is that none of this gets out.

We'll have to keep him here, and the whole thing under wraps, until after the results this evening . . . "

"What happens then?"

"Mathilde will be in power. Christos can say what he likes. None o f it will matter."

Christos raised his head. He seemed to sniff the hot air. "Ah . . . !" He shouted. "Just because of this hood, do you think I can't see?" His back was arched, straining against the chains which bound him. "That woman, the one who bandaged my arm—she smelled so *afraid*. But she needn't have fear. Fear is past. This is the end of everything. Do you understand?" Claude had to attend a reception at party HQ. It was the start of the party which would go on into the night—and beyond, we hoped, at the announcement of a socialist victory. I, though, was a lesser light, and I felt sorry for the man up in the rank heat of this warehouse, for all that I disagreed with everything he stood for.

Christos complained. Christos drowsed. Christos made demands, or said he was hungry, or uncomfortable, or in pain, or that this was all the end of everything and that he wanted nothing. I went back to our atelier and found towels, plates. I called in at the corner shop and bought food. Christos' white vans were out in force. So were his water sellers, and I bought half a dozen bottles from a thin, white-faced girl wearing a tee-shirt with a moving image of a bleeding, suffering Christ.

Back up in the warehouse, Christos was still complaining, but Tiger-Stripe Jill and Thibaut were ignoring him and watching the news on one of the many screens. I saw Mathilde looking happy and elegant and hopeful as she stood on the steps of party HQ, and then Boullard looking devious and smarmy and seen-it-all— in fact, the archetypal French politician—as he kissed the hands of nuns at some suburban nunnery. It was depressing to think that people accepted such obvious cynicism. Then, as the faces, the forest fires, the desert fields, the clogged or empty roads, flickered around us, we listened for word of Christos' disappearance. But he wasn't part of the regular round of interviews, police cordons, press conferences and scandals which fed the news channels. The only angle we found on the apocalyptic cults was the predictable one that they believed the end of the world would be brought even closer by whatever happened today in France. There were brief scenes of dancing circles and flagellating figures in one of the abandoned theme parks, then the news moved on to a ceremony commemorating the melting of the last snow in Africa on the peak of Kilimanjaro.

I walked over to Christos and gestured to Jill to turn down his helmet. Sensing a presence, he raised his chins. He smiled.

"I've brought you food," I said. "But perhaps you'd like a drink first . . . "

"Do you know how your friends captured me? No? Sometimes, I go out and sell water. People, the ones who say they advise me, they tell me not to. But I know I should. Not to stop someone taking me to this high place, but *because* of it. I always knew this would happen. It's part of the prophecy."

The chains went round his waist and legs, binding him to the chair, and they'd put some kind of padlock under the chin of his VR helmet. But his hands were free. Warily, as one might approach a snake, I laid the bottle in his lap, then quickly stepped back.

Christos took it in his left hand, smiling as he felt its shape. "It's my water, isn't it?"

"Yes. As if it matters."

"You're right. It doesn't." He tried to move his splinted right arm to open the bottle, winced, then held it out in my approximate direction. "I need your help."

I took it, uncapped it. Our fingers brushed as I gave it back.

Christos drank quickly and messily. Water ran around his stubbled cheeks and across his fat neck and soaked into the dirty collar of his smock. He gave a liquid belch.

"You're not French, are you?"

"What difference does that make? Now I'm going to put some food down for you on this plate."

"No food. I'm not hungry."

"You should eat."

"You sound like someone's mother."

"I'm not."

"No, you're not, are you?" He said it with sinister emphasis. Then he smiled again, but in a sour, different way. "I need to get off this chair."

"I'm not sure—"

"—You don't understand. I need to shit. I can do so anyway. But you've got to stay up here as well . . ."

I exchanged weary glances with Tiger-Stripe Jill and Thibaut. Over in the corner lay an old, empty paint tin. Seeing that neither of them had considered this obvious necessity, it would have to do. We ended up releasing Christos from his chair but leaving him chained by his left ankle to a bolt in the floor so that he was free to move within the circle described by all the now-useless recording equipment they'd set up around him.

Deciding I had no particular desire to watch Christos shit, I crossed the floor to stand at the edge of the wide opening which looked out across Paris. A variegated mid-afternoon smog—fruit of the mingled exhaust of all the supposedly cleaner non-petrol fuels—hung over the city and I could feel the damp heat of my own body wafting up from the shirt I was wearing as I breathed. I think Tiger-stripe Jill and her little group had expected more of Christos: that he'd live up to his name and sing psalms, or fight or curse them. They probably even hoped for miracles, and I could see them losing interest as the afternoon progressed. I, though, remained curious. We left Christos chained just by his ankle once he was finished on the basis that he could do no more harm that way, and I told Tiger-Stripe Jill to keep down whatever sounds she'd been feeding into his helmet.

"You're not afraid of me, are you?" he asked—or stated.

"Why should I be?"

"The rest of them are. That one over there—" he cocked his helmeted head.

"—especially."

Thibaut glared, but said nothing.

"You're just some . . ." I thought for a word. "You're just a man."

"Thank you."

"I didn't mean it as a great compliment."

"Do you fear God?"

I shook my head before I remembered that Christos couldn't see me.

With Mum, I told myself, I should know better. "Why should I?"

He gave a laugh. "You'd fear him, if you knew what I knew."

"What do you know?"

"You've heard me speak. Why do I have to say these things again and again? Especially now. When it's too late."

"So this is the end, is it? You're like the *sadhus* and holy men my mother—" I stopped.

"Go on. *Tell* me about your mother. I can't help the world, but perhaps I can help you. You're lost, you're deep in sin. But it isn't too late. So tell me. Do you think I don't know who you are?"

"Then say my name."

But he said nothing.

The minutes crawled. The heat deepened. The hours stood still. I considered going back to our atelier to try and rest before tonight's performance, but decided against it. The forced sweaty intimacy of this warehouse somehow felt like part of my preparation to play that eerie tune. The piece was still changing. Even at that meeting this morning, Claude had remained reluctant to settle on an absolutely final version. But then, he knew the value of publicity, of doing a high-wire act, and wanted to make sure that the buzz going around Paris about what would happen tonight at the Opéra was greater than that which surrounded the midnight unveiling of Harad's 6th floor.

I heard Christos' chains rattle. His breathing sounded irregular and asthmatic.

"Are you sure you're okay?" I asked, turning from looking out over Paris.

"What does *that* matter?"

"If you're in pain. If it's your arm. If something's—"

"*There's nothing*," he growled in a voice so sudden and ferocious that I almost took a step back. He stood bunched at the end of his chains, head bullishly raised, as if waiting for something, and the air reeked of our confinement.

"We'll let you out, you know, at the end of today."

He gave a quick laugh.

"We're not monsters."

"We're *all* monsters, sinners, demons—that's the point."

"With you, there seem to be many points. And there are people out there—people who listen to what you say and . . . " I felt the same frustration Claude must have felt in that debate. The misogyny. The money. The lies. The denials. The—yes—the kidnappings. The sheer *illogic*. But where to begin, when you knew everything would be evaded or ignored?

"If you're worrying about what happens when I leave here," he said eventually, "you needn't. I've told you—I won't get out of here alive."

"I wish you'd stop saying that."

Wish you'd stop saying that. His fat lips, eloquently disconnected from the hidden features of the rest of his face, mouthed the words in silent parody. "I'm sorry if it depresses you."

"You welcome it, do you—all this fire and brimstone you say is coming?"

He gave a shrug. "It's coming anyway."

"So why . . . " Giving up, I strode back over to the drop and leaned against the edge of the hot bricks. Distant thunder rumbled. Some-where, it might even be raining. But not here.

"I know who you are." Now, his voice was wheedling—self-consciously unpleasant.

"You've said that before."

"Then why do you doubt it? I've heard people say you have a God-given talent. I'm not so sure I can understand what that means—for surely every talent is God-given, even the meanest? And I know nothing, I *care* nothing, about the kind of music you play. I'm completely ignorant. So why don't *you* tell *me*?"

I continued to stare out, considering what he really knew. After all, my French was still tainted with an obvious English accent . . .

"Now you're sulking," he murmured. "But I bear you no resentment. This isn't your fault—not any of it. This is the start of the end of every-thing where all judgements will be made and the dead will return to life . . . "

Clever, I thought. He's toying with me when I should be toying with him. As I walked around the space beyond the tripods, I could tell from the pout of his lips and the movement of his helmet that his eyes were following me. I knew from Mum that the blind have a way of seeing which the sighted can find un-nerving. She exploited it shamelessly. So, now, did this man. But he's been here before, I told myself—in confined spaces with the hopeless seekers of faith who've been lured or dragged into those ghost vans. That's why he seems so comfortable, so amused.

The clouds were growing darker outside. I stepped to the very edge of the circle made by Christos' chain and he shuffled close to me. We were both breathing in unison. I could smell his body, feel its heat.

"How do we fill in these last hours?" he said. "What can we say? I suppose we could talk about your stupid tunes. I could tell you that all your so-called arts are all a trick of the devil. That those words you use about feeling and power and glory and honesty are misdirected. What you think you believe in as *truth* is the wind over the graveyard. It's the death rattle of lost souls turned into an ugly jig . . . "

"Who are you, really?" I breathed.

An arid chuckle. "You *really* want to know?"

Sudden, dry lightning crackled. I felt the hairs prickle on my arms.

Thibaut had fallen asleep beside the flickering screens, but Tiger-Stripe Jill was hunched forward and watching us, her face gleaming with sweat.

"Yes," I said.

Starting once again to pace in circles, hunched lopsidedly, his shifting voice punctuated by the rumble of thunder and the drag of chains across the ridged concrete floor, Christos began to talk.

"It isn't a lie, you know—that I've got no recollection of a life before these recent years. The first time I awoke, or it seemed like the first time ever, I was lying on fresh sheets in a clean white room, and I was in pain. There were wires, tubes, monitoring equipment and I was tended by figures who wore masks. They mopped my flesh, they gave me water..." He smiled and chuckled. "I remember how I loved its cool ease. Sometimes, I heard screams which didn't seem to be my own. Once, I thought I heard someone call out what sounded like *Christos*, and I clung to that name.

"Slowly, the pain lessened. One day, I was sitting on the side of my bed. Another, and I was walking—or learning to. Talking, as well—or at least giving voice to the words which already filled my head. The figures I saw still wore masks, but they seemed interested—impressed, even—by what they called my *progress*. They laughed when I told them I was called Christos... They often laughed. Helped by them, I began to leave my white room and I found that there were similar rooms fanning out along corridors, and that their occupants suffered on sheets amid wires and tubes much as I had and did.

"I came to understand that this place was on the fringes of the great city known as Paris. Sometimes, I'd be allowed to stand outside. There was wreckage and barbed wire. Many of the surrounding buildings were burnt out, but I saw the twisting projections of distant adverts, read wind-blown leaflets which talked of other places called heaven and hell. And still the screams and pleas from the occupants of the other white rooms mingled in my head. But the others all came and went—some-times alive, sometimes dead: the masked figures told me it really didn't matter—whilst I, *Christos*, stayed. And they were all I knew, and I wanted to impress them and I was keen to learn. I helped give injections. I mopped wounds. I laughed when they laughed beneath their masks. I tightened or loosened the straps by which the living subjects were held. I hauled the gurneys which bore out the dead..."

By now, I'd begun to understand what Christos was describing. Not that I'd ever believed the stories of illicit clinics which kidnapped the dispossessed and used them as unwilling donors for black market organs, but it explained a lot—not least, Christos' own white vans . . .

"Then I went out into Paris. The masked figures took me with them in their dark vans as they went in search of what they sometimes called *new donors*, and sometimes simply *fresh meat* and I saw all the lost and the helpless souls who lived on these streets. Ha—and imagine what could be made of *this*—I even helped capture and subdue them . . . "

Christos was growing more and more agitated now, sometimes talking of visions which even his terrible clinic would have failed to contain: of dead souls swimming the sewers, and of the sky above Notre Dame teeming with angels. But whether he wandered the clinic corridors or prowled the Parisian streets in search of fresh donors, all he saw was a fallen world. The unreachable skies teemed with promises of different flesh, intricate metals and plastics—new skins, new clothes, new perfumes, which cost more than the supposed worth of many people's lives. So he knew that this world was fallen and ending long before he understood the scriptures, for the word of the scriptures was already all around him. But the masked figures still merely laughed. And they complemented him on how well his skin had taken, and how well he had healed, and asked if perhaps he might care to help out again tonight in the operating theatre . . . ?

Lightning rattled. The dark afternoon was passing. Sometimes, Christos hunched or crawled. Sometimes, he squatted and whimpered as if he could no longer bear to speak. Yes, yes, look at me. He ripped his smock and stabbed at his pasty chest. You see this heart? You hear this voice? *You think you understand* . . . His words veered into English, or were smeared with a scatter of other languages which might have been German, Dutch, Gujarati, Swahili . . .

Once, he told me, he was taken to a place where it was so cold that you couldn't touch anything without ripping your flesh.

There, lined on shelves within shrivelled plastic, lay frosty lumps of meat. No, no, the masked figures told him, these weren't for *eating*—but look...Gloved hands picked up a frozen lump which Christos, who now knew about these things, recognised as a human heart. Then, peering up at him like a swimmer drowned under ice or a flower inside glass, lay the whole face of a beautiful woman, preserved until it was required by some rich crone...

"But here's the problem," he growled at me as he knelt amid his chains. "You can only keep people alive with a certain number of organs. After that, they die. It's how we're made, and freezing's a poor alternative to using fresh, live donor flesh—or perhaps you didn't know that? But what if...What if...? What if...What if..." The dead eyes of his VR helmet fixed me with their insect gaze. "Let me tell you what I am. I was more of a joke than a serious suggestion...That was what the masked figures told me, anyway. But what if..." Christos nodded to himself, as if the truth had only just struck him. Then he let out a hacking laugh, and nodded again. "But what if a few spare parts—organs and, yes, limbs and flesh as well—could be reassembled into something resembling a living whole? Might that not be a way of keeping the valuable meat fresh for longer?"

"You're saying that's what you were?"

Up in that high room, Christos rattled his chains. "That's what I *am*. I'm the fragments of dozens of helpless donors stretched over with a covering of borrowed skin. I'm the scattered tribes of Babylon made real..."

"What happened to you? How did you get—"

"These places—the place I thought of as my home—they don't last. There are competitors. There are market forces. There's even the gendarmerie, it they haven't been paid enough to look the other way. One day, I awoke and found that the masked figures had vanished. No rattle of trolleys. No humming generators. No slamming doors. All I could hear were the moans and screams of the imprisoned ones. I wandered the corridors. I helped some of the donors left behind,—loosening their bonds, giving them the crutches or medicines which might allow them to survive. Others, those past hope, I led into the next world. That was easy work to me—I knew what to do. Then, as I left, I noticed several cases of bottled water lying in a corridor. Remembering the sweetness and ease which water had brought me in my darkest time of pain when I first awoke, I decided to carry them out as my gift to the world . . . "

Christos smiled beatifically. "So here I am. *This* is who I am. Look at me. What do you see? One man or many . . . ?"

Thunder moved the air—I felt of the wash of its power—but it was getting late, and I needed to prepare for tonight's performance. Stumbling amid the sensors and tripods, I backed away. Christos' bare chest, his half-masked face, shone out through the hot darkness, seeming to twist and change as lightning stuttered and something new and dark and titanic unfurled beneath. I was genuinely afraid, but Tiger-Stripe Jill was laughing. "He's Michael fucking Jackson—he's falling apart!" She clapped her hands in delight as I ran down the metal stairs.

The shower still wasn't working back in our atelier, so I stripped and took the last bottles of Christos water from the fridge and tipped them over myself. For a few precious moments, I felt cool and clean. I wandered about, looking at the things Claude and I had bought together in Paris. Gazing at our watercolour of Venice, the frozen face of a woman rose up towards me from inside the glass. When I struck the keys of the piano, it gave off a dissonant clang.

The polling stations had closed, the traffic had faded, and Paris seemed oddly empty as my taxi bore me to the Opéra on that deepening evening. Only the water sellers were about. Looking up at the skies, I saw the perennial adverts still playing amid the continued flicker of lightning. Buy this or that. Everything was *Changed, Enhanced, Improved, Boosted, Redesigned* or *Classic* for the new era which was supposedly about to come, but I no longer believed a word . . .

My part of the performance wasn't due until after the interval, and I was able to make my arrival with the concert already in progress. I was beginning to relish the idea of simply turning up, playing, departing, just as Kreisler had done. Claude came in just as I'd finished changing into the crimson dress which Lujah Vaudin had helped me choose in Washington. Elegant as ever in his black silk tuxedo, he kissed me lightly on the lips, then propped himself on the edge of my dressing table.

"You look beautiful, Roushana."

"It's going well. So I hear."

"Great, but not brilliant. Have to keep them waiting, wanting—that little bit in reserve. Haven't seen Karl around, have you? After all, it's his premiere."

I shook my head.

"You should see who *is* out there, Roushana!"

"Mathilde, I suppose?"

"Of course." He smiled at me. "And that guy who's Boullard's so-called arts minister."

"We're alright both ways, then, aren't we?"

"Hardly that, but . . . " A short, frigid silence, different in character to anything I'd experienced with Claude, fell between us.

"Why are you—"

"You're—"

We both stopped.

"Tell me," Claude said, "is everything okay with Christos at the warehouse? Not that I don't trust Jill, but . . . "

"I stayed with him most of this afternoon. He seems . . . " There was no word for it. "He doesn't think and act as normal people would, Claude. He keeps saying he's going to die and the world's going to end. I'm not quite sure which it is, really . . . And he told me the strangest story. He says he's made up from the bits of other bodies taken by some illegal organ-snatching clinic."

"Hey, you mean like Baron Frankenstein's monster . . . !" Claude laughed almost as much as Tiger-Stripe Jill had done. "You didn't *believe* him, did you?"

"No. But I think he believes it himself."

"I suppose it fits." Claude nodded. "I am legion and all that."

"What?"

"It's just a phrase. From, I think, the Book of Revelation. You probably wouldn't have heard it, Roushana, seeing as it's from the Bible instead of one of those . . . " He waved a hand " . . . those Indian holy books. Anyway, I can't think that there's any reason not to let him out once we get the results after Harad's precious unveiling, can you?"

"We can hardly keep him forever."

"No, no." Claude picked a piece of fluff from his silk lapel. "Of course not. It's all just the sort of weird thing which happens at the time of elections—you should hear the stories Dad tells!—and Mathilde says—"

"I thought you said she couldn't possibly know about this?"

"Well, she *doesn't*."

My head swam. I was tired. I'd never felt less right in the moments before a big performance. "By the way, Claude, did you ever work out what it was that Christos said to you on *Rapport*?"

Claude shrugged a less than Gallic shrug. "I think it was something about destruction. You're going to be destroyed—something like that, anyway. Pathetic, I know."

Thinking for a moment that Claude meant that his own reaction was pathetic, I nodded.

"But it would suit him, wouldn't it?" Claude muttered. "To be let out after disappearing for a while, and then with that damaged arm. No matter what you do with these people, it plays into their hands. It would all just add another layer to his ridiculous aura of mystery. He doesn't deserve—"

Then a knock at the door signified we had five minutes to performance.

Sitting at the edge of the proscenium as I awaited my entrance, was able to watch Claude ascend the podium. Dry lightning sheeted through the glass dome overhead, catching on shirt fronts and cosmetically enhanced bosoms. There was a palpable sense of expectation amid the audience. Claude didn't need to win them over; they were yearning for this to be good. Still, he took the unusual step of turning to them. He explained how what they were about to hear was essentially a snapshot of Nordinger's new symphony, and that the piece would be different every time it was performed. There was scattered applause and much neck-craning up and down the aisles for a glimpse of Nordinger himself, but he still seemed to be absent. Silence fell. Lightning flickered again at the perfect moment, illuminating Claude's silhouette as he turned towards the orchestra. Like everyone else, I was urging him on.

There had even been enough leaks for the audience to have an idea of what to expect. They certainly wanted fine tunes, giddy pyrotechnics, wild peaks and troughs of sadness and exultation. And, as the symphony unfolded, all these elements were there— but, from the very first notes, they were filtered through a distraction of mistakes and fluffed entrances. Where Karl Nordinger's *Fourth Symphony* should have danced, it stumbled. Where it should have been steely, it was limp. By the end of the cacophonous first movement, there was already a changed mood in the Opéra de Paris Bastille. Of course, Claude had been here before, and I fully expected him to turn things around, but, by the end of the second movement, there were shuffles, and a few loud departures. When I made my entrance, I heard sympathetic cheers. We'd decided that my contribution would be more dramatic like this, but now it looked as if I was disassociating myself from the performance, and my sharp, angry tone as I played the *Song of Time* probably didn't help. When, as happened with the beginning of the fourth movement, an orchestra and a conductor fluff an introduction and have to start again, there's usually encouraging applause, for audiences love to think that even great orchestras can lapse from their usual high standards. This time, there were angry gestures and catcalls.

So it turned out that Nordinger's *Fourth Symphony* was an addition to that distinguished canon of works mangled at their first performance, but the applause after the ragged finale was surprisingly loud. Paris had come to witness the unveiling of a masterpiece, but was just happy to be given another tale of hubris to tell.

The reviews were being posted even before we reached the Marais for the unveiling of Harad Le Pape's 6th floor.

What can any critic say about a new work, when they haven't had a proper chance to hear it . . .

Claude Vaudin stepped up onto the podium. The only good thing that can be said of his and the orchestra's performance was that, eventually, he stepped down again . . .

The one shining light in an evening of missed opportunities was Roushana Maitland, whose intervention in the third movement was, as the English might say, a breath of fresh air . . .

We wondered at the start why Karl Nordinger wasn't attending his own premiere. Soon, we found out . . .

I knew about bad press, but this was gloatingly malicious. Claude, though, was kissing cheeks with the very people who'd said the worst things about him as they emerged into the hot night outside Harad's apartment. Still in a sleek suit and ruffed shirt, he cut the fine figure he always did. No, no, he insisted to everyone who asked—*of course* it hadn't been the symphony itself. That was undeniably a masterpiece. Nor was it the orchestra—less still was it the responsibility of Roushana for—yes—that brilliant cameo. Claude wanted everyone to understand that he bore every ounce of the blame. What he was doing, I realised as I watched him clap shoulders and laugh and ruefully shake his head, was to make the whole thing out to be a failure of such epic proportions that it could only be regarded as a success.

Word was spreading about the elections. Boullard, no, Irissou, was ahead. The computers were up—or they were down and there would be no announcement at all at midnight. Better, some said, weary as I'd grown of the whole thing, to have a theocracy, despotism, anarchy, civil war. But it was the computer glitch thing which rode the strongest in the waves of gossip which flooded Harad's foyer as the elite of Paris waited for the lift.

Here they all were, in their bright feathers, in their subtle furs, wilting a little, yes, but happy and bitchy and undaunted as they were borne up towards the canapés and champagne. Bracelets chimed. Hands evaded, or chose to settle like butterflies, on buttocks and breasts. There was so *much* to talk about. The water was a nightmare—at least for those poor souls who hadn't got a private supply. But anyway... And by the way... And did you see...? And haven't you heard...? It was amazing, really, to hear these people talk of arrogance and hubris. But *you*, my darling Roushana. What you did was stunning. Even more so in the circumstances. It was a breath of heaven amid those clouds of sulphur and shit...

Glancing into the mirrors which ranged the rococo walls across Harad's apartment, I found it hard to pick myself out. I was just another sleek dress, another pretty face—the violinist, yes, who played that tune: you know, the one who's screwing poor, poor Claude Vaudin... The fame, the fabrics, the simply *being here* seemed to matter far more than who you really were. Many of the men were wearing back-buttoned suits with high collars, which, it suddenly struck me, mimicked the smocks that Christos and his followers wore. Everything here had been reduced—or elevated— to gossip and fashion statement.

At eleven, and after a brief and largely inaudible speech from Harad Le Pape, the newly-constructed doors at the apartment's far end groaned open in a breeze of fresh paint. This, at last, was it— or at least would be until the next big *it*—and everyone agreed as we filed up the wide, new stairs that only dear, darling Harad could have ever persuaded a gathering such as this to queue like common entrants to a fairground ride. What an odd feeling it was, finally to be entering the fabled 6th floor which had long promised a redefinition of art—or perhaps of life itself. Harad had said so many things about this work that it was hard to recollect any of them, but it was immediately apparent as we fanned out along a maze of stark white walls that this project was at least as ambitious as expected, and that it was vigorously multi-sensory. There was much to admire as we wandered the labyrinth of installations and exhibits, and much that was intriguingly new, or interestingly familiar, or just down-right strange.

The journalists and the commentators were happy—you could see them revising their estimation of the Nordinger premiere even further downwards in the light of this—and there was certainly nowhere else to be seen, at least until the post-election parties. But I soon realised that I was fighting back a rising sense of disappointment. Here, for example, was the same mound of dog poo which Harad had once famously reviewed when it had lain outside the Pompidou Centre. Everyone oohed and ahhed, but surely this was ridiculously self-referential? And here were the precious glasses which the myopic Joyce had supposedly used to write *Ulysses*, shattered—but so what? And here were Impressionist street scenes, and wafts of sound and smell, and portentous voices reading stuff backwards. Was this woman vomiting copiously into a Ming vase an exhibit, or merely another guest? Harad would probably have been happy to have it either way, but I suddenly wasn't. Although cleverly and expensively presented, this was nothing more than just another one man—or woman—exhibition . . .

A study of the surviving contemporary reviews would probably suggest that Harad's 6th floor was uniformly received as a masterpiece, but in truth attention soon began to drift on that night of its unveiling. The thing, the problem, the computer or communications glitch which a few people had mentioned earlier in the context of the elections, seemed to be genuine. Bracelets weren't working. It was most frustrating, especially for the many who liked to read the reviews before passing judgement on anything. It was assumed for a while that Harad had cleverly put up a block on airwave transmissions, or that it was an effect of the endless dry thunderstorm which still rumbled outside. Perhaps it was even a virus attack. But none of those explanations made proper sense.

Claude was still performing. Claude was relentless. His voice was whipcrack loud. Harad, in comparison, seemed almost catatonically subdued. But here we all were in his or her 6th floor, and the odd thing was that, despite the gathering sense of ennui and the pull of the imminent post-election parties, people seemed reluctant to leave. I checked my own bracelet. It, too, was dead. Looking around for Claude, I heard a man moaning in what sounded at first like the throes of sexual ecstasy, but which then turned into a high wailing. There were titters. Looks were exchanged. *Most* strange. Perhaps Harad had another trick up his or her sleeve, after all . . .

It was getting harder to tell exactly where performance ended and reality began. The next big virtuality projection I encountered looked like nothing more than the lightning-shot Parisian sky above our heads, but the one beyond was far more fiery, and was perhaps an ironic play on the apocalypse which Christos and so many others had predicted. But I realised as I approached another roiling vision of flame and smoke that what I was seeing wasn't simply art. The display of a near-midnight sky above some great city shot through with a bleary sun fizzed and flickered with the logo of one of the main news channels. Those people who still hadn't realised that this was a realtime transmission relayed along the surviving landlines were smiling and clapping as they watched, but the rest of us had fallen into shocked silence, or were looking away.

The story kept changing. The Chinese, no, the Americans, had exchanged missiles. It was an asteroid or comet. It was 9/11 and 10/12 all over again, but bigger, smaller, better, worse. I caught a glimpse of Harad Le Pape standing amid the increasingly agitated crowds. Tears shone across his or her big cheeks, although whether in grief about what seemed to be happening in the world or at the fate of his great artistic statement, it was impossible to tell. Spillages of bicycles from last year's Tour de France faded from another of the expensive virtual screens and people screamed as smoke and rubble rolled out towards them in one vast, unending wave.

Bizarrely, the one name which kept re-emerging was Yellowstone, which we then still thought of as merely the home of Old Faithful and Yogi Bear. This wasn't a nuclear war, the talking heads which began to appear amid the scenes of devastation were beginning to explain, but a natural disaster—a volcanic eruption on a scale beyond any in human history. There was an odd mixture of commiseration and relief as this news swept through Harad's 6th floor. Yes, it was terrible. But it was only some *volcano*. And it was in America, by which in those days we still meant the USA. It really couldn't have been much further away . . .

Harad's guests finally began to move down onto the street and I found Claude outside as well, amid the milling noise and traffic. Paris had reawoken, and the scene was colourful, chaotic. It was past midnight and the election results had been delayed, but the planned fireworks went off anyway. They ripped overhead in angry volleys. Then, bells began to ring in their crackling wake. There was so much noise. Thunder still rolled. There were shouts, car-horns, the waving of flags and makeshift banners, and people were barging by us as the lit sky played over Claude's anguished face. It was as if all the contents of Harad's 6th floor had spilled out across Paris in a vast carnival wave. For who cared about the elections now? At the very least, it could wait. Cataclysmic projections played across buildings as I followed Claude north and west. There was street music. Dogs barked from balconies and the business in the cafes was huge. The water-sellers were in fine voice. Madmen and prophets of every conceivable religion wandered and raved . . .

To me, much of this was all too much like that day when I'd tried to get across Birmingham to Nan Ashar's house along the canals beneath the flames and barricades. Even beyond the images of roiling darkness which were playing everywhere, there was the same broken glass, the same smoke and flame. I thought at first as I hurried with him that Claude was hurryingly intent on discovering some proper source of information. Then, that he just wanted to escape all this light and noise. I already guessed that his home country was ruined and his parents were probably dead, but everything was too loud for talk, and had happened too quickly for us to have any proper understanding.

Claude grabbed my hand as we stumbled on through a sea of images. Paris was several cities at once that cataclysmic night. Wild parties of cheering youths went by, leaning from cars with banners and bottles, waving burning American flags. Moaning women clustered around news sources, broadcast images of flame and smoke playing torrents of emotion across their weeping faces. Gunshots or fireworks still crackled. Clustered in a side street— I'm still sure I saw it—was a cackling gaggle of penguins. The thunder still rolled. A van went by, its loudhailer proclaiming victory for one side or the other in the day's elections, although the words were distorted beyond any possibility of being understood. Claude was still holding my hand, dragging me on, and I submitted easily to the pull of his arms and the tumble of the streets towards Montmartre. I knew that he needed me, and I'd have held onto him even if he'd tried to let me go.

"**W**ELL?" ADAM REGARDS ME FROM THE CHAIR BY the window as I lie here on the red divan in the music room which he helped, half-carried, me down to this morning. "You were going to that warehouse—but what happened? Was Christos still there?" Curled amid a soft spill of blankets, I stare up at the beamed ceiling, feeling a dimming sense of noise and smoke. "You don't understand. It isn't that simple. Life isn't just one story. You make choices . . . Or you think you do. Anyway, you stumble along streets and up steps and duck openings. And somewhere along the line, events happen . . . But afterwards, when you look back, they're not always just one thing, but many."

All last night, all of this morning, I've talked, and Adam's listened. Now, outside, and far away from Paris, the clouds are pushing their stormy arms through the stuttering sunlight, and the wind is rising strongly enough to cause Adam's many reflections to flare and distort in the panes of the bay windows.

"I checked up on Christos' name," he says softly, "when I was looking at all that stuff about Claude. He's well documented—a totemic figure. Then, at about the time of the elections, he just vanished. Of course, there were all sorts of suggestions, but nothing concrete. He was simply there, and then not there. Of course, his organisation collapsed without him. And he never reappeared again . . . "

. The air that night tasted tipsy and hazy. The looted shops had spilled out onto the streets, and the windmill above the Moulin Rouge was in flames. Everyone was looking for someone to blame.

"Well, you hardly need me to tell you, Adam, do you?"

"Tell me what?"

"That Christos vanished."

"That's it?"

"What else do you want me to say? Claude and I, we got to the tobacco warehouse and we climbed the stairs. But Tiger-Stripe Jill and her situationist crowd were all already out on the streets—on this of all nights, it was where they belonged. Christos was gone as well. All that was left of him were the chains and that virtual helmet. What would you expect? After all, Jill and her mates were hardly the most diligent of warders. They'd probably have let him go just as soon as they realised what was going on outside. So Christos went out into that dangerous night and, just as you say, he vanished. You, Adam, should understand better than most how people can disappear—how they can change identities, transform themselves, or simply get irredeemably lost. I'm sorry to disappoint you, but I really have no idea what happened to Christos. He could have been deliberately killed in the riots—believe me, enough people wanted him gone. Or he might have died anonymously like so many others. Or perhaps, after Yellowstone, he thought his work was finished. Perhaps he simply gave up. Or perhaps he really was what he said to me, and the warring bits of his body simply fell apart . . . "

"And nothing else?"

"Nothing."

Adam stands up. Looking far more disgruntled than he should—after all, it's *my* life I'm telling him about—he leaves the music room. As the sounds of dinner waft in from the kitchen, I get myself up and move over to the desk. Something loud clatters across the floor—it's the empty plastic bottle of Christos water which Adam has been toying with. Too weary to bother to pick it up, I lean close to the windows. A frozen mask, withered beyond recognition, blurs as I struggle to re-focus outside. I can feel the wind as it forces its way through the gaps in the glass. The sea is turning jagged. It's going to be another savage night, on this savage earth.

How did we ever manage to care so much about politics back in Paris? None of it really mattered. We're just puny humans, and Mother Earth is Mother Earth. Cities can be put to the flood or capriciously saved in the blink of a cyclone. Comets can approach enough to give us the apocalyptic willies. Whole continents can be laid waste. All these things might happen, and it doesn't matter to anyone but us humans: that was what Yellowstone taught us.

A few scientists, doom-sayers, those in the know, had understood that one of periodic eruptions of the vast reservoir of magma which lay beneath much of Colorado was imminent, at least in geological terms. For the rest of us, it was just part of the background fuzz of sundry other threats of mass extinction. But the supervolcano erupted, and its after-math soured the skies across the whole planet, withered crops and brought five of the longest, coldest and hungriest winters in human history. The Seine froze—so did the Danube and parts of the Amazon. The snows returned to Kilimanjaro. There were rains across the Gobi and the Sahara. America and Canada were destroyed as functioning nations. The glaciers stopped retreating. The world economy, which had been relentlessly pumping carbon into the atmosphere, suffered an enormous recession. Before, there seemed to be no doubt that the seas would continue to rise and the deserts would spread, that many of the great cities, both the riches and the poorest—as if such distinctions mattered—would be consumed, but in those long winters and short summers, people began to speak of a new ice age instead. Of course, many have said that Yellowstone was the earth's way of restoring her equilibrium, but they haven't looked far enough back across her long record of catastrophes, inundations and extinctions. The earth doesn't care whether she's hot or cold, fecund or arid. She's just the tumbling ball of rock to which we, at least those still living, have to cling.

Adam goes to the kitchen and returns a seeming blink afterwards with lunch on a tray—that luxury which soon becomes a curse—which, after helping me to sit up, he lays on my knees. The food passes me by, although I don't doubt that it's predictably excellent, whilst he talks of Yellowstone, which of course he already knows all about. He tells me how my parents' generation must have feared the things we humans could do to each other— terrorism, viruses, the bomb—far more than what nature could do. I don't bother to contradict him. I can tell he wants me to continue with the story of my life all this afternoon, but I'd rather rest. Why this desperate need to push on today when by tomorrow, this coming storm—which I can feel and hear in the gathering crash of waves—will have blown itself away? Who knows, summer might make a return and we could go back to Bezant Bay. And I could re-visit my childhood. I could tell him more about living in Moseley—or Mum and Dad's parents, or our holidays in France. I could even walk down to Fowey again to stock up, if I'm feeling fit enough. Then, and just as I did last night, I'll play him some music before we both go to bed . . .

"I have a request to make," Adam says after he's cleared lunch away. "Could you play some of the *Fourth Symphony* for me?"

"It's hardly a solo piece. Anyway, the score isn't here. That's the whole point—there is no final score."

"But you can play the melody from the third movement. What do you call it—the *Song of Time*?"

I grunt. "Even that would have changed."

"But isn't that what Leo always used to say—from one performance to the next, no piece of music ever stays the same."

Submitting, levering myself up from the divan and shedding my blankets and shuffling across the strew of rugs and old scores and other memories, I open up the case. I shoulder the Guarneri. I lay my fingers on the strings. *Song of Time* . . . Was that name Karl's idea? Perhaps Harad's, or Claude's? I can't remember now when or where it came. Just one of those titles which a piece seems to attract from nowhere. Like Beethoven's *Emperor*, or Wagner's *Lay of Sorrows* . . . I take a breath. Concentrate, Roushana, concentrate . . . I visualise my hands' and then the music's shape, which is immortal, yet never ceases to change. I raise my bow.

Everything blends. A slow beat. A tremble of strings. One and two and—

The moment shatters, my betrayed fingers skid, and the Guarneri clatters and erupts from my useless hands with an agonised shriek.

I CAN'T HELP IT—I'M SOBBING. MY SIGHT IS BLURRED AND my ears are roaring as, carefully, respectfully, Adam prises the useless instrument from my numb hands and places it back inside its case. Then he helps me back over to the red divan, and eases me down, plumping cushions and then—I'm still gasping, shivering—he covers me with the same blankets with which I covered him just a few days before. I lie there with my face aching and the room spinning. For all that I've been dreading this moment, I realise now that I never believed it would come. Not really—not like this. And now that it has, nothing will ever be the same. The thing which defined my life has been taken from me. *It's down to you now Sis* . . . What Leo always wanted me to understand was that the music—lovely, organised sound which is gone too quickly to ever really be properly understood or analysed—was all that ever mattered, and that everything else is distraction, noise, empty static . . .

Adam draws the chair over from the desk and settles himself beside me. His fingers smooth the brittle hair away from my wet and withered face. "It's nothing. Just give it another chance . . ."

I shake my head.

"What can I do?"

"Just being here . . ."

"I won't go away."

The room pulses. Empty silence rings.

"Life's been so quick, you know."

"Don't talk like that."

"But it *has*. It's a like a fairground ride. One minute, you can't wait for it to start, you're queuing to get on. And the next . . . "

He takes my hands in his own. "Tell me more about Paris, Roushana. Tell me what happened after Yellowstone . . . "

I swallow, lick my salt lips. "Claude and I left soon after—it was just as the first of the long snows came. Oh, it wasn't a conscious decision to begin with. We still returned when the transport would let us, and we kept our atelier . . . "

"But what about the people?"

A whispery chuckle. "You should see Harad Le Pape now!"

"What?"

"Oh, it's nothing—Harad returned to journalism, and his or her views lost their urgency, although I believe he or she grew enormously rich. And the others, well they headed for greater fame or lesser obscurity, or they gave up entirely in the way that many artists do. You probably know that Jane Affray committed suicide in that bizarre way. Others succumbed to drink, drugs, starvation, that flu epidemic, or to their own self-importance. Of course, Mathilde Irissou did win the election, although most of the promised reforms broke on the rocks of national hardship. I mean, who remembers her now? I suppose there's that ridiculous theme park of lakes and offices—a counterpoint to La Defense, another monument to presidential impotence and vanity— although I doubt if either are still occupied . . .

"And Karl Nordinger . . . Karl retreated into the wealth that his music and programme-writing had created for him. There was talk over the years that he was working on some great oratorio, song-cycle, opera or symphony, or a new piece of software, but none of it ever emerged. The *Fourth Symphony* has remained his last, defining, work—the symbol of that changed era—and Claude's disastrous first performance on the night of Yellowstone is simply another part of its story. If you're wondering, Adam, Karl and I never did keep in touch. But then, Karl didn't keep in touch with anyone. There were just those odd sightings—one year seemingly bedraggled, long-haired, the next apparently swish and prospering. Knowing Karl, or at least having once nearly-known him, I always suspected that he sometimes paid others to imitate him and lived quietly somewhere in smug misery. I missed him, you know—of all the people in Paris . . . But, knowing what you do, I suppose you're not surprised . . . And Karl's work has remained, and that was all that most people had ever wanted of him, and I, too, have contented myself with re-visiting that great symphony. It was probably the best of him. It's always remained new and surprising. Yes—even now, even today . . . "

Claude and I, we travelled this newly damaged world seemingly endlessly. We were itinerant musicians, but on a global scale. We gave speeches. We organised festivals. We performed in the refugee camps in Georgia and Florida. People wanted the comforts of music in those times, and we were so much in demand that our public life, the inter-views and the rehearsals and performances and those endless journeys and freezing, stinking encampments and ramshackle hotels, often seemed all that there was. The world barely noticed when we got married on that rainy day in Santiago, for it had long been assumed that we already were. Claude Vaudin and Roushana Maitland. I can remember the disappointment which crossed people's faces if they thought they might not be getting us both. But we *were* a great double act. We knew it as well.

Oh, I could go on about the festival in Prague, or Claude at Bayreuth, or our long residency in Florence, but the recordings and the newscasts are all there already for anyone who cares to access them, and the programmes and posters cover these music room walls. The public life, the life of being who we wanted the world to think we were, absorbed us both in those years, and the private side, the few breaks we ever took and the house we bought in Beijing and the other one Claude insisted on keeping in the new dominion of Washington as a kind of memorial to his dead parents—all of those things seemed pale in comparison. We made music, and the world wanted to listen, and that, in the best of times, seemed like enough. Standing with Claude onstage, performing alone, or sitting marvelling as he manipulated some recalcitrant orchestra to new heights—all these many moments are filled in my memory with such a glow that it's hard to look clearly at them now, they all blur into one, and it's harder still to understand them. Was I really so absorbed, so uncaring, so dedicated to making sounds with my violin and bow whilst the world starved and suffered? Did Claude allow himself to become so much the great interpreter that that was even how he saw his own image in the mirror? But Leo, as always, was right. The music's there, and then it's gone. It's all beyond analysis. And, now that final silence seems to have overtaken me, I feel that that's how I should leave it.

Despite all the risks she took with her health, Mum survived and thrived in Gujarat long after the global crisis of Yellowstone. But, since that time she visited Paris, she became more distant. When she called me, I knew without asking that she would be seeking some kind of impersonal favour. A new endorsement, the grant of rights of performance, a word in the ear of someone she thought I might be meeting, another charity concert or media shoot. Just as Claude and I were, Mum seemed in those post-Yellowstone years to have become absorbed by the external personality projected to the world. On the occasions I visited her in Gujarat Two, she seemed to be so preoccupied that she barely had time to talk, whilst I, perhaps, might have seemed the same to her, with my endless calls and crises about the next hotel and the next concert. Then, ten almost unbelievably quick years after Yellowstone and Paris, and passing the time before a performance by flicking through the datastream in a hotel in Mexico City, I learned by chance from a stray news item that she was dying.

I couldn't get through when I tried calling her. But that was nothing unusual, and in any case the facts were all there, and repeated every quarter of an hour on the screens. The "Famous Champion of India's Poor" had lymphatic cancer. Treatment was certainly possible, but the best she could hope for was a couple of extra years in weakening health, and at a cost which would provide food and healthcare to thousands of the neediest Indians instead. What I felt as I sat down alone in that anonymous hotel was a mixture of irritation and sorrow. My mother had decided to do what she always did with everything, and turn her death into a fundraising event. She gave interviews, she published the scans and prognoses. She kept an online diary of her symptoms. Pointedly, publicly and repeatedly, she refused any kind of treatment. People, complete strangers, would come up to me after performances to give me the latest news on her slow public decline as she gave whispering inter-views to the world's media which, just as she surmised, remained more interested in portraying an individual's story than it was in the suffering of millions.

I went back to India in her last days, and Claude came with me as well. Plane travel was common for us, but for most people, this distant view of the earth had become a memory, and I often wondered if they realised just how much had changed. The seas seemed so much wilder and darker now, and it wasn't uncommon as you looked down to glimpse the cresting backs of whales. And the land, the land was always different, although perhaps we also saw it differently by then, admiring but no longer trusting our planet, looking at it in all its continuing beauty as one might the jewelled flesh of some dangerous snake. Nowhere but in India, as we flew long and low across its western reaches, did that metaphor seem more appropriate. The towns and cities were no longer cubist paintings in terracotta and stucco, and the fields, fishing beds and cattle enclosures had lost their neat boundaries. Everywhere, sprawling and irregularly beautiful, there were shimmering profusions of blues and greens. The people who looked up and waved at us as the shadow of our hopper passed over them seemed rare and solitary. Somehow, you could tell that they no longer tended the herds of white and brown cattle you saw tumbling their backs across the wide and open landscapes. This world of ours was turning beautifully wild, and the smells of India which you inhaled when you stepped out into the delicious heat of the old Blue Sector runway were no longer soured by dust, excrement and rotting meat. It was like inhaling an exquisite perfume. Everywhere, there were flowers.

The Blue Zone itself had crumbled, its wires were down, and the old UUN tanks and transporters had also been transformed by vegetation into giant, bizarre potholders, nests for enamel-bright lizards, birds and snakes, although the same hotel where Mum and I had stayed on my first visit was still struggling on in a make-do-and-mend way I'd come to recognise by now in other parts of the world, but which I still thought of as characteristically Indian. As I looked up at the jumbled edifice, part marble, part concrete, part stacked Portacabin, above which a neon sign poked and still seemed to be glowing in the vivid morning light, I was reminded of the great buildings of Washington which Claude and I had recently driven past on the way to perform a concert at the refurbished National Cathedral from which the lemurs from the nearby zoo had been evicted. So much about the rest of the world was changing. Only India seemed to me to have become more and more of what it had always been.

Inside, the hotel was more like an office. Screens bloomed ever-changing colours. Everywhere, there were desks and the murmur of meetings. Up many stairs—inevitably, the lift wasn't working—and along several corridors, Claude and I, dressed in our smart western clothes, were confronted by a brisk selection of ladies, all of whom gave a bow and a melting smile once they realised that I was the famous Sadhu-lady's daughter. More than ever, seeing my own mother felt like seeking an audience. A final doorway, a hurried discussion, and then Claude and I were admitted into what had once been a hotel bedroom but which, with all the tributes and statuettes of Hindu gods which had been provided by well-wishers, looked more like a temple. Soft music played. Incense smoked. Flags and silks plumed from the ceiling. At the centre of it, smiling her benediction at the departing team of journalists from the German Republics, and almost too small to be believed, sat the tiny husk of a woman.

I wasn't surprised by Mum's appearance—I'd grown used to seeing her dying image on the newscasts—but it still felt odd to be here with her, and I held back, standing at the far end of the giant pillowed bed whilst Claude, who'd always enjoyed the company of my mother, leaned over and kissed her hand. Mum's eyes and cheekbones stretched as she gave a thin smile. She was so pale now she resembled the dalits of Ahmedabad One, but she radiated a hot energy which still fuelled everything else which was going on in this hotel. Her eyes flickered away from Claude. Not towards me, but to the sensory tripods which corralled this crowded room. They were the centre of everything, through which Mum relayed her and India's plight to the world. Despite the ten years which had passed, the progress of technology had slowed in the wake of Yellowstone, and they were almost identical to those which had once surrounded the lost figure of Christos in that tobacco warehouse in Paris.

"Come Roushana," Mum whispered in faltering and heavily-accented English, "I want you beside us."

Still, I hung back. Even as Mum murmured to Claude about our journey, I could tell that she was thinking of the fine contrast they both made for the sensors as he leaned beside her, the black conductor come to visit the Sadhu-lady, and how much finer still a triptych we would make when I, the concert-violinist daughter, had joined them. She and Claude weren't so very different. I loved them both but, even as Claude held Mum's hand, I could see his other hand tapping a beat on the red silk coverlet whilst his gaze wandered in that way it always did when he was considering how to resolve some musical problem. You could spend a whole life trying to break through into whatever lay in their hearts without ever really succeeding.

"Well . . . " Mum sighed, as I finally sat down on the bed beside her. "Here I am. Just like John Lennon in the Toronto Hilton without Yoko."

I nodded, although I didn't understand the reference until I checked it later, and it was Amsterdam in any case. Then she asked me about my work, and about our journey, and soon I had to stop her pressing a button to call in one of her secretaries to discuss the details of the supposedly impromptu, but, by Indian standards, reasonably well-planned, recital Claude and I were supposed to be giving.

I revised my first impression. This *was* a shock. Mum had shriveled since even the last broadcast in which I'd seen her, and she seemed to shrink further with every breath, falling back into these gold-embroidered silks and cushions as nothing but bone and skin. Something angry flared within me. I kept glancing at those watching sensors. As if they—and the unwavering public eye which Mum had become even better than Claude and I at exploiting—were to blame for her illness. And she was in considerable pain by now. She told me as much, in her usual matter-of-fact way, but then I knew already, for she'd recorded every detail of her agony in her worldwide diary. This, I realised as I stared into the changed face of the once young, once beautiful woman who had waved to me from the shore with her limbs shining on French beaches, would be the last time I would see her alive. The saddest thing of all was that I didn't feel remotely like crying.

Dry silence fell. For all her tiredness, Mum seemed restless and frustrated. I guessed that by now our presence was stopping her from seeing someone else, or checking on the progress of some initiative. When I died, I vowed to myself then, I would do so alone, and quietly. Then I felt the bones of her hand make a small movement.

"Roushana, what are you thinking?"

I shrugged.

"Have you got there?"

"Where?"

She blinked slowly in that way she'd always done when she felt that her daughter was slow in understanding something. "The place you wanted to get to. With your life. With your music."

"I suppose I have," I said, wondering.

She made a small sound, and I thought it was some kind of spasm before I realised she was laughing. "Remember how we argued about your violin playing! That day we went to the shops in Fowey?"

"Yes." I met her stare. For a moment, we were both walking along those damp, fishy streets, trying on clothes and, yes, arguing. And with us, unspoken, then as now, was the lingering ghost of Leo. We didn't even need to say his name. He was there, just as always. "I do remember."

We left Mum shortly afterwards, and Claude went off to arrange things for our recital, whilst I, knowing that my husband, who was always wary and finicky about his health, wouldn't be comfortable going there himself, set about finding the quickest and simplest way of getting to Ahmedabad One. I tried asking at the hotel desk, and even thought about finding whatever remnants there were of the UUN, or of ringing my Indian-subcontinent agent. Then I just walked outside. It was past midday, fragrantly hot, and the roads along the main strips were spasmodically busy. Cyclists and cars crawled. There were a few lorries. Taxis as well. I tried hailing one. The driver touched his prayer beads when I asked him if he'd take me to Ahmedabad One. But he nodded.

What had once been shanty towns had now acquired a sense of permanence. Concrete, mud and stucco had replaced the flimsy tents and shacks, although they were still set with unexpected scavengings from the destroyed city, here a window of plate glass, there the rear-end of a van, which gave the landscape a collage-like effect. And it was all widely-spaced within large expanses of florid greenery. I scanned the skies for the carrion birds which had once circled over the funerary fields of the Parsees, but all I saw were sparrows, and a flock of flamingos rising like pink smoke from a lake in the mid-distance.

The early half-life of the radiation had decreased considerably, and the dead area within Ahmedabad One which the dalits inhabited had contracted. Still, there was a point where the houses gave out, and the road grew rougher until the driver finally stopped at a rise which looked down over the old city. The afternoon sun blazed down at us as we climbed out and he sat on a rock to mop his head and I crossed a short rise. What I saw in the wide bowl beneath, fanning out towards the blue bay, was nothing but softy steaming greenery. If the dalits were still down there, they'd become the lost tribe of a new jungle.

I laughed out loud, to think that the saddest of all places should look like this, and make me feel so happy. In a few days time, the husk of Mum's body would be bathed, dressed in white and surrounded by garlands. Then she would be burned, and no doubt it would all happen before the all-seeing eyes of those sensors. But I was remembering that ridiculous violin I'd once had, and which I'd sent back to this place, and which perhaps lay down there somewhere, burrowed by insects and embroidered by creepers. And then I was remembering the baby I'd never really thought of having, all for the sake of my career, and for the sake of music. Now, I was crying, and I knew in that moment that the performance Claude was organising would be my last for many years, and that I wanted us to find a house that I could really live in, and have children.

Claude was intrigued by my insistence after Mum's funeral that we find a house in Cornwall. But he was never one to turn away from change, and he loved exploring the neat little fishing villages which had been there for too long to be troubled by the world's recent difficulties. Nothing could have been more different from the clean lines of balconies and hissing road-ways of our flat in Beijing, but that was good as well. He said he was reminded of Cape Cod. He read *Jamaica Inn* and *The Hound of the Baskervilles* (Devon, not Cornwall, Dartmoor, not Bodmin, but then my husband was still an American) and rediscovered for repertoire the works of Arnold Bax. My initial vow that I would cease performing right after Mum's death proved impossible to sustain, and, between winding down my existing commitments and honouring Claude's, finding a house took many months, much of which we wasted looking for that cottage not far from Fowey were Mum and Dad and I had first stayed. I couldn't believe that somewhere so seemingly solid could have vanished, but Claude was prepared to humour me. Another joy which he'd discovered in Cornwall was driving by hand along narrow, winding roads. He was already talking of getting hold of some antique MG or Austin Healey.

It was a happy time for us. The Cornish landscape, which always seems to have the bones of autumn poking through even on the warmest of days, had coped well with the darker skies of the years following Yellowstone, and ancient landscapes of lichened churches and moor-lands unrolled as we explored abandoned farmhouses, Georgian seaside villages and ridiculously over-large estates. We liked Padstow, and Claude was attracted to Saint Ives, which had become cheap enough to harbour a bickering colony of artists once again, but, if for no other reason than my continuing insistence that that cottage still had to be there if we could only find the right turn along some country lane, we kept returning to Fowey. And then, one day, we found Morryn, long-empty and looking ridiculously romantic as it hunched black in the sunset against a massive crimson sky. As we walked around the low stone wall towards its waiting windows, we already knew that this would be the place. The rooks cawed. The gulls screamed. That saying that there is no first time for coming home is wrong, for here we were. Laughing, expectant, already half-made, our unborn children seemed to rush out to us on the darkening breath of the sea along with Morryn's characteristic scents of nettles and wood rot and old stone. I could already see their faces, could smell the pillowed crowns of their sleeping heads, and I knew that they would become everything that was best of Claude and I.

I became clerk of works for this house's restoration. After the abstractions of music, I found that I enjoyed the practical challenge. Claude came and went, continuing, as we'd agreed, on his world-hopping career whilst I put mine on hold. Scorning the idea of having children by the use of modern aids, and after the minimum of tests and interventions, we strove joyfully to conceive in the old-fashioned way. For Claude, for us both, those questing journeys across the Cornish landscape had become addictive. Now that we had our house, we began looking for his car instead. Old sports cars of the type Claude craved were ridiculously rare, and the idea of one left forgotten in a barn belonged in the sort of story you'd expect to hear in a snug Cornish bar on long nights when salt rain lashed the windows, but that didn't mean we didn't believe it. More questions, more drinks, other bars, and the car even acquired a marque. It was an Aston Martin, DB 4 or 5 (I learned from Claude there was little difference) abandoned in near-perfect condition by some local eccentric—up near St Austell, no, no, another voice in another bar insisted, it was down beside Penzance—who chased away with a shotgun anyone who expressed an interest in it.

We took dead ends. We risked roads that had been torn off from the cliffs. We stopped amid the heather to make love. Then, one grey after-noon, we found it. The house was large and dilapidated, but, instead of the whiskery old man we'd envisaged, the door was opened by a youngish woman in an open caftan with ornaments of glittering silver wire twined across her skin. The place was some sort of commune, and the answers we got about the car were vague. We surmised that, like ownership of the house itself, the turbulent years had eroded such certainties, but, settled in a damp birch copse more as if it had risen from the earth than ever been driven there, lay a mossy mound from which what might have been a wing mirror protruded. Still, the house's inhabitants knew the worth of what they claimed they had, and the price they asked was ridiculous.

The DB arrived here a week later. Claude meanwhile had had the builders divert the attentions of their machines from plumbing to have the old stables made sound. The thing just sat there, still barely a car at all, let alone that legendary near-pristine marque, but Claude was bliss-fully happy and I smiled with him as he prowled the mottled flanks whilst the smashed and blinded headlights stared towards the steel racks of his new tools. I hadn't fully appreciated that he hadn't wanted an antique car to drive, but something he could remake from almost nothing. Smelling of moss and rot, shedding leaf-falls of rust, the ancient DB wheezed and creaked as, leaning me back against the gouged and dented bonnet, Claude began to part my clothing and caress me.

Does a woman know? Does it have to be some special moment? It could have been any of the frequent times we made love in the few days before Claude headed off to a new guest-residency, but that was the moment we set aside for the making of Edward in our private mythology. Pregnancy came as a shock to me. I'd always

264

imagined my body was my own, and the sheer alienness of the symptoms, the sickness and the swellings and the changes to my senses, was disconcerting as well as discomforting. I never quite got to the point of wishing we'd had the baby grown in some fleshy pod, but it was close, and it never got closer than during the act and aftermath of giving birth. Claude had managed to call off his commitments to be with me, although he turned out be surprisingly squeamish. I'd never thought about men and women being particularly different, but now that I was leaking blood and milk from various orifices, we seemed like other races. Work on Morryn still hadn't finished, and Claude was soon back off to Stockholm, and I was moving through a fog of plaster dust and weariness, falling over dangerous bits of ambulatory machinery whilst I attempted to take care of this squalling parcel of new flesh which we'd decided to call Edward in commemoration of the greatest of English composers.

Maria came a year later, although she seemed like the eldest, the more responsible and burdened, even when they were—what?— only three or four. Kids, they change and grow so quickly. Blink, and you're back sitting in the old kitchen with the wheezing new Aga which had looked beautiful in the showroom but never worked properly here in Morryn, and that gassy smell of damp we spent years trying to eradicate until it vanished of its own accord. Blink again, and everything's gone. But no one had told me that motherhood would be lonely as well as so absorbingly busy—a spinning kaleidoscope of joy, exhaustion, irritation and times when your conscious self swirled off entirely and you realized as you grazed the soggy remnants of long-abandoned breakfasts that whole days had passed without thinking at all.

We had a Rumpus Room built in what is now part of this new kitchen. Far more than the climbing frame in the far garden which Claude, whistling and busy in the way he was when he did these projects, had made for them, the Rumpus Room was where our kids loved to play. A glory of what was then cutting-edge technology, it was their generation's equivalent of television or the internet, but all-invasive. Edward and Maria swam in hologram oceans

265

of cartoon pap. Some of it—a lot of it—was great fun. I still have a soft spot for those gaudy faces and bizarre voices. But it was all so *loud*, so *big*, so bossily *cheerful*, and there was so *much* of it. I was determined to be an involved parent, and not to use the Rumpus Room as a baby-sitter for the kids. So I sat with them in that padded cell, and swam in daydreams of candyfloss, and joined in all the games and songs. I'd already realised that I wouldn't be the great mother I'd intended, but at this I was at least determinedly adequate, sharing laughs and digitised adventures with my kids. Then we'd head down into Fowey, and I'd sit amid the roll-up mats with the few other similarly hollow-eyed females who'd made the increasingly rare decision to have offspring. Back at home I'd dole out the processed pap which was pretty much the only thing which Edward and Maria would eat until they were well into their twenties. Too tired to prepare anything else, I'd then eat the same myself.

There I was, humming *bouncy-bouncy-bounce* or some other inane Rumpus Room jingle each evening as I waited for that stupid Aga to at least *think* about finally bringing some water to the boil. Then bath-time—a whole round-the-house-chase—and fifteen last minutes and not a second more in the Rumpus Room before bed. And *humpy-bump* up the stairs.And so to bed bed bed bed bed . . . ! And, yes, a story. Just the one. Then, when I'd finally got them calm and settled, Claude would call from halfway across the world just like the doting father he really was. And the kids would be awake again as he got them wildly, newly excited with jokes and games and gifts. The last thing they wanted when he finally rang off was to climb back into bed and go to sleep. Okay. One *last* story. *One* last song. A kiss. Their sweat-and-talcum smell. Their eyes glinting from the dark like the wild, untamed things they truly were. And me heading downstairs, certain that they'd soon be gigglingly thump-creeping down after me. Not a perfect mother, no—and how that feeling hurt—but finally and at last I was able to make my longing way towards my violin.

My ears boomed. My eyes itched. My fingers and brain were numb. All I could see was Day-Glo dinosaurs. All I could hear was

266

bumpity-bump and the twittering thump of my exhausted heart, when what I longed for was the cool, clear certainties of Mozart and Bach. God, how I miss those times. God, how I hated not being the person I'd always thought I was. Doling out pap in the ruckus of our steamy little kitchen—the cramped hub of our house with the Aga dead or roaring and paper and toys everywhere—because Claude was doing the *Ring* in Cape Town and the kids and I were alone. That fucking, fucking, useless Aga. I'd never felt so tired, or so needed, or so happy.

Adam is still sitting beside me. Softly defining the frail hollow of my temple with his fingers, he asks, "Do you want to finish now?"

I know it's getting late. Outside, the weather is brewing something foul and harsh—I can feel it in my Cornish bones. It'll be one of those nights when the windows rattle and you sleep with the storm within you. White, flying clouds tear at your dreams. I can feel the sea gnawing at the land. One night long after this, and far beyond my caring, Morryn itself will be consumed. But I feel no sadness at the thought of these old walls and all my lost possessions tumbling through the shrieking arms of the wind. My memories, all that I am, will outlast any stone.

I shake my head. "There's really not that much left to tell."

"If you're sure? I mean, there are so many years."

"It isn't the *years* that matter, Adam. Time doesn't run that way. Life's quick and then it's slow and then there are grey spaces where it really doesn't seem to run at all."

He's studying me warily. I guess that it's a trick I've learned to use against him—saying things about time and memory to which he can't possibly reply.

"I'm sorry . . . " I sigh.

"Why be sorry?"

"I wish I could make better sense. Life isn't just one thing. As you get older, especially—and I don't mean old as I am now— nothing just has one story, one truth. If I said I'd never been happier that I was when the kids were young, I wouldn't be lying. But if I told you that I hated them, and thought of this house as a prison, that would be close to the truth as well."

"Children create complex emotions," he agrees. "I understand that much."

"But what I think about them, what I remember, it really doesn't matter..." I pause, wondering at the odd echo of my words. "My kids are still out there, living and alive. Oh, I could tell you more about them. I could bore you with their studies and bits of old drawing and endless family albums. There are whole sheaves of the stuff Maria used to do, charcoals like autumn smoke, collages like old stained glass, somewhere over there in that corner. I could go on about the happy times down on Bezant's Bay, but I've done that already, I suppose...? The thing is, Adam, they're not dead, and they can speak for themselves, and they have their own memories and their own opinions. They don't need me to be their scribe. And when I'm..." Untangling my hands from the blankets, I make a small gesture. "When I've passed, we can still talk. In fact, we'll talk even more. I'll be gone from here, but they'll remain. Just as you will. Had you thought of that, Adam? That you're as much a part of what I am now as..." I hesitate. "Anyone. But you're *here*. You don't need this thing in my skull to make you real."

Adam nods. He's looking down at me oddly again. "But you said," he says so lightly that I barely hear, "that you didn't want to stop..."

CLAUDE POSSESSED THINGS. NEVER JUST ONE PLACE OR enthusiasm or project, but several. Always, always moving on. If he were here now, if he were doing what I'm doing, it would be amid a blizzard of information, friends, enthusiasms, theories, performances. Instead of Morryn being empty, he'd have had another of his famous parties, which went on for days with bodies sleeping or doing other things in surprising corners. He'd have seen dying as another big performance, just as he saw everything . . .

Of course, there was the DB, which spent many years dismantled into endless pieces and looking even less like a car than it had on the day it arrived. Like those party guests, odd-shaped bits of oily metal, new tools, precious sheets of glass and containers of paints and dangerous substances made their way into Morryn's cupboards and hallways. I'd complain about the mess and the dangers when the kids were young, but the kids never minded—the kids liked the mess. I even think that Maria gained the sense of structure which she displays in her best buildings from the long afternoons she'd spend simply staring at some oddly shaped engine part which Claude had left out in the kitchen. For them, it was all just a part of what Dad was, and thus of our lives.

Did I come to hate the DB? Of course I bloody did—who wouldn't? But the thing you have to understand is that, just as I sometimes loathed and hated Claude, I also loved him deeply, and I loved that car as well. The time he finally got the engine turning, or the summer's day when we found that lost carburettor in a Truro scrapyard: times such as those weren't good just because Claude was happy. *I* was happy as well. Of course, sometimes I'd just have to laugh out loud to think that we felt the way we did over a ridiculous agglomeration of metal, but it was a red-letter day above all others when, and after many false dawns and false starts, the DB was finally finished—although it never really was—but at least was in a state when it could be driven out from the garage and along these Cornish lanes.

The kids came home specially. Edward from his work in London bearing that raffish air which then seemed to work so well with the girls, and Maria recovering from the first of what turned out to be many short but powerful relationships with other women, this one in a charitable project in the shanties of New York. The DB gleamed now. It was a car again. It smelled deliciously of clean-cut metal and new oil. We all walked around it, truly amazed. Standing proudly at the bonnet, Claude uncorked the champagne and tipped some over the silver paintwork before he poured us each a glass. We were all laughing, even Maria, getting tipsy on nothing but our all being here, then smilingly serious, as we each proposed our own toast to this marvellous car.

Time to open the doors and slide into the give of the seats and fresh aromas of walnut and hide. Maria and I crowded into the doggy seat at the back like giggling debutants, and the two men, in this timelessly old-fashioned car, sat mannishly in the front. But getting the garage doors open turned out to be a far bigger performance than anyone could have imagined, seeing as they'd never been fully opened before in all those years since the DB had first arrived. It nearly scuppered everything, until, with a creative use of one of his best wrenches, Claude finally broke and lifted one whole side out of the way. Standing out there in the sunlight with the wrecked and fallen door beside him, and but for the gleams of grey in his hair, he looked just as tall and strong as he had on that first night when I saw him up on that stage in Paris. He waved his wrench like a baton and gave an elaborate mock-bow. It was a perfect moment.

The kids only managed to stay with us a couple of days, although they were some of the best days in all human history. Claude did most of the driving, but, naturally, we all took our turns. People stared at us as we throttled past. Literally, they'd never seen anything like the DB before. And the little cars, those horrible modern things which drive themselves like the one I'll be taking to Bodmin tomorrow morning—they all stopped to cower on the verge at the first sight of the DB's gleaming grin. We took it on picnics, or it took us. We urged the sun to stop shining simply so we could watch the wipers work. I suppose that the days weren't quite like that, or didn't come quite so easily, for the DB was never that reliable, and getting any kind of petrol was always a chore, but that's how these days are in my memory, and that's how I want them to stay.

Musically, for me, things were also going well again by then. Now that the kids were off living their own lives, I was able to return to playing. After those jelly baby years in the Rumpus Room, and the teenage tantrums and uncertainties, I found I actually enjoyed the travelling, and the hassles, and the hotels. The world seemed to be in resurgence and performing, the whole business of having people listening to the music I played, often felt like a prolonged holiday. Claude was busy by then with his own famous partnership with the LSO, so I often with worked with other accompanists, new conductors, and explored new works. I enjoyed all the different tensions which doing this brought out, and I enjoyed going back to play with Claude again all the more. We knew by then that we were the great couple—it wasn't subject to doubt—and our playing reflected that fact, although I was famous by now in my own right, and had set aside the chilly pyrotechnics of my earlier persona as I performed with, as was often commented in the reviews, a new freshness and humanity around the world.

For Claude, these were the years of the big Mahler cycle he'd long been promising himself. As a solo pianist, he moved away from the percussive experiments. A Claude Vaudin recital of this time would most probably include works by

"WHY ARE YOU TELLING ME THIS, ROUSHANA?" ADAM interrupts, standing up, circling the tension from his big arms as he prowls the music room.

"I know you think you care about music—I know you imagine you understand, but it was the most important part of our *lives*. Apart from the children, of course . . . "

"I *do* understand. Why shouldn't I understand after all you've told me? That's not what I mean." He gestures at all the awards, and the books, and the recordings and other kinds of antique media which line these walls. "What do you think I've been doing this last week? I've *read* the interviews, Roushana. I've *listened* to you and Claude play. I *know* about the seasons, the key concerts, and where they took place. Good and bad, I've *seen* the reviews. There's no point in you telling me any of this. It's all been set down already. Your life, the public part of it, it's already here."

"In that case—" "In that case, you should tell the truth."

"The truth isn't—"

"The truth isn't something you can play around and interpret. It's not some performance!" Rain, it could almost be sleet, claws behind him at the windows and Adam seems lifted by the fury of the gale. "What exactly is it that you want to take with you, Roushana? Those glossy interviews—the fawning cover shots or the good performances, or the memorably bad ones, or perhaps all the many, many ones which you and the entire audience have long

273

forgotten about. After all, music's just entertainment, and playing some instrument is, when you come right down to it, just another kind of job. It's like these books and pictures. It's just another of your precious bloody *things*, Roushana. It's just *sound*. It's like this house, which, by the way, some-times smells of pee, or that car. The what—" he, the storm, shrieks and twirls "—the what is it, the right make and marque, the torque and the steel-framed aluminium bodywork? And, by the way, how did all four of you ever manage to climb into a two-seater? Still, I suppose if you love something that much, it ceases to become what it really was, which, if all the news reports I've read are remotely correct, is the vehicle that Claude died in. Or would you like to magic that away as well? Turn it into another of your precious things which you can mould into whatever shape you want?"

The lifting wind roars in Morryn's chimneys. It keens a shriller note across its eaves.

"What do you want me to say?"

"I want you to tell me," Adam murmurs on the breath of the storm, "what happened to Claude."

I T WAS ALL BEETHOVEN'S FAULT. BEFORE HIM, GREATS SUCH as Bach and Handel led orchestras through their compositions seated modestly at their own instrument. Then along came Ludwig. Being clumsy, disorganised, prone to fits of rages and tears, as well as being famously deaf, it was plain that others did a better job than he did at organising the performance of his increasingly difficult compositions.

—No, I'm not going to launch into some lecture about the role of the conductor in classical music, but there's something you need to understand if you want to know about Claude. Conductors were a product of the Romantic movement—the big gestures, the big egos, the big contracts, the big hair—and they somehow managed to cling on and remain at the centre of things and gesturing from the podium and being photographed with presidents when Romanticism faded to remind us of how important they were. But there aren't many pieces apart from the wilfully complex ones written by the big Romantics, conductors to a man themselves, for which a conductor's presence is essential. I've heard exquisite Bach, superb Messiaen and dazzling Nordinger played by orchestras without some man with a baton standing up in front of them. And it always *is* a man. For that's what conductors are—they're big, romantic, vain, and male. But understand, at the core of this great ego is the doubt, the worry, perhaps almost the certainty, that the music would continue without them.

Claude came late to this scene. There were so many role models, so many key performances, that it must have been hard to know where to go next. I think that explains something of his restlessness. No matter what he did, no matter how far he went, there was always some swallow-jacketed other figure who'd been there before him. So Claude decided that being black, being American, being socially-concerned and suavely handsome and speaking French and playing jazz and hanging out in low bars and living in Paris would be his trademark. Apart from the skin colour, which was no choice of his, none of this was particularly original, but Claude embraced it all as if it was uniquely him, and he was lucky to be there in Paris at the right time. Yellowstone changed everything, but for a few years, and amazing though it seems, classical music was in the kind of resurgence which will probably never be seen again. People had grown sick of big beats and clever virtualities, and they liked the idea of dressing up and going out for the evening to watch living people performing music which somehow sounded fresh and new despite its age. And there were the formers of taste like Harad, and all the other music-makers, most of whom are now forgotten, or remembered for their eccentricities and exploits rather than their work. But at least we had Nordinger, and one timeless genius is probably as much as any generation can expect.

So Claude, who never embraced anything less that whole-heartedly, made Paris his *leitmotiv*, and if Paris meant anything as the years went by and the myths proliferated and people began to look back fondly to that seemingly golden time, it meant Karl Nordinger, and his magnificent *Fourth Symphony*. Of course, Claude still loved the work. But he came to hate it as well, and, as other conductors learned from the mistakes he had made in dealing with an evolving piece of music, and a generation of critics far less iconoclastic than Harad Le Pape began to hail it as the masterpiece it always was, it haunted him far more than he ever dared admit. For all his stirring re-interpretations of Elgar and his re-discovery of Blore, it was the one thing which all the people he encountered knew about him. For here was Claude Vaudin, who had made a famous mess of the first performance of the one acknowledged work of symphonic genius to be produced in the twenty first century.

Claude was torn. That era in Paris had fitted him so well that he found it hard to discard it. He often tried to re-invent some different milieu which would do the same thing again—with him, there were always the next trend, a different philosophy or cause or tone-scale or way of living or dressing—but the effect grew thinner as he got older and began to turn a little fat. Sometimes, and for all my continued close-ness to him, I'd barely notice whatever fad he was currently chasing until it was gone. For me, it was always a lot simpler. I had my violin, and then I had the kids. But he was tied to the chains of Paris, of those great times of over-reaching failure and glorious success, which part of him, for all that he railed against it, never really wanted to shake off.

After Yellowstone, after Mathilde's election, after the mess of Christos and the fiasco of that premiere, it was inevitable that things would change between us, and I realise now far more strongly than I did at the time that I was already steeling myself to losing Claude. I knew the pattern by then. Claude took on lovers just as he took on his other passions, and the times when you were in the spotlight of his attention were glorious, but—inevitably, so it seemed—short-lived. After that night, though, something changed within Claude. In many ways, he became louder and more bombastic, more obviously the famous Claude Vaudin, but the Claude I knew, the quieter real man who lay underneath all the power and bluster, was less certain of himself, and in far greater need. I got lucky, if lucky is what you call it. If things had worked out differently in Paris, I might well have lost him. But instead of falling out of love with me and moving on to his next big passion, Claude Vaudin took me as the refuge he could return to from a world which had turned wintery.

I'm still not that sure that I was ever really that good at providing a welcoming mind and heart and body to soothe away all his frustrations and pains. Love, whatever it is, has always been mysterious to me: some-thing you feel, if you feel it at all, only when it's mostly gone. Was I ever that warm and womanly? Or is the icy tone which people have always heard in my playing, and the difficulty I still feel about giving either Maria or Edward the unconditional love I got from my own parents, what I really amount to? Did Claude stay with me because I loved him enough, or because he feared I didn't love him at all? It would certainly explain a lot. The angers, the demands, the tantrums, the breakages ...

And Claude liked a drink. In fact, he liked several, and so did I. Even after Paris, even when we had the kids, it long remained part of the fun of being with Claude. In fact, getting properly drunk became an act of nostalgic reunion. But then I realised one day that the soberups weren't working and the whole thing was getting in the way of my playing, and that was it. I simply quit. From then on, drink became another barrier Claude could never quite bridge between us. *Go on, Roushana. Just try. This is one of the last, ever, Californian whites. You can still taste the lost sunshine.* But the more expansive his cellar became, the less I wanted to submit. So Claude drank the whole expensive bottle—indeed, several bottles—himself.

None of it's easy, you know. Not living, or being famous, or being great and talented and handsome and knowing for most of your life that the best times have already gone. And being American; that as well. It wasn't just losing his parents. In the quick way they surely died, that was probably a sort of blessing. As the states divided in that terrible, messy war, and no matter which of the several sides you supported and how many fundraising performances you gave, there was soon no country left to call America, although being American was a big part of what Claude truly was. That passion. That optimism. That can-do. All of it gone, a harbour to which he could never return, especially when visiting what remained of the country itself was far more painful to him than India ever became for Mum.

So Claude kept up with his new passions and his new orchestras, and he held those famous parties and, yes, there was the DB. I remember he had this brief, searing enthusiasm for the music of Thin White Duke-era Bowie: sleek and soulless soul music sung by a white Londoner lost in cocaine and Los Angeles, all sheen and bluster and not much else. But Claude wouldn't have a word said against it. He got this machine from somewhere, a sort of cassette called an eight-track, which he installed into the DB's dashboard. He was always playing this particular song—*Young Americans*. He'd sing along at full volume about living for twenty years and having to die for fifty more as he drove, often drunk and dangerously one handed.

Not that it was just drink, or ever had been. In his hurry to keep up, a Thin Black Duke who didn't quite fit into his sleek suits because the diet hormones he took were cancelled out by the soberups, Claude was always game for the next big high. He never took serious risks—there was always some essential caution—but he could never ignore the chance of an interesting experience, and I had to grow used to a variety of different Claudes in the times he spent with me here in Morryn. There was always some new gateway which would unleash and explain everything until the next one came along, although it wasn't as simple by then as saying that drugs degraded your critical faculties. There were substances which did the exact opposite, just as there were those which allowed you to see your own private version of God.

Claude tried them all, or at least he said he did, for the story, the public performance, was always at least as important to him as the truth. And he *could* take it—he could take them all. He was big and he was strong and he was Claude Vaudin, whilst I, being me, drew back and said little and let him get on with it, knowing that any other course would only make matters worse. No matter how far he went, I always knew that he would come back, even if some of the journeys were very strange. I remember how he once returned from Singapore with what he was sure, absolutely convinced, was the way ahead not just in terms of creativity, but of understanding the human mind. Sitting beside him on our bed and wishing we could simply make love and go to sleep, I watched as he opened a prosaic matchbox-sized tin. Inside, there seemed to be two small-bore bullets. Then, by small expansions and contractions, the bullet-things started moving.

"Doesn't look very promising," he admitted, "but the whole insight they offer is entirely unique. They're not about changing consciousness. They're just about bringing two minds closer together. They allow you to share your dreams . . ."

I'd already decided I wasn't having any of it, especially when Claude explained you let them crawl into your ear.

"They're just like little transmitters. They form a holistic pattern of the entire sleeping brain, which they then impart, send out, to their host-twin. Imagine, what *this* will do to the world. And it'll be cool Roushana. It'll be great."

Exactly who, I couldn't help wondering, had Claude shared these things with already to know that they were so wonderful? And why on earth should I risk my mind and my hearing for the sake of some dubious technological stunt? But Claude had to demonstrate, tilting his head to let one of the things worm its way into his ear as if that would make me like the idea more. Then, playfully at first, and then more insistently, he tried to get me to do the same. A scuffle ensued and I ended up stamping repeatedly on the remaining bullet-thing as, shedding delicate wings of circuitry, it tried to crawl away across the bedroom floor.

I spent that night alone down here on this divan. I remember staring up at that ceiling and thinking of the thing in his head, sending out unreceived dreams into a changed and hostile world.

By then, Claude was returning for the first time in years to performing publicly on the piano. Gone were the percussive jazz experiments and treated strings of Paris. This was about a new simplicity, and he settled on the great body of work central to all solo piano music, which is of course Chopin. Slimming down a little, sobering up, getting himself some more appropriate suits, combing his hair in a way which covered his growing bald spot for which he was too vain to take treatment, Claude set out to re-conquer the world.

I was surprised that the critics still cared enough about Chopin, or even Claude, to be as harsh as they were. Essentially, they saw him as a conductor pretending to be a pianist, and the worst part of it all was that Claude knew they were right. He slunk home with half the tour cancelled, as sad and as needy as I'd ever seen him, although the humility and the sobriety were on hold. By then, he'd developed this thing about Leo. It was a kind of jealousy, I suppose. I must have told him once about hearing my brother playing the *Raindrop Prelude* on that New Year's morning, and so of course Claude got himself drunk enough to sit down at the piano and play it for me, and then turn and ask if it was anything like as good. Of course, it wasn't—how could I tell him otherwise when, with music if nothing else, we always kept to the truth?—and in his worst moments Claude came to see my lost brother as some kind of ultimate musical competitor: Ashkenazy, Barenboim, Prevent, Gould and Keith Jarrett combined . . .

What else can I say? How many other Claude-stories do you want me to tell? You know what happened—you know where this leads. It's so easy, with all this stupid hindsight, to make it seem as if it was always coming. Claude liking a drink. Claude loving that DB so much that I would sometimes sit inside it when he wasn't here and breathe its leather scent and feel far closer to him that when he was. There were the dangerous nights when I agreed to drive out with him for fear of what would happen if he drove alone. There was the talk—sometimes, he seemed to believe it—about the machine guns and ejector seat he was going to have fitted so he could finish off his James Bond car. And all the wild theories—stuff he'd have called reactionary nonsense when he was young. Best or worst, I always thought, was his idea that the Yellowstone eruption had been trigged by some Arab atom bomb. But that wasn't Claude. That wasn't *my* Claude, the man I still loved and still wanted to be with forever, and in precious moments—in soft mornings, walking the beach or just playing music here in this room or simply making love—still sometimes was.

Claude didn't have to die. It happened, but it didn't need to. There was so much he wanted to give, and I loved him so very dearly . . . It was just another night—inside Morryn, anyway, although outside the weather was brewing up a storm almost as bad as this. I'd come back lateish from town, cold and soaking wet from the rain, and I'd got changed and we'd eaten in the old kitchen, and Claude had drunk some wine, just as he always did. I was feeling tired. I think I was probably coming down with something—one of those stupid, snivelling diseases they've never worked out how to cure. We sat in here for a while, but I said I'd like an early night, and I stood up from this divan and went over to that chair by the desk, and leaned over and kissed his forehead. When I got upstairs, I could still hear him moving about, and then, after I'd laid down, I heard him lift the lid on the piano. He started playing. It was nothing special. No particular piece. He probably wasn't really thinking, just sipping a glass of wine or two and strumming, although Claude often played far more beautifully and soulfully when he did that than when he tried. If you could have trapped the moment, you'd have had the essence of my husband. Easy, relaxed, charming, profound—everything. Much as I was feeling achy and sniffly and part of me wanted him to simply come to bed, I felt happy like that, lying there listening to the delicate sound of my Claude's playing coming up through Morryn above the boom and swish of the storm. The music drifted, it paused—he probably went to open a fresh bottle—I was already half asleep when he started playing again, but I was sure he drifted into a twinkling rendition of *Les escaliers de Montmartre*, which made me want to laugh and cry. So I fell asleep sniffling and smiling, and I suppose Claude went on drinking and playing, and at some point he must have decided to take the DB out for a drive. If I'd been awake, I'd have tried to stop him. Worst come to the worst, I'd have even gone out with him as I'd done before. But he went out alone in the DB, out into that storm, which, being such a big soppy Romantic, and of course rather drunk, would have seemed to Claude like a very obvious and natural thing to do. He was probably planning on stopping above Bezant's Bay. It was one of the places he liked best, especially when the weather was this wild. He'd stand there above the cliffs like Mickey Mouse in *Fantasia*, conducting the storm. But instead he must have over-shot, misjudged—the road there was already failing and badly marked—and when I awoke the next morning, Claude, his DB, everything worth remembering, was gone.

ADAM'S PACED THE MUSIC ROOM, SAT DOWN, CROUCHED beside me, moved to stand at the window surrounded by reflections of the storm. He's stared at the automatic piano which Claude played, as if it might start playing again with a will of its own, although that would scarcely be a surprise to either of us now. The way he's reacted, the plays of rain-driven shadows across his face, are like those he displayed when I played him music. He's more than an audience. He's there—he's involved . . .

"That's where it ends?"

"I'm not saying Claude's death ended my life. I travelled. The kids grew. I performed. Life went on. Things changed . . . I could tell you about the year I spent in Bolivia, helping musically gifted kids who'd never otherwise have had a chance to play. All so very altruistic, I suppose it sounds, but what I was really doing was filling in the shadow of all the things done by Mum and by Claude. That, and trying to revive my enthusiasm for my instrument which five years of touring had exhausted. You see, that's how it always is with us artists, musicians. We're not even *self*-obsessed— we're simply obsessed with doing the thing that we do. Or I could tell you about the speech I gave—a rare thing for me by then, and I couldn't believe how nervous I felt—at one of the first conventions of the Reformed League of Nations. Not that it made the slightest bit of difference to the fate of the world, and I realised as I stood there and looked down at all those faces that the reason I was here wasn't because I was Roushana Maitland, but because I was the widow of the famous Claude Vaudin. And the reason *Claude* was famous—it wasn't his musical triumphs, it wasn't even the fiasco of Nordinger's *Fourth Symphony* any longer, it was because of all the speeches he'd given in places like this. *That* was how people remembered Claude, as a celebrity promoter of lost causes. It was the biggest, saddest irony of all . . . "

He looms over me. "What happened to his body?"

"You sound like some detective now. Does it really matter?" I feel so tired. I really do want to go to bed, and I wish he'd leave me alone. I'd love to sleep, if sleep were possible. But he's right to ask—this thing, this need to resurrect the past, won't let go of me now until it's done. "There were so many places Claude told me he wanted to be buried, scattered, cremated or commemorated over the years. You wouldn't believe . . . It just one of those things he had—something he'd say if he was happy, which usually meant he'd just presided over a particularly successful performance. *I want it to be here.* Partly a joke, although Claude's jokes were always in earnest. So it could have been Paris, or here in Morryn, or Bayreuth, or Sydney or any of a dozen places—including several not on this earth. But I didn't have to think hard to decide. I took his ashes over to Washington. The place reminded me of the way New Delhi had been, right after the war, and it reminded me of the time we visited Luxor. There were the same sights, the same flies and smells, the same toothless guides . . . The Washington Monument's still standing—did you know? Or at least it was back then. And still surrounded by rusty fences and huge walls of concrete, dykes to keep back the maniacal messiahs the Americans thought were trying to destroy their country. Of course, they were wrong. It was the very land itself which turned on them. The top of that monument's a windy spot now. All the old plate glass had been taken out—looted, I suppose. Claude's ashes just blew away, high across the ruins and swamps of the lost capital of a lost country where my husband once dreamed of changing the world . . . "

"You make it sound very poetic."

"That's the trouble with memory, Adam. The fact was, I was shattered by the enormous climb, and worried about being knifed by the seedy little guy who'd led me there, not to mention the prospect of the long climb down. The place stank of pee as well, just like the pyramids and New Delhi. Funny how people always seem to want to piss against the monuments of old empires, which is something Shelley forgot to mention when he was writing that poem. But that's not what I'm saying. You see, it's all gone. Not just Washington, but anything that matters. What I am is what I was. It all goes back to the people I loved, and to those times . . . The rest is just . . . Words."

"You mean you've finished?" he asks after a long pause.

I nod. After all, didn't Liang Ho tell me that the day would simply come, and that it could be there and then, just as I wanted, without preamble or fuss? So this is it—and it feels like nothing. It's like the end of the final concert, the last day of the tour. Packing up in your hotel room, or walking across an empty auditorium. All that struggle, all that planning. All the night-sweats and the nerves and the bleeding fingers. A huge mountain of effort which lies before you and bulks out the rest of your life, and which you dread and hate and long to finish. And then it *is* gone, and you're left with this empty feeling. I suppose I could go on. I could talk some more about Bolivia and those kids sitting around me under the jacaranda trees, nervy with talent and expectation. Sometimes, I just wanted to tell them to stop. Say—*Forget music; it isn't too late. Just go out and live instead* . . .

I look over at Adam. He's standing so quiet now, framed by the wings of the storm, when before he was so passionate . . .

"Stay here," I tell him. "Stay here when I'm gone. Not that I *will* be gone—we can still talk, sort things out. My kids, they don't want this house—they've told me as much. They don't need the money. I can leave it to you. Keep it, sell it, do whatever you want. If you have some kind of property, it won't matter who you are or aren't."

"You'd really leave me this house?"

"Why not? It's not as if the dead can't re-make their wills."

What *is* that expression I can barely see on his face? Is he sad, or amused? It's almost as if he's not taking it in, but it would solve everything, and it would rescue us both. It would save Morryn as well, before Edward starts treating it like another investment, or Maria uses it to work some more of her architectural angst.

"This isn't just some passing whim, Adam. I really will give you the rights to this house."

"To some stranger from nowhere who's befriended a dying, elderly woman?"

"We both know it isn't like that."

"I'm sorry, Roushana. This is your moment, not mine. Perhaps we really should just go to bed now...?"

The music room sinks back into the littered and homely place I've long known, but nothing much else happens when I tell my limbs to move. The old Leo's Smith Kendon tin gleams over on the desk. Maybe Adam and I should open it up—fill this room with antique smoke and push back the years just as Claude once tried to do. But whatever's there would be dried-up, worn out, drained of all its potency and power. The past is gone. So is the future. All that remains is me.

"Could you help me?" I ask.

Adam bends to slide the strength of his arms between me and the divan. It's not even like I'm being lifted; I'm that light, he's that strong. All the plans I had for these last living hours—the music I'd listen to, the food I'd taste, the things I'd touch, the messages I'd leave—seem worth-less now. I'm just a husk, I'm driftwood, I'm nothing, and to give up like this is far better. The hall ceiling floats above me, but I'm safe here in Adam's arms, far away from the fists of the storm. My body is redefined. Bits of me are floating above the water, but most lies beneath. And Claude was right—or was it Leo?—dying isn't hard. It's easy, a mere act of will. All I need to do is let go...

I let out a small mew of disappointment as Adam flops me down on the wide, cold space of my bed.

"You want me to stay?" he asks.

I smile a yes, too tired to talk. Once again, his hands slide under me, and I'm rolled and pushed. I'm feeling giddy now as well.

Adam's hands and the seasick roll of the bed won't leave me alone. I laugh a little, then give out small sobs of pain.

"Who do you want?" I hear him ask. "What?"

"Open your eyes, Roushana. Look at me. *Concentrate*. Tell me—who do you want me to become?"

Strange, strange question. Am I dreaming? Am I dead? But I open my eyes, and a storm-shadow which might still be Adam floats above me amid the grainy light.

"Just tell me!" it shouts. "I can be anyone!"

I cringe. The storm rises. I'm swept up by impossible arms. The shape above me is stretched, contorted—it could be Claude, dancing naked to Miles Davis in that big Parisian atelier. It could be Leo. It could even be the distant ghost of the child I never had. It's like all humanity, and everything Christos ever claimed, driven here and tossed together by this storm. Then everything retreats, Morryn regains substance as the sea beneath us beats its irregular heart, and I can make out Adam sitting hunched in the darkness at the far end of my bed.

"What *was* that . . . ?" I breathe. "What *are* you . . . ?"

He gives a dry chuckle. "I'm everyone and no-one—haven't I told you that before?"

I shrink back from him.

"*Why* are you so afraid now, Roushana? Nothing's changed between us. It's always been the same truth. I'm an empty vessel, I'm legion, I'm flesh unmade. But perhaps you *don't* understand—perhaps you really don't . . . "

He gets up. The storms quickens as he begins to pace the dark room.

"So look at it this way, Roushana. You think the dead really want to *stay* dead? You think they don't hate and lust and envy the way the living shit and sleep and fuck and breathe? Who the hell wants endless potentiality? What could be better, eh, than a live body—someone fresh and new and cheaply young? You could breed them specially, perhaps grow them in vats or simply kidnap them from the sink cities. Life's cheap, so who knows, who cares? Then you can wipe the mind, cleanse the body of its petty identity, fill it instead with a crystal field which will absorb all that you ever were. You've just got that thing growing in your *head*, Roushana. But look, look at this stuff—it's invaded me. It's all that I am..."

Adam's scattering drawers, strewing glass, searching for something long and sharp, which gleams a white arc as he lifts the hem of Claude's old sweatshirt and drives it into the wound in his belly and then, breathing in hard, angry snorts, begins to widen and deepen it.

" . . . look . . . "

His fingers scrabble at the lips.

" . . . look . . . "

There's flesh and tissue deep inside him—in this flickering light, I can even see the gleam of organs—but it all shines within a dense webbing of crystal through which the blood wells thickly as if through a layer of dense frost. Down there, deep within him, he's barely human at all.

"You were *made* like this?"

"It's what I'm for! Somehow, I suppose I must have escaped. I realised that long ago when I first looked at those marks on my legs and wrists—but why did the sea take me here, to you, and to Morryn? *That's* what I've been wondering, asking, all these days. It's taken me this long to understand . . . "

Despite everything, what he's saying makes a kind of sense. You don't have to keep up with the newscasts to understand what a good, young body stripped of all personality and identity might be worth. And perhaps the dead do envy the living. Perhaps they do seek to re-enter life through stolen flesh. Adam's certainly an empty vessel, just as he says. It all makes sense—all the things he knew—all the things he can do—the way he's *everything* but a single mind, a single collection of memories . . . Hunched on sheets which are now scrawled with his blood, watching him prowl this room, I believe.

Adams nods and smiles. He laughs. He spreads his dripping hands. "I'm nothing. I've looked into my heart, Roushana, and it's empty. But it doesn't *have* to be like this—can't you see why the sea brought me here?"

"What are you saying?"

"You don't have to go to that clinic tomorrow. You don't have to shed your flesh and take nothing in exchange. Or you can— but you can do it here, you can do it now with me, and you can have *everything* instead. Look at me, Roushana. I'm all you could ever want. You can take me, you can enter me. You can become all that I'm not. These days in Morryn, all I've ever had from you is an endless torrent of faces and places and memories. And the music, the music as well, lest we forget . . . You don't have to let go of any of it. Look at these hands . . ."he holds them out, still darkly bloodied " . . . *feel* them. Feel their strength. Imagine holding the Guarneri with *these*, Roushana, imagine listening with these ears, feeling with this heart, and fucking, yes, with this cock . . . Imagine all of that. Imagine what you could become . . . "

The spread hands are offered but he jerks them away just as I reach hungrily. It seems for a terrible moment that he's withdrawing, but instead he reaches to drag Claude's old sweatshirt off his shoulders, then the tee-shirt beneath, and he scrambles towards me across the bed, his chest covered with runnels of sweat, his whole body shining and shuddering.

" . . . here . . . "

His fingers make dark scrawls as they cross his belly to seek that wound on his left side. There's a shuddering gasp, a wet tearing, but there's no flesh, nor blood, nor even crystal, inside the rent he's made in himself. What I see instead is a vortex of gathering dark.

" . . . you see . . . "

A widening space of potentiality spreads towards me from within his spread arms. Everything he is lies within it—his sweet flesh, his new breath, his finely beating heart—and I could have it all. I could have everything. I could *become* him. Adam's right— he's merely a vessel, a swirl of disconnected information. He has nothing to lose, and I long to escape this stupid, failing, body and live on. All it takes is an effort of will. Already, withered hag reaching forward to grasp life with these useless hands, I see myself through his eyes. I feel his breathing. I can taste his tongue. I could leap. I could do it. I could live on. But something breaks and the moment dissolves in a clamorous rush.

"I can't do it!" A voice which could be Roushana's tries to howl, although it comes out as a dying whisper.

"You must—"

"—You don't understand. All the things I've told you. It isn't *me*. What I said about the truth being more than one thing, Adam . . . It's far simpler than that—I lied."

ROUSHANA MAITLAND'S CROUCHING ON HER BED IN her ruined body,looking out at the blur of Adam through her fading eyes. I'm her, and she's me. But it isn't that simple any longer—everything's much too clear. I can see Adam as well, sprawled beside me with that wound gaping and the blood drying on his hands. I can hear *the husky hurt in his disbelieving voice. What is the truth, Roushana? What are you, really?* Questions, questions, and the frail old creature hunched beside him which is still partly me mutters something about Morryn knowing, how Morryn has always known and kept its secrets, down in its cellar heart, down in its crystal granite bones...And she's right—I can feel it as well. But I can also feel the pull of the wind drawing me away towards drowned cities, gilded spires, crystal domes. From here, it would be so easy to let go. But I'm Adam as well. I could leave here, I could be him—I could be *everything*. But I, too, have to know . . .

There's no mystery about what happened in Paris. Christos really had vanished from that warehouse when Claude and I got there on the night of Yellowstone, leaving nothing behind but his chains. But, inevitably, Claude was angry to find that high space deserted whilst the world partied and his homeland lay destroyed in sulphurous fumes. He grabbed the abandoned chains and flung them, and then that virtual helmet. He kicked and smashed all the expensive recording equipment. Things skittered and bounced and flew. Not for the first time in one of Claude's rages, I had to duck out of the way.

Sometimes, things also got broken in our Paris atelier. We used to joke about it as we cleared up afterwards, saying it was one way of keeping the place free of clutter. Not that Claude was some madman—he was always careful. That Turner watercolour—even in his worst moods, he'd never have damaged that. Nor his Bechstein, or his beloved hi-fi, or his Miles Davis recordings. Claude always knew what not to break, and I had my moments, too. Not that I could match Claude's rages, for Claude was always passionate, Claude always *cared*. He loved, hated, hoarded, shared, made and destroyed, in equal measure. Even more than his being American, it was what he truly was, and rage was something he often used with his orchestras, for he was never one to hold in his frustrations and quietly sulk. There was a story going the rounds when I met him—of course, there were already many Claude Vaudin stories by then, but this one was of how he'd grown so frustrated in a rehearsal that he grabbed the principal second violin's instrument and stamped it to pieces. Next day, he returned with a huge bouquet and a replacement violin far better than the broken one. Of course, the woman played like an angel after that. Not that I know whether this incident ever really happened—that isn't the point—but if it did, Claude would already have been certain that the violin was of particular consequence before he smashed it, and that he could afford to replace it with a better one.

Claude was a careful tornado, a picky poltergeist, and I soon learned when to stand back, and when to get involved. Sometimes, for whole days, and without at first even my consciously noticing, I could feel the air sharpening as a fragile brilliance began to radiate from the objects which I knew he would eventually break. And yes, I sometimes grew a little wary—who wouldn't?—but when he flung things, when he ranted, I didn't believe for the longest time that I was being flung and ranted at as well. Yes, there was sometimes flying glass. Yes, there were occasionally beating fists and punched holes in the plasterwork. But the pain was always directed inwards, and what I remember most is tending Claude's bruises and grazes. I remember licking them, kissing them, oiling them with antiseptics and studying the slow progress of their sunset colours across his midnight skin. And if the flying plates and broken glass and those wall-punchings sometimes accidentally hurt me as well, that was also simply part of what we shared. As long as it didn't show, as long as it didn't stop me from playing, as long as he kissed those secret marks afterwards when we made love, I was proud to share and bear them. For the longest time, for all that magical summer which we spent in Paris, I felt safe and trusted, and I loved Claude beyond all doubt and across all bounds.

We were riding a rollercoaster, it's true, but, with Claude, I'd never expected anything else. Once, we took a holiday. It was a year or two after Yellowstone, but the skies across much of the globe remained dark, and it was hard to imagine anything more luxurious than a warm beach, warm skies, a warm sun. The place seemed like a dream even when we got there—although it was also a well-fortressed one, fenced, concreted and colonnaded against the threats of earthquake, tsunami, eruption, hurricane, virus and terrorist bomb. All we could hear from the window of our room was the innocent swish of sea and palm trees. We swam naked. I put on beads and henna to make love. It was everything we'd wanted, the escape we'd long promised ourselves, but Claude still had several projects he had to keep an eye on. I was prepared to switch off and trust my agent, but Claude was his own agent even when he employed someone else. We were nearly at the end of the holiday when news of some predictable crisis finally reached him. I can't even remember what it was, but he raged. He prowled off down the beach making his own dark clouds, swirled in his own sub-tropical storm.

Sitting waiting in our room, sipping a lurid cocktail, I stared at the big, white conch shell which rested on the cabinet opposite our bed. It had innards of pink mother of pearl, and I could see it growing that characteristic sharpness and brilliance with which I was now all too deeply familiar. I already knew what would happen when Claude returned, and still part of me thought that it was really pretty rock'n'rock to trash a room like this, here in paradise. And all of me waited. All of me stayed.

It was another accident—not anything Claude had ever intentionally meant—but that shell hit me full in the side of the face, and I remember staring at myself afterwards as the doctor tilted a mirror, seeing the sutures and swellings. For the first time, I realised that real accidents weren't things you could sense coming for days, weeks, ahead. I even briefly wondered if I was a victim. But I was wrong—I was always wrong. Claude was a totally different man next day: sweet and needy and endlessly apologetic. He was funny as well. He showered me with gifts. I'd never felt so wanted, so needed. We got deliciously drunk. We fucked and fucked and fucked. By now, part of me was thinking it was just some stupid accident and wouldn't happen again, and another part knew he'd be helpless without me, and the rest was wondering why I'd just sat and waited for him to return in the certain knowledge that something like this would happen, and that it was all probably my own stupid fault.

The bad times, the really bad times with Claude, were rare. And in fact, they were surprisingly tolerable, especially when I knew how much better things would be once we got to the other side of them. It was the long, brittle build-up which I always found hardest to take. I longed then to *do* something, to make him or me better, to re-shape his world. And I wanted to love him more—show him what I really felt so that he would stop hurting himself. But it was hard: it was walking on eggshells. Don't get me wrong. There were months, weeks, whole years, when Claude led a happy and busy and productive life, and so did I. The idea of being without my husband was almost laughably grey, and I missed his love and all the excitement which came with it dreadfully when he wasn't around. And the kids made a difference, too, just as I'd been sure they would. No matter how dark his rages became, some part of him could always put things down, turn away, go off to have another few drinks or head out into the garage and fiddle with the DB. If there'd ever been the slightest sign that Maria and Edward saw that side of him, I'd have left him in a moment. But, just as I had in that sun-tropical hotel room, I waited. I stayed.

I resumed my career after my maternal break, and Claude continued with his. For me, especially, things went well. As the critics noted, I and my playing had matured and people were soon talking about me without using Claude's name as well. And when they did mention Claude, he didn't always come first. To me, *Roushana Maitland and Claude Vaudin* always had an odd ring, and you can imagine how Claude felt. Professional jealousy, that terrible beast, began to squeeze its green scales between us. Claude took up other violinists—often female, always young—he tried re-interpreting Ligeti and popularising Schoenberg and there was that disastrous tour playing Chopin, but eventually he had to come to terms with the knowledge that people were most eager to see him conducting me. They weren't wrong, either. We produced some magical performances—key interpretations which the few who still care about such things number amongst the greats—but the more feeling Claude and I poured in the music, the less there seemed to be left over for our everyday lives. Claude still ranted, Claude still battered and ranged, but I'd seen it all by now, and the mood swings and the weeks of edgy expectation had begun to bore me. I no longer waited. I just stepped back and let him get on with it. In the darkest corners of my heart, I even began to pity him, and then to feel a gathering contempt.

I came to understand far more than Claude ever did about his moods. After his season at Glyndebourne performing *Der Rosenkavalier* to bored and uncomprehending crowds who'd never thought of Strauss as a sexually explicit modernist, I already knew exactly what lay ahead. Even when he returned home to Morryn as if nothing had happened and then stayed that way for days, I still knew the storm would eventually come. I even sometimes found myself standing in the garage when he was out walking the cliffs in the last days of that long, late summer, stroking the DB's silky paintwork, breathing its odours and watching the sharp sparks of sunlight which broke through the crack in the middle of the doors. It wasn't prescience by now. It was simply knowledge.

I got drenched when I went down to the market in Fowey on the afternoon when the blue skies finally dissolved in dark flurries of cloud. Hauling myself and my shopping back up the coast road through the rain in a soaked summer dress, seeing Morryn looking so warm and welcoming with all its chimneys smoking and its windows alight, I almost broke into a run, such was my hurry to get home. But I knew as soon as the wind slammed shut the front door that the simple evening of our being together wasn't to be. Claude was wild as the coming storm. Sounds, smells and crunchy glass filled the hall. It could almost have been one of those sensory collages he still claimed to like, but, even before I fully realised what was going on, I could tell that this was a creation of his own. Voices were calling from screens, and there were gaps amid the pictures along the walls. Music was playing—several tunes at once in a Charles Ives cacophony—and litter sprawled the stairs . . .

"All this crap!" Claude was bellowing. "Can you live as what you *are*, Roushana? Do you have to be like some fucking tortoise, dragging your whole life behind you? How the hell can you even *breathe* with the weight of all this stuff . . . ?"

I was beginning to understand. This stuff was all mine—or so Claude thought. My clothes—old ones I'd put aside because I was fond of them, or those which I thought might become fashionable again. My knicknacks and keepsakes—many of which had associations with the kids and our life here in Morryn. Paintings and objects—some of which went all the way back to Paris. Odd musical instruments we'd collected on our travels . . . In a surge of weariness, I put down my dripping bags. I could already see the mess I'd have to clear tomorrow, and the changed Claude who'd help me patch things up. The least emotion I felt was surprise. But the air was smoky, and that *was* a little more unusual. Picking up my bags again—although I knew by now that we'd never eat what was in them—I headed into our old kitchen where the Aga's furnace was open, and stuffed with crackling papers. Something fell out, its singed corners glowing. It was an old, flat, two-dee photo of Leo, standing smiling and alone in our back garden. Grabbing a poker, I raked out the rest of the smoking mess. It was all Leo. His commendations, his school reports. Books of his, some with the corners still turned back where he'd stopped reading. And more photographs. Then I understood. Quietly raging, I left the kitchen. It was the same throughout Morryn. Even the precious data about my brother I'd collected, recordings of his performances, school interviews, old e-mails, family videos, was freshly deleted from the screen in the music room . . .

Now, finally, I did feel a falling sense of surprise. But I was mainly angry—angry with Claude, and all the more with myself, for I really should have seen this coming. My husband had been working on this ridiculous inferiority complex he felt about Leo for years. I thought I'd learned how to handle it. Every time he said something harsh or foul, I'd quietly step back and let him stew, and then, when he was next away, I'd put another picture or memento of Leo up on Morryn's walls in quiet revenge. Now we'd both got what we wanted, which was the biggest scene of all.

I was so used to Claude's rages that I barely noticed what he was saying, or his attempts to shove me out of the way as I pushed my way past him and down the hall. In a cold rage, I ran out into the teeming yard and dragged open the garage doors. I'd always had a fascination for Claude's racks of tools. They were oiled, polished, the best, most expensive, brands, but to me they had that same odd mingling of aesthetic precision with pain which I'd once associated with the implements you glimpsed in dental surgeries and hospitals. Turning up the lights, I lifted one out, which made a sweet ticking sound and changed its displays as it swung in my hand. A torque wrench, I believe, and tipped with finely-machined angles of some terrific metal which—I could feel it before it happened—would slice with ease through the DB's fifteen layers of buffed and lacquered paintwork, then deep into the bodywork beneath.

The storm beat the garage's open doors and hammered across the roof as I set to work, but the delicious noise which the wrench made still carried. It was a kind of grinding sound—teeth against blackboards, steel across slate—but inordinately satisfying. I drew the keen metal back and forth across its front panels in painterly swirls. I inscribed hieroglyphs across the wide, fat bonnet. I felt as if I was changing the DB into some-thing else: no longer a car, but some totemic symbol of the wounded thing my marriage to Claude had become. My husband was watching. I could see his silhouette hunched outside where the storm raged at the edge of the light thrown from the garage. The air swirled. It was brittle. Sharp. Intense. Electric. Chewing my lip as I gouded more marks across the DB, I got a foretaste of blood.

"What the hell are you doing, Roushana?" he finally shouted. Such a bathetic comment, I thought, as he lumbered in, half-drowned.

"What do you think?" Mine was little better, but this was hardly a time for words.

"You're destroying something that's precious to us both!"

"No, Claude. That's what *you* were doing in the house." I still had the wrench in my hand. I lifted it higher, then brought it down hard across the DB's bonnet, and metal shifted its tensions and gave a protracted groan.

"For God's sake, stop, Roushana! This isn't about this car. It's about you and me. I can't go on living like this with you—I can't live in a fucking mausoleum!"

"Why not?"The wrench falls again; it has a will of its own.

"Because . . . *What* do you want me to be, Roushana. *Who* do you want me to be? Just tell me,and I'll do it . . . I'd be whatever you want,but I need to *know*. I can't read you mind—I never could. Do you want me to stop fucking someone? Is *that* what this is about? Or do you want me to start? I can do that as well. Who exactly *is* it that you want me to fuck, Roushana, because it sure as hell isn't you . . . "

I nod. Once more, the wrench falls. My husband's right about our sexual life, which has dried up in recent years. The energies we once directed in that way have found other channels. There's been this car. Morryn as well. Then the kids. Always, always, music.

298

The storm surges, the wrench falls, and the tang of wounded metal is salt-sharp as the blood-taste in my mouth.

"What *is* it, Roushana? I could be Leo. I mean, I've tried hard enough. Or I could be your fucking mother. I could even be the guy you once thought I was in Paris, or whoever else it is you think you see in whatever you really feel inside your head. I'll be what you want me to be, Roushana. Just tell me who."

He's so *weak*. I feel faintly disgusted—with myself, and with him. Nauseous, as well, although perhaps that's just the taste of sea and blood and metal. The image of the car blurs and redoubles as the wind sweeps in. So does the figure which might or might not be Claude. He's right. He really could be anything—anyone. "All I want you to be," I say patiently, "is the man I once thought I loved. That's not so very much to ask, is it? What I don't want you to be is some weak-willed victim—a half-decent pianist and failing conductor who's going to flab and drinks too much. I don't want you to be *pathetic*, Claude. And I'm sick of you being merely good, and I'm tired of what passes for our life together, and of being better at most things than you are, and then feeling that I ought to apologise. And I'm sick, above all, of this car. Just grow up, Claude, or go away and kill yourself like you sometimes say you will. But you can't even manage that, can you? You can't get anything right . . . "

The figure hunches, glowering. Time slows. This is like the moment when you become the thing you're playing, when you and the music unite. There's that same sense of pure inevitability, yet of having absolute control. This is how God must feel, I tell myself. I can do whatever I want. I can re-make or destroy him— and myself. I'm crystalline, I'm everything, and I'm held in the frozen moment, and endlessly looking down.

"You're *nothing*, are you, Claude? You're powerless. You haven't even got the nerve, the self-belief to . . . But why don't you do something properly for once, eh, and forget all the posturing? You've been longing to do it for enough years. All the throwings and the tantrums, the grabbings and the pushings. All the yes Roushana no Roushana this Roushana that. All the pathetic sobbing and the wasted glass. But why, for just once in your life, don't you do what you want to do, Claude? Why don't you stop distracting yourself and trying to be everything and do something properly for a change? Why don't you just hit me?"

It comes as a blur—as the bite of the rain, as the hammering storm, as more of the taste of salt. My head rings. This feeling is far too familiar to be strange, and yet the pain is as distant as I remain from myself. And then I hit him back—my hand has an amazing weight, a will of its own—and Claude crumples instantly, and I'm looking down on him and looking down on myself as I stand there holding the dripping, ticking wrench.

I'm still riding the moment, still in complete control, but this *now* is endless, the past and the present are one. Morryn's seen it all, held it all, in the crystal of its granite bones, and I can see it, too, through its chimneys and windows as an old woman and a young man struggle out from its maze of memories and down and out into the storm as if that were any escape. Perhaps they're heading towards the garage, which I know has long been empty, and so does the frail and barely recognisable old creature I've somehow become. Wind and lightning crackle as she and Adam slip and slide across the wet lawns. Roushana's weakening, but Adam carries her down the sluicing steps towards the boiling sea, just as she once carried him. Concrete crumbles, they almost fall. Then they are down beside the raging waves and the boathouse, part hewn-stone, part cliff, part cavern, Morryn's last outreach, at which the sea tongues and mauls, lies ahead. Blinding white froth rolls out of the blackness, draws back, rolls in again. Shingle slides. The old causeway is mostly gone, but the place still clings to its rotted doors. Muscles bulk as Adam drags at its seaweed chains, then something gives and the door tumbles as drift-wood across the slate and granite sky.

The storm, the wind, rush greedily in, driving into a space which is barely sheltered, although something—a changed but familiar shape, sea-lit by roaring phosphorescence—bulks within. The DB now has barnacled eyes. Rotting weeds beard the radiator's misshapen grin. The oystered bonnet rides up and the engine's torn innards protrude their fronded lips within. The windshield's the green-teethed maw of some dead, submarine predator, and the hanging doors are its broken fins. Its shines, darkens, with the thrust of the waves. A thing of the sea, it's too beautiful to be ugly, too wonderful to be strange. This ship-wrecked car is the essence of something—that's what I and Morryn have both long known . . .

Things don't need to be decided when you're in this heightened state—I can tell that Claude's dead as I stand in the garage even before I feel his pulseless chill as I stoop to touch the bared skin of his neck. There's little blood—there's little of anything apart from the strange indentation the wrench has made in the side of his skull—although I let out a sound, either a sob or a giggle, to think how ridiculously wrong and messy this scene is. I can't leave things like this! After all, he's Claude Vaudin, and I'm Roushana Maitland, and this is nothing like the way we ever were. Not to our kids, not to the world, not to anyone, and least of all to ourselves . . .

Moving quickly, slowly, I half–lift and manage to heave him in across the DB's passenger seat as I elbow open the door. I get odd flashes as I slam it shut and move around to the driver's side of the car. The DB's panels already look sea-corroded, its windows are greened. The sea is everywhere, flooding in gleaming fingers as I climb in and fumble along the DB's dashboard for the ignition key. I pull the choke, and *Young Americans* comes pouring out at full volume as the big engine roars until I claw at the buttons to make it stop.

Work the gears, work the clutch. A dance with feet and hands. *For fuck's sake, Roushana, you're wrecking the transmission* . . . This was never easy, and the DB bounces off the gatepost with a scream of hurt metal as I swing it out towards the road. Claude's body is keeling against me—a massive weight I can't believe I ever managed to lift—and I can't see a thing. There. Wipers. Lights. Never did get that ejector seat, or the guns, but at least the road leaps out, blurrily illuminated through the thwacking blades. Tyres scream. The wheel's heavy, and the DB continues sliding as I swing it to a halt on the verge above Bezant Bay and I'm losing control. But it stops, it stops, and the headlights gleam into nothing but wind-driven rain.

The storm hits me as I stumble out, and I'm so close to the drop that I can't get around the front of the DB. The engine's still rumbling as I fight the wind to open the passenger door, leaning in and putting my arms under Claude's as I attempt to lift him over into the driver's seat. My husband's been bleeding—the hide and the carpets gleam dark in the dashboard lights—and the gearstick and the handbrake keep getting in the way. One huge effort, and he finally begins to shift. Almost easy now, and I can feel him pushing back against me. *Don't ratchet the fucking handbrake, Roushana, you'll wear it out* . . . I try to grip the thing to release it, but my hands are freezing and slippery with blood. Then it snaps down in one ferocious lunge and the car resumes its slide towards the rage of sea just as I fall back out and Claude lets out a bubbling groan.

Lights streaming, the DB sails off into the night. The tide's high, pushed up by the autumn moon and tonight's storm, and the car hits the waves head-on, falls back, exhausts still pluming, is lifted, turned. I start to scramble down scree and sheer rock just as its rear begins to stain the surface with blurs of red. I don't know how long it takes, but suddenly I'm down in the waves. And I'm cold, cold, cold. I've lain down here on these summer rocks on days with the kids, but now I'm driven against them in a series of bruising shocks. Lost, gasping, I dive down. There it is, the DB, not so very far out, but sinking towards the swirling sand with its all lights glowing, its chromium wheels still turning. Silver-lit, mottled by churning shadows, it shifts and wavers with the beat of the storm. Its windscreen has broken in glittering shoals, and I kick towards it, rise into the roaring night, then dive again. Claude's been pushed half-through onto the bonnet by the shock of the impact as the DB hit the sea, and he's surrounded by a dark haze. Clawing my way down, I try to grab something, anything— flesh, hair, clothing—but my head is bursting. My lungs are ready to explode. Then, as I push back towards the surface, something

302

cold and hard grips one of my legs. Looking down, all I can see is a haze of blood-darkness and the windshield's glinting maw. I feel as if I've been caught by a predator, something which will drag me down into a last, terrible place. In a ferocious surge of failing energy, I kick myself away and start to rise.

The waves haven't finished with me yet, but, finally, I haul myself away from them and crawl out onto the rocks. And I lie there for the longest time, shivering and gasping as the sea still breaks around me, sometimes almost clawing me back, staring up at the roiling sky as the storm slowly retreats, and wondering how difficult it is—to let go, to die, to drown . . .

T HERE ARE OTHER CLINICS—PLACES WHICH DEAL WITH the living instead of the dead, and I took myself to visit my friend Adam in such a place this morning, travelling in one of those strange bubble-shaped cars which are everywhere nowadays, and helping myself out onto the wide, dizzying gravel with the aid of my walking stick. In fact, not so much a clinic as a large, pleasant, house, done in the same sort of understated Arts and Crafty style as many of the houses once were on the Calthorpe Estate, but this one sits at the lip of a glen which winds down to the sea and the wind sighs its Cornish breath over the tips of the bared trees. I was greeted, I think, by the woman who has greeted me here previously. A doctor, I believe, or at least of some kind of specialisation which involves humanity, she helped me into the hall and sat me down beside the crackling fire as Adam's presence was sought out in some imperceptible way.

"You still have no better idea of who he was?" I asked, although what I could make out of her expression suggested that this was a question I'd asked too many times before.

"I don't think we ever will, Roushana," she replied—loudly, slowly, patiently, firmly, as one might when speaking to a child. "Nor am I sure that it would be a good idea if we did. Adam's body has been wiped of every trace of identity, as has his mind—he was deliberately made into a blank slate. If he has any lingering memories, they wouldn't be his, but those of the invading personality…"

I nodded my understanding. Before this lovely fire, I was drifting in warm haze, but yes—I *had* been told all of this before, or something very much like it. Not that it's permitted or legal, if such terms still mean anything, but there are tales, rumours—indeed, recorded cases—of attempts by the passed to regain possession of a new, living body. Such a thing could be purchased easily enough, I suppose, for flesh has always been cheap, and then, once it had been wiped of all traces of what it had previously been, it would undergo a more invasive version of the process which was inflicted on me. Crystal would spread across emptied synapses, grow between bone and sinew, and into that would be poured the memories and personality of a different being. Looked at like this, the whole concept doesn't seem that difficult. Isn't that what I nearly did myself—a different kind of possession? All it would take is an effort of will. And isn't this exactly what Adam told me on that last night we spent together in Morryn?

"But what," I still persisted, "happened to that dead person who took over Adam . . . " I allowed myself a mischievous pause. "Not supposed to say *dead* now, are we? Oh dear—and now I've gone and said it again."

As the firelit woman beamed her understanding, I realised how I can get away with anything now, say fuck or shit or piss or any of the bad old words, or stand up and do a stupid jig for that matter, if I still could. "As I said, it's strictly against all the protocols for a living body to be possessed by someone who has passed, and I understand that the technology is sketchy and unreliable at best. It's highly likely that the invading personality was simply—well, I suppose *rejected by the host* would be the most obvious term. The data would be lost forever."

"Then why did he come to me . . . ?"

"Pure chance, most likely, although I suppose it's possible the passed personality had some kind of connection with you or the area—that there was some trace of a memory drawing him on. I believe there are records of a confused young man showing up in Mevagissey a few days before you found Adam. Those rope bindings you said you saw around his ankles and wrists, and that nasty gash we found in his abdomen, may be evidence of some final crisis as the remnants of the invading personality fought against losing its host. And then, I guess, he managed to stumble on along the shore in pretty much the state you found him in—as you and he were detected and rescued on that night of the storm. But look—if you have any more questions, Roushana, you really don't need me to answer them . . ."

Adam's a little thinner, a little sharper—a little older, indeed. It seemed odd for him not to be wearing Claude's old clothes as he helped me up from my place beside the fire and led me through the house and out into the cold gardens beyond.

"How are you feeling, Roushana?"

I chuckled, wavering between him and my walking stick. "I should be asking *you*."

"But I'm fine. They say I can leave shortly."

"Where will you go?"

"I thought I might explore around here for a while—I mean Cornwall. And I'd love to go north, perhaps do some walking and climbing, see the Scottish glaciers. Then I'll probably visit Paris."

"It won't be the same, you know."

"No." We'd reached the steps leading into the deepening glen, where thick frost still rimed the trees beyond the sunlight's wan edge. "That's why I want to see it."

Our footsteps crackled as we made our way down into a place of shadows and ice. It was another kind of crystal, and I thought as we wandered through it of the alien presence which Adam and I had once shared, and of which we are now both being drained. Liang Ho was as understanding about my change of heart when I went to Bodmin as he's been about all my other doubts and vacillations. All it took was a small amendment to my medications, then a day or so of slight sickness, and an odd taste in my mouth which lingers even now. I'm sleeping properly again already—dreaming, as well—and I laughed out loud as I walked through that frosted glen with Adam to think of the twisted version of my past which returned to me last night.

"I'm not getting any younger, you know," I muttered as the sound of the sea grew nearer.

"Neither am I," Adam countered—although he doesn't know what he means. He can't do; he's far too young.

The steps levelled in a space of frosted grass where the sea and sky beyond were both incredibly clear and pale. The ruins of a small building were etched amid the white fronds and I peered around again, trying to reposition my thoughts within this strange yet oddly reminiscent place.

"How far are we," I asked him, "from Fowey, here?"

"You should know, Roushana. Isn't that the journey you've just taken . . . ?"

Our breath plumed, fading and changing everything, but I was sure by now that I really was seeing the remains of the cottage where I'd stayed with Mum and Dad when we first came to Cornwall.

Adam was talking again, saying how things would never have worked out like this if it hadn't been for me. I stopped him by laying my hand across his own.

"Morryn's yours. It's all been arranged. That woman—the one who was with me before you arrived—she was saying how you might have come that way along the shore because of something about what you are—or were. Some kind of a trace of a memory . . . "

Adam gazed at me—his hair is longer now and his eyes, in this winter frost, were coldly grey—and then something, a twinge of distaste, almost of horror, seemed to cross his face. "I don't *want* to know, Roushana. I mean, why should I? Where would it get me? Whatever personalities I once possessed are gone—they're irretrievable."

"But don't you sometimes wonder . . . ? Don't you wish . . . ? I mean—to have some proper memories?"

"You're forgetting, Roushana. I do have proper memories—and most of them are about you."

That's it, I suppose. There was a moment, on that last night together in Morryn, when Adam would have let me have his body as a repository for everything I could possibly become. I can still scarcely believe such an act of self-sacrifice was possible, but neither now, I think, can he. After all, he's young, and he's talking of going to Paris, exploring Scotland, and isn't that just the way things should always be? I'm the only one now who's obsessed with knowing who Adam might once have been. Studying the changing light in his eyes as we sat there in that forgotten place and the pale sun edged over the whitened trees, I thought of how he'd listened to me in the times when I still could master my violin, and the intensity of the emotions which had played across his mobile face. Even now, he tells me, he devotes a great deal of his time to discovering—or re-discovering—music. The way Adam listens, the way he *is*, he's far more than just a spectator. He can already pick out complex melodies by ear on a piano, is beginning to understand chordal structures, and he's always scowled at anything resembling a wrong note. But I *like* that scowl. It's part of what he is, even if it takes me back—well, to Paris, and to playing my violin in our atelier on those nights when Claude was out trying to re-arrange the world and Karl Nordinger and I were alone.

I can't help it. With or without the jewel in my head, sitting here in Morryn, or standing with Adam this morning in that frosted place, the past remains inescapable. Only yesterday—recently, anyway—I caught sight of something red when I opened an old wardrobe filled with clothes I'll never wear again. I lifted it out, momentarily surprised, then remembering . . .

And Paris. Paris especially. I really can picture you, Roushana, in that red leather raincoat . . .

I'd shaken my head when Adam had said that, firmly told him I'd never possessed such a thing, but I was completely wrong, for that coat and I had been inseparable in the rainy Paris spring. I'd worn it when I first visited Harad Le Pape's 5th floor apartment in the Marais, and again on that afternoon when Claude and I had been sitting in that bar after a fraught rehearsal at the old radio building and a lonely, dripping figure had burst in. Such a ridiculous thing to forget . . .

Adam gazed at me with those eyes which are winter-cold, yet

remain filled with an openness and faith which I hope will never be abraded in the way that Karl Nordinger's was. But, yes, I can well imagine how Karl might have clung on to life no matter how sour he found it, until it was possible for him to make the leap which his own early software was partly responsible for creating. And I can also see how Karl would have grown as disillusioned there as he would anywhere else—in fact more so, with the sheer terror of endless potentiality, and having no excuses left for feeling anything but sheer joy. Karl would still have been Karl, and he'd soon have been pondering other ways of escape.

Karl? Is that you . . . ?

Part of me longed, and still longs, to ask Adam that question, but I know as well that he's right. Whatever he was, whatever happened, has gone. It's not even a memory. And I feel the cold so much more now—my lips were freezing as I stood leaning beside him, my eyes were turning to ice—and there was still something else, something important, which I'd planned to say.

"I know you'll probably say I've given you enough already, Adam. But there's one last thing I want you to have, and it's not a gift—not really. It's more of an inheritance, or a responsibility. I know, I can tell, that you have it in you to be an exceptional musician, and I'm sure you'll get there, if that's where you to want to go. So, Adam, anyway . . ." I took a slow breath, feeling more of the Cornish cold pouring into me. " . . . I'd like to give you my Guarneri."

There was a long pause. Then he simply nodded and hugged me a little tighter. "Yes," he said. "I'd like that. I'd love to learn how to play."

"Just as long as you don't expect people to *care*, Adam. Or anything like instant results. You'll probably need to get yourself a simpler, less tricksy instrument to cut your teeth on. And you should always remember to *listen*. Practise on its own is nothing. You need to make sure you plan to . . ." My breath faded into the frozen air. I was starting to sound like Claude, or Leo. "No—forget all of that. Just enjoy it, Adam. That's all I want you to do."

Soon I was seated again shivering before that fire in the hall of the clinic, and people were hovering around me and Adam was holding my frozen hands, and asking me if I was alright, if I felt okay? Then it transpired that the car to take me back here to Morryn was already here and waiting, or perhaps had never gone away. We parted with a smile, a hug that buried me in the broad warmth of his chest, and a promise that next time he would save me the journey and come and visit me here in Morryn. I felt relieved, for I've taken more than enough journeys lately, and I'm not sure I have the energy to ever travel again.

Heading back home in that bubble vehicle through this newly glittering world with the waterfalls frozen and the failing roads unwinding their dirty-bandage trails, I thought of Blythe, and remembered my recent trek to Birmingham, and the different city I found. Birmingham is feral now—there's no other word. The tower blocks have rotted and fallen, and the roofs of the many terraces have slid screes of tile and rubble across what once were roads. Windy and sere with fern and bramble, the landscape is returning to the open heath which Birmingham was before we living humans invaded it. Even with the assistance of the devices which had helped to bring me there, it took a wearying effort to find the part of the area which had once been called Moseley, and then Augusta Road. Our house now smells of foxes, trapped rain, feral cats, and it's shrunken even more than I have. I couldn't believe as I peered through at the tiny spaces from the ivied hall that this was where so much *life* had once been contained. The stairs are too dangerous to climb now, the roofwork is rotting, the piano's keys have grown green, a lopsided grin, and the bath into which Mum would retreat after a long day's teaching has fallen through into the lounge. It squats there like some alien presence with its once-white belly filled with moss and leaves.

I was already exhausted by my journey, but there was one other place I wanted to visit before the machines bore me back to Cornwall. The Calthorpe Estate where the Munros once lived was always verdant, although the trees and palms which had once prospered there are succumbing to these seasons of deeper cold and the dwellings, which had always hidden behind high hedges and long walls, seemed even further in retreat now, and even more deeply consumed by wilderness. It's amazing to think how I've managed to survive when so much else which seemed immovable has fallen and crumbled, although the swimming pool at the back of their house is still recognisably there, even if its waters are greened and the plastic loungers have been strewn like strange sculptures across the heathered slopes which were once lawns. Fighting brambles, I made my way down towards the place where Blythe had led me on a summer afternoon long ago. And there it was—those sheltering trees and that same stone bench. I was suspicious, and peered for runnels of crystal just to check that this was real, for nothing else I'd seen had been anything like the places I remembered. It was another season, but this glade remained a charming place. Sitting on that same stone bench, conscious of the empty space where the living Blythe, a prim wood-nymph in her bikini, had once sat beside me and made me promise I'd take care of Leo, I finally noticed something different, and I stood up and rustled through the leaf-fall to investigate. Just an outcrop of stone, another piece of garden statuary, but large and grey and square. Even before I'd leaned close enough to read the inscription, I already knew what it was. It seemed so unlike Blythe, and oddly gothic, to have arranged for her body to be laid here, but perhaps even the dead need to grieve . . .

Now, as I sit here in Morryn, at my music room desk, I'm still surrounded by memories. Here's a Polaroid photo of Mum and Dad on the day I was born, whitened in one corner by the ghost of a carelessly placed thumb. Mum looks as tired and drawn and relieved as you'd expect any new mother to look, and her eyes are even more reddened by the flash, whilst Dad is caught in one of his perpetual moments of surprise, and not quite fully sitting on the bed nor standing up either. I don't look like anything much; just a blue hospital blanket and one tiny hand. And here's Leo later on that same day in that same blue-walled room, dragged out from school with his hands stuffed into the pockets of his looped and Velcroed shorts as he feigns unsurprise at this new arrival who will undoubtedly twist around his entire world. Of course, he looks much younger than I remember him, with a smudgy nose and a sticking out little-boy crown of hair. And then here I am again and again, on rugs and in bouncy chairs, awake or asleep or crowned with suds, squalling in reluctant family groups on the shoulders of aunts who grin hopefully back at me as if they're expecting me to remember their names. I was a spring baby, so there are many glimpses of the garden of our house on Augusta Road. A golden rod of forsythia, a mossy cold-frame, a dandelion-strewn patch of lawn, and what these images cannot provide I can easily fill in. The glint of Nana Ashar's many-ringed fingers and the murmur of her voice as she slips back into Gujarati as she leans over me with that wetly regretful look which never quite left her eyes. Ice cream chimes against blue skies scratched with passing of tiny aeroplanes. The smell of next door's tom.

Here, floating on the screen above my desk in the music room, is the video of my first birthday. Our old dining room, racked with cupboards and plates, didn't change much in the time I knew it. It's another bright spring day, and the lens of Dad's video camera flares as it dances around the jelly-strewn table. A couple of Leo's friends are here to placate him over my queenly domination of the day, and here also are my two Nans, both of whom are offering contradictory and unwanted advice as Mum scurries in and out of the kitchen with bits of streamer in her hair until the wooden blind clatters down and the CD stops burbling Disney tunes and the cake, resplendently single-candled and adorned by fondant icing Teletubbies, finally emerges. Disturbed by this sudden focus upon me, I look suspiciously around from my high chair, my hair a neat black bob now and my cheeks reddened from teething. Predictably enough, I start crying, and the camera is plonked down in close-up of a half-eaten sausage as Dad reaches to lift me up before the scene cuts. We're out on the street now, walking down towards the park, and Mum's bagged the camera and is zooming in on him in mild revenge for all the times he's zoomed in on her. He smiles but looks wryly uncomfortable to be caught on the wrong side of his Panasonic, and Mum's disembodied voice is warm and close.

"No speeches, then?"

Dad shakes his head as he steers the push chair around a heap of dog poo on the pavement. His ginger hair is close-cropped, and the crown gleams in the sunshine where it's starting to thin as he leans over to speak to me. "You'll be watching this one day, Roushana," he says.

And here's Leo, jog-trotting to catch up. His two friends must have gone home now, as have my two Nans. It's just us, the Maitlands, walking in and out of the shade along the car-lined, tree-lined streets beside the tall redbrick Victorian houses. The scene snows before we get to the picnic, but Moseley remains. I remember the circular barometer set in the wall beside the doors of the Fighting Cocks on the Alcester Road, the pointer wavering beneath its grimy glass between STORMY RAIN CHANGE FAIR, and I remember the peeved hiss of the buses. I remember the high ceilings of our house with their peeling covings and the dusty Ikea paper lampshades and patiently zigzagging flies, and the night-time heat of the boiler which came through the wall beside my bed, and the stormy commotion of the spin cycle of the old washing machine. I remember the orange faces on the telly and the exercise books Dad brought back to mark from Selly High strewn in a leaf-fall on the back seat of the Citroen. I remember Mum letting me eat as many Smarties as I wanted from a magical jar just as long as I counted them correctly. I remember gates clanging and car doors banging and the taste of the scabs I picked from my knees, and I remember the white boat house on other birthday picnics at the park, and the fishermen fishing and the dragonflies floating as if on metal threads and the green smell of warm stagnant water. Leo was right—the moment's there, and then it's irredeemably lost—but he thought he was merely talking about music, when what he really meant was life.

It's all still there, or almost all of it, and I think Claude knew even on that last terrible night that he could never destroy my past without destroying me as well, which was something he could never do. The only thing Claude ever really hurt when he tried to break things was himself. In his heart, he was always a healer, a maker, but he dragged something with him into this adult life, something which came from those desolate suburbs of once-golden Georgetown and the smooth, lost certainties of his parents which he could never really face or resolve. Oh, I'd love him to be here with me now—I'd love to lean again into his arms—but I suppose I've grown used to loneliness, and to loving him for dancing naked to Miles Davis with a spectacular hard-on in those times in Paris when it sometimes seemed as if we'd need to keep stones in our pockets to stop ourselves taking flight, or playing some ridiculous game of his own invention with our kids, or driving in that fine car which no one but him could ever have re-made. Claude's like Leo now, he's like Dad and Mum, he's like everyone else who has ever lived apart from a recent few, and that's how I will also soon be—and for that I rejoice. Life, living, is such hard work. There are so many things to arrange, choices to consider, faces, places, commitments and aches, that I really don't mind joining all the rest of the long-lost in whatever place they happen to be now, be it heaven, hell, or oblivion. At my age, I feel I've earned the rest.

It's taken me many broken years, the imminence of death, to come to terms with the loss of Claude, and even then I don't think I could ever have managed without Adam. I've looked Abaddon up, and it's the name of some kind of angel from the fiery pit, a creature of medieval myth and nightmare, but I'm not that credulous—not even now. Nor do I believe in miracles, but if there was one in my life, it was him, and I really do hope he'll come and visit and stay with me here in Morryn again before it's too late. I'd like to sit and listen to Karl Nordinger's *Fourth Symphony* with him for one last time. Not that I expect it to mean anything more to him than any other great piece of music, but I want us both to rediscover how the piece has evolved. Once stormy and tempestuous, as famously bitter and ironic as Karl himself, it's changed into something far quieter. In fact, there are stretches in the third movement, and especially in the *Song of Time,* when the strings are so muted, the orchestra so subdued, that they're barely there at all, and seem to be falling towards silence. If I can remember, I might

314

also admit to Adam that the other story I told, the one about lying in bed listening to my husband getting softly drunk as he played the piano down here in this room on our last night together on this earth, was true as well. Or almost . . .

We'd long had our differences and difficulties by then, and Claude had had his liaisons and affairs, but I was still happy when, instead of going out in the DB as I'd feared, I heard him climbing the stairs after the piano had fallen silent, and I turned unhesitatingly into his arms as he lay down in our bed. We made love on that night for what must have been one of the last times, and it seems to me that we already knew some kind of ending was looming between us, and that we clung to each other all the more passionately, and that the moment was all the more sweet. I'd long given up by then with all the tests and protections which a younger, more sexually active, woman would have taken. The possibilities of our having another child were getting very remote—I wouldn't have minded, anyway—and as for the idea of some other risk—well, part of me always understood the chances I was taking with Claude because I knew of the chances he took himself. So it was probably on that night, or a night much like it, that he passed on to me the virus which, like the unadmitted secret of my guilt, remained dormant in my system for many years before it finally began to destroy the little that remains of this flesh, these thoughts.

Are you still there, jewel, crystal? Can you hear me now? I know you're fading, dissolving, but I think that you probably can. Outside, dusk is darkening the sea and thinning the sky as another day turns to its end, and the implements which tend to me in this enchanted house will soon be preparing dinner, but there are still tasks I need to perform. I must speak again to Maria, and then to Edward. They're both coming to stay here with me soon, and something about their expressions as we've discussed times and arrangements tells me that they're already expecting what I now realise must be obvious news. In fact, I can barely understand why I've spent so long putting the moment off. More to do, perhaps, with knowing that Edward will want me get myself to a clinic like the one in Bodmin, and that Maria will be against it. That, and the ways in which I lost Mum and Dad, and Claude and Leo. Not that I'm afraid of death—I realise that now—but I've long been afraid of dying.

I still am.

Barely anything's changed, and this is still my life, the little that's left of it. Maria and Edward can think as they like, do whatever they want, but, more than ever now, I realise that it's time for me to let go. The world is theirs, and they can take it—they've taken it already—and bear it on towards the unknown and unknowable future. Still, I've come to understand that the one thing a parent owes their child is honesty, and I will take them down to the old boathouse to show them what's left of the DB before this winter's storms wash it away. I won't burden them with the circumstances of Claude's death, for that terrible weight belongs to me alone, but I do feel that I owe it to them to share the bitter, unspoken truth of what a harsh and infuriating—as well as a charming, funny and loving—man their father, my husband, was. That, and to tell them how much I love them both, and how poor I've often been at showing it, and how proud I am of what they've become.

This is the future, Sis... but it's gone now—and this day is dying, crystal, just as surely as you and I both are. Still, if I can summon the energy to get up from this chair, then perhaps find a warm coat, there might still be enough time left for us to take one last walk along the shore before it gets dark.